PAST POISONS

An Ellis Peters Memorial Anthology
of Historical Crime

Edited by Maxim Jakubowski

HEADLINE

First published in hardback in 1998 by
HEADLINE BOOK PUBLISHING

First published in paperback in 1999 by
HEADLINE BOOK PUBLISHING

10 9 8 7 6 5 4 3

ISBN 0 7472 6027 3

Typeset by Palimpsest Book Production Limited,
Polmont, Stirlingshire
Printed and bound in Great Britain by
Clays Ltd, St Ives plc

HEADLINE BOOK PUBLISHING
A division of Hodder Headline PLC
338 Euston Road
London NW1 3BH

TABLE OF CONTENTS

Introduction

In Memory of Ellis Peters

The death of Edith Pargeter, who wrote both under her own name and as Ellis Peters, left a major void in the thriving field of historical mysteries, a category of crime fiction she had almost made her own. Loved by readers and other writers alike, her passing evoked much nostalgia and sadness that there would be no more Brother Cadfael stories.

Before Edith created the much-loved medieval monk in 1977 in *A Morbid Taste for Bones*, combining her passion for history and storytelling, she had already published eighteen books as Ellis Peters, including the still popular series featuring Inspector George Felse and members of his family, two whodunnit novels as Jolyon Carr (now prime collectors' items) and twenty-seven books as Edith Pargeter, including several important historical yarns.

It is ironic that after half a lifetime of writing, fame came to her so late in life as the endearing medieval monk took a strong grip of readers' imagination worldwide and she finally enjoyed the benefits of fame.

Long before Derek Jacobi portrayed the twelfth-century sleuthing Benedictine on screen and became every television viewer's incarnation of the clever historical investigator, the sub-genre of historical mysteries had already exploded and burgeoned under the influence of the novels of Ellis Peters, with a plethora of authors enjoying the genre as a perfect domain for entertaining and educating.

By now, almost every period in history has been mapped by mystery authors, from Ancient Rome, Greece and Egypt, to Edith's beloved medieval times, to Restoration, Elizabethan and Victorian times and even much further afield in time and geography. This would not have happened without the influence of Ellis Peters. The mystery genre is a perfect medium for exploring the past, bringing it and its colourful protagonists to life again. Whether variations on actual historical characters or imaginary ones, the sleuths of the past now enchant tens of thousands of readers and the historical mystery is one of the fastest growing commercial areas in crime writing.

Edith was much loved. A modest and warm person, she was quite unaware of the amount of affection fans and other writers had for her and I will always remember with great joy the splendid look of surprise on her face when, after several years of trying to convince her to come down to London from her beloved country retreat, she finally agreed to do a signing for *The Potter's Field* at the Murder One bookshop, despite her poor state of health. She genuinely believed no one would turn up to see her. Lo and behold, there were queues inching their way past the front door on to the Charing Cross Road, most holding magnificent bouquets of flowers. Apart from a few local appearances in Shropshire, she had never until then made a public appearance as a writer and the pleasure on her face at witnessing her readers and their pleasure at meeting her was unsurpassed. She stayed on much longer than scheduled and had a kind word for every fan laden with books to sign. Amusingly enough, encouraged by this, she then agreed to do a gruelling publicity and signing tour of the USA a few months later, where the response to her appearance was as enthusiastic. Remember that by now Edith was in her eighties, and moved with great difficulty!

We now miss her very much, but I retain the consolation that in her final years the popularity she attained became apparent to her, and there is no greater reward for a writer.

This anthology celebrates her life and work. With the blessing of her estate, I asked some of the major British and American mystery writers working in the historical mystery field to pen a brand-new story in her honour. All were delighted to do so, acknowledging quite openly the debt many owed her. Some novelists are featured here with their first ever short stories, others with their usual series characters and some with new characters altogether. A multitude of historical periods have been selected, giving a wonderful idea of the scope historical fiction affords the writer. In addition, we introduce a new author, David Howard, who was discovered through a competition in *Crime Time* magazine which, had Edith still been alive, she would have wished to be a patron of, in view of the warmth and encouragement she always provided for newcomers in the field.

A memorial is also a celebration. Once again, the past comes magnificently alive in these pages and so does the spirit of Ellis Peters.

Maxim Jakubowski

I cannot really decide when I became interested in history or historical novels. It seems as far back as I can remember! I was brought up on Robert Louis Stevenson's *Treasure Island*, *Quentin Durward* and then on to Walter Scott and Charles Dickens. Perhaps the greatest influence were two authors who write for both adults and children: Rosemary Sutcliffe and Henry Treece. They both had this marvellous ability of transporting you back in time: of being able to create past civilisations. Both novelists were brilliant at being able to take legends and put them into historical context. I still believe Sutcliffe's *Sword at Sunset* is the best book ever written on King Arthur whilst Treece's novel on *Jason and the Argonauts* was spellbinding. Others came my way. George Shipway's *An Imperial Governor*, Nigel Tranter's novels about Scotland and, of course, Mary Renault.

My real interest in historical detection was fuelled by my thesis on the murder of Edward II in 1327 as well as Josephine Tey's *Daughter of Time* where the novelist brilliantly used historic techniques to resolve a real historical conundrum. Umberto Eco's *Name of the Rose* (perhaps the film more than the book) also influenced me. I must admit I have never read any of Ellis Peters' Cadfael novels. It is a treat I am looking forward to some day. However, I did find Ellis, writing under

1

her own name, Edith Pargeter, a brilliant historical novelist and her *Bloody Field By Shrewsbury* still ranks as a classic.

Paul C. Doherty

A Counter-Blast to Tobacco

Paul C. Doherty

S ir George Carey knew he was dying. He sat back in his chair clutching at the hideous pains turning his belly and chest into a sheet of flame. It must be poison! He could not rise or move whilst his mind, for some strange reason, kept going back to those mist-hung glades in the forests of Virginia; dark and green, menacing yet quiet, shapes shifting amongst the trees. Another image – Sir George tried to move but still found he couldn't – the *Fire Drake*, sails furled, battling head winds in the grey swell of the Atlantic which rose, hurling itself up at the dark, lowering skies.

The pain was so intense, Sir George found breathing difficult; an icy sweat dampened his face despite the roaring fire. His hand went out to the hand bell but it was too far, almost as far as those mist-hung glades. His hand brushed the white clay pipe full of rich tobacco. He had been about to light it when the pains first began. What could it be? He had eaten and drunk hours ago! No wine, no food here in his private chamber. He stared blearily at the door, firmly locked and barred, then at the leaded, mullioned glass window: this seemed to disappear. He could see the trees, smell the rich, rotting vegetation of the Virginian forest. Copper-skinned Mohawks, eagle plumes in their hair, were coming towards him, running at a half crouch, arrows to bows. Some carried tomahawks. Sir George's head went back. He must get within the stockade. He would be safe there. Or had he been struck already? This terrible pain! The window began to whirl as Sir George Carey, captain of His Majesty's ship the *Fire Drake* collapsed and died over his desk.

'You are, sir?' The manservant stood in the doorway ready to block this stranger's entrance. After all, there was enough trouble with the master dead – some whispered poisoned – in his chamber. Lady Carey was having the vapours, the servants and wenches in the kitchen and buttery were filling the house with their lamentations whilst he, Carnabell, butler to Sir George Carey, had not yet finished the funeral arrangements. There was black lawn cloth to drape over the pictures and furniture. The house should be in mourning. Sir George, a stickler for discipline and protocol, would have insisted on that. Now it was all chaos and, to make matters worse, strangers were rapping on the door in the dead of night. Carnabell narrowed his eyes. The visitor was tall, not dressed like a courtier. His cloak was of grey wool and the black doublet beneath sported silver buttons; a white linen shirt open at the neck; leggings of dark kersey-blue pushed into polished, high-heeled Spanish riding boots. The stranger didn't seem at all perturbed. He kept his hand on his sword hilt, the other grasping a cream-coloured scroll tied with a scarlet ribbon.

'I asked if I could enter?' The stranger's weather-beaten face showed no emotion though Carnabell glimpsed a flicker of annoyance in the dark blue eyes. Carnabell liked to judge visitors. This was a soldier, yet one with authority. Was he from the court? Yet he wore no wig or powder on the black hair which fell uncombed to his shoulders. No paint decorated his eyes or lips like those fops who constantly sought the eye of King James.

'I am Robert Nightingale,' the stranger declared. 'I have been sent by His Majesty's Council. Now, sir, I could stand here all night.' He waved the scroll. 'This is the King's writ.'

Carnabell hastily stepped back and gave the deepest bow. 'I am sorry, sir,' he stammered. 'My wits are wandering; Sir George's death!' Carnabell could have kicked himself. He had heard of Nightingale. The King's man, with a long nose for trouble. Sir George had once mentioned him. Nightingale, however, was already taking his cloak off. Carnabell caught it and hung the cloak on a hook just inside the doorway. Nightingale walked in with a slight swagger, a man sure of his power and authority.

'I'd best take you, sir.' Carnabell brushed by and led Nightingale down the wooden-panelled passageway into the small comfortable parlour specially reserved for the Master and his visitors. Here the panelling only covered half the wall. Above it the pink plaster was washed and cleaned. Portraits hung, paintings of ships and a drawing of a native. On the great mantel hearth, which housed a roaring fire, stood objects and curiosities from Sir George's travels to the Americas. A decorated axe, curiously shaped pots, a figurine made out of polished wood, a large white tusk. Some said this came from a dragon. Sir George had laughed when he had heard this and told Carnabell it came from a Narwhal. The manservant would have asked Nightingale to sit down but the royal emissary had already done so, turning a quilted chair towards the fire. He even had the temerity to pick up the copper-headed poker and was pushing at a log until it broke in a crackle of sparks.

'Ah, yes,' Nightingale murmured. 'No wine but a cup of posset. It's cold as death outside. They say the Thames will freeze this winter. You'd best tell Lady Carey I am here.'

Carnabell hurried off. He told a weeping servant girl to heat a cup of posset, make sure it was spiced and hot, bind it with a velvet cloth and give it to their visitor.

'The King's man,' Carnabell whispered warningly. 'Eyes like a hunting dog!'

The maid hurried into the kitchen. She took a pewter cup and a jar of nutmeg then pushed a hot iron into the fire. She'd wait until it was almost white with heat and use it to warm the wine. She wanted to ask more questions but Carnabell was already away to warn the family, assembled in the dining hall, that the King's man had arrived.

Lady Margaret Carey found it difficult to understand Carnabell's message. Her fat, doughy white face was soaked in tears. Those little black eyes, which could become so imperious and hot-tempered, were now red-rimmed from worry and lack of sleep. She clutched her servant's arm.

'Woe is us!' she moaned. 'Sir George lies dead in his chamber. I cannot even tend his corpse! Now the King's man is here!'

'Hush now, madam.' Dr Thomas Somerset, sitting on her left, grasped her cold hand. He rubbed it between his. Lady Margaret forced a smile and blinked prettily. Sir Thomas truly was a handsome man with his gold, swept-back hair, rubicund cheeks and dancing blue eyes. He would surely be a comfort in the months ahead! Oh yes – there would be changes! She glared down the table. No more talk of sea voyages now, she thought viciously. No more sea charts! No more whispers in his chamber! No long months, even years, of separation and loneliness. Lady Margaret *hated* the sea. She couldn't abide even to cross the Thames whilst she knew that, despite thirty years of marriage, Sir George always had another love – that damnable ship, those mysterious places across the far horizon.

Lady Margaret's pebble-black eyes quickly studied the others. Aye, and it would be farewell to her, Sophia Littleton, how old, eighteen summers? 'Beautiful as a rainbow,' Sir George had described her and so she was, with those gold, clustering ringlets, light blue eyes and that perfectly formed face. Now she sat in a dark-coloured damask dress, its lace ruff brushing her chin. Sophia was grieving, but quietly, the tears rolling silently down her face. She had been the only daughter of Sir George's great friend, a fellow sea captain whose ship had left for Virginia but never returned, so Sophia,

6

as a young girl, had entered their household. Sir George had been so proud of her!

Lady Margaret's lower lip trembled and, ignoring Carnabell, she launched into another fit of tears. A cunning ploy so she could study more closely the expression of the young man sitting beside Sophia. A strange one that, she thought, with his copper-coloured skin and eyes as black as night: hair swept back like raven's wings; a strong cruel face with high cheekbones, hooked nose and thin, bloodless lips. What had George said when he had brought him home? A native, a member of what tribe? Ah yes, the Mohawk. Sir George had found him, the only survivor after a massacre. Her husband had brought him home. Yes, he had dared to bring him here: a dirty heathen with his strange looks and clacking tongue! Oh, he had been baptised at the font in St Mary Le Bow and he was dressed as smartly as any young man in London but he was still a demon! He would have to go! Ah yes, there would be changes all round.

'My lady?' Dr Somerset squeezed her hand again, his eyes now not so merry but watchful. 'Robert Nightingale, a scurrier from the royal council, is here.'

'This is ridiculous!' Lady Margaret drew herself up, plump shoulders quivering.

'It is not ridiculous, ma'am.'

Charles Carey, Sir George's only son from a previous marriage, joined his hands together and stared down the table. His auburn hair was dishevelled. He plucked at the sleeping robe round his shoulders. Lady Margaret smiled sweetly back. She hated this young man with his airs and graces, a relic of Sir George's passionate youth when he'd married the brat's mother! She had died in childbirth. Now Charles was a physician at St Bartholomew's in Smithfield; he'd successfully resisted his father's urge to go a-wandering.

'Mother,' Charles insisted. 'I believe Father died from poisoning.'

'But that's ridiculous.' Sir Thomas spoke up. 'I have not examined your father's corpse but . . .'

'I have! I believe he was poisoned.'

'By the foul tobacco he smoked!' Lady Margaret tried to sound jocular but realised she had said the wrong thing. 'We will see him now,' she declared defiantly. 'Bring this council man in here. Oh, and Carnabell, no servants.'

A short while later Robert Nightingale, one hand on the hilt of his sword, the other clasping the velvet cloth around the posset cup, walked into the hall. He placed the cup down, unbuckled his sword belt and looped it over the back of his chair, then sat down at the far end as calm as you please. He sipped from the cup as Lady Margaret made the introductions. Nightingale's eyes rested on each and then moved on when Lady Margaret did. She tried to maintain her calm poise but, secretly, she was frightened of this man who showed her no courtesy as the widow of a famous sea captain. He reminded her of a kestrel Sir George had once kept. The bird would sit on its perch and scrutinise whoever caught its attention. That's what you are, she thought, a bird of the night! The sooner I get you out of this house the better!

'And now, sir,' she concluded, 'I have made the introductions.'

The emissary leaned back in his chair, running a thumbnail along his upper lip.

'I am Robert Nightingale, a lawyer attached to Star Chamber. I advise His Majesty on –' he paused – 'on affairs of state.'

'What affairs?' Dr Somerset asked. 'I have heard of you, sir.'

'What have you heard?' came the sharp reply.

'That you are a lawyer.'

'I've said that.'

'A Scotsman by birth?'

'So is the King.'

'And a former Catholic priest.'

The word hung like a noose in the air. Nightingale lowered his eyes.

'They say you came here,' Somerset continued, 'to bring popish practices back to this island. That you were captured by the Judas men, and after a short stay in the Tower, recanted your errors.'

'Some of that's true,' Nightingale replied languidly. 'And some of it isn't.'

'So what is the truth?' Lady Margaret jibed.

'I'll tell you what, my lady.' Nightingale moved in his chair. 'If I find the truth here, I'll tell you all the truth you want.' He brushed some dust from his white lace cuffs. 'Sir George Carey,' he began, 'was captain of his His Majesty's ship the *Fire Drake*. A man who sailed to His Majesty's colony in Virginia and brought great profit to the King and to his realm.'

'Yet found little favour at court,' Charles Carey broke in.

'True, true.' Nightingale steepled his fingers. 'Sir George was one of Raleigh's men.' He paused.

Lady Margaret put her hands on the table. Raleigh had been executed in Palace Yard and Sir George had never forgiven the King. Perhaps that's where the breach had occurred?

'My father was always loyal,' Charles insisted. 'He bore the scars of many a brush with the Spanish and other enemies of His Majesty.'

Nightingale waved his hand apologetically. 'I'm here, sir, at the personal request of the King. I believe *you*, Master Charles, sent a letter to Whitehall saying that your father had died in mysterious circumstances. The council was then in session. I was despatched here immediately. If there was a breach between your father and His Majesty,' Nightingale continued evenly, 'then it was not so much Raleigh but what Raleigh brought back to England.'

'Tobacco!'

Lady Margaret glared. How dare the native speak without permission?

'I beg your pardon, sir?' For the first time Nightingale allowed himself a smile.

'Tobacco,' the Mohawk replied. His voice was harsh, rather nasal. He turned slightly to stare down at the King's emissary. 'My master, my *father* –' he emphasised the last word – 'believed in the properties of tobacco.'

'Yes, yes, he did,' Nightingale agreed. His smile widened. 'And, as you know, His Majesty is the author of a very famous tract against the damnable substance: "A Counter-Blast to Tobacco". Sir George, I believe, challenged him on this, posted a proclamation at St Paul's Cross and elsewhere in the city.'

'He was writing a rebuttal,' Charles broke in. 'A pamphlet he intended to take to the stationers.'

'Yes, I know,' Nightingale replied. 'His Majesty was most interested in this. Indeed, even before I left the council, His Majesty was insisting that this tobacco substance actually caused Sir George's death.'

'So, all this nonsense about poison?' Lady Margaret glared at her stepson.

'We must investigate,' Nightingale intervened. 'Now, my lady, what exactly happened tonight?'

'We had dinner as usual, just after dark, about six o'clock. Sir George retired.'

'At what hour?'

'Shortly after seven. The meal was frugal. Sir George always retired to his chamber for two or three hours. He left instructions to his manservant here –' Lady Margaret flickered a hand at the Mohawk – 'that he was not to be disturbed until the bells of St Mary Le Bow began to toll for curfew, ten of the clock precisely.'

'And then what?'

'He left the dinner table here,' Charles broke in.

'Did he take any food with him? Or drink?'

'No,' the Mohawk declared. 'Sir George was always frightened of wine tumbling over and staining his manuscripts. He was a most regular man, Sir George. Before dinner I had prepared two of his clay pipes, filled them

10

with tobacco and, when he retired, I went with him. I lit the capped candles on his desk as well as oil lamps round the room. Sir George was very eager to continue. He was at his desk and . . .'

'And you noticed nothing untoward?' Nightingale asked.

'No.' The Mohawk's face creased into a smile. 'Sir George was a very precise man. Nothing was out of place. I left the chamber. As usual Sir George told me to stay on guard outside.'

'And did you?'

'Yes.' The Mohawk turned and glanced quickly at Lady Sophia. 'Except I went down to the buttery for something to eat and drink. Sir George was safe enough. It was a custom which he always insisted on at sea: I would stand on guard outside his cabin.'

'And what happened then?'

'As normal.' Carnabell spoke up from where he stood behind Lady Margaret. 'Once the bells of St Mary Le Bow chimed ten, I went and knocked on Sir George's door. You see, sir, he always locked and bolted it from the inside. Anyway, I knocked and knocked.'

'Yes, yes,' Lady Margaret snapped. 'Continue.'

'No answer,' the aggrieved Carnabell replied, raising his eyes heavenward. 'So I squatted down and peered through the key hole but I couldn't see anything because the key was still in the lock. I turned to the Mohawk: he was seated in the stairwell, a lantern beside him. He was looking at a book Sir George had lent him. He joined in the knocking.'

'Then they came for me.' Lady Margaret spoke up. 'Sir Thomas and I were sitting in the parlour, sharing a jug of mead.'

'We both went upstairs,' the good doctor declared. 'There was more clamour.'

'By which time I had returned,' Charles added. 'I had left shortly after dinner to visit a patient at St Bartholomew's. It was my decision to break the door down. We used a bench

11

from one of the galleries. Inside Sir George lay sprawled in his chair, eyes popping, mouth open. I felt his wrist, there was no life pulse, or blood beat in the neck.'

'Was his flesh warm or cold?' Nightingale asked.

'Cold,' Sir Thomas replied.

'So Sir George must have died shortly after he retired.'

'That is so.'

'Why did he lock and bolt the door from the inside?'

'It was part of the custom of the house,' Charles replied. 'When Father said he didn't want to be disturbed, he meant he didn't want to be disturbed.'

'And inside the chamber?'

'Nothing was disturbed.' The Mohawk spoke. 'The windows were closed. Some of the candles were guttered out.'

'And?' Nightingale waved his hand. 'There was no strange smell or . . . ?'

'Nothing, sir, except tobacco. Sir George's two pipes lay on the desk.' The Mohawk passed a hand over his eyes as if eager to hide any emotion. 'Sir George was a good master. He lived a good life and should have died a good death. Not like some rat poisoned in a hole.'

'Watch your tongue!' Lady Margaret snapped.

'My tongue is my own as are the thoughts of my heart,' the Mohawk replied. 'I will pray for Sir George, in the manner of my tribe, that the Great Spirit will receive him. He was a noble man and a brave warrior.'

'Enough of such pagan nonsense!' Lady Margaret drummed her fingers on the table. 'Master Nightingale, what is all this?'

'Just a few questions, my lady, and then I'll be gone.' Nightingale smiled quickly. 'Though, of course, I must examine the corpse. What did Sir George eat and drink at dinner?'

'The same as us,' Charles replied. 'I was sitting opposite him. The same wine from the same jug. Roast goose from the common platter.'

'I know that.' Sophia spoke up. Her voice was soft but very clear. She seemed to be lost in a reverie but now stared

12

narrow-eyed at Nightingale. 'Everything he ate and drank at this table we all ate and drank. When he left the table, Michael here –' she touched the Mohawk gently on the wrist – 'led him up to his chamber.'

'And he ate nothing else?'

'Nothing whatsoever.'

'And where were you all during the hours Sir George was in his chamber? Master Charles, you went to St Bartholomew's? Lady Margaret and Physician Somerset, you stayed in the parlour? And Sophia?'

'I was in my chamber,' she replied tersely. 'I was reading – Michael has the second volume – the first of Sir George's travels to Virginia.'

'And you never left your chamber?'

'I came out.' The young woman coloured. 'To meet Michael.' Sophia chose to ignore Lady Margaret's withering glance of disapproval.

'Did Sir George favour your friendship with Michael?' Nightingale asked tentatively.

'He more than favoured it!' Lady Margaret snapped. 'He positively encouraged it.'

'We are hand fast,' Sophia declared. 'Michael and I are betrothed to be married.'

Nightingale nodded and stared down at the table. He spread out his fingers, moving them so the light from the candles glittered in his silver and gold rings. A dandy and a fop? Sophia wondered. A hanger-on at court? Except there was something sharp about the emissary's eyes, a slight cast to his mouth. Sophia, who had been lost in memories of her dead guardian, felt a chill of apprehension. This court limner, this royal sniffer-out, would not give up so easily or trot back to Whitehall unless he was satisfied.

Nightingale leaned back in the chair. 'Sir George drew up a will?'

'Yes,' Charles replied. He glanced along the table. 'On that we are all united. The will has not been changed for years. Sophia has her own wealth. I have already been given my patrimony. There are most generous bequests for Michael whilst the rest, including the house, goes to the Lady Margaret.'

'Well, well, well.' Nightingale pushed back his chair and rose. 'I ask you all to stay here. Perhaps, my lady –' he gave the most superficial of bows – 'Master Carnabell could show me Sir George's room?'

Lady Margaret shrugged one shoulder.

'And the corpse?' he asked.

'It lies in my father's bedroom,' Charles declared. 'His chamber is undisturbed though I stripped my father's body for burial.'

'So soon?' Nightingale asked.

'I wished to examine him for any cuts, marks or bruises.'

'And were there any?'

'None that were fresh. Old scars. As Michael says, he was a warrior.'

Nightingale followed Carnabell out of the room. They went into the hallway and up the great oaken staircase. The balustrade and newel were of the finest polished oak. Portraits and damask cloths hung on the plaster above the line-fold panelling.

'A wealthy man, your master?'

'Sir George was successful in his trade,' the manservant replied tentatively.

'And in love.'

Carnabell paused on the stairway, pigeon chest slightly heaving. 'He was loved by his family. His relationship with the Lady Margaret was formal but friendly enough.'

'And his children?'

'I am glad you asked that.' The manservant smiled. 'Sir George regarded Charles, Sophia and Michael as his off-spring.'

'Do you like the Mohawk?'

'A brave man, he loved my master and therefore, sir, I like

him. He is kind enough, polite, self-effacing. He worshipped the ground Sir George trod on. If the good captain had sailed to the ends of the earth Michael would have gone with him.'

'And Sophia?'

'What you see, sir. A lovely young woman much smitten by the Mohawk.'

'And Charles?'

'A good physician, a man who cares for the poor. Sir George was disappointed that he did not follow him to sea but their relationship was strong.'

'Except in one thing?'

'Yes, sir.' Carnabell sniffed then smiled. 'Charles totally disagreed with him about the taste of tobacco: he claimed it was a poison spat out by hell.'

'And the good physician Somerset?'

'Oh, a kindly enough man. He was helping Sir George with his tract though I suspect that he, like young Charles, had a deep distaste for tobacco and its properties.'

Nightingale walked on. They reached the first gallery, a comfortable, warm place. Capped braziers stood in the window embrasures, hooded candles glowed in their bright brass sockets. Sir George's chamber stood at the far end just off the stairwell leading up to the next gallery. The door hung askew, its woodwork smashed, as was the lintel around it. Nightingale crouched down and examined the battered lock and the bolts pulled from their clasps on the lintel inside. Carnabell moved around lighting the candles and oil lamps. Nightingale sighed.

'This door was certainly forced.' He rose and gazed round the chamber. It was comfortable with velvet drapes on the walls. The painted windows were closed. A small cot bed in the corner; shelves full of books, chests and trunks. The chamber was dominated by a huge oaken table with a high-backed, red leather chair, its high arms carved in the shape of snarling lions.

'And Sir George was found here?'

He sat down on the chair and stared round the leather-topped desk. There were ink pots, pumice stones, parchment, knives, rolls of vellum. A large brass candlestick and a copper bowl containing two blackening clay pipes; beside them a cluster of half-burnt tapers. Nightingale pulled across a sheaf of documents and stared at the heading written in a clerkly copperplate hand.

'THE BENEFICIAL PROPERTIES OF TOBACCO A Respectful Answer to His Majesty's Recent Work on the matter, by Sir George Carey.'

Nightingale leafed through the document. Sir George had presented a concise case giving the history of tobacco, its medicinal properties and its use by the natives of His Majesty's colony of Virginia. 'Tell me, Carnabell, were you here when the door was broken down?'

'Yes, sir.'

'And you noticed nothing untoward?'

'Nothing whatsoever, sir. Except the air was thick with tobacco and Sir George was just slumped there.'

'Had he been writing?'

Carnabell's fingers went to his lips and he closed his eyes. 'No, sir, he had not. I remember that. The quills were still in their holders and the ink pot unstoppered.'

'So, what did Sir George do when he came here?'

'I suppose the same he did every night, sir. He would sit, light his pipe and think. A great thinker, the master.'

'And then he would write?'

'Oh yes, sir, he'd become all feverish.'

'And the pipes were here?'

'Yes, sir, they were in the copper bowl.'

Nightingale pulled this across, and picked up the pipes. They both smelt, as did the room, faintly aromatic, tinged with that rather pleasing fragrance Nightingale had experienced in the cook shops and taverns in the city. He studied the pipes curiously: they both had large bowls and long thin stems. One was full of feathery ash but the other, he felt with his little finger, contained some tobacco halfway down the bowl. He put the pipe to his lips, ignoring Carnabell's gasp at such impunity, yet all he could taste was tobacco. He noticed both pipes were discoloured, in some places yellow and, around the top of the bowl, a crusty black. The mouth pieces had both the same indentations where Sir George had grasped them between his strong teeth. Nightingale put the pipes back and crossed to the fireplace. Taking the poker he sifted amongst the white feathery ash but there was nothing there. He looked at the bookshelves and moved to the mantelpiece. He sniffed at the aromatic pot holding more tobacco and the six pipes in a rack beside it.

'Sir George always brought tobacco from Thurstons in the Strand,' Carnabell declared. 'He loved this chamber.' He added wistfully: 'It was the only place Lady Margaret allowed him to smoke. I think that's why he really came here.'

'No one else in the house partakes of tobacco?'

'Oh no, sir.' Carnabell shook his head disapprovingly. 'This was Sir George's smoking chamber.'

Nightingale again looked round the room. 'And nothing has been taken in or out?'

'No, sir. I know this chamber like the back of my hand, better than anybody. Apart from Sir George,' he added mournfully.

'We'd best see the corpse,' Nightingale declared.

Carnabell led him back down the gallery. He took a candlestick from a holder and opened the door. The place smelt of death. Already black lawn cloths had been placed across cupboards, chairs and portraits. Nightingale waited while Carnabell tiptoed across and lit two lamps on either side of the great four-poster bed. The dark green curtains were drawn but these were now pulled back. The body lay covered by a white linen sheet. Carnabell gently took this off and Nightingale studied the thickset corpse. A strong body, muscular and sinewy, pink scars on the chest, stomach and thighs. The face was liverish, eyes half-open. One of the coins had slipped off. At Nightingale's insistence Carnabell turned the corpse over but Nightingale could see no mark or wound.

'You'd best send for the physicians,' he advised. 'Master Charles and Dr Somerset.'

Once Carnabell left, Nightingale studied the corpse more closely. He had some knowledge of poisons and the effects of apoplexy. He wasn't sure, but the discoloration of the face, the slightly blueish tinge to the cheeks and the eerie red rash which appeared on the lower chest and stomach indicated poisoning might have taken place. Holding the candle carefully, Nightingale opened the stiffening mouth. The teeth were strong and fine but the tongue was blackish, slightly swollen.

'Poison it must be!' Nightingale murmured and hastily got up as he heard footsteps outside.

Somerset, followed by Master Charles, bustled into the room with Carnabell behind them.

'What made you think he was poisoned, Master Charles?'

'The swollen blackened tongue, the discoloration of the skin on my father's chest and stomach. His hands, too, are swollen, as are his cheeks and the inside of his throat. Dr Somerset, would you agree?'

The physician pulled a face. 'It is possible.'

'And what poison would you say was used?'

Master Charles blew his cheeks out. 'Sir, there are more types of poison in London now than there are rats. Arsenic, antimony and different other chemicals. Some can kill within a matter of minutes, even seconds.'

'Could it have been the tobacco?' Nightingale asked.

Somerset looked over his shoulder at Master Charles. 'It is possible, sir. The London Pharmacopoeia published in 1618 says a juice can be distilled from tobacco which, under observation, has killed a rabbit in a matter of seconds.'

18

'But this is not the case now. Is it?' Nightingale asked.

'Again, all things are possible,' Somerset answered briskly. 'We have yet to put Sir George's tobacco under some form of chemical distillation. It may have been a putrid strand but, sir, if it *was* poison what proof do you have? I agree, the discoloration of the corpse . . .' His voice faltered. 'Anyway, who would murder Sir George?'

He looked accusingly at his companion.

'I have not said that,' Charles stammered. 'I am simply talking as a physician.' His eyes fell away. 'The poisoning could be natural.'

'Thank you.' Nightingale turned his back on them. 'Oh, if I may? Could I sleep in Sir George's chamber this evening? I saw a small cot bed there. I would like to be alone before reaching a satisfactory conclusion.'

Charles and Somerset agreed. Carnabell offered to bring up a jug of wine and a platter of dried meat, cheese and some freshly baked bread. Nightingale absent-mindedly agreed. After the others left, he stood for a while staring down at the corpse.

'You were poisoned,' he whispered. 'And, do you know, sir, I believe you were murdered. No accident could occur so fast, so speedily.'

'I agree.'

Nightingale whirled round, hand going to his sword hilt. The Mohawk stood just within the doorway. Nightingale caught his breath.

'Sir, you surprised me. You move . . .'

'Like a shadow?' The Mohawk drew closer. Nightingale was struck by how handsome he looked. His face was now not so fierce but strong, resolute; his unblinking black eyes held his gaze.

'Why do you think your master was poisoned?'

'Death came too swift.' The Mohawk tapped the side of his head. 'You have been in danger, sir?'

'Many times.'

19

'And you know when danger is present, even though you can't see, hear or touch it.'

Nightingale nodded.

'In the same way I know Sir George was poisoned.'

'By whom?'

'If I knew that, sir . . .' The Mohawk's hand went to the short stabbing dirk which hung from the side of his belt. 'Master Charles,' he continued, 'has talked of poison. My people have poisons which can kill in two breaths. I have been across this city. It is no less dangerous than the glades and forests of my valley.' He walked towards the door. 'You will sleep in Sir George's chamber.' He turned, his hand on the latch. 'They say you were once a priest?'

Nightingale didn't reply.

'Pray to his spirit,' the Mohawk declared. 'And perhaps the truth will come.' He pushed back his long black hair. 'And I will mourn him my way.'

The Mohawk left as quietly as he came. Nightingale walked out along the gallery; Carnabell was standing outside Sir George's writing chamber.

'Sir, is there anything you wish before I retire?'

'Did Sir George always keep his room locked?'

'Oh no, sir. Only when he went in. It was his sanctuary. Will the corpse be removed tomorrow, sir?'

Nightingale looked back down the darkening gallery. From below he heard the sound of voices, the opening and shutting of doors.

'This old house fair creaks,' Carnabell murmured. 'Sir George said it was like a ship riding at anchor. Tonight it will be his ghost.'

'What do you mean?' Nightingale asked.

'Sir George is bound to walk.' Carnabell's eyes gazed quickly down the gallery. 'I have smelt him, sir.'

'Smelt him?'

'Yes, sir, tonight, after Sir George's corpse had been found. I went back into the parlour. Do you know, sir, I smelt his tobacco smoke, I am sure of it! Now Lady Margaret would never let him smoke there!'

'Could it have come from up here?' Nightingale asked.

'But I didn't smell it elsewhere, sir. A keen nose I have. You need it, sir, when you check on servants' work or cooks preparing food in the kitchen and buttery. I am sure I smelt smoke in the parlour. I told the Lady Margaret.'

'And?'

'A short while later she summoned me to the parlour but I couldn't smell it any more.'

'Good night, Carnabell.' Nightingale opened the chamber door then pulled it closed. The lock was damaged but the door held fast. Carnabell had lit candles and a lantern horn. A tray bearing a jug, a goblet and a pewter platter with some food had been placed on the table. Nightingale sat down in the chair and absent-mindedly filled the cup and nibbled at the cheese and bread. He leaned back, cradling the cup in his hands, and stared at the closed window. He recalled the Mohawk's words. '*Requiem dona ei Domine,*' he whispered. 'Eternal rest grant unto him O Lord.'

What had really happened here? Nightingale put the cup down. He picked the rack up and placed it on the table. All the pipes were clean, the bowls empty. One caught his eye and he pulled it out and stared curiously at the stem. Unlike the rest it bore no indentation or teeth marks. The bowl was yellowing, blackened round the rim, but the stem itself looked clear. Nightingale, mystified, put the pipe back and picked up the two from the copper bowl. He shook the dust of the first down on to the desk and with the tip of his dagger cleaned the second one. The wadge of tobacco which fell out was only burnt slightly. There was a top film of grey ash but the rest of the tobacco was soft, untouched by flame. Nightingale held it to his nose. It was sweet, aromatic; Nightingale took the pipe and went across to the small porcelain tobacco pot. He took a pinch out and put it on the desk, kneading it gently between his fingers. It was slightly damp and left a brown

21

mark. He filled the pipe, took a taper from the mantelpiece and, crouching down near the fire, lit the taper and then the pipe itself.

Nightingale had taken tobacco before but the first breath he drew made him cough and retch; his eyes watered. He took the taper and again lit the pipe, this time drawing deeply then blowing the smoke out. He felt slightly nauseous but continued. After a short while he stopped. He squatted down by the grate and cleaned the pipe. Most of the tobacco had burnt to ash from the deep draughts he had taken.

Nightingale returned to the desk. He ate some more of the cheese and sipped at the wine.

'Sir George came here,' he murmured. 'He lit one pipe and finished it. He had barely started on the second when he became unwell. He put the pipe down and shortly afterwards he was in deep distress. What if?' Nightingale sat, face cupped in his hands, watching the tobacco smoke he had blown out curl and drift towards the mullioned window.

Where were the rest? he thought. Master Charles had gone, the Mohawk was on guard outside and the others? Nightingale felt a tingle of excitement in his stomach. He got up and opened the door but he could still hear sounds from below. He went back into the chamber, picked up the pipe which had first evoked suspicion and sat on the edge of the cot bed. He felt tired and swung himself up, still clasping the pipe, and drifted into sleep.

He woke hours later. Most of the candles had guttered out. He felt cold and, crouching by the fire, thrust on some more kindling and another log. He sat and watched the flames lick and, in a burst of sparks, catch hold. He drank some wine and left the chamber. The house was now silent. Nightingale crept downstairs. He pushed open the parlour door. The place was in darkness and, for a while, he stumbled about quietly cursing. At last he lit a candle and soon had every light in the chamber glowing. He arranged some of the candles in a circle, picked up the matting and shook it gently into the pool of light. Kneeling down Nightingale sifted through bits of the debris which had fallen out. There was a pin, a button, but then he saw the dark strands, like pieces of wiry thread. He picked these up and rubbed them carefully, pressing them between his fingers. He noticed the dark brown stain they left. He then examined the chair but could find nothing and, taking the candle, sifted amongst the white ash in the fire grate, only giving up when he found the traces of a burnt taper lying to one side. He took a small money pouch from his belt, put the items he had found inside and returned to his chamber.

For a while he squatted on the floor next to the fire. Nightingale suspected a terrible murder had taken place but how could he prove it? What real proof could he offer? The assassin, with the aid of an astute lawyer, would make nonsense of the meagre evidence he'd found. Nightingale sighed and went back to bed, wrapping the blankets around him. He slept fitfully, listening to the sounds outside. A chambermaid trudged wearily up the stairs so he went out and asked if she would be so good as to bring Master Michael to his chamber as soon as possible.

Nightingale sat behind the desk. He started when the door opened and the young Mohawk slipped into the room. If it hadn't been for the voice, the eyes, Nightingale would have thought he was dreaming. The Mohawk had stripped himself of all his fine raiment. Now he wore buckskin leggings, a small kilt of leather over his groin. His chest was bare except for the war belt slung across one shoulder. Yet the changes to his face and hair were the most remarkable. His hair had been shaven except for a black tuft which ran from the forehead back to the nape of his neck. His cheeks were now covered in white paint, his eyes ringed by red ochre. Two black streaks on either cheek emphasised his fearsome looks and on his chin was daubed a red arrowhead which stretched up to his lower lip. From his hair at the back of his head two eagle feathers sprouted. He carried a long, strange-looking pipe and, in the other hand, a small axe, its black blade winking in the firelight. His bare feet hardly made any sound. When Nightingale offered him a stool the Mohawk just shook his head. He squatted by the desk, cross-legged, looking up at him.

'You mourn your master?' Nightingale asked.

'I mourn him in the manner of my people,' Mohawk replied. 'I have not slept but watched the night so his spirit is not lonely before he makes that final journey.'

'And how long will you mourn?' Nightingale asked curiously.

'According to my people, a warrior's spirit will stay three days in the place of his death.' He stretched out his hand in a cutting movement. 'Only then can he make that long journey into the West.'

'And if that man is murdered?'

'He will travel in peace knowing that justice will be done.' The Mohawk's black eyes gazed unblinkingly at Nightingale. 'And you have found the truth?'

'I have found the truth,' Nightingale confirmed.

The Mohawk nodded. 'I know, it's in your heart as it is in mine and Master Charles'.'

'Yes, yes it is, but,' Nightingale sighed, 'the truth and the law are different. Master Charles has his suspicions but he cannot speak them.'

The Mohawk lifted his axe and tapped Nightingale gently on the knee. 'But you have the truth of this murder?'

'Yes, and I shall tell you how. Last night, before supper, someone came to this chamber. He took one of Sir George's pipes from the rack and replaced it with another. This pipe had been especially prepared to look as if it was used, not to be distinguished from the rest. I wouldn't have noticed it –' Nightingale opened his mouth and touched one of his canines – 'if Sir George's bite had not been so strong. The assassin took the pipe he had replaced so as to use it later.'

The Mohawk let out a long sigh.

'Now, Sir George came up here. He bolted and locked the door. He sat thinking about his treatise and smoked one of the pipes you had prepared for him. When he had finished that, he picked up the second.'

'I had left two here,' the Mohawk confirmed.

'Yes, yes, you had, though this second one had been tampered with. The assassin came here before dinner. He, or she, not only replaced a pipe but took one you'd prepared, removed the tobacco wadge, poured in a small pool of deadly poison and the tobacco was then replaced. Sir George quickly finished the first pipe and then started the second. He would find it hard to light, suck vigorously on it and, in doing so, draw the poison up into his mouth and down into his gut. A few drops but, like most powerful poisons, it would work immediately. Sir George became unwell. He probably didn't realise how he had been poisoned. He put the pipe back in the bowl, thinking it was something he'd eaten or drunk. The poison worked fast. Sir George may have known a little but it was too late.'

The Mohawk stared impassively.

'The hue and cry are raised,' Nightingale added dryly. 'The door is broken down. The assassin ensures that he is one of those who enter the room. In the confusion, the examination of Sir George's corpse and its removal to his bed chamber, the assassin simply replaces the poisoned pipe, which he would know by some mark, with the one he'd taken earlier.'

The Mohawk rocked backward and forward staring down at the floor. 'But you have proof?' he asked, not raising his head.

'I have proof but it is meagre.' Nightingale picked up the pipe he had discovered and passed it to the Mohawk. 'This looks an old pipe but I do not think it was Sir George's. Look, there are no teeth marks.'

'Why should he replace a pipe?'

'Just in case a count was made by someone like Carnabell who knew the chamber well, and a pipe was found missing. The poisoned pipe had to be removed and destroyed without suspicion being raised.'

'And what else?' the Mohawk demanded.

'Carnabell said he detected smoke in the parlour. He thought it was Sir George's spirit. I went down there. I found traces of tobacco in the matting – it was fresh, ready to use – as well as the remains of a taper at the back of the fire grate. Now, the only two people who used that parlour yesterday evening were Lady Margaret and the physician Dr Thomas Somerset. Lady Margaret cannot stand the odour of tobacco, can she?'

'It is true,' the Mohawk replied.

'But last evening she made an exception,' Nightingale continued. 'She and Dr Thomas were waiting for Sir George to die. They had taken the pipe; now they must use it to lull any suspicion. Dr Thomas has brought a taper. He lights the pipe he has stolen from Sir George's chamber and, for a short while, smokes it. Lady Margaret would have opened the window. The pipe is now ready to be returned. The window is closed and the taper is thrown into the grate whilst Dr Thomas puts the pipe into his pocket. When the door to Sir George's chamber is forced, Somerset takes the poisoned pipe and replaces it with the one he brought from the parlour. People may suspect but who can prove it? The same number of pipes are in the rack. The two Sir George allegedly smoked are in the bowl on his desk and, apart from the absence of a few teeth marks, a manservant's sharp sense of smell, a few grains of tobacco and a scrap of burnt taper . . .' Nightingale shook his head. 'I can offer no proof. Yet, I tell you this, Mohawk. Dr Thomas wears a long frock coat, does he not? If you can, when I leave, search the pockets of that coat carefully. You will find some trace of the two pipes he carried.'

Nightingale got to his feet and went to the window.

'I shall collect my sword belt and cloak. I shall return to Whitehall and tell His Majesty how Sir George Carey died because of the taste of tobacco.'

'But justice?' the Mohawk spat out.

'You communed with the Spirit?' Nightingale replied without turning round. 'You are my jury, Mohawk. Watch! Wait! Listen! Search! And if I have spoken the truth, then you can be judge and executioner.'

He heard a sound and turned. The Mohawk was on his feet, axe thrust into the sash around his waist. Nightingale clasped the Mohawk's outstretched hand.

'In God's time, sir,' the emissary murmured, 'and at a place of your choosing. If I have spoken the truth, sentence is to be carried out!'

In the balmy days of June, following the sudden and mysterious death of her husband, Lady Margaret Carey and her close and constant companion, Dr Thomas Somerset, left London. They took the Epping Road to the physician's country house which stood in its pleasant grounds on the edge of Theydon Bois. The road wound through deep forest but it was high summer and an easy ride, so no one really understood what could have happened on such a pleasant journey. Lady Margaret and Dr Thomas never reached their destination. No trace, despite the most scrupulous search, was ever found of them or their horses. Lady Sophia and her new husband, the Mohawk warrior Michael, together with Master Charles, could only attend a brief memorial service for them in the church of St Mary Le Bow. Robert Nightingale, the King's special emissary, heard of their disappearance whilst in his writing chamber at Whitehall. He smiled grimly at the news. He thought of those two assassins journeying so merrily along the Epping Road, and that dark, death-bearing shadow, with war paint on his face and eagle feathers in his hair, slipping through the trees in hot pursuit. A good place to attack! Epping, with its soggy marshes and deep morasses, could hide an army. Nightingale sighed, lit a clay pipe then went and opened a window. After all, His Majesty, God bless him, could not tolerate the damnable odour of tobacco.

When I was invited to contribute a new historical mystery for this Ellis Peters Memorial Anthology, my first thought was to set the story in England, in the same general period as the memorable Brother Cadfael novels. I was thinking particularly of the late thirteenth century, about 150 years after Cadfael, and a possible plot came immediately to mind. It would involve a leper, but first I thought I'd better reread the solution to *The Leper of Saint Giles* to make certain I wasn't inadvertently copying it. I wasn't, but I could see uncomfortable similarities in the two plots.

In fact, as I reviewed my entire collection of Ellis Peters novels, it became clear that she had covered the setting and period of her Cadfael books quite thoroughly. I could think of nothing more to add, and it seemed I would have to search in a far different time and place for my plot. I found it in Vienna in 1897, a long way from medieval England.

The historical mystery has always held a special fascination for me, as it did for writers as different as John Dickson Carr and Julian Symons, each of whom turned to period novels late in their careers. Part of its appeal, I think, is the challenge and enjoyment of researching a past era, finding odd little facts to entertain both author and reader.

Though Ellis Peters did not invent the historical mystery,

it was the popularity of the Brother Cadfael novels and television adaptations that played a large part in the current emergence of history as a whodunit. In America and Britain an increasing number of anthologies and single-author collections are devoted to historical mysteries, and it's a rare issue of *Ellery Queen's Mystery Magazine* that does not include at least one such tale.

Certainly the contributions of Ellis Peters and Brother Cadfael will be remembered as long as history and mystery can be merged so fortuitously.

Edward D. Hoch

Wheel in the Sky

Edward D. Hoch

By the autumn of 1897 Oswald Lustig had been retired two years from the Vienna Police Department. His life had fallen into a weekly routine that had changed little since the death of his wife Lisa the previous year. On Fridays he still went to the new police headquarters, barely eleven years old, to collect his pension and speak with old friends. Their greetings had grown more perfunctory with the passage of time, consisting mainly of a hasty word or two from Captain Hesse in the midst of a busy day.

Then, if the weather allowed, Lustig would take a horse-drawn streetcar down the Schottenring to the Danube canal. It was a long, pleasant walk along the canal, with the mammoth new Ferris wheel at the Prater growing larger in his vision as he neared it. He often wished his wife had lived to see the completion of this marvel of architecture, a true rival of Paris's Eiffel Tower. Each Friday when he crossed the canal bridge and reached the Prater he would stand patiently in line before the pleasant young lady selling admission tickets to the wheel for little more than the cost of a beer.

There were abundant green spaces in which to stroll, but it was the amusement park and its new Ferris wheel that dominated the area. He would wander among the hundreds of structures on the Prater grounds, exploring the tents and

31

stalls and taverns that sold everything from beer and wine to ice-cream, coffee and pastries. It was in the Prater dance halls that the waltz became the rage of Europe during the Congress of Vienna nearly ninety years earlier, and that was where Lustig and Lisa learned to dance it much later during their courting days.

Occasionally he would even take a ride on the merry-go-round, but always it was the wheel that drew him. Some two hundred feet in diameter, constructed of huge steel girders held in place by one hundred and twenty spokes of steel cable, it moved at about two and a half feet per second. Its thirty red wooden cabins swinging gently from their supports seemed like foreshortened railway coaches, each bearing a number.

Lustig had soon discovered he was not the only one who made a routine of Friday visits to the Ferris wheel. There was the woman in the hooded cape who regularly fed the pigeons, and the old man (older than Lustig!) who came to sit on one of the benches until the ticket office opened for business. There were young people too, especially the romantic couple who met there, apparently on their lunch hour, to share food from a paper bag. He was never sure of their names, though once he'd heard the young man call out in English to the blonde woman, 'Magdalen! Over here, Magdalen!'

These four plus Lustig were in the habit of getting into cabin number 30 at one o'clock each Friday afternoon. Often they were the only passengers, though each cabin could hold twenty people. Perhaps the number was lucky for them, or perhaps like Lustig they chose it as the least crowded cabin since passengers were loaded starting with number 1.

The city from more than two hundred feet up was a thing of rare beauty. The old man, whose name was Fritz Kralik, told the others of coming here at night during the opening week, seeing the beauty of Vienna in the scattered sections of the city where electricity had been installed. The young couple, obvious lovers, said very little, hugging each other tightly as the swaying car began its assent. One complete revolution took ten minutes once all the cabins were loaded. Since they were enclosed, the Ferris wheel was expected to operate every day, rain or shine.

The woman who'd been feeding the pigeons turned to Lustig and said, 'I see you here often on Fridays. Are you retired?' She was younger than him, probably still in her early fifties, and quite attractive now that she'd pushed back the hood of her cape. Her name was Mina.

'Yes, from the police department.'

'Oh! How interesting!'

With a boyish smile on his lips, Oswald Lustig settled back to enjoy the ride.

The following Friday was a chilly October morning. Lustig awoke and dressed with a certain unease. Neighbours had reported a prowler in their building the previous evening while he was out to dinner, and he'd found scratch marks around the lock of his door. Nothing seemed to be missing but he planned to mention it when paying his usual visit to police headquarters. Before he could do so, Captain Hesse waved him into his office. Hesse was a slender man of military bearing, in his early forties, who'd risen quickly in the department. When off duty he was something of a dandy, attending the State Opera or dining at the Sophienbad in evening clothes complete with top hat and a gold-headed cane, usually in the company of attractive young women. Even in the office he kept an open box of bonbons for visitors and Lustig occasionally took one. 'You may be able to help us with a case,' he said casually. 'You mentioned once that you sometimes go over to the Prater and ride the new Ferris wheel on Friday afternoons.'

'Almost every week,' Lustig acknowledged. 'That wheel has enriched the life of our city.'

'Do you see the same people?'

'Some,' he admitted. 'Why do you ask?'

Captain Hesse sighed. 'There's been a murder. Both the

33

victim and her killer seem linked to the Prater Ferris wheel.' He reached into his desk and took out an envelope. Opening it, he let the contents slide on to the top of the desk. It was a torn admission ticket to the Prater Ferris wheel. The number 30 had been written across the face of it.

'Where did you find this?' he asked the captain.

'Clutched in the victim's right hand, along with a torn piece of cloth.' He produced the cloth next, a ragged dark blue triangle that he tried unsuccessfully to square up with the edges of his desk. Hesse had always been a meticulous man.

'Tell me about it,' Lustig suggested.

'The body of a young woman, Karen Kritzer, was found yesterday morning in her apartment about two blocks from the entrance to the Prater. It's difficult to place the exact time of death, but we believe she was probably killed on Tuesday evening. The landlady hadn't seen her since then and she didn't report for work Wednesday. Interestingly enough, she was a ticket seller at the Prater Ferris wheel. She was beaten to death, but we haven't found the weapon.'

'The ticket might have come from her own pocket,' Lustig pointed out.

Captain Hesse shook his head. 'We already checked that. The man who loads the cabins actually rips them in two as people board. Of course we questioned him. His name is Helmet Scrole.'

'I know Helmet,' Lustig told him.

The captain nodded. 'He described a retired police investigator who came on Fridays. I thought it might be you. Did you know Karen Kritzer?'

'I might have known her by sight but not by name.'

'Any of the other regulars?'

Lustig mentioned the woman who fed the pigeons, and the young couple who ate lunch together. 'There's an old man named Kralik too. I don't know the names of the others, but the woman who feeds the birds is named Mina. I've spoken with her.'

34

'Will you be going there now?'

'I expect so. The day is chilly but I ride the horsecar part of the way.'

'Keep an eye out for someone with a torn pocket.'

'I'll do that, Captain.'

'And take this ticket with you. It might help.'

The idea that one of his fellow passengers on the Ferris wheel might be involved in the killing was beyond Lustig's belief. In fact, he hardly believed the fact of the young woman's death until he arrived at the Prater that afternoon. Someone new, a middle-aged woman he'd never seen before, was selling tickets at the Ferris wheel.

'Where's the young lady who usually works here?' he asked.

'She was killed.'

'What happened?'

'I don't know anything,' the woman responded, grim-lipped.

He saw Mina tossing seed to the pigeons and walked over to join her. She smiled and greeted him. 'I see the cooler weather has not kept you away.'

'Nor the others,' he said, gesturing toward the line of people already waiting for the first ride. The Ferris wheel continued to be a prime attraction months after its opening. 'Did you notice there's a new woman selling tickets in the booth?'

Mina shook her head. 'I don't talk to them. I just buy my ticket.'

His wandering eyes were attracted to a man who stood in line, near the front. Middle-aged, balding, without a hat. Where had Lustig seen him before? Then Fritz Kralik appeared, with his old man's pace, head down as if searching for a lost coin. The balding man in line looked away.

'Over here, Fritz,' Lustig called. 'I've saved you a place.'

'Thank you, sir!' The old man shivered a bit. 'The dampness almost kept me away today.'

Helmet Scrole had come forward to tear the tickets and direct people to their cabins. Each had fourteen windows on the sides and ends, giving a panoramic view of the city and the river. When all thirty cabins were filled to capacity some six hundred people could ride the wheel at one time. Today it was less than half-full, but Lustig and the others still waited for number 30, the final cabin.

'The world will never see the likes of this again,' Mina said as the cabin swayed gently and began to rise. 'In Paris the Eiffel Tower just sits there.'

Old Fritz Kralik, who liked to correct people, quickly said, 'The original wheel built by Ferris in Chicago four years ago could hold more than two thousand people, and the ones in London and Blackpool are taller than this.'

'Ah, but can you see the Danube from them?' she countered.

Lustig wondered what had happened to the young couple who usually joined them on Fridays. There were only the three of them in the cabin today. But the thought left his mind as the swaying cabin approached the top of its arc. Looking out at his city he could see the tower of St Stefan's Cathedral, and far away to the south-east he could even make out Schonbrunn, the eighteenth-century Habsburg palace.

'Every day is different here,' he said in admiration. 'I wait for the winter when snow and fog will add a special beauty.'

'They may not open the wheel then,' Kralik pointed out. 'It might be dangerous with the weight of the snow added to a full load of passengers.'

But Mina was staring at Lustig. 'I can't believe you were once a policeman. You are a man with a sensitive soul.'

He smiled, pleased but embarrassed by her words.

The cabin of the Ferris wheel had reached the top and started down. It would make another complete circle before it started unloading passengers and bringing them on board for the next ride. Sometimes Lustig bought more than one ticket so he could remain on the wheel, but when he reached into his pocket all he found were torn stubs. Two of them. He remembered that Hesse had given him the ticket stub found in Karen Kritzer's dead hand.

Lustig studied the ticket again and noticed something new. Following the 30, written very faintly, was the word 'Horl'. There was a Horl-Gasse in Vienna, a street just a few blocks from the Ring that circled the city's main area. The 30 was not the number of the cabin they rode in, but an address on Horl-Gasse. Mina and old Kralik decided to ride again, but Lustig left the wheel when his cabin was unloaded and headed for the park's exit. He noticed that the balding man left too.

The address he sought was back to the west, beyond the police department, so Lustig retraced his steps, boarding a horsecar for the final portion of the journey along the brick streets of the city. Vienna had grown and prospered with a period of rapid economic expansion as the new century approached. Carriages and horsecars filled the wide avenues of the Ring, and customers crowded the shops. The Vienna Opera, newly under the direction of Gustav Mahler, was more popular than ever. As a member of the city's police, Lustig had been part of it all. Now he felt like an outsider, especially since his retirement and Lisa's death.

When he reached it, number 30 Horl-Gasse was an unexceptional apartment house on a street of similar older buildings. Lustig entered the tiny, shadowy lobby and looked over the list of tenants, but none of the names seemed familiar. Then he noticed something by one name, a spot of red like paint or blood. He wiped his finger across it but it was dried. *Magdalen Suter.*

In a sudden flash of memory he remembered the young man at the Ferris wheel calling to his girlfriend. 'Magdalen! Over here, Magdalen!'

He rang the bell for the third-floor apartment and started up the curving staircase. For a moment he expected her to appear on the landing above him. When she didn't, he hesitated as he reached the door. If she was out, he'd made the trip for nothing. Then he noticed the door wasn't quite closed. It was standing open a fraction of an inch, and he knew he didn't want to see what was on the other side.

The first thing to catch his eye was the bloody hammer in the centre of the sitting-room rug, almost as if it had been carefully positioned there. Her body was off to one side, in front of the apartment's fireplace. A fire started in it had died before fully igniting the logs, and the place was chilly as a result. He knelt to make sure the young woman was dead, then straightened up slowly. He'd seen enough bodies to make a rough estimate that Magdalen Suter had been dead since early morning, over six hours judging by the extent of rigor mortis.

The apartment was not equipped with one of the new telephones, so there was no way he could call for help. He left the door ajar as he'd found it and hurried downstairs to the street. It was the balding man who stopped his flight a few steps from the door. 'Just a moment, sir,' he said.

Lustig tried to push his way past him. 'I've seen you before today. Have you been following me?'

He ignored the question and asked one of his own. 'May I ask what you were doing in this building?'

Lustig sighed in exasperation. 'I'm a retired police officer. My name is Oswald Lustig.'

There was a flash of the badge he knew so well. 'Detective Danzig. I'm investigating the murder of the woman from the Prater. You frequent the Ferris wheel where she sold tickets.'

'Yes, but I'm hardly a suspect! Look here, there's a woman's body in this building. I was trying to find a police officer.'

The man named Danzig took a deep breath. 'You'd better show me, sir.'

*   *   *

Lustig had sat in the little room with the hissing radiator many times during his career, questioning people about every imaginable crime. Sometimes with a particularly difficult suspect, especially one with a prior criminal record, he would even have them taken to the basement room. He never went down himself, though, and preferred not to know about the questioning that occurred there.

Now for the first time he sat on the other side of the table. When Captain Hesse entered the little room he stood up and held out his hand. Hesse ignored it and said, 'I'm sorry about this, Lustig. Do you have anything you wish to tell me?'

The radiator hissed. 'About what, Captain?'

'About the killing of this woman Magdalen Suter. And about the previous killing of Karen Kritzer.'

'I've told your man Danzig everything I know. It was that torn ticket from the first victim's hand. The number 30 was part of an address. The street name was written faintly. I went to the address and recognised Magdalen's name. There was a spot of something, perhaps blood, next to the name on the bell downstairs. When no one answered the bell I went upstairs and found the apartment door ajar. Her body was inside.'

'You knew this woman?'

'Only from the Prater. We would nod or say hello to each other. She was always with her boyfriend. I knew her name because I'd heard him call her that.'

'Detective Danzig reported he encountered you fleeing the scene.'

'I was searching for a police officer. I saw no telephone in the apartment. And Danzig didn't encounter me. He was following me. I saw him at the Prater earlier.'

Captain Hesse sighed. 'He was acting on my orders. We were investigating everyone who had contact with the murdered woman. Now we have a second victim who also has ties to the Ferris wheel, and you are at the scene.'

'You must know she was dead hours before I found her.'

'But you might have returned to the crime scene, Lustig.'

'I had nothing to do with either killing,' he told the captain, growing impatient. 'What about the young man Magdalen met each Friday at the Prater? Have you questioned him?'

'No one seems to know his name.'

Lustig's anger was growing. 'Search her room for letters! Talk to her neighbours! Do something, for God's sake! What about the hammer? Is it the same weapon used on the first victim?'

'We can't be certain, though the wound is in the same area of the skull. I fear he'll kill again if not apprehended.'

Lustig allowed himself a slight smile. 'Like that Englishman? That Jack the Ripper?'

Hesse was dead serious. 'It could happen in Vienna as easily as London.'

Lustig stood up again. 'I see no object in continuing this conversation. Unless you wish to arrest me and charge me with these crimes, I must be leaving now.'

'You are free to go. I only ask that you contact me personally if you learn anything about these killings. You were always a good detective.'

Lustig glared at him. 'Will Danzig still be assigned to follow me?'

'With this second murder I have given Danzig new duties.'

When Lustig left the police department he hurried back to the Prater. Though it was late afternoon he was hoping some of the regulars would still be at the Ferris wheel. He was in luck. The first one he spotted was Fritz Kralik and he made his way through the crowds to the old man.

'You've returned for another ride,' Kralik said, obviously pleased to see him.

'I have to find someone. Have you seen the young man who often eats lunch with the blonde woman?'

'Ah, yes! He was looking for her just a short time ago. He may be up on the wheel, trying to spot her in the crowd.'

Lustig stared at the giant Ferris wheel with a sense of frustration. He could spend a quarter-hour waiting until it stopped and all the cabins were unloaded. Then suddenly he spotted the young man he sought, not on the wheel but over among the trees, seated on one of the park benches. He hurried over and introduced himself.

'Yes,' the man said. He couldn't have been more than thirty, with dark eyes and a melancholy expression. 'You often ride the wheel with us on Fridays, Mr Lustig. My name is Reggie Swan. I'm English. The woman I meet here, Magdalen – have you seen her today?'

'I have,' Lustig answered truthfully. 'I'm afraid I have some bad news for you, sir.' He told him as concisely as possible of Magdalen's fate.

Swan cried out in anguish and buried his head in his hands. He sat for some time like that. Finally when he'd recovered himself a bit he shook his head in despair and told Lustig, 'It was her husband. Who else would have done such a thing?'

'Her husband?'

'A man named Klaus Suter. He was brutal to her and she left him back in the summer. He's made her life hell ever since. He followed her everywhere and became enraged if he saw her with another man. That was why we arranged secret meetings here at the Ferris wheel on her lunch hour.'

'Where did she work?'

'At the confectionery shop near the park entrance.'

Lustig thought for a moment and then asked, 'Did you or Magdalen know the young woman who sold tickets to the Ferris rides? A woman named Karen Kritzer?'

'The one who was killed? Only by sight. You don't think the two deaths are related, do you?'

'I don't know,' Lustig said, though he knew there had to be some relation when Magdalen's street address had been found written on the ticket clutched in Karen's hand. 'You'd better go home now. There's no point in waiting around here.'

But Reggie Swan continued to sit there alone. Lustig left him and headed for the confectionery shop where he bought a box of bonbons. 'Our own exclusive brand,' the clerk told him. 'I love them.' She was barely out of her teens, with large, bright eyes, a striped blouse and a wide grey skirt that hung to the floor. He realised it was the same colour uniform the dead girl had worn on those lunch-hour trysts.

'I know,' Lustig said with a smile as he accepted the wrapped box of chocolates. 'I had some recently.'

'You're a regular customer? Forgive me for not recognising you. This is my first day on the job.'

'You replaced Magdalen?'

She nodded. 'She didn't come to work today. Do you know her?'

'Slightly.'

The following morning's newspaper reported that police were detaining Klaus Suter in connection with the murder of his estranged wife Magdalen. Lustig read through the brief account twice before putting down the paper. There was no mention of the first killing.

By the following Friday Suter had been formally charged with the murder. At headquarters that day Lustig asked Hesse about it. The captain shrugged and said simply, 'He confessed.'

'To both killings?'

'Just to hitting his estranged wife with the hammer. Apparently the two murders weren't related.'

'Then the Suter case is closed?'

Captain Hesse nodded. 'It's closed.'

At the Prater that day there was no sign of the Englishman, Reggie Swan. Lustig rode the wheel with Fritz Kralik and Mina. It was a pleasant day, but he couldn't stop thinking about the two dead women.

Some Fridays during that Vienna winter Lustig was unable to keep up his routine visits to the Ferris wheel. When an influenza-like illness laid him low for two weeks in January, Mina even appeared at his apartment one day to see what had happened to him. No one ever talked of Karen Kritzer's murder. Magdalen Suter's husband had been sent off to prison for her killing, even after recanting his confession. The police had beaten it out of him, he insisted, and Lustig knew it could have happened that way.

With the coming of spring, crowds again returned to the Prater. A woman named Marie Kindl, a professional circus performer, was hired to help promote the new Ferris wheel. She would hang by her teeth from a cable attached to one of the cabins as the wheel revolved. The stunt was scheduled for a Sunday afternoon to attract the most people, and Lustig decided to attend. In retirement his life had become inexorably entwined with that great wheel in the sky, visible from every part of the city. Even on his regular Friday visits he often ended the day by inviting Mina to join him at a *Kaffehauser* for coffee and a pastry.

For this day, being a Sunday, he decided to wear a dark blue suit that had been in his closet since the previous summer. He took it out on its hanger and held it up to the light. That was when he noticed the torn pocket on the suitcoat. A triangular piece of fabric was actually missing from it. He sat holding the coat for some time, staring at it.

The Prater was crowded when he finally arrived there, wearing an older suit that was a bit tight on him. Lisa had wanted him to dispose of it, but he was glad now that he had kept it, buried away at the back of the closet. When Mina saw him coming, at the entrance where they often met, she exclaimed, 'You have a new suit!'

'No, only a very old one.'

She took his arm as they made their way past the rows of stalls, drifting with the Sunday crowd toward the main attraction. 'You know who I saw not ten minutes ago? That Englishman, Swan. He told me it's the first time he's been back here since Magdalen's death.'

Lustig nodded. 'Many people are probably coming for the first time this year.'

As they neared the Ferris wheel they saw old Kralik dozing on one of the benches. Mina woke him with a tap on the shoulder. 'Come with us, old man, or you will miss the performance. Then Mr Lustig is taking me for a ride on the wheel.'

He smiled up at them. 'I come here on a Sunday to see a circus performer! Soon I will be living here like a gypsy in a tent!'

'There are worse places,' Mina assured him.

The three of them proceeded on to the open area before the great wheel. The best view of Marie Kindl's performance would be from the ground, so no customers were riding inside at present. Marie arrived on schedule, dressed in her circus costume and accompanied by a Prater dignitary who introduced her with great fanfare. A cable was lowered from one of the cabins to where she stood. After testing it to make certain it would support her weight, she attached a leather bit to the end of the cable. Then, opening her mouth wide, she took the leather between her teeth and signalled the operator to start the wheel.

'That's quite a stunt, isn't it?' someone said from Lustig's side. He half-turned his head to see Captain Hesse standing there in civilian clothes, carrying his gold-headed walking stick.

'Indeed,' Lustig agreed. 'I never knew you came to the Prater wheel, Captain.'

'This is something that should not be missed.'

They watched as the Ferris wheel began to rise, lifting the young woman with it. She kept her arms at her side, face to the sky. Knowing it took ten minutes for the wheel to complete its circuit, Lustig wondered if she'd be able to hang on that long. 'Strong teeth,' Mina commented. 'I wouldn't want to try that with my dentures.'

Lustig agreed. 'Ten minutes is a long time.' He stepped to

the other side of Captain Hesse, where the others could not hear him above the noise of the crowd. 'Sometimes women die much quicker than that, don't they, Captain?'

Hesse turned a smiling face towards him. 'What do you mean?'

'Karen Kritzer and Magdalen Suter. Are you really going to let Suter's husband rot in prison for your crime?'

While the wheel turned and the crowd held its collective breath, Lustig and Hesse were walking away towards the Danube canal. Captain Hesse swung his gold-headed cane in the air like the dandy he was, and Lustig talked on, telling his former superior how he'd happened to solve the crimes.

'It was a mistake, you know, trying to frame me for it. Why me? I suppose it was because you knew I came to the Prater every Friday. I had contact with Karen Kritzer when I bought my ticket from her, even though I barely noticed her. If you framed me, you could immediately establish the connection between us as part of your so-called evidence. But why did you kill her?'

Hesse shook his head. 'You have always been a smart detective, Lustig. I should not have underestimated you. As for the killing, it was just something that happened. I didn't mean to kill her. I'd met her here at the Prater, selling her tickets to the Ferris wheel. I went up to her apartment that night and we argued. She wanted money or she'd say I tried to rape her. It would have ruined my chances for promotion, perhaps even cost me my job. I struck out at her, hitting her with this cane. It was an accident.'

'What followed wasn't.'

'No,' he admitted.

'You picked the lock on my apartment and got into my closet. You ripped a piece of cloth from the pocket of one of my suits, then returned to the dead girl's apartment and left it in her hand as a clue. You also left a ticket stub from the Ferris wheel, with an address scrawled faintly upon it.

To make sure I'd see that address you even gave me the ticket stub, an important piece of evidence. What police captain would ever do that, hand over evidence to a retired detective?'

'I needed to get you to that address,' Hesse admitted. They'd reached the canal now and were walking along the footpath.

'Of course you did, because Magdalen's dead body would be there, waiting for me, her name even marked with a drop of blood so I wouldn't miss it. You killed her early Friday morning, a day after Karen. The hammer that you used was there too, so it would appear to be the same weapon that killed Karen. You didn't want anyone thinking about a gold-headed cane. You assigned Danzig to follow me, and he was supposed to find me with the body. This was where you made your only mistake. You left her body in front of the fireplace and started a fire in it, so the heat would slow rigor mortis and make it appear she was killed more recently. But the fire went out before the main logs ignited. I was found at the scene but it meant nothing when the autopsy showed she was killed more than six hours earlier.'

'There is nothing to connect me with Magdalen Suter.'

'Except that she too worked at the Prater, in a confectionery shop that sells an exclusive brand of bonbons. I recognised them because I'd eaten one recently from the box you kept on your office desk.'

'Her case is closed. Klaus Suter confessed to the crime.'

'After you beat it out of him in the basement. I worked for you, remember? And now I want him freed.'

Captain Hesse turned to him with a look of triumph. 'Oh, haven't you heard? Klaus Suter hanged himself in his cell last night. If your motive was to free him you are too late.'

Lustig saw the gold-headed cane coming up then and waited no longer. He grabbed the cane and gave Hesse a hard shove that sent him off the path and into the canal. If there were any sounds or shouts they went unheard over the thunderous roar of the Prater crowd. Marie Kindl was safely back on the ground.

Lustig waited a moment and tossed the cane into the canal. Then he turned and hurried back to meet Mina. He still owed her a ride on the Ferris wheel.

Reading Ellis Peters' novels (particularly those written as Edith Pargeter) made me realise that the past could be as alive as the present. She had the gift of taking readers into a world as recognisable as the one in which they lived. It was only when I first tried to write an historical novel that I realised how extremely hard that was and the depth of research needed to recreate a past time.

However, I remained fascinated with history. I loved trying to recreate all the sights, sounds and other elements of past ages, studying how morals and behaviour can be affected by different standards in different societies and identifying what remains true whatever the era. Eventually I was inspired to write the first of a series of historical crime novels featuring Canaletto, the famous Italian view painter. The idea of an artist, one who would have the entrée to all levels of society and who could apply an observant eye and the detachment of an outsider to investigating crimes in the mid-eighteenth century, was irresistible.

The following story, though, doesn't feature Canaletto, nor is it set in his era. It arose from a visit to San Simeon, William Randolph Hearst's fabled fantasy Californian castle. As I followed the various tours around his incredible creation and viewed his priceless collection of Renaissance treasures,

I was gripped by the aura of the enigmatic tycoon and his relationship with Marion Davies. Her filmstar fame in the early days of Hollywood was inextricably intertwined with Hearst's patronage. In the following story, Daisy, Archie and Isabel are fiction but most of the other details are founded on fact. I've just used a certain amount of imagination in putting them together!

Janet Laurence

Starstruck at San Simeon

Janet Laurence

When I heard that Marion Davies had died, time rolled back and the memory of those unforgettable days at San Simeon were as fresh as a restored painting.

I promised her I would never tell anyone what happened while either William Randolph Hearst or she was alive. W.R. died ten years ago and now she has gone.

San Simeon! It was something out of a dream. Renaissance exuberance in a ranch setting, Castillian splendour resting on the top of a Californian mountain. The fact that the entire place was actually built of plain concrete faced with priceless coverings was an irony I only appreciated much later.

Over thirty years have passed since I was there and so much has changed. Now John F. Kennedy is blowing his presidential winds of change, we live in a technological age and you can jet around the world in little more than twenty-four hours. Then, I took over two weeks to travel from London to Los Angeles by boat and train.

When I announced I was going, my father said in disgust that I was starstruck. My mother feared for my virtue. I just wanted to be in the movies.

'Well,' said my mother at last, 'whatever you do, don't contact your cousin Archie.'

Cousin Archie Fortescue had made my growing years both

a pain and a delight. A pain because he was a cruel teaser, a delight because he was incredibly dashing. He'd been cast into the outer darkness when he abandoned a faltering career with a city bank for the stage and his father had finally lost patience with his rakehell younger son. Odd whispers of some new scandal arrived from time to time, including the news he'd signed a contract with MGM.

I arrived in Los Angeles in late spring and took the train to Hollywood. I retain a confused impression of oil wells, citrus groves and long, long beaches with crashing white surf.

Hollywood was a heartbreaking combination of dreams and disillusion. I'd been told the place was booming, that as many films were being made as there were days in the week. But the casting offices were brisk and ruthless. If you were to get on you had to have an agent. If you didn't have an agent, you went to Central Casting for a walk-on part. The first thing you saw at their Western Avenue offices was a large sign outside saying: DON'T TRY TO BECOME AN ACTOR, FOR EVERY ONE WE EMPLOY, WE TURN AWAY A THOUSAND. I ignored it, of course. And when they heard I had my own evening dress, it seemed as though I might get an offer. Then they discovered I didn't have an Alien Resident's Visa.

I'd ignored the instruction about not contacting cousin Archie as well. The only address I had for him, though, was the MGM studios. I wrote to him there and eventually the landlord of my decrepit lodging house told me I had a call.

'Daisy, is it really you?' asked Archie's voice.

'Sure is,' I said delightedly.

'Have you a car?' What a ridiculous question. As if I could drive! 'Then I'll pick you up. Half an hour, OK? And pack a bag for a stay with some people.' Before I could ask any questions, he'd rung off.

I quickly changed into my best linen frock, tried to second-guess the sort of clothes I'd need, then pulled on a hat and gloves and waited for him in the hall.

'Daisy!' he shouted as I opened the door. 'Gee, how

could such a long-legged, pigtailed brat grow into such a beauty!'

In the old days I'd have punched him one. Now I dipped my head demurely. 'You always knew how to flatter a girl, Archie.'

'No time for dalliance.' He picked up my case. 'We've a plane to catch.'

'A plane!' I squeaked.

He helped me into a smart roadster.

'I've arrived,' he said smugly. 'You see before you a major star of the future.'

Looking at him, I could believe it. He'd always been good-looking, tall and blond with dark blue eyes and a wide mouth, but his California tan emphasised the fairness of his hair, longer than I remembered, and he was leaner and, somehow, more *dangerous* looking. Perhaps it was the moustache. He started the car then turned to me with a wicked glint. 'I expect you've heard some terrible tales about me.'

'Gone to the dogs,' I riposted, holding my cloche hat tightly as the car leapt forward. 'It's reckoned you must be living off immoral earnings, running a gambling den, or have married a woman of means.'

'Don't spread such rumours around here.' He looked at me in mock alarm. 'The studios are awfully tight on stars these days. Moral clauses in your contracts, no hint of scandal and bachelors are best! I think it's considered immoral for shop girls to lust after a married man. Now, I have to pack my own case.'

He was living in a chalet-style one-storey house at the top of North Vista Street, its living room filled with polished mahogany and overstuffed chairs. Archie opened a side cup-board. 'Can I mix you something before I fling a few things in a case?'

I gazed at the bottles in awe. 'I thought alcohol was prohibited in America!'

He gave me a wide grin. 'It is. That doesn't stop people

drinking and it's too easy to get hold of. This is my poison.' He lifted out a bottle of whisky and poured the last of its amber liquid into a glass. Archie had always been fond of his tipple. Then he brought out a new bottle. 'Will you join me? Or shall I mix you a cocktail? Dry martini is the latest rage.'

'I know,' I said tartly. 'In case you've forgotten, England isn't the jungle.'

'Well, how about it?'

His eyes challenged me, reminding me of the boy who could make my life a misery, and I longed to say, shake me one. 'Have you a sweet sherry?' I asked primly.

'Oh, Daisy, what a coward you are.'

I sat, crossed my ankles and smiled sweetly at him. 'If you're introducing me around, you need me sober.'

That seemed to hit home and he gave me a smallish glass of respectable sherry. 'Now tell me all about the family while I pack my things.' He picked up his whisky and I followed him into the bedroom.

Life in England seemed a long way away from the palm trees, sun and Spanish-influenced architecture of Hollywood but I did my best, though Archie seemed more interested in choosing between this tie and that and finding a clean pair of tennis shoes.

He started to close his case then said, 'Heavens, nearly forgot.' He found a couple of hip flasks and filled them from the full bottle of whisky. 'Our host believes in rationing alcohol,' Archie explained.

'Where are we going?' I asked as we got back in the car.

'To Mr Hearst's ranch.'

'A ranch? I didn't bring my riding habit.'

'You don't ride side-saddle out here,' he mocked me. I decided he was still the boy who could put frogs in your bed and salt in the sugar bowl.

'Who is Mr Hearst?'

'William Randolph Hearst is a very, very rich man. He owns over twenty newspapers, and magazines, gold, silver and copper mines, any number of homes and –' he paused for dramatic effect – 'a movie company.'

'The one you signed with?'

He nodded. 'Sort of. Mr Hearst's Cosmopolitan Productions is in association with MGM. Their biggest star is Marion Davies and I've just made a film with her. Now she wants me to star in her next.'

I was impressed. Even my father had heard of Marion Davies.

'That's why we're going to the ranch; Marion wants to discuss the project with the writer and me and Mr Hearst.' He paused then said in an elaborately casual way, 'Marion and Mr Hearst, well, they're sort of together.'

'Together? Together for what?'

'Honestly, Daisy, don't tell me you haven't learned anything about the world,' Archie snapped.

I felt small and remembered how much I could dislike him.

He relented a little. 'Mrs Hearst lives in New York and isn't interested in divorce. A woman can make a man's life very difficult if she won't divorce him.'

We drove in silence then he gave me one of his best smiles. 'Sorry, sweetie, it just makes me mad sometimes how Marion jumps at his slightest word. He thinks he owns her.'

Oh, dear, I thought. Trouble ahead!

'What sort of film will it be?'

'It's based on a book all about the Borgias. Marion's to play Lucrezia and I'm to be Cesare.'

'You don't mean *Borgia Bastardy*? I've read it, it's wonderful!' I was really excited. The story depicted Lucrezia as a vulnerable woman manipulated by two evil men, her father, the Pope, and her brother, Cesare Borgia.

Archie sighed. 'That's the one.'

'Don't you think it's wonderful?'

He shrugged his shoulders. Then we reached the airfield and I forgot all about *Borgia Bastardy*.

The plane looked horribly flimsy and frail but Jim, the pilot, seemed confident enough. 'Glad you're no later,' he said as we came up. 'If the afternoon fog rolls in, the cliffs can be treacherous.'

I was helped up and strapped in. Then Archie settled himself beside me. A mechanic swung the propeller, there was a coughing followed by a roar and the whole plane vibrated and shook. I grabbed Archie's hand. He grinned at me.

We started rolling down the runway; then, above the roar of the engine, came a frantic shout. A young man was chasing after us, waving a newspaper in his hand. The pilot reached down for it. 'Mr Hearst's *Herald*,' he shouted to us. 'If I'd forgotten that, I'd be lynched.' We started rolling forward again, going faster and faster until, suddenly, we were in the air. I gasped with the feeling of freedom.

To see the ground unfold beneath us, the sweep of the hills broken by dark canyons, the sparkling blue of the sea fringed with white foam, was pure magic. I wanted to stay up forever.

After about an hour Archie grabbed my arm and pointed. The plane banked and I saw fairytale towers glittering below us, dominating a small cluster of luxurious Mediterranean-type villas in a sea of greenery. All poised on top of a hill that swept down to the sea. You couldn't believe it was real.

The plane straightened out and started to descend. We bumped along the ground and then we were still.

The silence was almost shocking. Even more shocking was the fact that that extraordinary sight had completely disappeared. I looked up at the hill above us and all I could see was grass and the odd bush or tree. Something moved and I thought it was a small herd of deer then cried out as I realised they were zebra.

'Mr Hearst's got quite a menagerie up around here,' Jim said laconically, helping Archie and me down. 'Wait till you see the monkeys, the lions and tigers.'

'Lions? Tigers? Archie, where are we?'

'William Randolph Hearst's ranch,' he said blandly. 'I told you.'

I gave up.

A car drove us up the hill to the bottom of a huge flight of steps.

'Archie!' A blonde bombshell danced down the steps in delight. 'I h, h, heard the plane and knew you were h, h, here.'

Archie was out of the car in a second. 'Marion, how wonderful to see you.'

He kissed her lightly on the cheek then stood looking down at her. Heavens, what a good-looking couple they made! His fair hair flopped over his wide brow, hers waved around a face that was both as lovely and more characterful than on the screen, they both exuded a radiance compounded of beauty, high spirits and good health.

After a heart-stopping moment, Archie turned back to me where I stood awkwardly by the car, linen frock horribly creased. 'Marion, this is Daisy.'

She came down the last couple of steps, her face alive with welcome. 'D, D, Daisy, great to meet you.'

'Awfully good of you to have me,' I muttered, feeling out of place.

'Archie rang and said a long-lost c, c, cousin was in Hollywood and I s, s, said, b, b, bring her.' The slight stammer was enchanting because she hardly seemed aware of the hesitation in her speech. But on paper it looks so odd that I think I shall ignore it from now on.

'Everyone else has gone horseback riding,' Marion said. 'Why don't we swim?'

'I didn't bring a costume,' I said, wondering why it had never occurred to me there might be bathing. Hunger gnawed at my stomach; we hadn't had time for lunch.

'You'll find every size in the changing rooms,' Marion said. 'Now, let me show you to your rooms. Archie, you're in the same guest house as before. Charlie Chaplin's there

57

as well and Brewster Millhausen; he's to be supervisor on the picture. Only he wants to be called a producer, says it's more dignified.' She giggled. 'Ted will bring your luggage, you know the way, don't you?' She made it sound intimate, a secret they shared. 'Meet us at the pool.' She tucked her arm through mine, we were of a height, both five foot four inches. 'Now, Daisy, we can get to know each other.'

She led me briskly up the flight of steps and then up more steps interspersed with little walkways, all in patterned tiles and edged with white walls and green hedges. Her arm felt friendly inside mine and she talked all the time. 'You're funny, you know that? You've got such a funny little nose, all tip-tilted. Archie says you want to be in films. Well, I can say it's a fine life if you like working hard. One time I did two films at once, you know? I worked on *The Red Mill* from nine till five and then on *Tillie the Toiler* from six to four in the morning.'

'When did you sleep?' I gasped. Then we stopped and I didn't hear what she answered because we were on a terrace in front of the twin-towered building I'd seen from the plane and it was even more incredible than it had seemed from the air. It looked like a Spanish cathedral.

'Something, isn't it?' said Marion.

'Oh, yes,' I breathed.

'W.R. built it, he built everything here –' She waved a hand around us. 'In fact he's still building. I tell him he'll never be finished.'

You could have thought yourself in a particularly lovely little town square in Spain, with trees and statues and urns and shrubs and I don't know what else all around. And this immense building in front of us that seemed to stretch back forever, with towers and galleries and balconies and bits everywhere.

'Archie said we were going to a ranch,' I blurted out at last.

Marion laughed. 'W. R. named this place La Cuesta

58

Encantada, the Enchanted Hill, and this is La Casa Grande, but he always calls it the ranch. It is a ranch too. As far as you can see.' Her arm swept out, encompassing the sweeping hills and undulating landscape growing blue-grey in the distance till it turned into mountains. 'It's all W.R.'s.'

I revolved slowly, taking it all in, unable to believe that this immensity was owned by one man.

But if the outside had staggered me, inside reduced me to silence. 'We have cocktails here before dinner,' Marion said, leading me through the entrance doors into an immense reception room that ran the whole width of the building. Sun-dazzled, my eyes took a little time to adjust to the gloom, then I saw carved panelling that went halfway up the high walls before marvellous tapestries took over; huge stone fireplaces, heavy polished tables and cabinets that looked as though they'd come from some Renaissance castle, bronze statuettes, tall brass candlesticks, silver platters, antique boxes, treasures everywhere, together with a collection of extremely comfortable-looking chintz-covered chairs and sofas.

Marion's breathless, stammering voice chattered away as she led me through the splendour and it took me a little time to realise that La Casa Grande had no sweeping staircase to make an entrance down. Instead there was a series of small elevators, wound around with steps.

'Tell me about Archie. I think he's just divine. He'll be wonderful in the Borgia film. Actually, I prefer comedies, I like having fun and lots of laughs, but W.R.'s convinced I'm a dramatic actress.' Then, sadly, she said, 'He doesn't realise I'm no good.'

'I loved *When Knighthood Was in Flower*,' I said stoutly. 'I thought you were wonderful as Mary Tudor.'

'Your Prince Edward thought the same, but it bombed in England. They hated for an American to play an English princess.'

'More fool them,' I said and squeezed her arm.

'I do like you,' she said happily.

We emerged eventually on to an open gallery. Off it were bedrooms. 'This is yours, dear.'

It was a twin-bedded room nicely furnished in mahogany without, thank heavens, the grandeur we had passed through.

'Here's your bathroom,' said Marion. My own bathroom! I was so excited, even more so when I saw it had that latest device, a shower. I'd never used one before. 'I'll wait while you freshen up. Finding your way around here isn't always easy.'

The swimming pool took my breath away again. It was the largest and loveliest you could imagine. It was all marble, with a Greek temple at one end and Greek sculptures in a little pool at the other. Greek columns and more statues curved round the edges. Through them you could see, far, far below, the sea.

Archie was already showing off a fast crawl. But by the time I'd found and changed into a chic navy-blue swimsuit, he was sitting with Marion, now svelte in a black costume with white polka dots.

'I've had them bring sandwiches,' Marion called. 'I bet you're hungry!'

As I was to find over the next few days, she was the perfect hostess.

We were splashing about in the water, pushing each other around, laughing and having a splendid time, when Marion suddenly stood quite still. 'They're back,' she said. She pulled herself out of the pool, slipped on a wrap, thrust her feet into mules and clip-clopped up the steps.

'Archie, why didn't you warn me?'

'Warn you?'

'About all this. Or haven't you been before either?'

'Oh,' he said with a slight smile, 'I've been before. Several times during filming we all came up for the weekend. W.R. laid on a special train to San Louis Obispo.'

'So why didn't you?' I demanded.

'Warn you?' His smile faded. 'Darling Daisy, what could I say? Would you have believed me?'

No, I probably would have thought he was teasing, the way Archie always teased. Not very kindly either. Stick legs, he used to call me, or tell me to be careful with my elbows or I'd stab someone.

'I'm sorry I'm not staying in the guest house with you; I'm never going to know what to do or how to find my way anywhere.'

'W.R. won't have girls and boys anywhere near each other, could lead to things, don't y'know.'

At first I thought he was teasing again.

Down on to the pool terrace came what seemed a flood of people in riding clothes. Taller than anyone else was a man in his sixties with a face that went on forever: long forehead, longer nose, long chin, big ears. His mouth was wide and his hazel eyes were set in attractive creases. There was something babyish about the smooth contours of his face. His figure was incredibly solid, like a tree, and hanging on his arm was Marion, chattering along in her stuttering way.

'W.R. meet D, D, Daisy D, D, Driver. She's Archie's cousin; you know I told you she was coming?'

The big man brushed a hand through the brown cowlick that fell across his forehead. 'Welcome to the ranch, Miss Driver.' He spoke in slow tones but as his hazel eyes looked at me, I felt he could read me right through. There was nothing comfortable or babyish about this big man after all.

Mr Hearst turned that piercing gaze on Marion. 'And your headache is quite gone now?' His hand fell on her shoulder.

She looked up at him, her big blue eyes clear and limpid. 'Quite, W.R. And wasn't it good I was able to welcome Daisy and Archie when they arrived?'

'Delighted to see you again, Mr Hearst,' Archie said.

The hazel gaze stripped him with one keen glance.

Marion added quickly, 'Your Los Angeles *Herald* is in the library.'

'You people enjoy yourselves now,' William Randolph Hearst said and left us.

'You can never keep W.R. away from his papers,' Marion said with a gurgle of laughter. 'Come on, everyone, pool time.'

The crowd disappeared to the changing rooms. All but a slight woman in her twenties, with a reserved but not unattractive face and dark hair pulled back into a knot. 'How nice to meet you, Mr Fortescue,' she said in a precise English voice, advancing with hand stretched out towards Archie. She had a neat figure that was well displayed by her riding clothes, not a habit but a divided skirt. Archie had been right about not riding side-saddle here.

'Miss Blandish, I believe,' he said gracefully, taking her hand.

'Isabel Blandish?' I asked. 'The author of *Borgia Bastardy*?'

Her head gave a little dip of acknowledgement. 'Have you read my poor little book?'

'Hey, don't pull yourself down,' Marion cried, seating herself on one of the long pool chairs. 'You're a bestseller.'

'Why yes, everyone's read your book,' I said.

'May I introduce my cousin, Daisy Driver,' Archie asked; his manners had always been perfect.

A graceful eyebrow raised itself. 'How charming for you to have a cousin out here, Mr Fortescue.'

'She's just arrived,' he said.

'I know we're going to have just a great time,' Marion interposed brightly. 'W.R. is so looking forward to discussing your book.'

Isabel Blandish flushed slightly. 'To think it could be turned into a photoplay, well!' She held out her hands, palms upwards, in an expressive gesture of astonishment. 'And with sound!'

'Sound?' I breathed. I'd seen *The Jazz Singer*, of course, and to hear Al Jolson sing 'Sonny Boy' had been so moving. But everyone said that talkies were just a novelty.

Marion looked at me and Archie, her eyes dancing. 'My film musical *Marianne* will be screened right after dinner. They shot both a sound and a silent version. Guess which we're showing!' She threw us a wicked smile, kicked off her mules, flung off the wrapper and plunged into the pool. Archie dived in after her.

When I look back at that time now, what I see are vignettes.

During cocktails in the assembly hall before dinner, when I hardly noticed the sumptuousness of the surroundings, my attention was totally focused on the gathering. There were, I suppose, some two dozen people there, a small number compared to some, I learned later. I was introduced to so many, my head spun. Names I recognised included Charlie Chaplin, small, neat and argumentative, and Marie Dressler, majestically large. It was a glittering assembly, politicians mixing with filmstars, high society with literati. Most seemed to know each other; I gathered there was an almost perpetual house party at San Simeon, particularly when Marion wasn't working. People came and people went. 'You watch where your place card is on the table,' said one to me. 'When it starts getting near one of the ends, that's the time to move on.'

Archie was already there when I arrived. 'Brewster wouldn't let me tank up,' he grumbled. 'It's too bad because they only allow you one drink before dinner. But I've brought my flask for a quick nip in the cinema afterwards.'

Not sensible, I thought, as Marion took him off to meet someone. What if W.R. saw him? First flirting with his hostess, then flouting the house rules. Did Archie want to be thrown off the enchanted hill?

'I wanted to talk to Mr Hearst but I gather he never attends the cocktail hour.' Isabel Blandish appeared at my side. 'No doubt writing one of his editorials.' She was wearing a severely tailored brown dress in knitted silk and smoking a cigarette through a long holder. Her gaze fell upon Archie and Marion, laughing together, looking very happy.

I thought that as a writer she was no doubt used to observing people.

I can never forget my first sight of the massively long refectory table set out in a dining room the size of a medieval hall, hung with faded banners from France and Italy, more precious tapestries, and furnished with a long side table loaded with an incredible collection of silver. All the trappings of Renaissance high society. It would have made a perfect setting for *Borgia Bastardy*. Then I saw that down the centre of the magnificent table were clusters of tomato ketchup and brown sauce bottles and paper napkin holders. Italian political machinations and the plight of Lucrezia vanished as I thought that my mother would have had a fit!

The showing of *Marianne* was a great success. The amazing thing was that Marion never stammered. But after it ended, Mr Hearst argued with Charlie Chaplin about the future of talkies. Mr Chaplin said they had no future. Who could afford to re-equip all the cinema theatres with sound? And what about all the people who couldn't speak English? Silent films could be understood by anyone.

Mr Hearst wouldn't acknowledge any of that was true; soon silent films would have had their day, he said with an air of finality. Charlie Chaplin got quite angry and stalked out. 'There goes the king of mime,' someone muttered.

'Don't write him off,' retorted someone else.

Entirely unmoved, Mr Hearst jovially asked who would like some Welsh rarebit and led us off to the kitchen. It was empty, neat and ordered without a servant in sight. He reached for a pan.

I was amazed; was this millionaire really going to cook?

'Too many in here,' he said. 'Miss Blandish and Miss Driver, would you like to help?'

Everyone else but Marion left. She got out plates, I was given cheese to grate and so was the authoress, who started opening drawers to find a grater. Mr Hearst himself added mustard and Worcestershire sauce to his pan. 'Miss Blandish,' he said. 'Your book deals with a time in history that interests me particularly. Do you not agree that that period when one able man could take control of the destiny of a state meant great things could be achieved?'

Miss Blandish handed me a grater, took another for herself and started reducing her block of cheese to fragments. 'Why, yes, Mr Hearst, as long as the man was honest and right thinking. More often it meant, as I think my book demonstrates, states suffering while powerful men fought amongst themselves. Surely it is safer to have a situation where ambition can be controlled by what I believe your state calls a system of checks and balances?'

Mr Hearst placed his pan on the stove. Marion busied herself with toasting bread, humming under her breath. She was neat and efficient in all her actions. 'It is merely a matter of the right man being in charge,' our host continued. 'I believe there are times when it is essential for a man of action to take control without let or hindrance.'

I tipped my grated cheese into his pan and wondered if William Randolph Hearst saw himself as the right man of action. Had he dreams of taking charge of America and running it? Archie'd told me W.R. had been a congressman at one stage. I thought of all the Renaissance splendour of La Casa Grande. Was W.R. soaking himself in the treasures and atmosphere of that time because he saw himself as one of its political princes? I thought of that clever Spanish family, the Borgias, migrating to Italy and using their brains and muscle to acquire wealth and power. To become Pope *and* to manage to legitimise your children was no mean trick.

Whatever W.R.'s ambitions, he made really excellent Welsh rarebits.

Later Marion led a small group of us to the Roman pool. Unlike the Greek, it was indoor and, impossible though it might seem, even more beautiful. Gold and lapis lazuli tiles covered walls and ceiling and the inside of the pool. Marble statues stood on the surround. The space was shaped like a short-stemmed T with a diving bridge over the join. Opalescent globes on long stands provided a romantic glow. Just like the Greek pool, the water was heated and the changing rooms full of costumes.

I climbed the little staircase to the bridge. As I dived, I saw Archie and Marion in the stem of the pool, alone. I couldn't be sure as I flashed down, but I thought his arm was around her and certainly their heads were very close together. As I came up, I saw Archie climb hurriedly out of the pool and someone come forward to help him. For a mad moment I thought it was Mr Hearst, then I saw that it was a guard, no doubt checking to see we were all afloat. Archie clamped a hand to his mouth and ran out.

I tried to follow but Marion detained me. 'Archie's n, n, not well,' she stuttered, looking upset. 'I hope it wasn't something he ate. I'll s, s, send someone to s, s, see how he does.'

When I came down to breakfast the next morning, Archie wasn't there. 'Your cousin isn't at all the thing,' Brewster Millhausen, pot-bellied and energetic, said. 'Been up all night puking his guts out.'

'Gee, that's awful.' Marion jumped up. 'He was given a p, p, powder and I hoped that would s, s, sort him.' Then Archie's stomach upset was forgotten as we heard that Charlie Chaplin was leaving the ranch. 'Hates to be crossed,' Marie Dressler muttered.

I managed to visit the guest house where Archie was staying in the morning, while Marion, Mr Hearst, Brewster Millhausen and Isabel Blandish discussed the screening of *Borgia Bastardy*. Archie was relaxing in a simply splendid living room furnished with more amazing antiques. 'The bedrooms are just the same,' Archie said, looking fine but sounding a little frail. 'I'm sleeping in Cardinal Richelieu's bed!'

'Are you better?' I asked.

'Much,' he said determinedly. 'Let's go and find some other guests and go for a walk.'

So a group of us strode out along a pergola-shaded path that stretched several miles in a hairpin round the hill. But Archie flagged quite quickly and we turned back without completing the circuit.

Lunch was served outside and we helped ourselves to hearty fare from a long table set with steaming dishes.

Naturally discussion centred on Isabel's book. Dressed in a silk crêpe de Chine frock she looked charmingly formal amongst the more casually dressed guests.

Someone asked about her research; I think it was Mr Hearst.

'There have been those who accuse me of solecisms,' she said. 'For instance, it was suggested arsenic couldn't have been available at that time. Well –' She looked at us provocatively. 'It's been used as a poison since pre-Christian times. In the seventeenth century arsenical powders were called *les poudres de succession*. Apt, don't you think? They were probably something like the poison on fly papers today. Did you know they usually contain arsenic? And that it's possible to soak it off?' She hesitated for a moment, her eyes downcast, then she looked at Mr Hearst. 'I hope you will forgive me if I mention this, sir, but I noticed in your kitchen last night fly papers of that very sort.'

We were all looking at him, fascinated. His expression remained bland and benign. 'Frank,' he called to the butler assisting with the picnic. 'Did you hear that? I suggest we do something about those fly papers or we may all wake up dead.'

The butler smiled and several people laughed but others looked speculatively at Archie.

Marion leapt to her feet. 'Why don't we visit with the animals? Let's go see the zoo!' If it was meant as a diversionary tactic, it worked. Several of us, including Isabel and, of course, Archie, walked down to the cages.

Marion threw biscuits to one of the lions. He looked up sleepily but wouldn't play. 'Oh, you're so mean,' she shouted at him and passed on to another cage with a huge ape sitting in the shade of a little tree. 'This is Jerry.'

'Why, he's adorable,' said Isabel. 'Come here, big boy!' she called skittishly. The ape paid no attention. 'Oh, come and say hello,' she pleaded and rattled the wire of the cage.

One of the keepers came forward. 'I wouldn't do that, ma'am, he can be a right mean son of a bitch.' He pointed to a sign that said, DON'T TEASE.

A minute later Jerry pooped neatly into his hand and threw the result with unerring accuracy at Isabel. The unpleasant mess clung to her sprigged crêpe de Chine. We all looked at her in horror but all she said was, 'Oh dear.'

Marion was horrified. 'Honey, that's too bad, naughty J, J, Jerry! Come with me and I'll help you change. Don't worry about the f, f, frock, I'll see it's cleaned or we'll get you a new one.'

When Archie and I returned to the luncheon area, most of them had dispersed, including Mr Hearst.

Another little vignette. A group of us gathered around a table after dinner, doing a jigsaw puzzle, some fiendishly difficult Constable scene, I think it was. There was a lot of laughter and jostling and much flirting as pieces were reached for.

Then Mr Hearst appeared and the flirting vanished as he asked who would like scrambled eggs. Apparently everybody did. It seemed as though no one wanted to refuse the genial host. So out came these plates of scrambled eggs. And we all said how good they were, and they were.

Later I wanted to know how long we were supposed to stay. I was nowhere near the end of the table yet but I didn't want to see myself sliding down the hospitality scale. But I couldn't see Archie.

'It seems your cousin was taken ill again,' Mr Hearst said quietly. I almost jumped. I hadn't realised he was quite so near. For a big man, he moved very quietly. And how had he known I was looking for Archie?

'I'm sorry, I'll go and see how he is.'

A big hand restrained me. 'That would be most improper,' my host said and I felt rebuffed. 'We look after our guests,' he added in gentle reproof.

'Of course,' I agreed weakly.

At breakfast next morning once again Brewster told me Archie had had a wretched night but was now beginning to feel a little better and would probably join us later. I began to feel really worried.

No one felt like going far afield that day. Cars came for several people catching the Los Angeles train from San Louis Obispo. There was a party by the pool and I joined them.

A newspaper editor contrived to get me apart from the rest and said, 'If I were your cousin, I'd remove myself from here without delay.'

I looked at him in surprise.

'Remember Thomas Ince!'

'Thomas Ince?' I asked. The editor looked both excited and guilty, like a child about to enter into some pleasurable but forbidden activity.

'An actor who became a supervisor in the movies –' His urge to tell the story was almost tangible. 'Marion took a real shine to him. He came on board Mr Hearst's yacht for a cruise one Thanksgiving, oh, some four, five years ago. Never got off alive!' The editor put down a glass of root beer with a small, definitive click.

A congressman had moved within earshot. 'What poppycock!' he said vehemently. 'He did so get off. Didn't die till he got home.'

'W.R. shot him,' the editor went on ghoulishly. 'Couldn't be proved, of course. Everyone knew W.R. took pot shots at seagulls but Louella Parsons swore there was never a gun on board and that's how she got her start as a columnist on W.R.'s papers.'

'But what has this got to do with Archie?'

'Ain't you got eyes in your head?' the congressman asked with asperity. 'Ain't your cousin and Miss Davies cosying up to each other? I tell you, W.R. couldn't get back here fast enough the day you arrived. As soon as we heard that plane, he turned the party around and said we were going back.'

'You want to be careful what you say,' Marie Dressler said quietly. I don't know how long she'd been listening. 'Thomas Ince died of a heart attack following indigestion several days after leaving Mr Hearst's yacht. There was no gunshot wound and only one New York newspaper ever ran the story. If there'd been an ounce of credence behind it, the whole pack would have had it.'

'But he was sick when he left the yacht,' insisted the congressman.

'But not of a gunshot wound like they said,' persisted Marie. 'And Louella Parsons was already working for Hearst newspapers.'

'So,' mused the editor. 'If the story had been that Thomas Ince had been poisoned, perhaps it wouldn't have been so easy to hush up.'

'You can't believe Mr Hearst would do anything like that. It's impossible!' I said.

'Is it?' the editor asked quietly.

I got up, determined to find Archie, when, suddenly, there he was, dressed in cream slacks and shirt with rather a dashing striped blazer.

There was a rush to ask him how he was.

'Fine, thanks,' he said brightly with an attempt at his usual wicked smile.

Marion joined us soon afterwards and was very solicitous. I could feel everyone's eyes on the two of them and I wished she had stayed away.

When lunchtime came, Archie had a bowl of soup that Marion had ordered specially for him, then he said he would rest again.

Later, Brewster Millhausen came and told me that Archie had had a relapse. 'If you don't get him away from here, he'll be a goner,' he told me ghoulishly.

Archie joined us for the cocktail hour, looking almost flushed with health. He took me aside and said, if I didn't mind, we'd catch the train back to Los Angeles in the morning. He had another bowl of soup for dinner, then disappeared immediately afterwards. Isabel Blandish touched his sleeve as he passed her on the way out and asked how he was. He answered her shortly so it was quite a surprise to hear Marion say to her a little later, 'I think Archie is crazy about you, you know? You should give him a little encouragement. You know, sort of look at him . . .' She gave a sultry glance from under her eyelashes that would have stopped any man in his tracks at twenty paces.

Isabel was taken aback. 'I'm sure Archie isn't, Marion. And, even if he was, I, well, I'm practically engaged already.'

'Engaged!' Marion clapped her hands. 'You sly thing! Who's the lucky man? I adore romances. You must get married here, it's a wonderful place for weddings. And I'm always a bridesmaid; well, I have to get a new dress somehow, don't I?' She was laughing and appeared completely at ease.

Isabel became positively frosty. 'Please, Marion, say nothing, it isn't official. And, anyway, he's in New York.' She didn't actually say the last thing she would want was a wedding at San Simeon, but that's how it seemed.

Archie had another terrible night and in the morning was still suffering from stomach cramps and diarrhoea. W. R. insisted we were flown back to Los Angeles.

He and Marion said goodbye to us at the bottom of the steps. Archie still looked fine but I could tell by the way he held himself he felt awful.

I was beside myself with worry. All the insinuations had got to me and I couldn't accept that he was suffering from some gastric ailment. Yet neither could I believe that the large, quiet, smiling man who was telling us to come back soon could be so jealous of my cousin that he was poisoning him.

Then I remembered W.R.'s power and stature, his affinity with the Renaissance, the way he'd created this castle from the trappings of that ruthless age. Surely if he wanted to, he could get away with anything?

We sat in the plane, waiting to take off, Archie shivering beside me. He pulled out a flask. 'Damn,' he said, 'it's empty.'

'Archie, alcohol is the last thing you need.'

'I'm just so thirsty.'

'Then drink water. I'll make you some nice soup when we get back.'

He shuddered. 'Don't mention the word!'

The journey was torture for Archie, not because he was sick but because of leg cramps. Strapped into his small seat he found it impossible to ease them out.

When we landed, I suggested we take a taxi and leave his car but he snapped that he was perfectly capable of driving.

He insisted on dropping me off and wouldn't hear of my preparing anything for him. 'Do you want to poison me?' he asked waspishly. 'Don't you remember trying to cook devilled kidneys? Even the dog wouldn't eat them!'

'That was years ago,' I protested.

I called on him the next morning.

'How are you?' I asked anxiously. He was in his pyjamas, his complexion freshly pink but sheened with a fine sweat.

Archie made a deprecating face and shrugged his shoulders. 'Not too good, actually.'

This was so unlike him, I knew he must be feeling terrible. 'Have you eaten?' I demanded. My mother has always declared that food cures all ills.

He shook his head. 'I can hardly swallow.'

I went to his bedroom door. As I suspected, the bottle of whisky was by his bed. 'Oh, Archie, I told you alcohol was no good for you.'

'It's the only thing that's keeping me going. What do you want, anyway?' His irritability was another sign he was worse than he had been at San Simeon and, curiously, that made me feel more cheerful. W.R. couldn't be poisoning Archie in his own home so, if he wasn't getting better, it had to mean he had some gastric disorder. The relief was huge.

'Where's your kitchen?'

'I told you, food's out.'

'Steamed fish will be just the thing,' I asserted.

His strength obviously wasn't up to arguing and when I brought the dish through he did try and eat a little.

Then the doorbell rang.

Marion stood there, looking as beautiful and chic as though she was about to start filming.

'D, D, Daisy, how is he?' she asked urgently and moved through without an invitation. 'Are you any better, honey?' she demanded.

He shook his head.

'Have you seen the doc?'

'What can he do? Only tell me I've got gastro-enteritis, give me some pill that won't make any difference and charge the earth. No, I'll be fine in a few days,' he said listlessly.

Marion sat and took a piece of paper from her purse. She leaned forward earnestly. 'Archie, do you feel sort of gritty in the mouth?'

He looked surprised. 'You could say that, yes!'

'And, like, you can't swallow? Does your stomach hurt?'

He nodded.

'You got the runs? Muscle cramps in your calves? Headache?'

More nodding.

Marion sat back, she looked very pale. 'Archie, I sp, sp, spent hours yesterday in W.R.'s library. He's got a book there on –' she consulted her paper then said carefully – 'toxicology; that's poisons.'

'What are you suggesting?' I asked anxiously.

'I couldn't stop thinking about Isabel telling us of the fly papers, see? It took me time but f, f, finally I drew enough sense between the long words. And, and then I told W.R. I had to fly down here because I had to do some sh, sh, shopping. I'm always shopping!' Marion scrunched the paper up nervously. 'I had to check with you because, well, you don't know what people say about W.R.!'

'You mean, he's responsible for Archie's illness?'

She turned on me, eyes flashing. 'That's the stupidest thing I've heard! W.R. wouldn't hurt a fly! Why, one time his little dog frightened a mouse that was in a plant pot, and he took the mouse with his own hands and put it in a hole and cut my lovely blanket to keep it warm. I tell you, W.R. is just so tender-hearted!'

The picture of that big man cosseting a mouse was irresistible but I couldn't help thinking that rescuing a rodent was quite different from allowing your mistress to be stolen from under your nose.

Archie pushed away his plate and got to his feet. 'Sorry,' he mumbled, 'back in a minute.'

He shuffled out and Marion mewed like a kitten in distress.

'Do you mean people think he's poisoning Archie?' I asked.

'I'm not brainy but I've got ears. And everyone's gone. I mean they should have but so often someone asks if they can stay a day or so longer, or W.R. will propose some outing, you know? But not this time. It's all happening again.'

'You mean like with Thomas Ince?'

She nodded. 'There was an investigation and everything but people believe what they want. And I can't stand for W.R. to be put in that position again.'

She seemed totally sincere.

'People think I'm with him because of his money, but I had a career before I met him and I don't need all that publicity rubbish in his papers.' She looked very sweet in her earnestness. 'Anyway,' she hurried on. 'As I was saying, it's too b, b, bad what people say. I thought Archie must be sick to his stomach of something normal, like gastric troubles. I mean, gastric troubles are normal, aren't they?' Her huge eyes, blue as cornflowers, were as earnest as a five-year-old's. 'But I thought I'd sneak a look, you know, to see what arsenic poisoning is like. I mean, W.R. has books on just everything. Usually if it hasn't a story, I can't read it, but this was just so important. It was hard but I find if you really concentrate you can work things out, don't you find?'

She seemed honestly anxious for my opinion, so I agreed with her.

'You're really nice, you know that? Anyway, there were lots and lots of medical words and things I didn't understand but it said that taking arsenic means you're sick very soon after and that if it's food poisoning, you're not for over twelve hours. And all the time Archie was ill soon after eating and then he appears well, doesn't he?' I had to agree that he looked in the pink. 'And the book said that when you first take arsenic it gives you a "milk and roses" complexion. Apparently some people used to take it for the look!' She paused. 'Fancy actually choosing to take arsenic!' It stunned me too. 'So, you see, I just had to come and see if Archie had all these symptoms.'

The patient returned, wiping his sweating face with a handkerchief.

'Archie, Marion thinks someone's been feeding you arsenic,' I said baldly.

'That's a ridiculous suggestion,' he said wearily, slumping into his chair. 'Who would want to kill me?'

When you're well over sixty and have got a pretty girl who's thirty years younger and you can't marry them, I suppose it could be natural that you think she could be impressed by a younger man. What interested me was that Marion actually seemed to think W.R. capable of putting a powdering of arsenic in a rival's Welsh rarebit, however tender-hearted she claimed he was.

'Did the book say you got better if you stopped taking arsenic?' I asked.

She frowned and still managed to look enchanting. I could understand W.R.'s fascination with her. 'I think so but there were just so many long words!'

'Archie's getting worse,' I said firmly. 'So he can't be being poisoned. If only he'd see a doctor!'

'If he's still taking arsenic, he would be worse,' Marion said doggedly.

'I wish you wouldn't talk about me as though I wasn't here,' Archie said irritably.

I ignored him. 'But his diet's completely different now.' Then it came to me. 'Archie, your whisky!'

Marion clapped her hands together. 'I knew it! W.R. hates people to drink a lot so the servants remove any bottles from guests' cases. But people are so cute and use so many tricks.'

'I kept my flasks in my back pockets until my things were unpacked, then hid them under the mattress. A man has to have a shot every now and then,' Archie said in injured tones.

I fetched the bottle from the bedroom. Marion took it from me and ran to the bathroom – she seemed to know exactly where it was – and started to pour its contents carefully down the basin.

'Hey, that's my whisky,' protested Archie.

'You want to be poisoned?' asked Marion. Then she grabbed a glass from the shelf and emptied the last remaining finger of whisky into it. 'Look,' she said.

Mingled with the remains of the whisky was a white sediment. 'I've never seen whisky like that,' Marion said with a note of triumph.

'But if it's bootleg?' I suggested.

'Not even if it's bootleg,' she asserted. 'The book said arsenic dissolves in hot liquid but comes out a bit in cold.'

Archie returned to the living room. He flung open the drinks cabinet, picked out another bottle of the same make and lifted it high so he could study the bottom. 'Looks like more sediment,' he said. He grabbed another and then a third. All were the same.

He slammed the bottle down. 'The bitch!'

'Who?' Marion and I asked in unison.

Archie rubbed his face. 'My beloved wife.'

'Your wife?' I squeaked.

'You're married?' gasped Marion.

'I regret, yes,' groaned Archie.

'Who to?' I asked.

'Isabel,' Marion said excitedly. 'I always know when there's something between a couple. I'm always getting romances going. I tell the man so-and-so is mad about him, why doesn't he show her a good time. Then I tell so-and-so the man's crazy for you, he told me so and they're away!'

'We married a couple of years ago,' Archie said. 'Isabel's real name is Hilda Black. She was working on a magazine and came to do a backstage story. I was understudying the lead. I was attracted and, well, one thing led to another. Then she told me she was pregnant, so I had to do the decent thing.' His voice was bitter.

'But you didn't ask us to your wedding!' I protested.

'It was a registry office. Father had cut me off already and I knew Mama would be upset.'

'What about the baby?' Marion asked in a quiet voice.

'Oh, she lost it. At least, that's what she told me. I don't think there ever was a baby. Things went wrong very quickly then and I decided I'd had enough. I jumped at the chance of a new start when an agent suggested there could be work out here and asked Hilda for a divorce. She said she was damned if I was going to desert her.' He sounded sulky and outraged at the same time. 'But she'd just had that Borgia book published and it was doing well so I left. I struggled here and there then managed to get my MGM contract. Just as I thought everything was hunky-dory, I get a letter from her at the studio, saying she'd met this millionaire in New York and wanted to get married. Well –' he looked up with an injured expression – 'I'd told the bosses I was a bachelor and a divorce would have caused no end of a ruckus. So I refused to provide evidence. The whisky arrived a few days later, a couple of weeks ago it was. Six bottles. I filled my flasks from the first one. I never thought she could be vicious, though, just difficult, devious and a liar.' I wondered how she had ever managed to attract him.

'My, it's amazing how we girls can get our man,' said Marion. 'Ring her, Archie. Get her round here, say you want to talk to her about a divorce.'

'But I don't know where she's staying.'

'At the Bel Air, of course.' Marion sounded as though there could be nowhere else. She picked up the telephone, gave the operator a number then handed the earpiece to Archie.

Twenty minutes later, Hilda arrived.

Marion and I were hidden in the bedroom. Archie hadn't thought much of this part of the plan but Marion had insisted. He needed witnesses, she said.

'Hello, Archie,' Hilda's cool voice said. 'Come to your senses at last, have you?'

'Have some whisky.' Archie's voice was uneven.

'You know I never touch the stuff.'

'And anyway you wouldn't want to take arsenic, would you?' he said venomously.

'Really, Archie, I don't know what you mean.'

'Yes you do, you bitch. You're trying to kill me.' I hardly recognised my cousin's voice. 'Well, it won't work, I'm on to you now.'

'Archie, I think whatever you're suffering from has affected your brain.' Hilda's voice was very steady. 'I came round to discuss divorce not to listen to the ravings of a lunatic. Now, if you'll just give me back my manuscript, I'll see everything goes smoothly. It's as much in my interest as yours that there be no publicity.'

'I don't know what you're talking about,' Archie said unsteadily.

'The manuscript you stole from me.' Hilda raised her voice. 'The one you've been using to blackmail me.'

Marion and I looked at each other in astonishment.

'Now that you've got your contract, you don't need my money.' Her voice dropped and it sounded as though she'd come close to Archie. 'We had some good times at the beginning. Can't we be friends now? I never wanted to hurt you.'

'Th, th, that's it,' Marion shouted out. 'She's c, c, confessed!' She rushed into the living room.

'Confessed? What do you mean?' Hilda turned to Archie. 'You're trying to trick me, you black-hearted bastard.'

Archie looked sick, the way he used to as a boy when found out in some misdemeanour.

'What's this about blackmail?' I asked sternly.

'I was a fool for ever thinking I could get away with it,' Hilda said with a sigh. '*Borgia Bastardy* was written by my aunt. I found it among her papers after she died. I typed it out and sent it off to a publisher's with my name as author. She'd left everything to me anyway. But Archie found the original manuscript and he's been making me pay ever since.'

'And that's why you want me dead,' he said violently.

'Anyone who says I'm poisoning you is a liar,' Hilda said with great aplomb.

I remembered her control when the ape had thrown his droppings at her. The clever way she had introduced the subject of arsenic and managed to make everyone suspect Mr Hearst. Marion had been too precipitate, we would never get her to confess now.

'I'm going to admit the truth.' Hilda held her head high. 'I've already told my fiancé. You won't be able to blackmail me any longer, so you might as well return the manuscript.'

'And the divorce will go through with the minimum of publicity?'

'The public knows me as Isabel Blandish not Hilda Fortescue. No one knows you yet,' she said cruelly. 'Change your name before your first film comes out and no one will be interested in our divorce.'

'Right!' Marion said enthusiastically. 'Archie Fortescue sounds real poncey anyway; you need something short, something like, like Rory C, C, Cable. I'll get the studio on to it.'

'The day we have our divorce,' Archie said to Hilda, 'I'll give the manuscript back. But if you have another go at killing me, I'll publish and be damned.' He was every inch the matinée idol.

Hilda looked contemptuously at him. 'Archie Fortescue, you're a liar and a blackmailer but, God help me, I once loved you and I'd never poison you. Goodbye!'

Archie slid into a chair as the door closed behind her. 'Christ!' he said. 'I'm dying.'

Marion gave him a straight look. 'Call a doc. The book said what you need is a stomach washout. And I hope it bugs the ass off you.'

'Marion, darling!'

'Don't you darling or honey me! Blackmailing that poor girl indeed.'

'That poor girl tried to murder me.'

'And if you'd done that to me, I'd a done the same. You look good on screen but off it you st, st, stink! We can't p, p, prove a word of this and if either of you breathes a word about arsenic, you'll b, b, both be finished in Hollywood, unnerstand?'

Mesmerised by her metamorphosis into avenging angel, I nodded. 'It won't do Archie's reputation any good if this story gets out,' I said.

Marion picked up her purse and left.

'What happened?'

'Archie, I can't forget you're my cousin but you haven't behaved like a gentleman.'

'Daisy, not you too? I married the stupid cow, didn't I?'

'That's the only decent aspect to the whole story.'

'And you got to go to San Simeon.'

I softened ever so slightly. 'I'll never forget that, Archie. Now, for heaven's sake, phone the studio and get the name of a discreet doctor. You need attention.'

I went to the kitchen to collect my bits and pieces. I felt totally confused. Horrified that Archie had been drinking arsenic-loaded whisky, outraged that he was capable of blackmail. No wonder Mother hadn't wanted me to contact him.

When I returned, Archie was looking through a mess of bills and papers in a desk.

'I'll manage in Hollywood without you, Archie.'

He wasn't paying attention. 'Look what I've found. It came with the whisky.'

It was a Cosmopolitan Productions card with the message, 'To Archie Fortescue, here's hoping for great things with the Borgias.' There was no sender's name but the card looked like the real thing. Could Hilda have picked it up on a visit to the studios?

'One thing I don't understand,' Archie said slowly. 'How did she know where I was living?'

'You didn't tell her?'

'What, and have her come round here and bend my ear? She sent the money direct to my bank and you heard me on the phone just now telling her where I lived.'

'She might have found out your address when she visited the studios and only pretended she didn't know it.'

'But she hasn't been to the studios yet; she's going next week. She must have rung someone.'

If she hadn't been to the studios, how had she got hold of the card?

The question never seemed to occur to Archie, but he'd never been very bright and perhaps the arsenic had affected his brain power. I saw no useful purpose in pointing it out. But I did start to wonder about the way Marion had insisted an ambiguous phrase was Hilda's confession.

Like I said, I promised Marion I wouldn't breathe a word of any of this while W.R. or she lived. *Borgia Bastardy* was never made but Hilda married her millionaire and gave up writing. Archie made a couple more pictures then took to the bottle and his contract was suspended. By then I'd married and given up my career, such as it was, to raise a family. I'd discovered I wasn't starstruck after all.

And W.R. and Marion? You could say they lived happily ever after, at least until Mr Hearst died in 1951 at the age of eighty-eight. They'd been together for over thirty years by then. Marion married afterwards but it didn't work out and she died the other day, ten years after W.R., at the comparatively young age of sixty-four.

All I know for certain about the episode is that I can never forget those days at San Simeon. Whatever else William Randolph Hearst was, he built an unforgettable castle.

My first introduction to Ellis Peters, and still my favourite of her novels, was not a Brother Cadfael book but a much earlier mystery, *Death Mask*, originally published in 1959. The setting was England and Greece. The period was contemporary, not historical, but the mystery hinged on archaeological evidence and an ancient artifact; those elements, and a curious bit of Mary Renaultish male bonding between the characters, were what made the novel so appealing to me. Knowing that Ellis Peters had a taste for the Classical world, even if at a remove, inspires me to ponder one of those imponderables: what if she had chosen to write a historical series set not in the medieval England of Cadfael, but in ancient Greece – or in the volatile Roman Republic of Cicero and Caesar?

But the task of reviving Rome was left to others, including myself. Gordianus the Finder first appeared in my novel *Roman Blood*, and most of his sleuthing has been in the vicinity of the Seven Hills. Occasionally he travels, however, and it seemed to me appropriate, in memory of *Death Mask*, to place him in a Greek milieu (Neapolis on the Bay of Naples, 75 BC), and to draw on Greek elements. (The inspiration for 'Death by Eros' can be found in Theocritus' 23rd Idyll, which gives the gist of the story, though as a moral fable rather than a mystery.) The theme, too, would be familiar to Ellis Peters, who frequently cast lovers (secret and otherwise) among her characters. In her tales, for the most part, love is vindicated and lovers triumph; would that it could have been so for the various lovers in this story.

Steven Saylor

Death by Eros

Steven Saylor

'The Neapolitans are different from us Romans,' I remarked to Eco as we strolled across the central forum of Neapolis. 'A man can almost feel that he's left Italy altogether and been magically transported to a seaport in Greece. Greek colonists founded the city hundreds of years ago, taking advantage of the extraordinary bay, which they called the *Krater*, or Cup. The locals still have Greek names, eat Greek food, follow Greek customs. Many of them don't even speak Latin.'

Eco pointed to his lips and made a self-deprecating gesture to say, *Neither do I!* At fifteen, he tended to make a joke of everything, including his muteness.

'Ah, but you can *hear* Latin,' I said, flicking a finger against one of his ears just hard enough to sting, 'and sometimes even understand it.'

We had arrived in Neapolis on our way back to Rome, after doing a bit of business for Cicero down in Sicily. Rather than stay at an inn, I was hoping to find accommodations with a wealthy Greek trader named Sosistrides. 'The fellow owes me a favour,' Cicero had told me. 'Look him up and mention my name, and I'm sure he'll put you up for the night.'

With a few directions from the locals (who were polite enough not to laugh at my Greek) we found the trader's house. The columns and lintels and decorative details of the façade were stained in various shades of pale red, blue and yellow that seemed to glow under the warm sunlight. Incongruous amid the play of colours was a black wreath on the door.

'What do you think, Eco? Can we ask a friend of a friend, a total stranger really, to put us up when the household is in mourning? It seems presumptuous.'

Eco nodded thoughtfully, then gestured to the wreath and expressed curiosity with a flourish of his wrist. I nodded. 'I see your point. If it's Sosistrides who's died, or a member of the family, Cicero would want us to deliver his condolences, wouldn't he? And we must learn the details, so that we can inform him in a letter. I think we must at least rouse the doorkeeper, to see what's happened.'

I walked to the door and politely knocked with the side of my foot. There was no answer. I knocked again and waited. I was about to rap on the door with my knuckles, rudely or not, when it swung open.

The man who stared back at us was dressed in mourning black. He was not a slave; I glanced at his hand and saw a citizen's iron ring. His greying hair was dishevelled and his face distressed. His eyes were red from weeping.

'What do you want?' he said, in a voice more wary than unkind.

'Forgive me, citizen. My name is Gordianus. This is my son, Eco. Eco hears but is mute, so I shall speak for him. We're travellers, on our way home to Rome. I'm a friend of Marcus Tullius Cicero. It was he who—'

'Cicero? Ah, yes, the Roman governor down in Sicily, the one who can actually read and write, for a change.' The man wrinkled his brow. 'Has he sent a message, or . . . ?'

'Nothing urgent; Cicero asked me only to remind you of his friendship. You are, I take it, the master of the house, Sosistrides?'

'Yes. And you? I'm sorry, did you already introduce yourself? My mind wanders . . .' He looked over his shoulder.

Beyond him, in the vestibule, I glimpsed a funeral bier strewn with freshly cut flowers and laurel leaves.

'My name is Gordianus. And this is my son—'

'Gordianus, did you say?'

'Yes.'

'Cicero mentioned you once. Something about a murder trial up in Rome. You helped him. They call you the Finder.'

'Yes.'

He looked at me intently for a long moment. 'Come in, Finder. I want you to see him.'

The bier in the vestibule was propped up and tilted at an angle so that its occupant could be clearly seen. The corpse was that of a youth probably not much older than Eco. His arms were crossed over his chest and he was clothed in a long white gown, so that only his face and hands were exposed. His hair was boyishly long and as yellow as a field of millet in summer, crowned with a laurel wreath of the sort awarded to athletic champions. The flesh of his delicately moulded features was waxy and pale, but even in death his beauty was remarkable.

'His eyes were blue,' said Sosistrides in a low voice. 'They're closed now, you can't see them, but they were blue, like his dear, dead mother's; he got his looks from her. The purest blue you ever saw, like the colour of the Cup on a clear day. When we pulled him from the pool, they were all bloodshot . . .'

'This is your son, Sosistrides?'

He stifled a sob. 'My only son, Cleon.'

'A terrible loss.'

He nodded, unable to speak. Eco shifted nervously from foot to foot, studying the dead boy with furtive glances, almost shyly.

'They call you Finder,' Sosistrides finally said, in a hoarse voice. 'Help me find the monster who killed my son.'

I looked at the dead youth and felt a deep empathy for

Sosistrides' suffering, and not merely because I myself had a son of similar age. (Eco may be adopted, but I love him as my own flesh.) I was stirred also by the loss of such beauty. Why does the death of a beautiful stranger affect us more deeply than the loss of someone plain? Why should it be so, that if a vase of exquisite workmanship but little practical value should break, we feel the loss more sharply than if we break an ugly vessel we use every day? The gods made men to love beauty above all else, perhaps because they themselves are beautiful, and wish for us to love them, even when they do us harm.

'How did he die, Sosistrides?'

'It was at the gymnasium, yesterday. There was a city-wide contest among the boys – discus throwing, wrestling, racing. I couldn't attend. I was away in Pompeii on business all day . . .' Sosistrides again fought back tears. He reached out and touched the wreath on his son's brow. 'Cleon took the laurel crown. He was a splendid athlete. He always won at everything, but they say he outdid himself yesterday. If only I had been there to see it! Afterwards, while the other boys retired to the baths inside, Cleon took a swim in the long pool, alone. There was no one else in the courtyard. No one saw it happen . . .'

'The boy drowned, Sosistrides?' It seemed unlikely, if the boy had been as good at swimming as he was at everything else.

Sosistrides shook his head and shut his eyes tight, squeezing tears from them. 'The gymnasiarchus is an old wrestler named Caputorus. It was he who found Cleon. He heard a splash, he said, but thought nothing of it. Later he went into the courtyard and discovered Cleon. The water was red with blood. Cleon was at the bottom of the pool. Beside him was a broken statue. It must have struck the back of his head; it left a terrible gash.'

'A statue?'

'Of Eros – the god you Romans call Cupid. A cherub with

88

bow and arrows, a decoration at the edge of the pool. Not a large statue, but heavy, made of solid marble. It somehow fell from its pedestal as Cleon was passing below . . .' He gazed at the boy's bloodless face, lost in misery.

I sensed the presence of another in the room, and turned to see a young woman in a black gown with a black mantle over her head. She walked to Sosistrides' side. 'Who are these visitors, Father?'

'Friends of the provincial governor down in Sicily – Gordianus of Rome, and his son, Eco. This is my daughter, Cleio. Daughter! Cover yourself!' Sosistrides' sudden embarrassment was caused by the fact that Cleio had pushed the mantle from her head, revealing that her dark hair was crudely shorn, cut short so that it didn't reach her shoulders. No longer shadowed by the mantle, her face, too, showed signs of unbridled mourning. Long scratches ran down her cheeks, and there were bruises where she appeared to have struck herself, marring a beauty that rivalled her brother's.

'I mourn for the loss of the one I loved best in all the world,' she said in a hollow voice. 'I feel no shame to show it.' She cast an icy stare at me and then at Eco, then swept from the room.

Extreme displays of grief are disdained in Rome, where excessive public mourning is banned by law, but we were in Neapolis. Sosistrides seemed to read my thoughts. 'Cleio has always been more Greek than Roman. She lets her emotions run wild. Just the opposite of her brother. Cleon was always so cool, so detached.' He shook his head. 'She's taken her brother's death very hard. When I came home from Pompeii yesterday I found his body here in the vestibule; his slaves had carried him home from the gymnasium. Cleio was in her room, crying uncontrollably. She'd already cut her hair. She wept and wailed all night long.'

He gazed at his dead son's face and reached out to touch it, his hand looking warm and ruddy against the unnatural pallor of the boy's cold cheek. 'Someone murdered my son.

You must help me find out who did it, Gordianus – to put the shade of my son to rest, and for my grieving daughter's sake.'

'That's right, I heard the splash. I was here behind my counter in the changing room, and the door to the courtyard was standing wide open, just like it is now.'

Caputorus the gymnasiarchus was a grizzled old wrestler with enormous shoulders, a perfectly bald head and a protruding belly. His eyes kept darting past me to follow the comings and goings of the naked youths, and every so often he interrupted me in mid-sentence to yell out a greeting which usually included some jocular insult or obscenity. The fourth time he reached out to tousle Eco's hair, Eco deftly moved out of range and stayed there.

'And when you heard the splash, did you immediately go and have a look?' I asked.

'Not right away. To tell you the truth, I didn't think much of it. I figured Cleon was out there jumping in and out of the pool, which is against the rules, mind you! It's a long, shallow pool meant for swimming only, and no jumping allowed. But he was always breaking the rules. Thought he could get away with anything.'

'So why didn't you go out and tell him to stop? You are the gymnasiarchus, aren't you?'

'Do you think that counted for anything with that spoiled brat? Master of the gym I may be, but nobody was his master. You know what he'd have done? Quoted some fancy lines from some famous play, most likely about old wrestlers with big bellies, flashed his naked behind at me, and then jumped back in the pool! I don't need the grief, thank you very much. Hey, Manius!' Caputorus shouted at a youth behind me. 'I saw you and your sweetheart out there wrestling this morning. You been studying your old man's dirty vases to learn those positions? Ha!'

Over my shoulder I saw a redheaded youth flash a lascivious grin and make an obscene gesture using both hands.

'Back to yesterday,' I said. 'You heard the splash and didn't think much of it, but eventually you went out to the courtyard.'

'Just to get some fresh air. I noticed right away that Cleon wasn't swimming any more. I figured he'd headed inside to the baths.'

'But wouldn't he have passed you on the way?'

'Not necessarily. There are two passageways into the courtyard. The one most people take goes past my counter here. The other is through a little hallway that connects to the outer vestibule. It's a more roundabout route to get inside to the baths, but he could have gone in that way.'

'And could someone have gotten into the courtyard the same way?'

'Yes.'

'Then you can't say for certain that Cleon was alone out there.'

'You are a sharp one, aren't you!' Caputorus said sarcastically. 'But you're right. Cleon was out there by himself to start with, of that I'm sure. And after that, nobody walked by me, coming or going. But somebody could have come and gone by the other passageway. Anyway, when I stepped out there, I could tell right away that something was wrong, seriously wrong, though I couldn't quite say what. Only later, I realised what it was: the statue was missing, that little statue of Eros that's been there since before I took over running this place. You know how you can see a thing every day and take it for granted, and when all of a sudden it's not there, you can't even say what's missing, but you *sense* that something's off? That's how it was. Then I saw the colour of the water. All pinkish in one spot, and darker toward the bottom. I stepped closer and then I saw him, lying on the bottom, not moving and no air bubbles coming up, and the statue around him in pieces. It was obvious right away what must have happened. Here, I'll show you the spot.'

As we were passing out the doorway a muscular wrestler

wearing only a leather headband and wrist-wraps squeezed by on his way in. Caputorus twisted a towel between his fists and snapped it against the youth's bare backside. 'Your mother!' yelled the stung athlete.

'No, your shiny red bottom!' said Caputorus, who threw back his head and laughed.

The pool had been drained and scrubbed, leaving no trace of Cleon's blood amid the puddles. The pieces of the statue of Eros had been gathered up and deposited next to the empty pedestal. One of the cherub's tiny feet had broken off, as had the top of Eros' bow, the point of his notched arrow, and the feathery tip of one wing.

'The statue had been here for years, you say?'

'That's right.'

'Sitting here on this pedestal?'

'Yes. Never budged, even when we'd get a bit of a rumble from Vesuvius.'

'Strange, then, that it should have fallen yesterday, when no one felt any tremors. Even stranger that it fell directly on to a swimmer . . .'

'It's a mystery, all right.'

'I think the word is murder.'

Caputorus looked at me shrewdly. 'Not necessarily.'

'What do you mean?'

'Ask some of the boys. See what they tell you.'

'I intend to ask everyone who was here what they saw or heard.'

'Then you might start with this little fellow.' He indicated the broken Eros.

'Speak plainly, Caputorus.'

'Others know more than I do. All I can tell you is what I've picked up from the boys.'

'And what's that?'

'Cleon was a heartbreaker. You've only seen him laid out for his funeral. You have no idea how good-looking he was, both above the neck and below. A body like a statue by

92

Phidias, a regular Apollo – he took your breath away! Smart, too, and the best athlete on the Cup. Strutting around here naked every day, challenging all the boys to wrestle him, celebrating his wins by quoting Homer. He had half the boys in this place trailing around after him at one time or another, all wanting to be his special friend. They were awestruck by him.'

'And yet, yesterday, after he won the laurel crown, he swam alone.'

'Maybe because they'd all finally had enough of him. Maybe they got tired of his bragging. Maybe they realised he wasn't the sort to ever return a shred of love or affection to anybody.'

'You sound bitter, Caputorus.'

'Do I?'

'Are you sure you're talking just about the boys?'

His face reddened. He worked his jaw back and forth and flexed his massive shoulders. I tried not to flinch.

'I'm no fool, Finder,' he finally said, lowering his voice. 'I've been around long enough to learn a few things. Lesson one: a boy like Cleon is nothing but trouble. Look, but don't touch.' His jaw relaxed into a faint smile. 'I've got a tough hide. I tease and joke with the best, but none of these boys gets under my skin.'

'Not even Cleon?'

His face hardened, then broke into a grin as he looked beyond me. 'Calpurnius!' he yelled at a boy across the courtyard. 'If you handle the javelin between your legs the way you handle that one, I'm surprised you haven't pulled it off by now! Merciful Zeus, let me show you how!'

Caputorus pushed past me, tousling Eco's hair on his way, leaving us to ponder the broken Eros and the empty pool where Cleon had died.

One after another I managed that day to speak to every boy in the gymnasium. Most of them had been there the previous day, either to take part in the athletic games or to watch. Most of them were co-operative, but only to a point. I had the feeling that they had already talked among themselves and decided as a group to say as little as possible concerning Cleon's death to outsiders like myself, no matter that I came as the representative of Cleon's father.

Nevertheless, from uncomfortable looks, wistful sighs and unfinished sentences I gathered that what Caputorus had told me was true: Cleon had broken hearts all over the gymnasium, and in the process had made more than a few enemies. He was by universal consensus the brightest and most beautiful boy in the group, and yesterday's games had proven conclusively that he was the best athlete as well. He was also vain, arrogant, selfish and aloof; easy to fall in love with and incapable of loving in return. The boys who had not fallen under his personal spell at one time or another disliked him out of pure envy.

All this I managed to learn as much from what was left unsaid as from what each boy said, but when it came to obtaining more concrete details I struck a wall of silence. Had anyone ever been heard uttering a serious threat to Cleon? Had anyone ever said anything, even in jest, about the potentially hazardous placement of the statue of Eros beside the pool? Were any of the boys especially upset about Cleon's victories that day? Had any of them slipped away from the baths at the time Cleon was killed? And what of the gymnasiarchus? Had Caputorus' behaviour toward Cleon always been above reproach, as he claimed?

To these questions, no matter how directly or indirectly I posed them, I received no clear answers, only a series of equivocations and evasions.

I was beginning to despair of uncovering anything significant, when finally I interviewed Hippolytus, the wrestler whose backside Caputorus had playfully snapped with his towel. He was preparing for a plunge in the hot pool when I came to him. He untied his leather headband, letting a shock

94

of jet-black hair fall into his eyes, and began to unwrap his wrists. Eco seemed a bit awed by the fellow's brawniness; to me, with his babyish face and apple-red cheeks, Hippolytus seemed a hugely overgrown child.

I had gathered from the others that Hippolytus was close, or as close as anyone, to Cleon. I began the conversation by saying as much, hoping to catch him off his guard. He looked at me, unfazed, and nodded.

'I suppose that's right. I liked him. He wasn't as bad as some made out.'

'What do you mean?'

'Wasn't Cleon's fault if everybody swooned over him. Wasn't his fault if he didn't swoon back. I don't think he had it in him to feel that way about another boy.' He frowned and wrinkled his brow. 'Some say that's not natural, but there you are. The gods make us all different.'

'I'm told he was arrogant and vain.'

'Wasn't his fault he was better than everybody else at wrestling and running and throwing. Wasn't his fault he was smarter than his tutors. But he shouldn't have crowed so much, I suppose. Hubris – you know what that is?'

'Vanity that offends the gods,' I said.

'Right, like in the plays. Acquiring a swollen head, becoming too cocksure, until a fellow's just begging to be struck down by a lightning bolt or swallowed by an earthquake. What the gods give they can take away. They gave Cleon everything. Then they took it all away.'

'The gods?'

Hippolytus sighed. 'Cleon deserved to be brought down a notch, but he didn't deserve that punishment.'

'Punishment? From whom? For what specific crime?'

I watched his eyes and saw the to and fro of some internal debate. If I prodded too hard, he might shut up tight; if I prodded not at all, he might keep answering in pious generalities. I started to speak, then saw something settle inside him, and held my tongue.

'You've seen the statue that fell on him?' Hippolytus said.

'Yes. Eros with his bow and arrows.'

'Do you think that was just a coincidence?'

'I don't understand.'

'You've talked to everyone in the gymnasium, and nobody's told you? They're all thinking it; they're just too superstitious to say it aloud. It was Eros that killed Cleon, for spurning him.'

'You think the god himself did it? Using his own statue.'

'Love flowed to Cleon from all directions, like rivers to the sea – but he turned back the rivers and lived in his own rocky desert. Eros chose Cleon to be his favourite, but Cleon refused him. He laughed in the god's face once too often.'

'How? What had Cleon done to finally push the god too far?'

Again I saw the internal debate behind his eyes. Clearly, he wanted to tell me everything. I had only to be patient. At last he sighed and spoke. 'Lately, some of us thought that Cleon might finally be softening. He had a new tutor, a young philosopher named Mulciber who came from Alexandria about six months ago. Cleon and his sister Cleio went to Mulciber's little house off the forum every morning to talk about Plato and read poetry.'

'Cleio as well?'

'Sosistrides believed in educating both his children, no matter that Cleio's a girl. Anyway, pretty soon word got around that Mulciber was courting Cleon. Why not? He was smitten, like everybody else. The surprise was that Cleon seemed to respond to his advances. Mulciber would send him chaste little love poems, and Cleon would send poems back to him. Cleon actually showed me some of Mulciber's poems, and asked me to read the ones he was sending back. They were beautiful! He was good at that, too, of course.' Hippolytus shook his head ruefully.

'But it was all a cruel hoax. Cleon was just leading Mulciber on, making a fool of him. Only the day before yesterday, right in front of some of Mulciber's other students, Cleon made a public show of returning all the poems Mulciber had sent him, and asking for his own poems back. He said he'd written them merely as exercises, to teach his own tutor the proper way to write a love poem. Mulciber was dumbstruck! Everyone in the gymnasium heard about it. People said Cleon had finally gone too far. To have spurned his tutor's advances was one thing, but to do so in such a cruel, deliberately humiliating manner – that was hubris, people said, and the gods would take vengeance. And now they have.'

I nodded. 'But quite often the gods use human vessels to achieve their ends. Do you really think the statue tumbled into the pool of its own accord, without a hand to push it?'

Hippolytus frowned, and seemed to debate revealing yet another secret. 'Yesterday, not long before Cleon drowned, some of us saw a stranger in the gymnasium.'

At last, I thought, a concrete bit of evidence, something solid to grapple with! I took a deep breath. 'No one else mentioned seeing a stranger.'

'I told you, they're all too superstitious. If the boy we saw was some emissary of the god, they don't want to speak of it.'

'A boy?'

'Perhaps it was Eros himself, in human form – though you'd think a god would have a better haircut and clothes that fit!'

'You saw this stranger clearly?'

'Not that clearly; neither did anybody else, as far as I can tell. I only caught a glimpse of him loitering in the outer vestibule, but I could tell he wasn't one of the regular boys.'

'How so?'

'By the fact that he was dressed at all. This was just after the games, and everyone was still naked. And most of the gymnasium crowd are pretty well off; this fellow's tunic looked like a patched hand-me-down from a big brother. I figured he was some stranger who wandered in off the street, or maybe a messenger slave too shy to come into the changing room.'

'And his face?'

Hippolytus shook his head. 'I didn't see his face. He had dark hair, though.'

'Did you speak to him, or hear him speak?'

'No. I headed for the hot plunge and forgot all about him. Then Caputorus found Cleon's body, and everything was crazy after that. I didn't make any connection to the stranger until this morning, when I found out that some of the others had seen him, too.'

'Did anybody see this young stranger pass through the baths and the changing room?'

'I don't think so. But there's another way to get from the outer vestibule to the inner courtyard, through a little passageway at the far end of the building.'

'So Caputorus told me. It seems possible, then, that this stranger could have entered the outer vestibule, sneaked through the empty passage, come upon Cleon alone in the pool, pushed the statue on to him, then fled the way he had come, all without being clearly seen by anyone.'

Hippolytus took a deep breath. 'That's how I figure it. So you see, it must have been the god, or some agent of the god. Who else could have had such perfect timing, to carry out such an awful deed?'

I shook my head. 'I can see you know a bit about poetry and more than a bit about wrestling holds, young man, but has no one tutored you in logic? We may have answered the question of *how*, but that hasn't answered the question of *who*. I respect your religious conviction that the god Eros may have had the motive and the will to kill Cleon in such a cold-blooded fashion – but it seems there were plenty of mortals with abundant motive as well. In my line of work I prefer to suspect the most likely mortal first, and presume divine causation only as a last resort. Chief among such suspects must be this tutor, Mulciber. Could he have been the stranger you saw lurking in the vestibule? Philosophers are notorious for having bad haircuts and shabby clothes.'

'No. The stranger was shorter and had darker hair.'

'Still, I should like to have a talk with this lovesick tutor.'

'You can't,' said Hippolytus. 'Mulciber hanged himself yesterday.'

'No wonder such a superstitious dread surrounds Cleon's death,' I remarked to Eco, as we made our way to the house of Mulciber. 'The golden boy of the Cup, killed by a statue of Eros; his spurned tutor, hanging himself the same day. This is the dark side of Eros. It casts a shadow that frightens everyone into silence.'

Except me, Eco gestured, and let out the stifled, inchoate grunt he sometimes emits simply to declare his existence. I smiled at his self-deprecating humour, but it seemed to me that the things we had learned that morning had disturbed and unsettled Eco. He was at an age to be acutely aware of his place in the scheme of things, and to begin wondering who might ever love him, especially in spite of his handicap. It seemed unfair that a boy like Cleon, who had only scorn for his suitors, should have inspired so much unrequited infatuation and desire, when others faced lives of loneliness. Did the gods engineer the paradox of love's unfairness to amuse themselves, or was it one of the evils that escaped from Pandora's box to plague mankind?

The door of the philosopher's house, like that of Sosistrides', was adorned with a black wreath. Following my knock, an elderly slave opened it to admit us to a little foyer, where a body was laid out upon a bier much less elaborate than that of Cleon. I saw at once why Hippolytus had been certain that the short, dark-haired stranger at the gymnasium had not been the Alexandrian tutor, for Mulciber was quite tall and had fair hair. He had been a reasonably handsome man of thirty-five or so, about my own age. Eco gestured to the scarf that had been clumsily gathered about the dead man's throat, and then clutched his own neck with a strangler's grip: *to hide the rope marks*, he seemed to say.

'Did you know my master?' asked the slave who had shown us in.

'Only by reputation,' I said. 'We're visitors to Neapolis, but I've heard of your master's devotion to poetry and philosophy. I was shocked to learn of his sudden death.' I spoke only the truth, after all.

The slave nodded. 'He was a man of learning and talent. Still, few have come to pay their respects. He had no family here. And of course there are many who won't set foot inside the house of a suicide, for fear of bad luck.'

'It's certain that he killed himself, then?'

'It was I who found him, hanging from a rope. He tied it to that beam, just above the boy's head.' Eco rolled his eyes up. 'Then he stood on a folding chair, put the noose around his neck, and kicked the chair out of the way. His neck snapped. I like to think he died quickly.' The slave regarded his master's face affectionately. 'Such a waste! And all for the love of that worthless boy!'

'You're certain that's why he killed himself?'

'Why else? He was making a good living here in Neapolis, enough to send a bit back to his brother in Alexandria every now and again, and even to think of purchasing a second slave. I'm not sure how I'd have taken to that; I've been with him since he was a boy. I used to carry his wax tablets and scrolls for him when was little and had his own tutor. No, his life was going well in every way, except for that horrible boy!'

'You know that Cleon died yesterday.'

'Oh, yes. That's why the master killed himself.'

'He hung himself, then, *after* hearing of Cleon's death?'

'Of course! Only . . .' The old man looked puzzled, as if he had not previously considered any other possibility. 'Now let me think. Yesterday was strange all around, you see. The master sent me out early in the morning, before daybreak,

100

with specific instructions not to return until evening. That was very odd, because usually I spend all day here, admitting his pupils and seeing to his meals. But yesterday he sent me out and I stayed away until dusk. I heard about Cleon's death on my way home. When I came in, there was the master, hanging from that rope.'

'Then you don't know for certain when he died – only that it must have been between daybreak and nightfall.'

'I suppose you're right.'

'Who might have seen him during the day?'

'Usually pupils come and go all day, but not so yesterday, on account of the games at the gymnasium. All his regular students took part, you see, or else went to watch. The master had planned to be a spectator himself. So he had cancelled all his regular classes, you see, except for his very first of the day – and that he'd never cancel, of course, because it was with that wretched boy!'

'Cleon, you mean.'

'Yes, Cleon and his sister Cleio. They always came for the first hour of the day. This month they were reading Plato on the death of Socrates.'

'Suicide was on Mulciber's mind, then. And yesterday, did Cleon and his sister arrive for their class?'

'I can't say. I suppose they did. I was out of the house by then.'

'I shall have to ask Cleio, but for now we'll assume they did. Perhaps Mulciber was hoping to patch things up with Cleon.' The slave gave me a curious look. 'I know about the humiliating episode of the returned poems the day before,' I explained.

The slave regarded me warily. 'You seem to know a great deal for a man who's not from Neapolis. What are you doing here?'

'Only trying to discover the truth. Now, then: we'll assume that Cleon and Cleio came for their class, early in the morning. Perhaps Mulciber was braced for another humiliation, and even then planning suicide – or was he wildly hoping, with a lover's blind faith, for some impossible reconciliation? Perhaps that's why he dismissed you for the day, because he didn't care to have his old slave witness either outcome. But it must have gone badly, or at least not as Mulciber hoped, for he never showed up to watch the games at the gymnasium that day. Everyone seems to assume that it was news of Cleon's death that drove him to suicide, but it seems to me just as likely that Mulciber hung himself right after Cleon and Cleio left, unable to bear yet another rejection.'

Eco, greatly agitated, mimed an athlete throwing a discus, then a man fitting a noose around his neck, then an archer notching an arrow in a bow.

I nodded. 'Yes, bitter irony: even as Cleon was enjoying his greatest triumph at the gymnasium, poor Mulciber may have been snuffing out his own existence. And then, Cleon's death in the pool. No wonder everyone thinks that Eros himself brought Cleon down.' I studied the face of the dead man. 'Your master was a poet, wasn't he?'

'Yes,' said the slave. 'He wrote at least a few lines every day of his life.'

'Did he leave a farewell poem?'

The slave shook his head. 'You'd think he might have, if only to say goodbye to me after all these years.'

'But there was nothing? Not even a note?'

'Not a line. And that's another strange thing, because the night before he was up long after midnight, writing and writing. I thought perhaps he'd put the boy behind him and thrown himself into composing some epic poem, seized by the muse! But I can't find any trace of it. Whatever he was writing so frantically, it seems to have vanished. Perhaps, when he made up his mind to hang himself, he thought better of what he'd written, and burned it. He seems to have gotten rid of some other papers, as well.'

'What papers?'

'The love poems he'd written to Cleon, the ones Cleon

returned to him – they've vanished. I suppose the master was embarrassed at the thought of anyone reading them after he was gone, and so he got rid of them. So perhaps it's not so strange after all that he left no farewell note.'

I nodded vaguely, but it still seemed odd to me. From what I knew of poets, suicides, and unrequited lovers, Mulciber would almost certainly have left some words behind – to chastise Cleon, to elicit pity, to vindicate himself. But the silent corpse of the tutor offered no explanation.

As the day was waning I at last returned to the house of Sosistrides, footsore and soul-weary. A slave admitted us. I paused to gaze for a long moment at the lifeless face of Cleon. Nothing had changed, and yet he did not look as beautiful to my eyes as he had before.

Sosistrides called us into his study. 'How did it go, Finder?'

'I've had a productive day, if not a pleasant one. I talked to everyone I could find at the gymnasium. I also went to the house of your children's tutor. You do know that Mulciber hanged himself yesterday?'

'Yes. I found out only today, after I spoke to you. I knew he was a bit infatuated with Cleon, wrote poems to him and such, but I had no idea he was so passionately in love with him. Another tragedy, like ripples in a pond.' Sosistrides, too, seemed to assume without question that the tutor's suicide followed upon news of Cleon's death. 'And what did you find? Did you discover anything . . . significant?'

I nodded. 'I think I know who killed your son.'

His face assumed an expression of strangely mingled relief and dismay. 'Tell me, then!'

'Would you send for your daughter first? Before I can be certain, there are a few questions I need to ask her. And when I think of the depth of her grief, it seems to me that she, too, should hear what I have to say.'

He called for a slave to fetch the girl from her room.

'You're right, of course; Cleio should be here, in spite of her . . . unseemly appearance. Her grieving shows her to be a woman, after all, but I've raised her almost as a son, you know. I made sure she learned to read and write. I sent her to the same tutors as Cleon. Of late she's been reading Plato with him, both of them studying with Mulciber . . .'

'Yes, I know.'

Cleio entered the room, her mantle pushed defiantly back from her shorn head. Her cheeks were lined with fresh, livid scratches, signs that her mourning had continued unabated through the day.

'The Finder thinks he knows who killed Cleon,' Sosistrides explained.

'Yes, but I need to ask you a few questions first,' I said. 'Are you well enough to talk?'

She nodded.

'Is it true that you and your brother went to your regular morning class with Mulciber yesterday?'

'Yes.' She averted her tear-reddened eyes and spoke in a hoarse whisper.

'When you arrived at his house, was Mulciber there?'

She paused. 'Yes.'

'Was it he who let you in the door?'

Again a pause. 'No.'

'But his slave was out of the house, gone for the day. Who let you in?'

'The door was unlocked . . . ajar . . .'

'So you and Cleon simply stepped inside?'

'Yes.'

'Were harsh words exchanged between your brother and Mulciber?'

Her breath became ragged. 'No.'

'Are you sure? Only the day before your brother had publicly rejected and humiliated Mulciber. He returned his love poems and ridiculed them in front of others. That must have been a tremendous blow to Mulciber. Isn't it true that when the two of you showed up at his house yesterday morning, Mulciber lost his temper with Cleon?'

She shook her head.

'What if I suggest that Mulciber became hysterical? That he ranted against your brother? That he threatened to kill him?'

'No! That never happened. Mulciber was too – he would never have done such a thing!'

'But I suggest that he did. I suggest that yesterday, after suffering your brother's deceit and abuse, Mulciber reached the end of his tether. He snapped, like a rein that's worn clean through, and his passions ran away with him like maddened horses. By the time you and your brother left his house, Mulciber must have been raving like a madman—'

'No! He wasn't! He was—'

'And after you left, he brooded. He took out the love poems into which he had poured his heart and soul, the very poems that Cleon returned to him so scornfully the day before. They had once been beautiful to him, but now they were vile, so he burned them.'

'Never!'

'He had planned to attend the games at the gymnasium, to cheer Cleon on, but instead he waited until the contests were over, then sneaked into the vestibule, skulking like a thief. He came upon Cleon alone in the pool. He saw the statue of Eros – a bitter reminder of his own rejected love. No one else was about, and there was Cleon, swimming face-down, not even aware that anyone else was in the courtyard, unsuspecting and helpless. Mulciber couldn't resist – he waited until the very moment that Cleon passed beneath the statue, then pushed it from its pedestal. The statue struck Cleon's head. Cleon sank to the bottom and drowned.'

Cleio wept and shook her head. 'No, no! It wasn't Mulciber!'

'Oh, yes! And then, racked with despair at having killed

the boy he loved, Mulciber rushed home and hung himself. He didn't even bother to write a note to justify himself or beg forgiveness for the murder. He'd fancied himself a poet, but what greater failure is there for a poet than to have his love poems rejected? And so he hung himself without writing another line, and he'll go to his funeral pyre in silence, a common murderer—'

'No, no, no!' Cleio clutched her cheeks, tore at her hair and wailed. Eco, whom I had told to be prepared for such an outburst, started back nonetheless. Sosistrides looked at me aghast. I averted my eyes. How could I have simply told him the truth, and made him believe it? He had to be shown. Cleio had to show him.

'He *did* leave a farewell,' Cleio cried. 'It was the most beautiful poem he ever wrote!'

'But his slave found nothing. Mulciber's poems to Cleon had vanished, and there was nothing new—'

'Because I took them!'

'Where are they, then?'

She reached into the bosom of her black gown and pulled out two handfuls of crumpled papyrus. 'These were his poems to Cleon! You never saw such beautiful poems, such pure, sweet love put down in words! Cleon made fun of them, but they broke my heart! And here is his farewell poem, the one he left lying on his threshold so that Cleon would be sure to see it, when we went to his house yesterday and found him hanging in the foyer, his neck broken, his body soiled . . . dead . . . gone from me forever!'

She pressed a scrap of papyrus into my hands. It was in Greek, the letters rendered in a florid, desperate hand. A phrase near the middle caught my eye:

> One day, even your beauty will fade;
> One day, even you may love unrequited!
> Take pity, then, and favour my corpse
> With a first and final farewell kiss . . .

She snatched back the papyrus and clutched it to her bosom.

My voice was hollow in my ears. 'When you went to Mulciber's house yesterday, you and Cleon found him already dead.'

'Yes!'

'And you wept.'

'Because I loved him!'

'Even though he didn't love you?'

'He loved Cleon. He couldn't help himself.'

'Did Cleon weep?'

Her face became so contorted with hatred that I heard Sosistrides gasp in horror. 'Oh, no,' she said, 'he didn't weep. Cleon laughed! He laughed! He shook his head and said, "What a fool," and walked out the door. I screamed at him to come back, to help me cut him down, and he only said, "I'll be late for the games!"' Cleio collapsed to the floor, weeping, the poems scattering around her. '"Late for the games!"' she repeated, as if it were her brother's epitaph.

On the long ride back to Rome through the Campanian countryside, Eco's hands grew weary and I grew hoarse debating whether I had done the right thing. Eco argued that I should have kept my suspicions of Cleio to myself. I argued that Sosistrides deserved to know what his daughter had done, and how and why his son had died – and needed to be shown, as well, how deeply and callously his beautiful, beloved Cleon had inflicted misery on others.

'Besides,' I said, 'when we returned to Sosistrides' house, I wasn't certain myself that Cleio had murdered Cleon. Accusing the dead tutor was a way of flushing her out. Her possession of Mulciber's missing poems was the only tangible evidence that events had unfolded as I suspected. I tried in vain to think of some way, short of housebreaking, to search her room without either Cleio or her father knowing – but as it turned out, such a search would have found nothing. I should have known that she would keep the poems on her person, next to her heart! She was as madly, hopelessly in love with Mulciber as he was in love with Cleon. Eros can be terribly careless when he scatters his arrows!'

We also debated the degree and nature of Cleon's perfidy. When he saw Mulciber's dead body, was Cleon so stunned by the enormity of what he had done – driven a lovesick man to suicide – that he went about his business in a sort of stupor, attending the games and performing his athletic feats like an automaton? Or was he so cold that he felt nothing? Or, as Eco argued in an extremely convoluted series of gestures, did Mulciber's fatal demonstration of lovesick devotion actually stimulate Cleon in some perverse way, inflating his ego and inspiring him to excel as never before at the games?

Whatever his private thoughts, instead of grieving, Cleon blithely went off and won his laurel crown, leaving Mulciber to spin in midair and Cleio to plot her vengeance. In a fit of grief she cut off her hair. The sight of her face in Mulciber's atrium pool gave her the idea to pass as a boy; an ill-fitting tunic from the tutor's wardrobe completed her disguise. She carried a knife with her to the gymnasium, the same one she had used to cut her hair, and was prepared to stab her brother in front of his friends. But it turned out that she didn't need the knife; by chance, she found her way into the courtyard, where the statue of Eros presented itself as the perfect murder weapon.

As far as Cleio was concerned, the statue's role in the crime constituted proof that she acted not only with the god's approval but as an instrument of his will. This pious argument had so far, at least as of our leaving Neapolis, stayed Sosistrides from punishing her. I did not envy the poor merchant. With his wife and son dead, could he bear to snuff out the life of his only remaining offspring, even for so great a crime? And yet, how could he bear to let her live, knowing she had murdered his beloved son? Such a conundrum would test the wisdom of Athena!

Eco and I debated, too, the merits of Mulciber's poetry.

I had begged of Sosistrides a copy of the tutor's farewell, so that I could ponder it at my leisure:

> Savage, sullen boy, whelp of a lioness,
> Stone-hearted and scornful of love,
> I give you a lover's ring – my noose!
> No longer be sickened by the sight of me;
> I go to the only place that offers solace
> To the broken-hearted: oblivion!
> But will you not stop and weep for me,
> If only for one moment . . .

The poem continued for many more lines, veering between recrimination, self-pity, and surrender to the annihilating power of love.

Hopelessly sentimental! More cloying than honey! The very worst sort of dreck, pronounced Eco, with a series of gestures so sweeping that he nearly fell from his horse. I merely nodded, and wondered if my son would feel the same in another year or so, after Eros had wounded him with a stray arrow or two and given him a clearer notion, from personal experience, of just how deeply the god of love can pierce the hearts of helpless mortals.

All historical fiction, including mystery stories, invariably betrays and portrays the time it was written as much as or more than it accurately presents the time in which it is set. This is a) inevitable and b) generally not openly acknowledged. No matter how well we do our research we experience our sources through twentieth-century sensibilities. One cannot, for instance, examine a piece of coarse worsted worn next to the skin from the point of view of a medieval peasant – however hard we strive to fight it, awareness of Marks and Spencer's lingerie remains indelibly at the back of the mind and elsewhere.

This is just as true when we consider works of fiction written in the past but adapted or dramatised, and even more so when we read modern sequels to, say, *Emma* or *Frankenstein*. No amount of care with historical reconstruction of costumes, manners, etiquette, horses, carriages and the rest can hide the fact that we are looking at or reading a construct made by contemporary minds for contemporary consumption. All this is all right if one accepts that a historical fiction is a straightforward commercial venture designed to sell to a substantial and paying audience a product it will enjoy and from which it may even learn something about our times, here and now. But let us not imagine that the experience has opened up to us an understanding of the real Jane Austen or the real nineteenth century.

It was with thoughts like these in mind that I wrote *Damned Spot*. In the context of the heavy artillery deployed in this anthology it is a mere squib, but not, I hope, a damp one. At any rate it may serve to remind readers (though not without providing some entertainment as well) that historical fiction wittingly or otherwise reflects the way we are now far more than the way we were then.

Julian Rathbone

Damned Spot

Julian Rathbone

Tall windows, leaded in diamond patterns, looked out on a knot-garden of box. Around it gravel walks were edged with formal borders of gillyflowers and tulipans . . .

Hang on! Already I am performing one of the tricks of the history fiction writer's trade. You, dear readers, well, some of you anyway, have no idea what a gillyflower is and you're guessing hopefully that a tulipan is a tulip. But because I have used these unfamiliar names for common flowers, I have won your trust. I have disarmed any suspicion of anachronism, and if you have no idea at all of what you are meant to be visualising, no matter – you have been transported into the past. Whereas if I had written wall-flowers and tulips you would have suspected a historical solecism and seen, in your mind's eye, a modern municipal garden.

You would, however, have been right to think late April–early May, especially as I am about to describe the cherry trees in full but falling blossom beyond the knot-garden. Not, of course, your flamboyant vulgar Japanese ornamentals, possibly pink, but a decent, modest, fruit-bearing English tree. The merry month of May then, the first week, and the year is 1593.

Tall windows and two men looking out of them – one of them old, very old for those times, already in his seventies,

113

supporting himself on an ebony stick and occasionally dabbing with a lace-edged linen handkerchief at a drooping lip which leaked spittle, the other middle-aged, sturdier, a coarser version of the older man who was his father. Both were dressed soberly in black velvets trimmed with fur and enlivened with discreet flashes of gold and polished gems – nothing flashy, you understand, but not mean either.

There was a large oak table behind them, with bulbous fluted legs, covered with papers and some parchments, the latter fastened with red tape and heavy seals. There was also a posy of spring flowers – not there particularly to give pleasure but to ward off plague. 1593 was a bad year for plague which was why all this was happening well away from London.

I nearly wrote 'dark oak', epithets which I thought would also do for the oak panelling decorated with fruits and flowers carved by . . . but no, Grinling Gibbons came a century later, and even worse, as we well know if we think about it, new or newish oak is pale, honey-coloured, it darkens slowly with age, and the oak furniture and panelling in Hatfield House in 1593 would have still been pale.

But we don't imagine our Tudor grandees surrounded by pale oak, do we? And now, damnit, I find Hatfield House did not belong to the Cecils until ten or so years later . . . but it was a royal residence in 1593, so without laboriously checking the fatter history books I think we can say that the Cecils were there not because they owned the place but because that was where the Queen was. And the Court. Yes, why not. And in fact a meeting of the Privy Council has just taken place; most of the members have withdrawn, leaving William and Robert behind to set in train the execution of the results of the council's deliberations.

There was, however, one other person hovering in the shadows at the back of the room, furthest from the window. Not, yet, a member of the council, though he thought he should be, a prim, pompous man, lean and hungry, with permanent five o'clock shadow, already noted for his cleverness and lack of humour. He was a cousin by marriage of the Cecils and could not quite understand why he still lacked preferment beyond the Bar where he practised his trade with a punctilious observation and knowledge of the law which annoyed judges but which they could not gainsay.

The older of the two men by the window held a piece of paper under its cool light. That was why they were by the window – not to admire the wall-flowers and tulips or even the cherry blossom, but because the old man especially was suffering from failing eyesight.

'This confession,' he wheezed – he had been suffering from a rheumy chest since Easter – 'that Thomas Kyd is supposed to have made, what's it worth? I mean, will it hold up in a court of law?'

The younger man in the background uttered a different sort of cough.

'Oh, I think so, my lord. Fear of hellfire produced it. Hellfire following whatever unpleasant death is now deemed suitable for heretics.'

He looked smugly at his nails.

'You mean he wasn't tortured?' The old man's son, Robert, sounded incredulous.

'Well, of course he was tortured. Enough for recollection of the experience to make him vow that this confession was offered freely.'

'Even the bit involving this blighter –' William peered again at the close-written italic hand – 'Christopher Marlowe? Is he really going to shop him?'

'Certainly. For heresy. Marlowe is an atheist, and an antinomian. No need to say he was a secret-service asset who betrayed us. We'll get him on a heresy rap.'

'I don't see how he can be both,' Robert chipped in again. 'Both atheist and antinomian.'

'Personally,' his father commented, after giving the matter some thought, 'I prefer atheism. At least an atheist

115

might recognise the importance of moral imperatives. An antinomian has *carte blanche* to do what the hell he likes. If he's one of the chosen he'll get to heaven anyway, however evil his life; if he isn't chosen he'll go to hell anyway, however worthy his life. Such a doctrine is not conducive to good order in the state or observance of the Commandments, and it undermines degree; untune that string and all you get instead of harmony in the general polity is pandemonium . . .' As old men will, he was off now.

The young man behind him tried to dam the flow.

'There are, my lord, examples in Holy Writ, especially in Romans four and five, which being interpreted by over-cunning and zealous minds . . .'

'Francis, I have managed this kingdom for its monarch for more than three decades and throughout I have been guided by one principle alone. Whatever threatens the stability of the state must be contrary to Holy Writ – and there's an end to it. I leave others, clerics, theologians and the like, to find the bits of Holy Writ that will serve. And they find them. Or else they lose preferment. Ask Richard Hooker – he's not yet forty years old but on the back of that book he's writing he should make Canterbury before he dies. Now, where were we?'

'Christopher Marlowe.'

'Off with his head! He always was a pain, a threat. Double spy, taking Dutch gold for spying on us as well as our gold for spying on them, totally immoral, a jerkin-lifter from all accounts, writes lewd poetry, thinks a great deal too highly of himself, and then there are those dreadful plays . . .' The old man was beginning to spit properly now, and his colour had risen, rouging the soft, wrinkled old skin on his cheeks. 'Openly seditious as well as lewd. I mean, come on, that Edward the Second piece, grossest disrespect for the Crown. Of course he was protected by that toad Walsingham, to whom he was I believe related, but Walsingham's been

116

pushing up pied daisies and blue violets these last couple of years. Off with his head, I say.'

'Problem, Father. Walsingham's gone, yes, but Marlowe's got other friends . . . scholars, scientists. William Harvey . . .'

'Tush, man. Whoever heard of a scientist who wouldn't perjure his learning for the sake of a good seat in a university or to escape burning? Give them enough carrot and stick and they'll tell you the earth's flat, or goes round the sun, any nonsense they think you want to hear . . .'

'Sir Walter Raleigh is also an intimate.'

'That's not, just now, in his favour.'

He was referring to the fact that Sir Walter was at that time in internal exile in Sherborne having seduced and later married one of the Queen's ladies-in-waiting without asking her first. The Queen, that is.

'There is one other problem.'

'Yes?'

'Marlowe's in hiding. We don't know where he is.'

Francis Bacon again cleared his throat.

'But he is also penniless. He's got to come out, show himself, if he's going to eat. If we approach his actor friends, and people whom he owes money to, and promise them he's in the way of getting some money, they'll lead us to him.'

'That's that settled then. You find out what Marlowe has he can sell and who will buy it, get them together in some tavern or dive somewhere and we'll move in on him.'

William Cecil, Lord Burghley, dropped the small sheet of paper he was still holding and reached towards the table for the next. Then he paused. 'He's not worth a trial and all that fuss, you know? Flush him out and have him skewered in a brawl over a bummer-boy, something of that sort.'

Some tales based in the past are *quotha* tales and some are not, and some fall between two stools – not aping the speech of the time, but maintaining a spurious dignity which chimes with our perception that people spoke with more weightiness and less forcefulness than they do now. The problem is particularly acute when dealing with the Tudor period. So much of the literature purports to represent spoken language there is a temptation to pastiche it. Some have managed successfully – one thinks of Robert Nye or Anthony Burgess, but Burgess or Nye I am not, so I must ask you, dear reader, to accept some dialogue at least transliterated into modern. You can waste a lot of time checking the NED to see whether or not a particular word was current in the 1590s, and if you're not going to be thorough about it, you might as well take the modern option. And having, um, grasped that nettle, you might as well go the whole hog. Enough. Let us get on with it. More matter, less art, I can hear you saying.

What, Francis asked himself as he trundled down what was later to be the A1 towards London, has Marlowe got that other people might want to buy? His art. His ability to turn out copper-bottomed, sure-fire theatrical hits, the like of which no one has ever seen before. *Tamburlaine*. *The Jew of Malta*. *Dr Faustus*, for Christ's sake. He'll be working on something right now. Because he's in the shit he won't be able to get it put on. But he can always sell it to someone else who can have it done under their own name or a pseudonym or whatever. But who? To whom? Thomas Kyd's *Spanish Tragedy* was much in the same style, and he won't be writing anything on his own account again, not with his thumbs in the state they are in now. But, since he's just shopped his old mate on an atheism-heresy rap, which was why he was in hiding in the first place, it isn't likely they'll get together amicably to do a deal. Who else? Well, the players will know.

Thus the wily lawyer contemplated as his cumbersome cart climbed the hill towards Highgate. He'd make the rounds of the companies, buy the right people a few drinks, even a square meal . . . Kill two birds with one stone, he might even get a line on where Marlowe was hiding out.

Problem. All the London theatres were shut and had been for a year. First there had been riots, now plague.

It took him until the end of the month to set it all up. And, though the fact the theatres were closed did make it harder to track down the sort of people he wanted to meet, it did also mean that once he had found them they turned out to be more than usually hard-up and susceptible to bribes, or the promise of getting their hands on a box-office hit to put on as soon as the theatres opened again. The competition to find a really hot script was fierce – whichever company scored with the sensation of Christmas '93 or the '94 season would make a killing. Indeed the rewards seemed so promising that he began to think he might try his hand at this play-writing lark himself. He'd already circulated a few short pieces he called 'essays' which were quite highly thought of by those who hadn't read Montaigne.

The upshot was, you might say, satisfactory. A whisper here, a clandestine meeting there, money passed beneath a table in a tavern, a promise offered in one of the Inns of Court all led to an understanding that Chris Marlowe did have a script he was willing to sell and that he'd be at a certain lodging house cum tavern cum brothel in Deptford on the twenty-eighth of May shortly after dusk. He'd have the play with him and he'd only part with it for twenty pounds. Lot of money in those days. The party of the other part was quite happy too. The play was apparently very much in the Marlowe mould, a rampaging piece about a Bohemian duke who murdered his way to the throne of Wenceslas, taking out young princes and raping the widow of one of his victims on the way – the usual Overreacher Theme that had done so well for him in his other plays. The only stipulation the buyer had apparently made was that the play should be re-jigged to round off a trilogy he had already had performed based on the Wars of the Roses. It had been pretty tedious stuff and the players he had worked for weren't at all sure that they wanted any more in the same vein. The guy was a poet really, not much of a dramatist at all. Lousy actor too.

And he it was, rather than the lawyer, who turned up at the Deptford house of ill-repute to buy a play and lure the playwright out into the open. He ordered some cakes and ale, and waited. Then, to pass the time, he pulled out of his bag a well-thumbed copy of Holinshed's *Chronicles*, some scrap paper and a pen and ink-horn. He began to make notes.

Eventually, an hour late, Marlowe came sauntering languidly down the stairs from the upper room just as the serving girls were bringing in the candles. He was tucking in his shirt and yawning at the same time since he had spent a fair bit of the afternoon buggering one of the stable lads.

'Oh Christ,' he said, as he took in the short, prematurely balding, plumpish young man who was waiting for him, 'it's young Waggle-dagger, the Warwick grammar-school boy. Little Latin and no Greek. Upstart crow who steals our feathers. Budge along, there's a good chap.'

He pushed himself on to the bench beside the scribbler and slapped down a thin folio tied with ribbon.

'There you are then. It's all good stuff, I promise you. Got the chinks have you?' He rattled the bag the man he had called Waggle-dagger had put on the table next to his book. He picked the book up and sneered again. 'Don't shade your eyes, plagiarise. It's still your shout so I'll have a pint of sack.'

And he signalled to the landlord.

'Sack's off,' said mine host, and snapped his fingers and winked at the three ruffians who were concealed behind a high-backed settle. 'Got some good Kentish ale though. Good ale hath no fellow.'

'Stratford actually,' said the aspiring playwright, and began to undo the ribbons.

'Eh?'

'Stratford-on-Avon. Not Warwick.' He smoothed out the title page. The Troublesone Raigne and Lamentable Death of Sigismundo, King of Bohemia . . . except the words Sigismundo and Bohemia had been crossed out.

Marlowe laughed, the high bray of an Oxbridge graduate.

'The Bard of Stratford-on-Avon,' he crowed. 'Got quite a ring to it.'

At that moment the three ruffians jumped out from behind the settle, armed with daggers and clubs. Marlowe also had a dagger, but he fumbled the drawing of it and poked his eye with the point. Thus incapacitated he could not defend himself from the one lunge a man variously named as Archer or Ingram managed to get on target. At this point the landlord, seeing the business was done, and mindful of his reputation, began to holler for the constable and the ruffians legged it.

Marlowe fell to the floor. The Warwickshire Bard placed a handy cushion under his head and examined the wound.

'It is not,' he said, 'as wide as a church door, nor as deep as a steeple, but . . .'

'What the devil are you talking about?' Marlowe groaned. 'How in blazes can a steeple be *deep*?'

And died.

While waiting for the constable, the Bard could not help congratulating himself on how things had turned out. He had, of course, had his suspicions about the whole set-up. Dick Burbage had told him he thought something fishy was going on, especially when that lawyer chap volunteered to put up the twenty pounds in gold himself. Putting two and two together he had guessed it was a ruse to get Marlowe to show himself. Well. Serve the bastard right. Always putting on airs with his university ways. 'The name's Marlowe –' that smooth drawl – 'Marlowe with an e.'

The way looked pretty clear now. Seven or eight actors' companies around and with Kyd out of the way and this bleeding lump of flesh shortly to be laid to rot in cold obstruction . . . Obstruction? What did that *mean*? Never mind, it had a ring to it . . . he was the only one left with any sort of halfway respectable track record. He'd soon show them who was the king shake-scene on the block.

Meanwhile he couldn't resist turning the title page. 'Now is the winter of our malcontent made glorious . . .' He frowned, picked up his quill, crossed out *mal* and wrote in *dis*.

There was a splodge of Marlowe's blood on the top of the page. He used his penknife to scratch away at it but it wouldn't shift.

'Damned spot,' he muttered.

I blush to admit that I must be alone among the contributors to this volume in having never read an Ellis Peters novel. I am woefully behind with my reading of crime fiction. Yet, like all writers of historical mysteries, I was hugely encouraged by her enormous success – and long before Cadfael got on to television. I knew of her early forays into the genre through George Hardinge, the editor we shared at Macmillan. Edith, as he always referred to her, remained with George when he moved from Collins to start a crime list at Macmillan. Over lunch he would tell me ruefully of the difficulties of promoting an author of great originality and charm who rarely ventured out of Shropshire. Eventually, on one of the rare occasions she did come to London, I met Edith myself, and it didn't matter at all that I was unfamiliar with her writing. She was gracious, unspoilt by success, sensitive and amusing.

My own crime stories barely qualify as historical. I came to know and enjoy the Victorian period through an interest in the history of athletics. My first novel, *Wobble to Death*, published in 1970, was a whodunit based on an ultra-long-distance race. Seven others followed, each featuring Sergeant Cribb and centred on Victorian pastimes and enthusiasms. After that I wrote some 'one-offs' ranging in settings from

1916 to 1946. Later I returned to the Victorian period and recruited Bertie, the Prince of Wales, as an amateur sleuth.

The one that follows, set in 1860, and dealing largely with sensational events in 1827 and 1828, is the farthest back in time I have dared to go.

Peter Lovesey

Showmen

Peter Lovesey

'Getting rid of the bodies was never a problem for me, sir. Sure, we got rid of so many I lost count.'

'Sixteen, they said.'

The cracked lips parted and curved. Sixteen was a joke. Everyone knew the official count had been too low.

'You got away with it, too.'

'I wouldn't say that.'

'Come now, you're a free man, aren't you? Thirty years later, here you are, drinking whisky in the Proud Peacock.'

'God bless you, yes.'

'A reformed character.'

'Well, I'm not without sin, but I've not croaked a fellow creature since those days. I was wicked then, terrible, terrible.'

'Does it trouble you still?'

'Not at all.'

'Really?'

He roared with laughter. 'Jesus, if I thought about it, I'd never get a peaceful night's sleep.'

Talking of trouble, it had taken no end of trouble to find the fellow. Rumour had it that he was now an Oxford Street beggar – but trying to find a particular beggar in Oxford Street in 1860 was like looking for a pebble on Brighton beach.

From Hyde Park to Holborn a parade of derelicts pitched for pennies, pleading with passers-by, displaying scars and crippled limbs, sightless eyes and underfed infants. They harassed the shoppers, the rich and would-be rich, innocents up from the country trying to reach the great drapery shops, Marshall & Snelgrove and Peter Robinson.

It took a long morning and most of an afternoon of enquiries before William Hare was discovered outside Heath's the Hatmakers, a lanky, silver-haired, smiling fellow offering bootlaces for sale and not above accepting charity from those who didn't need laces. 'A spare wretch, gruesome and ghoulish,' the court reporters had once called him, but at this stage in his declining years his looks frightened no one. Animated, grinning and quick of tongue in his Irish brogue, he competed eagerly for the money in the shoppers' pockets.

To listen to Hare trading on his notoriety, discussing his series of murders, was supposed to be 'high ton', the latest thing in entertainment, the best outside the music halls. He was a good raconteur, as the Irish so often are, with a marvellous facility for shifting the blame on to others, notably his partner, Burke, and the anatomist, Dr Knox.

Of course, he had to be persuaded to talk. He denied his own identity when first it was put to him. The promise of a drink did the trick.

Now, in the pub, he was getting gabbier by the minute.

'Did y'know I was measured by the well-known bumps-on-the-head expert, Mr Combe, at the time of the trial, or just after? Did y'know that?'

'The phrenologist.'

'You're right, your honour. Phrenologist. There's something called the bump of ideality and mine is a bump to be marvelled at, prodigious, greater than Wordsworth's or Voltaire's. With a bump like mine I could have done beautiful things if my opportunities had been better.'

'You made your opportunities.'

'Indeed I did.' The mouth widened into the grin that was Hare's blessing and his curse.

'You robbed others of their opportunities.'

'That's a delicate way of putting it, sir.'

'No one murdered so many and lived to tell the tale.'

He almost purred at that. 'A tale I don't tell very often.'

'Unless you're paid.'

That nervy smile again. In court, all those years ago, the incessant twitch of his lips had displeased the judge and drawn hisses of contempt from the public gallery. The people of Edinburgh had hated him. The grin inflamed them.

It seemed Hare didn't feel comfortable with his new patron, despite the whisky in his hand. 'Tell me, sir, is it possible we met before?'

'Why do you ask?'

'The familiar way you talk to me.'

The nerve of the man – as if his crimes had made him one of the elect. 'You're notorious, Hare. I know all about you, if that's what you mean.'

'I bet you don't, sir, not *all*. You know the worst, but no one ever told you the best. People shouldn't believe what they read in the newspapers. The queer thing is, I never planned it, you know. The papers made me out to be a monster, but I was not. It was circumstances, sir, circumstances.' He was into his flow now. 'The first one, the very first, wasn't one of those we turned off. He was an old soldier, a lodger in the house, the lodging house my woman had in West Port. He faded away of natural causes.'

This caused some macabre amusement. 'Come now.'

'I swear before God, that's the truth,' Hare insisted, planting a fist on the table. 'Mag and I didn't hasten his leaving at all. We wanted him to live a few days more. His rent was due. Four pounds. And fate cruelly took him to his Maker before his quarterly pension was paid. How can you run a lodging house without the rent coming in?'

'So the circumstance was financial?'

'You have it in a nutshell, sir. He left nothing I could sell. I couldn't go up to the Castle and ask the military for his pension. I was forced to go elsewhere for the arrears.'

'By selling the corpse.'

Hare nodded. 'With the help of another lodger, my fellow countryman, Mr Burke, whose name has since become a byword for infamy. Sure and William Burke was no angel, I have to admit. But I couldn't have managed alone. We removed old Donald from his coffin and weighted it with a sack of wood and gave it a pauper's burial. After dark that evening we carried the body up to the College on the South Bridge, with a view to donating it to science.'

'Selling it, you mean.'

'To recover the rent. All of Edinburgh knew the schools of anatomy couldn't get enough corpses. At the time I speak of, 1827, there were seven anatomists at work in the city, doing dissections to educate the students, and that wasn't enough. The dissecting rooms were like theatres, sir, vast places, crammed to the rafters with students, five hundred at a time. Is it any wonder there was a trade in bodysnatching? Not that Burke and Hare rifled graves. Say what you like about us, we never stooped to that. Ours were all unburied. We had this innocent corpse, as I told you, and we went in search of Professor Monro.'

'Why Monro?'

'You have an item to sell, you're better off going to the top, aren't you? And here's a strange twist of fate. We were standing in the quad with our booty between us in a tea-chest when a student happened to come by. I asked him the way to the School of Anatomy. This is where fate interfered, sir. The student wasn't a pupil of the professor. He was one of Dr Knox's canny little boyos. He sent us down to Cowgate, to 10 Surgeons' Square, the rival establishment.' He drew himself up. 'That, sir, is the truth of how we got drawn into the web of the infamous Dr Knox. If we'd got to the professor first, the story might have ended differently.'

'Why is that?'

'Because of what was said, sir.'

'By Dr Knox?'

'His acolytes, the people at Surgeons' Square. We didn't get to see the old devil that night. We dealt with three of his students. You have to admire his organisation. He had students on duty into the night meeting visitors like ourselves and purchasing bodies, and no questions asked. They paid seven pounds ten. We should have insisted on ten, but we had no experience. The students seemed well pleased with what they got, and so were we, to speak the truth. And then they spoke the words that touched our Irish hearts: "Sure, we'd be glad to see you again when you have another to dispose of." Ha – and didn't our ears prick up at that!'

'"*Glad to see you.*" Glad to see the contents of your tea-chest, more like.'

A cackle greeted this. 'And do you know who those students were that night? They became three of the most eminent surgeons in the kingdom. Sir William Fergusson, Thomas Wharton Jones and Alexander Miller. And here am I, who assisted so handsomely in their education, reduced to begging on the streets.'

'Shall I fetch another whisky?'

'I won't say no.'

Left alone at the table, William Hare pondered his chances of extracting something more than drink. He had a suspicion the expenses were being met by a newspaper. There was still plenty of macabre interest in the story of Burke and Hare. It was like old times: the law of supply and demand at work again. A paper with an interest in famous crimes ought to be paying him a decent fee for this interview. He might even negotiate a week in a proper hotel.

'Would you mind telling me who you represent?' he asked his companion when he returned to the table.

'Myself.'

'You wouldn't be from the press?'

129

'Certainly not. I'm a showman.'

Hare stood up, outraged. 'I'm not going into a freak show.'

'Please calm down. I haven't the slightest intention of offering you employment. This is simply a quiet tête-à-tête over a whisky.'

He remained standing. 'What's the show?'

Dismissively, the showman said, 'It's totally unconnected with this conversation. If you must know, I am employed for my voice, in a circus, acting as interlocutor, lecturer and demonstrator for a travelling party of Ojibbeway Indians from North America.'

If anything could silence Hare, it was a man who spoke for a troupe of Ojibbeway Indians.

He resumed his seat. 'What do you want with me, then?'

'I'm curious about what happened.'

'It's all been told before.'

'I know that. I want to hear it from the lips of the man who did it. Tell me about your method. How was the killing done?'

'For the love of God, lower your voice,' said Hare. 'I don't want the whole of London knowing my history.' He'd suffered enough in the past from being named in public.

More quietly, the showman said, 'You've always insisted that Burke was the prime mover in the business.'

Leaning across the table, Hare responded in a low voice. 'He did the suffocating, and that's the truth. He always held the pillow.'

'But you assisted.'

'Only in a passive manner, sir, by lying on the subject, to discourage the arms and legs from interfering. I did it well, too. There was never a mark of violence. Never. That was what saved me from the hangman.'

'That, and your gift of the gab.'

Hare sniffed. 'You're a fine one to comment, by the sound of things. Say what you like, we were professionals, through and through. We didn't take any Tom, Dick or Harry. They were hand-picked. They were not missed usually, being derelicts, simpletons and women of the unfortunate class. And it didn't matter what sort of scum they were when they were lying on Dr Knox's slab. He called them his subjects.' He laughed. 'Straight, that's the truth. His subjects. You'd think he was the King himself.'

'What did you call them? Your victims?'

'Our shots. Did I say a moment ago that none of them were missed? I'd better correct that. We did have an enquiry from the daughter of one of our shots, a grown woman, a whore. She came looking for her mother.' He paused. His timing was part of the act. 'We got sixteen pounds for the pair.'

'Did you ever sell a corpse to anyone else?'

'No, sir. Only to Dr Knox. I'll say this for him – and I won't say much for that odious sawbones – he knew how to guard his reputation. There was one we took to his rooms known in the city as Daft Jamie, a bit of a character this one had been. Jamie always went barefoot, winter and summer, and they were queer feet, if you understand me, misshapen. Well, when we pulled him out of the tea-chest in the dissecting room, three or four people, including the janitor, said, "That's Daft Jamie!" But Dr Knox would have none of it. He said it couldn't be. Burkey and I guarded our tongues and took the money.'

'You believe Dr Knox was pretending?'

'I'm sure of it.'

'Why?'

'Because later there was a bit of a hue and cry about Jamie. His mother and sister went around the town asking questions. And as soon as old Knox heard of that, he ordered the corpse to be dissected and the parts dispersed. Mr Fergusson took the feet away and one of the others had the head, so that if the police came calling, no one would know the rest of the body from Adam's.'

There was a pause in the conversation. The appalling

details didn't make the sensation that Hare expected. Surely the story was worth another drink? But no. 'And this lucrative career of yours came to an end after only nine months.'

'You must have been a-checking of your facts,' he said caustically. 'Yes, it was no fault of mine. I was having trouble with Burke. There was a falling-out at one point, you know. In the summer, Burkey went visiting his woman's people in Falkirk, and when they returned, he smelt a rat. Thought I'd done a little work on my own account, taken a shot to Dr Knox and pocketed the reward without telling him. The leery devil trots off to Surgeons' Square to get the truth of it. When he's told they paid me eight pounds for a female, he leaves my lodging house in a huff. Found new lodgings.'

'That must have put a blight on your arrangements.'

'Not for long, sir. Burkey got short of money and came skulking back with a new proposal. A cousin of his woman's, a young girl he'd met in Falkirk, came to stay. He asked me to take the first steps in the matter, the girl being a relative.'

'You did the smothering on this occasion?'

'As a kindness to his family. A ten-pound shot. But Burke never lodged with us any more.'

'You were back in business, though.'

A twitchy smile. 'We did a few more, and then the fates put a stop to our capers. Burke asked me and my woman Mag to his lodging to celebrate Halloween. What a disaster! If only I'd had the sense to refuse. He'd found another shot, of course, some old beggar woman called Docherty. Sure, she was Irish, like Burkey and myself, and only too willing to join the party. But all he had was the one room to do it in. What's more he had lodgers, a family called Gray, who slept on straw on the floor. To simplify matters, I said the Grays could remove to our place that night, and they did. So it was just Burke and his Nell, me and my Mag, and old Mrs Docherty. Well, we all had a few drinks too many, and the old woman screamed "Murder!" and one of the neighbours went to look for a policeman.'

'You were arrested?'

'No, sir.' The smirk again. 'You know how it is with the guardians of the law. They're like the bloody omnibuses. You can never find one when you want one. What did for us was Burke's incompetence. When the Gray family came back next morning, the corpse was still in the room, under the straw they slept on. Can you believe that? Like a bat out of hell Gray goes to the police.'

Hare's companion took a thoughtful swig of his drink. He wasn't writing any of this down. 'You don't have to talk about the trial,' he said. 'How you turned King's Evidence to escape the noose.'

'To assist the law, sir. They had no case without me. As I told you a moment ago, there wasn't so much as a scratch on the bodies.'

'You had a few more brains in your head than Burke.'

'He swung, as you know, sir.'

'And his corpse, fittingly enough, was presented to Professor Monro to be dissected.'

'Yes,' said Hare cheerfully. 'And did you hear about the lying-in-state?'

'The *what*?'

Hare laughed. 'Burkey was never so popular as when he was on the slab. The judge in his wisdom decreed that he should be anatomised in public and the public demanded to see the result. Thirty thousand filed through the room. Most of Edinburgh, if you ask me. The line stretched for over a mile.'

'Your companion, flayed, salted and preserved, packed into a barrel – for science, as you would put it. His skin cut into pieces and sold as souvenirs. I believe his skeleton can still be seen at the University.'

This was not part of the script, the audience taking over. Hare didn't care for it. Moreover, he had detected a note of censure. He stated emphatically, 'It was no bed of roses for me, sir. They tried their damnedest to make me go the way of

Burke. A private prosecution, followed by a civil action. They failed, but it was mental persecution. And when I finally got my liberty I was in fear of my life from the mob outside. They wanted to lynch me.'

'And no wonder.'

'I had to be smuggled out of the gaol, disguised. I was put on the southward mail coach. As bad luck would have it, one of my fellow passengers had featured in the trial as a junior counsel, and he recognised me, and blabbed to the others. The news was out. At Dumfries, I was practically mobbed. It was ugly, sir, uncommon ugly. I holed up in the King's Arms for a time, but it wasn't safe. The authorities removed me to the gaol for my own safety, and the jackals outside bayed for my blood all night. It took a hundred specials to disperse them.'

'But you got away.'

'Under armed guard. The militia escorted me across the border.'

'You're a fortunate man, Hare.'

'You think so? A ruin, more like. Look at me. I'll tell you who was a fortunate man, and that's the piece of excrement they called Knox. He was in it up to his ears, as guilty as Burke, and guiltier than me.'

'Why so?'

'Knox was the instigator, wasn't he? He knew everything, everything. He dealt with us in person a dozen times. Oh, he denied it of course. For pity's sake, where did he think the bodies were coming from, freshly dead and regular as clockwork? The people weren't fooled, just because he was a doctor.'

'Surgeon, in fact. You should be careful with your choice of words. The people you just referred to were the same crowd you described as the mob a moment ago.'

Hare laughed. 'Mob they may have been, but they knew all about Knox. I know for a fact that they met on Calton Hill and made an effigy of the bastard, and carried it in procession all the way to his house in Newington Place, where they burned it in his garden and smashed all his windows.'

'So they did.'

'You heard of it, too?'

'Indeed,' said the showman. 'Moreover, they attacked his dissecting rooms. Like you, he fled. He was thought to have gone into hiding in Portobello, so they made another effigy and hanged it on a gibbet at the top of Tower Street there. You were not alone in being an object of hatred.'

'He got his job back,' Hare pointed out. 'The same year he was back in Surgeons' Square cutting up bodies.'

'Ah, but he was obliged to suffer the indignity of a University committee of inquiry. They found nothing actionable in his past conduct. There's the difference, Hare. You stand condemned – or you should have, if there were any justice. Dr Knox was exonerated of blame in the matter.'

'Absurd,' muttered Hare.

'What do you mean?'

'They would never sack him. He was a god to his students. They adored the bastard. His classes numbered over five hundred.'

'However, his career was blighted. You may not know this, but he twice applied for Chairs of the University, and was twice humiliated. He was compelled to relinquish his career at Edinburgh. He moved to Glasgow.'

'And I'm moved to tears,' said Hare. 'I hope he died spitting blood in the poorest tenement in the Gorbals.'

'You're still a bitter man.'

'I've reason to be bitter. Dr Knox underpaid us for the last one.'

'The last one? I don't understand.'

'The old Irish woman I was telling you about. Mrs Docherty, on Halloween. You see, we delivered her to Knox the day the game was up. We had to get rid of it. He only paid us half. Said we could have the rest on Monday. We never got our second five pounds.'

'And that still irks?'

'No man has treated me with anything but derision . . . until today.'

'Just a couple of drinks so far.'

The 'so far' emboldened Hare to say in the wheedling tone that worked best for him, 'Would you see your way to the price of a bed in return for all the inside information I've given you in confidence, sir?'

'I can do better than that. If I give you money, you'll only blow it on drink. I can offer you accommodation. I have rooms in Hackney. A humble address, but better than the places you inhabit, I'll warrant.'

'Hackney. That's not far.'

'Shall we treat ourselves to a cab ride?'

Hare beamed. 'Why not, sir? And if you want to introduce me to your friends and neighbours, I won't object.'

'That won't be necessary.'

'I am the only man to be exhibited in the Chamber of Horrors in his lifetime. Baker Street – my other address,' he joked, 'care of Madame Tussaud.'

'Shall we leave?'

'If you're ready, then so am I.' Hare finished the last of the whisky and stood up. He reached out with his right hand, groping at the space between them. 'It would help me if I took your arm, sir.'

'Of course.' The showman enquired with what sounded like a note of concern, 'How did you come to lose your sight?'

'That was after I came south, sir. I got a job. Labouring – that's my occupation. It was all right for a time. I got on well enough with the others. Then – pure vanity – I confided in one of my mates that I was the smarter half of the old partnership. Smart! You know what? They set upon me. Threw me into a lime-pit. Vicious. Destroyed my eyes. I've been a vagrant ever since. Do you know what I most regret?'

'I've no idea.'

He permitted himself another smile. 'I shall never see myself in the Chamber of Horrors.'

'Careful, there's a step down.'

'Down to what, sir?' quipped Hare. 'A meeting with Old Nick?'

They made their way out of the pub and took the first cab that came along. Heading east, it was soon lost to view in the Oxford Street traffic.

The encounter just described is a fantasy based on accounts of the case, but the story can end with facts. William Hare, who combined with Burke to commit the West Port Murders of 1828, was said to have been a familiar figure, blind and begging in Oxford Street until about 1860.

The famous anatomist Dr Robert Knox also ended his days in relative obscurity, as a general practitioner in Hackney, and latterly as 'lecturer, demonstrator, or showman to a travelling party of Ojibbeway Indians'. He died of a stroke in 1862 at the age of 71.

Hare just disappeared.

We live in an age of instant global communications, space probes, microwave ovens, and special-effects extravaganzas featuring spectacular explosions and muscle-men with Uzis. So why, in the final run-up to the twenty-first century, should modern readers be hopelessly enchanted with the exploits of a medieval monk?

There could be any number of reasons: the intelligence and clarity of Ellis Peters' prose, the ingenious plotting, the historical detail . . . But I think it's because Ellis Peters realised that, despite the passage of more than seven hundred years, deep down we're not that different from the people of twelfth-century Shrewsbury, or any other place and time.

She made us see our ancestors in a different light: not the dry, distant figures of academic tomes, but flesh-and-blood men and women with hopes and dreams, passions, fears and foibles just like our own.

She made us feel at home with people we could understand and care about, and that is what, in my opinion, made her writing so irresistible.

Molly Brown

The Padder's Lesson

Molly Brown

Robert rode his horse at a slow canter along the quiet country lane, feeling more than usually pleased with himself. In his long blond periwig, his matching satin coat and breeches and hat trimmed with satin ribbon, he felt he would not look out of place among the courtiers of Whitehall Palace. Someone had once told him that vanity would be his downfall, but the remark had obviously been prompted by jealousy. Surely his proud carriage and long hours spent in front of the glass had brought him only benefit.

The early summer air was mild and filled with the scent of wild flowers, the path shaded from the sun by the over-hanging branches of trees. Lulled by the steady rhythm of his horse's hoofbeats, he soon lapsed into daydream, reliving the previous day's momentous events, over and over again.

He was jolted from this pleasant reverie by the sight of a figure leaping from the bushes at the side of the road. The figure caught hold of his horse's bridle, bringing it to a sudden stop.

Robert looked down to see an oaf armed with a club.

'Stand and deliver,' the oaf demanded. He had a low forehead and narrow eyes much too small for the rest of his features.

Robert kicked the man hard in the face. The other grunted

140

and reeled backwards, his head hitting the ground with a resounding crack. Robert leapt from the saddle and drew his sword, pressing the tip of the blade into the soft flesh of the other's neck. 'I should slit your throat, you cur!'

The robber's small eyes darted down to look at the blade. He tossed away his club, his stupid face a mask of terror. 'Have mercy, I beg—'

'Silence, rogue! I am the Duke of Tunbridge Wells,' Robert said, naming the first place that came into his head. 'I have no need to summon a magistrate to sentence you to the gallows. I shall sentence you to death myself, right here and now.'

Tears began to well in the other's eyes. 'Please, your grace, I beg you, have pity! I have never done this before, I swear it!'

'I could have guessed that,' Robert said, enjoying being addressed as 'your grace'. It was hard not to laugh. 'I have never seen one so inept at robbery! What is your name, villain?'

'Joseph, your grace,' the other sobbed.

'And your age?'

'Seventeen years, your grace.'

'A big-boned, lusty lad of seventeen,' Robert observed drily. 'A pity you shall not see eighteen.'

'I beg you, your grace, have mercy! I was never a thief until this day. I have worked all my life as an honest servant. My master's house is but two miles from here.'

Try as he might, Robert could not stop his mouth from curving upwards into a smile. 'I see. And pray, what reason have you, an honest servant, to turn padder?'

Joseph sniffled, his voice unsteady. 'I wanted to know what it was like to sleep in a bed.'

This was not an answer Robert had expected. 'What?' he asked, no longer smiling.

'All my life I have slept on straw beneath another's roof. I wanted to lie in a bed of my own. May God forgive me, that is all I have ever wanted.'

The sight of this big strapping boy lying snivelling on the ground had ceased to be amusing. 'Get up,' Robert said, putting away his sword. 'I grow weary of this jest.'

Joseph remained where he was. He stared up at the sky for several seconds, his mouth opening and closing without sound. 'Jest?' he repeated at last.

'It was no more than you deserved,' Robert said. 'You tried to rob me, so I decided to teach you a lesson.'

'Lesson?' Joseph still didn't move. 'You're not a duke, then?'

'No, I am a king.'

Joseph's mouth began to work again, his eyes widening in alarm.

'A king of the road,' Robert explained.

Joseph's expression didn't change.

'A gentleman collector.' He saw by the other's face that he still didn't understand. 'A highwayman, you fool!'

'A highwayman?' Joseph considered this a moment, then slowly pulled himself into a sitting position. Once upright, he tentatively touched the back of his head, then examined the tips of his fingers. There was blood on them. 'A thief?' he said, wiping the snot from his nose on the sleeve of his smock. 'You are a thief like me?'

Robert picked up Joseph's club, weighing it in his hands. It was solid and heavy; he had been lucky his would-be robber had so little knowledge of how to use it. 'I am nothing like you. I am not a young fool with no experience of the trade who has lost his only weapon and must now return to his master with a sore head and the certainty of facing a whipping. Or did you ask your master's permission before you left his house to try your luck on the road?'

Joseph grimaced and touched the back of his head again.

'I thought not,' Robert said. 'Your master will feel the need to teach you a lesson, and it will be a much harder one than I have given you. I wonder how many lashes you will receive

. . . Still, you must admit you were remarkably fortunate to have chanced upon me as your first victim.'

'Pray, how was I fortunate?' Joseph asked him. 'As you yourself have pointed out, I have lost my weapon, I have a sore head, and I am certain to face a whipping. When I set out this morning, this was not the result I had in mind.'

'If you had bungled your first robbery with any victim but another thief, you would be on your way to the gallows by now. On the other hand, if your laughable attempt to rob me had been successful I should not have dared to prosecute, as everything I have is stolen.' Robert climbed back into the saddle and made to resume his journey. 'For one who has made such an ill start at the trade, I would say you have much to be thankful for.'

'You are right, sir,' Joseph exclaimed suddenly, as if the truth of it had just occurred to him. 'You are right, I should be thankful. For what better fortune could I have than to meet someone like you, a master of your chosen trade?'

Robert stayed his horse. It would not be dark for several hours; he had time to listen to a little praise. 'Not a master,' he said modestly.

'Oh, I disagree, sir. I may lack your gifts of intellect and refinement, but I am not so ignorant that I do not recognise such superior qualities in others.'

Robert paused a moment, considering. 'Perhaps you are not so simple as I first took you for,' he observed.

'Simple or not, I was a fool to take to the road with no experience or knowledge of the trade.' Joseph sighed and wiped his face with a grubby hand, leaving black streaks across his cheeks. 'Now I must pay the price for my stupidity and accept whatever punishment awaits at my master's house. God speed you on your journey, sir.' He bowed and started to walk away.

'Joseph, wait,' Robert called.

The servant turned around, his face expectant.

Robert smiled and tossed the would-be padder his club.

'You are more fortunate than you know, for I have decided to help you.'

Robert rode his horse at a slow walk along the shady lane, the servant accompanying him on foot.

'When you have a mind to rob a man on horseback,' he said, 'never do as you did today and merely take hold of the bridle. The first thing you must do is knock him to the ground. Then, if he should try to speak, hit him another stroke with your club and say, "Do you prate?" Then you have the advantage and can take what you will.'

'If I can get him on the ground, he will be at my mercy?'

'Generally speaking, yes. Though you must not let him reach for his sword. Tell him if he tries for his blade you will break his arm.'

'But what if he still should try?'

'Then break it. It is no good making threats you are not willing to carry out.'

'I see,' Joseph said, thoughtfully tapping the club against his thigh. 'Pray, sir, is it true what you said earlier, that everything you have is stolen?'

Robert laughed. 'Nearly everything.' He reached forward to touch the white star on his horse's forehead. 'See this? Paint. So are the markings on his legs.'

Joseph frowned. 'You paint your horse? Why?'

'To avoid identification.' Robert winked and tapped his nose. 'The horse I stole had no markings.'

'You are a clever man, sir,' Joseph said admiringly.

Robert shrugged. 'It's a common enough practice, and if you knock a man to the ground to rob him, you would be wise to take his horse as well.'

'Why is that, sir?'

'Fie! Would you leave your victim his horse while you escape on foot? How far do you think you would get?'

'Of course you are right, sir. I had not thought of that.'

'You must learn to think of everything, Joseph, or all I have

144

tried to teach you today will have been wasted. A man needs wit to survive as a thief; without it he will soon find himself being dragged on a hurdle to Tyburn.'

'But you have no shortage of wit, sir, do you?'

Robert laughed and tapped his nose again. 'I pray I may honestly say I am no fool.'

'Oh, you are no fool, sir. But you speak of needing wit merely to survive and I can see just by looking at you that you have managed much more than mere survival.'

Robert chuckled. 'I have indeed.' He patted one side of his jacket. 'On my person at this moment, I am carrying more than fifty guineas. Enough for a man of less expensive tastes to live the rest of his life at ease. And here,' he said, patting the other side, 'I have something for which I am sure to get an excellent price in London.'

They continued on for another mile or so, Robert explaining the finer points of his art to the servant, until they came to a fork in the road. 'Here I must leave you,' Robert said, 'for the time is getting late and I must reach London before dark.'

'Farewell, sir. I am forever grateful for all your help and instruction.'

'Farewell, padder.' Robert waved one hand in a gesture of careless magnanimity before proceeding to take the road to the left.

'Forgive me, sir,' Joseph called after him, 'but I should not go that way if I were you!'

Robert halted and turned around. 'This is the road to London, is it not?'

'It is *one* road to London, but not the road to take if you wish to reach the city by dark,' Joseph said. He pointed to the road on the right. 'There is a shorter route up here.'

'How so?'

'Follow this road until you come to a gate leading on to a field. Go straight across the field and at the far side you will find a row of hedges. Beyond lies the main coach road to

London; riding that way will take at least an hour off your journey.'

Robert thanked him and took the other road.

He found the gate and set out across open fields, enjoying the rush of air against his face as the horse broke into a gallop. The contents of the pouch inside his jacket jangled and rattled, bringing a smile to his lips.

He still could not believe his good fortune. It was like a delicious dream from which he never wanted to waken. His eyes glazed over, the open countryside around him fading into an unseen blur as once again he relived the events of the previous evening.

It had been early afternoon when he received a message from the landlord of an inn halfway between London and Tunbridge Wells: *The Duchess of Portsmouth stops to dine here on her way to take the waters.*

His hands had trembled as he read the note. The Duchess of Portsmouth was none other than Louise de Kéroualle, the favourite mistress of Charles II.

He left his lodgings a few moments later, carrying a mask and two pistols. He rode to a spot a few miles up the road from the inn and waited behind some bushes.

The coach, when it arrived, was a beautiful sight, bright red trimmed with gold, drawn by six horses in feather head-dresses.

He emerged from behind the bushes, his horse rearing up on its haunches as he pulled back on the reins. 'Stand and deliver!'

'How dare you?' a heavily accented woman's voice shouted. 'Do you know who I am?'

He rode round to the coach window and came face to face with Louise de Kéroualle, the King's French papist doxy. With her large eyes and lustrous dark hair, Robert might have thought her beautiful – if it were not for the harshness of her expression.

'I know exactly who you are,' he said, eyes gleaming behind his mask. 'You are a whore kept by the King at the public expense.'

'*Mon dieu!* Never have I heard such insolence! His Majesty himself shall see you pay for this.'

'Your haughty French airs will not help you, my lady,' Robert told her. 'For I am king here, and my rule is absolute. And just like His Majesty in Whitehall, I also have a whore which I keep on the public's contributions.'

That silenced the woman.

Robert laughed out loud at the memory of the look on her face as she had handed over her money, followed by a diamond necklace, a gold ring set with rubies, and finally, a diamond and emerald bracelet. Cautious as always, Robert had later spent most of the night taking the stones from their settings so they could not be identified.

When he thought about that poor would-be padder and how easily the young servant had believed him to be a duke, he laughed out loud again. Thanks to the collection of precious stones rattling about in the pouch inside his jacket, he would soon be living as well as a lord.

He slowed the horse as he came to the row of tall hedges at the far side of the field. He found a gap large enough for a horse and rider and went through, expecting to find the London road.

A sudden blow knocked him from his saddle.

He found himself flat on his back on the ground, staring up at Joseph.

'What?' Robert sputtered angrily. 'Is this how you repay me for all my help and advice?'

'Silence, villain!' Joseph shouted, waving his club. 'Do you prate?'

Robert's hand went for his sword. He screamed in pain as Joseph smashed the club down on his arm, breaking it.

'Move again, and I shall break your skull,' Joseph said. He

reached down, pulled Robert's sword from its sheath and pressed it to his throat.

'My hearty congratulations to you, sir,' Joseph said as he mounted Robert's horse. 'You make an excellent teacher. Now if you'll pardon me, I must be on my way if I am to be in London before nightfall.'

'But why?' Robert croaked. 'After all I did for you, why?'

Joseph shrugged his massive shoulders. 'Why not? As you yourself pointed out, for stealing from another thief, I need have no fear of prosecution.' He held up the pouch containing the duchess's jewels and shook it. 'Do you think there is enough here for a man to buy himself a bed?'

I first read Ellis Peters' Cadfael novels when I was a student in Durham, and her books helped me appreciate the tremendous atmosphere of history in that city far more than I would have done left to my own devices. Her vivid descriptions of life in a medieval abbey in a war-torn shire must surely have inspired many people to want to learn more about the Anarchy and its politics and people. That the abbey church at Shrewsbury is now such a recognised tourist spot is another testament to the profound impact Ellis Peters has had on popular history. Perhaps more than any other writer of her genre, she has proved that reading books about events that occurred hundreds of years ago in places that we still know today can be fun.

Invited to contribute a short story for a volume published in her memory, it seemed appropriate to select the period for which Ellis Peters is best known – the 1100s – and to choose a monastic setting. In the 1180s, the Cistercian foundation at Kingswood was nowhere near as grand as the noble Benedictine abbey at Shrewsbury, but fragments of it survived the Dissolution of the Monasteries and the looting that followed as the people of Kingswood built themselves finer homes with abbey stone (including the house on the

High Street that belonged to my grandparents, and is in the care of English Heritage).

As it is possible to walk the ancient thoroughfares of Shrewsbury and imagine Brother Cadfael hurrying along the Foregate to solve another crime, so it is possible to stand in the peaceful Cotswold village of Kingswood and imagine the chime of bells calling the monks to their offices and the chanting of their plainsong. It was through reading Ellis Peters' novels that I first learned to appreciate Kingswood Abbey's sense of forgotten grandeur and the timeless quality of the few medieval stones encroached by modern houses. It is an appreciation that I will treasure and for which I will always be grateful to her.

Susanna Gregory

To Dispose of an Abbot

Susanna Gregory

Kingswood Abbey, Gloucestershire: Christmas 1180

Snow fell softly and silently, smothering the churchyard in a thin white blanket and coating the rough wooden coffin with flakes that glistened wetly in the dull noon light. Richard of Berkeley watched two monks struggle to lower the body of their abbot into the grave, wincing as the box tipped precariously and threatened to fall. Next to him, his wife Alys gave a sigh of relief as the coffin touched the frozen bottom with a hollow thump. She touched her husband's arm.

'There, you have done your duty by coming here. Now come home before the weather turns worse and we find ourselves stranded in this godforsaken place for the night.'

'Just a few more moments,' he said. 'Ask Cynan the groom to saddle the horses. By the time he has finished I will be ready to leave.'

She sighed again to register disapproval at his lingering, but walked away to order the horses prepared for the short ride from Kingswood Abbey to Richard's prosperous little manor of Hillseley. Richard turned his attention to where the two monks were hurrying to shovel earth into the open grave, desperate to return to the abbey's roaring fires. Lost

151

in memories of the abbot who had been a friend, Richard did not hear Brother Hugh, the victualler, approaching, and jumped at the sudden closeness of the voice at his side.

'It was good of you to come,' said the monk, although the tone of his voice suggested Richard's presence at Abbot Pagan's graveside was more irritation than honour. 'Will you join us for some refreshments before you leave?'

Richard dragged his attention away from Pagan and turned to the monk, anticipating and seeing no welcome in the arrogant face. Hugh had a florid complexion and greasy black hair, and he and Richard had never liked each other. 'Thank you, no. My wife wants to leave before the snow settles.'

Hugh glanced down at the mound of earth his colleagues were slapping into shape with the backs of their spades. 'I understand it was Pagan's doing that you have a wife. I heard you would have joined our Order had he not recommended that you pursue another vocation.'

Richard nodded. As the youngest son of the powerful Lord Berkeley, Richard had been expected to take the cowl and had been placed in the abbey that his great-grandfather had founded. But even the unworldly Abbot Pagan had not needed Richard's flagrant indiscretions with Alys to tell him Richard was no monk in the making, and he had persuaded Lord Berkeley to grant his son a small manor instead. With Alys at his side, Richard was happier than he would have believed possible, and a day seldom passed when he did not want to thank Pagan for saving him from a life in the cloister.

'I spoke to your groom just before the funeral,' said Richard, not inclined to discuss his personal life with Brother Hugh. 'He told me Abbot Pagan died of a violent sickness, but your message said he choked on wine. So which is true?'

Hugh shook his head impatiently. 'Really, Richard! I am surprised you have time to listen to the gossip of servants. I expected better of you.'

Richard grabbed his arm as he began to stride away. 'I

would like to know what happened,' he said quietly. 'Pagan was a good friend to me.'

'He was a good friend to many people,' muttered Hugh, freeing his arm roughly. 'That was his problem.'

'What do you mean by that?' demanded Richard, angry that a man like Hugh should be criticising the gentle abbot.

'Exactly what I said,' snapped Hugh. 'Pagan was an old man whose increasing feebleness and insistence on seeing the good in everyone was proving a liability to the abbey. He should have resigned years ago in favour of a younger, more able man.'

'And I suppose that younger, more able man would be you?' asked Richard coldly, disgusted by the man's transparency. 'But you have not answered my question. How did he die?'

'He died, as I told you, because he was too ancient even to drink his wine without gagging over it. We took him to his chamber where he died during the night. And now, if you will excuse me, I cannot stand here all day. I have important matters to which to attend.'

Not normally a man given to violent impulses, Richard nevertheless had to clench his fists tightly to prevent himself from wrapping his hands around the monk's throat and squeezing until he would never speak against Pagan again. Pagan had served Kingswood Abbey for more than thirty years, and did not deserve to have his good nature sneered at by a man like Brother Hugh.

Richard stood in silent contemplation for a few more moments, and then went to find Alys. She was arguing with the porter because Cynan the groom was nowhere to be found and she wanted to look for him in the stables. Women were not allowed in the abbey, but the porter would not leave his warm lodge to trudge through the snow to seek out Cynan himself, so they were locked in a fierce debate.

'Let her in, for the love of God!' snapped Hugh as he stalked past, clearly as keen to be rid of them as they were to be away. 'How can they return home if they have no horses?'

'Your graciousness and hospitality never cease to amaze me, Brother,' said Alys tartly, before disappearing through the gate in the direction of the stable.

Seeing Hugh splutter with indignation at her effrontery went some way to restoring Richard to better humour. While he waited, looking around at the ramshackle collection of stone buildings and huts that comprised the abbey, three men approached him, all wearing the white habit and black apron of monks of the Cistercian Order. Two he knew already: Brother William, the cellarer, was fat and had a withered right hand that he kept tucked inside his sleeve; Brother Eudo, the infirmarian, was red-haired and handsome with a ready grin and a wry sense of humour.

'This is Father John of York,' said William, turning to indicate the third monk with his good hand. 'He is the Visitor from our mother abbey at Tintern.'

'Visitor?' asked Richard uncertainly.

Eudo laughed and gave him a nudge in the ribs. 'Have you forgotten all you learned from your sojourn with us, Richard?' he asked teasingly. 'The Visitor is the man who will tell us who our next abbot will be.'

'It was fortunate I was in the area when news came that Abbot Pagan had died,' said John. He was a tall man who wore a fur-lined cloak over his habit, so that he, unlike the others, did not seem to mind the snow that settled on his shoulders. He spoke Norman French like an aristocrat, and Richard had no doubt that John was a man who would rise far in the ranks of the Cistercians. 'Because I am here, I am able to name Pagan's successor without any inconvenient delays.'

'I see,' said Richard, trying to conceal his distaste that the monks should be considering such matters quite so soon after Pagan's death.

'Hugh is certain it will be him,' said Eudo, eyes twinkling

with mischief. 'But Father John will not tell us what he plans to do until he makes a formal announcement after compline tonight.'

'Not all of us think Hugh will make a good abbot,' said William to Richard, although Richard saw perfectly well that the comment was intended purely for John's ears. 'He has too quick a temper and will alienate prospective benefactors with his poor manners.'

John arched elegantly sculpted eyebrows to express interest, but made no reply. It was well known in the abbey and village that William considered himself the most appropriate candidate for Abbot Pagan's position.

'Benefactors such as Lord Berkeley?' asked Eudo impishly, who also had his eye on the position left vacant by Pagan. 'I just heard Hugh arguing with Richard across poor Pagan's grave. Antagonising Berkeley's son is scarcely the best way to encourage healthy donations from the wealthiest family in Gloucestershire. What was he saying to incite you to consider wringing his scrawny neck as he strutted away, Richard?'

Richard grimaced, embarrassed that his display of anger had been observed. 'I just asked him how Pagan died.'

The merry twinkle faded from Eudo's eyes. 'He slipped away in his sleep.'

William shook his jowls in irritation. 'Nonsense, Eudo. Pagan died from choking on the vile bread Hugh served us that night. But regardless, his death was God's will and nothing more.'

'Died in his sleep? Bad bread?' asked Richard, looking from one to the other in confusion. 'And Hugh said the wine killed him, while Cynan the groom said he had a violent sickness. Why so many different stories?'

The two monks began to bicker. Bewildered, Richard watched them, aware that the Visitor, John, was doing the same.

'It seems to me that we do not really know how Pagan died,' said John, when the argument eventually faltered into an uncomfortable silence. 'Perhaps he had a sickness induced by sour wine or dry bread; perhaps he died naturally in his sleep. All we know for certain is that he was taken ill after compline, and that he was found dead in his room before dawn the following day.'

'But someone must have been with him,' protested Richard. 'Surely you did not see an old man sicken over his supper and leave him alone for the night?'

'Pagan said he felt better once he was in bed,' objected Eudo. 'Hugh, William and I offered to stay with him, but he dismissed us all.'

'It is irrelevant now, anyway,' said William pompously. 'Pagan is buried, God rest his soul, and we must look to the future of the abbey, not its past.' He took John's arm solicitously and ushered him away from Richard and towards the gate. Before Eudo could follow, Richard grabbed the infirmarian's sleeve.

'What is going on?' he asked. 'Did Pagan die a natural death, or are there so many monks in your abbey who are keen to take his place that one of them decided to hasten his end?'

'That accusation is both unpleasant and dangerous,' said Eudo, showing a rare flash of temper. 'We are friends, Richard, so take my advice: keep such vile aspersions to yourself.'

Richard was about to question him further, when there was a piercing scream. His stomach lurched as he recognised Alys' voice, and he darted through the gateway and raced towards the stables. Alys was running towards him, holding both hands in front of her. Even from a distance, Richard could see they were stained red.

'Cynan!' she cried. 'He is in the stable with his throat cut!'

Richard paced restlessly, while Alys huddled near the fire, shivering as the wind rattled the window shutters and whistled down the chimney. The first flurries of snow that had fallen during Pagan's funeral had heralded the onset of a furious blizzard. By the time Richard and the monks had inspected Cynan's body and Alys had been calmed with sips of mulled wine, the weather had degenerated so much that riding the few miles back to Hillseley was out of the question.

None of the monks, however, had seemed pleased that Richard and Alys were obliged to take refuge in the abbey's guest house – a handsome room above the gateway with real glass in the windows and a generous fire blazing in the hearth – sensing perhaps that Richard would not be satisfied until he had learned exactly what it was that had snatched the life away from the old abbot, and who might have had a hand in it.

'Monks are nothing but trouble,' said Alys, watching her husband walk back and forth. 'I would have them all removed from the country if I were King.'

'Pagan was not trouble,' said Richard, pouring himself some claret. 'He was a virtuous and kindly man, who wished nothing but good to everyone. Do you want more wine?'

'No,' said Alys with a grimace. 'It is as sour as vinegar. No wonder poor Pagan choked on it; it is poison!' Realising what she had said, her eyes opened wide and her hands flew to her lips. 'Do you think that was what made Pagan choke over his supper? Poison?'

The notion had certainly crossed Richard's mind. Whether Pagan had died of a sickness or in his sleep, it had been after his curious reaction to what he had had for supper. He nodded slowly. 'It seems a reasonable assumption to make.'

Alys' eyes went to the goblet in Richard's hand. 'Then do not drink that! Anyone desperate enough to slay an old man to further his own ambitions will not hesitate to dispatch a meddlesome sheep farmer – and the fact that you are Lord Berkeley's son will not save you.'

Richard had been in the process of raising the goblet to his lips, but he lowered it again, gazing thoughtfully at the dark

157

liquid that swirled in the bottom of the pewter goblet. 'What do you think is going on here, Alys?'

She shrugged. 'It is obvious. Pagan has ruled the abbey for thirty years and someone decided it was time for a change of leadership. That arrogant Brother Hugh has made no secret of the fact that he considers Pagan's death a stroke of good luck, while William and even your smiling friend Eudo clearly believe they would make excellent successors.'

'Do you believe one of these three killed him?'

She frowned, staring into the crackling fire. 'They are the ones with the obvious motive, and they have concocted so many lies that it is difficult to know what is truth and what is fabrication. Hugh claims Pagan choked on wine; he is the victualler, and so would not want the bread blamed. On the other hand, William, the cellarer, maintains that the bread was at fault, because he wants to keep suspicion away from the wine. Meanwhile, Eudo says Pagan died in his sleep because, as infirmarian, he has unlimited access to strong medicines and does not want anyone poking around in his store room for possible poisons. Who knows what is the truth in all this?'

'Someone knows,' said Richard bitterly. 'Whoever killed Pagan knows!'

'And let's not forget poor Cynan, murdered and lying in the stables with his throat cut. Tell me exactly what he said to you when he suggested that Hugh's message about choking on the wine was false?'

Richard frowned and rubbed his chin. 'When we first arrived in Kingswood, he came to take our horses and commented how we were only just in time for the funeral. I told him Hugh had not sent word until early this morning – hoping, no doubt, that we would assume it would be too late to come and would stay away.'

'Then Hugh does not know you very well,' said Alys, smiling. 'What else did Cynan say?'

'When I told him Hugh's message had been that Pagan had choked on wine, he said he saw Pagan being escorted from the refectory to his room by Hugh, William and Eudo. All three were still there when he went to douse the fire in Pagan's room. That was when he saw Pagan had some kind of sickness.'

'And Eudo told you that Pagan had recovered and had dismissed all three from his presence,' mused Alys. 'If Pagan was ill enough to be escorted from the refectory and was still ailing later when Cynan went to tend the fire, then it seems unlikely that he would have recovered so abruptly. He must have been poisoned, while Cynan was killed to make sure he did not tell anyone else what he had seen that night.'

'But what *did* he see?' asked Richard, frustrated. 'Cynan said nothing that would warrant ensuring his permanent silence – and he had already told me what he had seen anyway, so the damage had already been done.'

'Then that raises two questions,' said Alys thoughtfully. 'First, does the killer know Cynan has already told you what he knew? And second, will he now consider us a danger to his plans and have us slain too?'

Her eyes were huge in the dim light, and Richard pulled her towards him, breathing in the clean, fresh scent of her hair. 'I have been invited to dine in the monks' refectory tonight – you are expected to eat here alone – and I will find out all I can. I suspect the only way we will be safe is if we uncover this murderer and deliver him to justice. But when I go, I want you to lock the door and open it to no one but me.'

She nodded uneasily and he felt a lurching fear that his determination to attend the funeral of a friend had dragged the person he loved more than any other into all kinds of unseen dangers.

A fire roared in the hearth of the spacious room the monks used as their refectory. As Hugh ladled out mutton and bean broth and William poured the wine, Eudo whispered that they usually dined more frugally, but that the presence of the

Visitor had prompted Hugh to provide rich soup and fresh bread for supper.

The atmosphere in the refectory was tense, everyone anxious to hear who was to be the next abbot. There were about forty brothers present, all sitting at two long tables that ran the length of the room. At the table placed at right angles to them sat the three most senior monks – Hugh, William and Eudo – with Father John and Richard.

Richard sipped the wine, but it tasted sour to him and made his stomach feel knotted and acidic. While he did not imagine the killer would risk poisoning a second person in front of the entire convent, Richard was in no mood for festivities while his friend lay murdered in the frozen soil of the churchyard outside the abbey gates.

'How did Pagan die?' he asked. He had already decided that the best way to protect himself and Alys was to make his suspicions public in the hope that the killer would realise their subsequent deaths in the abbey would lead to a good many questions being asked. He had intended his question to be for Hugh, William and Eudo, but the very mention of the abbot's name was sufficient to still all conversation, and the hall was suddenly silent except for the crackling of the fire. Disconcerted by the effect his query had on the community of monks, Richard swallowed hard and blundered on. 'Pagan sickened at supper, I understand. All of you must have seen him taken ill. What happened?'

'He was called by God,' said Hugh, feigning weariness at the subject. 'And that is all that need concern you. What happens inside these abbey walls is none of your affair.'

'But it is my father's affair,' said Richard, meeting his pale blue eyes steadily. 'He will not like to hear that the saintly man who served the abbey our family founded has been murdered.'

There was a hubbub of raised voices, some angry, some denying, some accusing. Richard looked around at the assembled faces and sensed he was not the only one uncomfortable over the blurred facts concerning Pagan's death.

'Silence!' Hugh's outraged voice stilled the clamour instantly. He turned to Richard, his voice shaking with fury. 'You are a guest in our house. You have no right to make such foul accusations! If you cannot act with courtesy and honour, you may leave immediately!'

'Please!' cried Eudo, his normally jovial face distressed. 'We laid one of our most loved members to rest today. Let's not sully his memory by squabbling.'

'And I will not sully his memory by allowing the man who killed him to walk free,' shouted Richard furiously, leaping to his feet. 'Did he choke on wine or bread, or die in his sleep? Or, as I suspect, was he poisoned?'

There was another hush. Father John sat back with his arms folded, his face etched with concern at the discomfiture Richard's accusations were causing the others.

'Pagan was not poisoned with wine,' said William stiffly. 'I can vouch completely for my brews. And anyway, we all drank from the same jug, so if it had contained something toxic, Pagan would not have been the only one buried this morning. If he choked on anything, it would have been the bread.'

'Do not blame my bread to exonerate yourself,' snarled Hugh, his bellicose face suffused with anger. 'We both know the wine was at fault.'

William's disdainful expression made it clear he did not consider Hugh's words worth a response. He spread flabby hands and addressed Richard. 'Please, sit down and enjoy the remainder of your meal with us. Hugh's words were over-hasty; none of us wish you to leave tonight.'

And why was that? thought Richard. So it would provide the killer with an opportunity to dispatch him? Eudo tugged on Richard's arm to make him sit. Reluctantly, Richard complied.

'You are grief-stricken and do not know what you are

saying,' said Eudo gently. 'Pagan had not been well these last few days. He refused remedies from me, but at compline even sipping wine was too great an effort for him. He did choke, as Brother Hugh claims, and was taken to recover in his chamber. I am sure he sensed his end was close and so we were dismissed – he wanted to make his peace with God alone. Afterwards, I imagine he slipped away in his sleep. Do not forget he was seventy years old.'

'Cynan said he had a sickness,' said Richard stubbornly.

'Cynan is not qualified to judge such a matter,' said Eudo. 'However, he was right: Pagan was sick, just when Cynan came to douse the fire. But the purge seemed to relieve him, and afterwards he said he felt much better, so he dismissed us. He died of natural causes, Richard.'

'And what about Cynan,' demanded Richard. '*He* did not die of natural causes.'

'Cynan was unpopular with the villagers,' reasoned Eudo, unruffled by Richard's persistence. 'One of them probably killed him when we were all conveniently absent at Pagan's funeral mass. The abbey will investigate the matter, of course, but Cynan's murder is totally divorced from Pagan's natural death.'

Richard had never been more uncertain of anything in his life. Who was telling the truth? Cynan, who had no reason to lie that Richard could see? The ambitious Hugh, who was clearly delighted by the old man's death? The cunning William, who wanted the bread and not the wine blamed for Pagan's choking? Or the jovial Eudo, who had access to strong medicines that might kill an old man? All three monks had been with Pagan before he died, and therefore had the opportunity to poison him, and all three wanted to be abbot, and so had the motive.

Reluctant though he was to accept the word of Hugh or William, Eudo's explanation sounded plausible. Richard had not seen Pagan for several weeks, and so could not say whether the old man had been declining in health or not. He rubbed his head tiredly.

Seeing Richard was not going to speak again, John pushed back his chair and stood. There was an instant hush.

'I am pleased to announce the name of the man who will be your new abbot.' John paused and looked at the expectant faces. Richard saw Hugh's eyes burning with fierce hope, while William was smug, as though it was a foregone conclusion who represented the best choice. Eudo's face was blank, although Richard noticed his hands shook.

'I have spent hours seeking divine guidance,' John went on, 'and I have observed all of you at work and at prayer. You understand, of course, that it is in my remit to appoint an outsider to the post.'

Richard saw Hugh start to raise an objection, but he saw that it would not be prudent to question the Visitor and his words died in his throat. William's fat face was a mask of sweat and he flexed his withered hand in agitation. Eudo simply sat as still as a statue.

'But I have decided there is one member of the community who stands above all others, and whom I believe will make you a splendid abbot. Brother Hugh will be Pagan's successor.'

'Hugh?' cried Alys in disbelief when Richard informed her of John's choice later. 'What is John thinking of? Hugh is an ignorant pig who, as far as I am concerned, is the chief suspect for Pagan's murder!'

'Eudo made a death by natural causes seem very plausible,' said Richard tiredly. 'Perhaps we are allowing our grief to misguide us.'

'Then what about Cynan?' demanded Alys.

'Eudo says Cynan was unpopular and thinks one of the villagers killed him.'

'Eudo seems to have a good many convenient explanations at his fingertips,' said Alys. 'But he is wrong, Richard:

Cynan's murder is related to Pagan's death. I am sure of it.'

'I am too tired to think about this any more tonight,' said Richard. 'We should sleep, and things may appear differently in the morning.'

'I will never be able to sleep here,' said Alys, looking around the chamber in revulsion.

But she, like Richard, was exhausted by the day's events, and she began to drowse almost immediately. The abbey's beds were soft and warm, and the fire sent a comforting glow around the room, locking out the bitter cold as the snow fell heavily outside. Richard's dreams teemed with visions of Pagan calling him to avenge his untimely death, while Cynan struggled to speak through a gashed neck. Richard raised his hands to find his throat too had been cut, so that he started to gag for breath. He could not suck enough air into his lungs and he began to panic, thrashing around with his arms.

'Richard!'

Alys' scream slowly dragged him from his nightmare world, but his eyes smarted and stung as he tried to open them and he still could not breathe. The room was full of white, swirling smoke, so thick he could barely see. Gasping and choking, he seized Alys' arm and hauled her towards the door. It was locked from the outside. Desperately, he staggered to the window, throwing it open to lean outside and drag in great lungfuls of snow-laden air. Next to him, Alys sobbed as she fought to catch her breath.

Voices could be heard in the hallway, and someone pounded on the door. Richard did not have the voice to reply. Then, an ear-splitting crack suggested someone was applying an axe to the door with considerable force. Within moments, the lock had been smashed and Eudo stumbled inside. Behind him were William and Hugh, gazing around the smoke-filled room in horror. Father John elbowed past them impatiently and ran to unlatch the other windows, allowing fresh air to pour in and dissipate the choking fumes.

'Thank God you are unharmed!' cried Eudo in relief, striding towards Richard and Alys. Alys shrunk away from him. 'We were on our way to lauds when William smelled smoke.'

'Someone set a fire in the porch outside your room and sealed the doors,' said Hugh. 'The smoke might have killed you had you been soundly asleep.'

'We *were* soundly asleep,' said Alys unsteadily. 'I only woke because Richard was hitting out with his fists in the grip of some nightmare; he landed a blow that woke me.'

'Whoever did this was clever,' said John, looking to where other monks doused the smouldering pile with water. 'He chose damp straw and green twigs that would not set the abbey on fire, but that would smoke and so suffocate you in your beds.'

'But why?' asked Eudo in horror. 'Who would do such a thing?'

No one replied, although the answer was clear enough in everyone's faces. Richard's accusations the previous evening had not made him safe from an attempt on their lives after all, and had only encouraged the killer to strike again. Richard drew Alys closer towards him and wished with all his heart that he had never brought her with him to Kingswood Abbey.

Richard fell a third time in snow that was so deep it reached his waist. The sky was a dirty grey-brown, suggesting that it would not be much longer before yet more snow would fall. He hauled himself up and took a few more steps before falling again.

'This is hopeless,' said Alys, sitting astride her palfrey as she watched him struggle. 'We are barely out of Kingswood High Street and you cannot walk. We will never reach home – we will lose our way and die from the cold when night falls.'

'It is only just past dawn; we have all day,' said Richard, taking another step and sinking almost to his chest in a deep drift against what was probably a hedge. Behind him, the horse he was leading whinnied in fright as it was unable to extricate itself.

'We will have to return to the abbey,' said Alys reluctantly.

'No!' said Richard fiercely. 'I do not want you there. I want you away from those murdering monks and their vile ambitions, safe in our own home.'

'The killer will not make a second attempt on our lives so soon,' she said, although her voice lacked conviction. 'We will take it in turns to sleep tonight, and we can spend the day in the church. No one will harm us there.'

Richard was not so sure, but saw there was no other option open to them. The snow that had fallen thick and fast all night was just too deep for walking in, and there was no way he and Alys would reach home before dusk. Unfortunately, all the shabby houses that lined the High Street were already packed to the gills with people – mainly shepherds who had brought their flocks to the village byres when the first snows began to fall. There was no room for Richard and Alys anywhere except the abbey. With grave misgivings about throwing themselves on the dubious hospitality of the monks again, Richard took the reins of his horse and reluctantly began to retrace his footsteps.

'At least we now *know* Pagan was murdered,' said Alys as they walked. 'Had his death been natural, as Eudo claimed, then no one would have needed to smother us in our beds to prevent us prying further into the affair.'

'The killer must be Hugh,' said Richard, panting with the effort of plodding through the snow that lay knee-deep along the High Street. In places it had blocked the doors of houses, and lay in untidy piles where the occupants had shovelled it away. 'He never liked Pagan, and he hates me.'

'But it might equally well be William or Eudo,' said Alys. 'They, too, wanted Pagan's position, and they were among the first of our rescuers to arrive last night.'

'But it was Eudo who smashed open the door,' said Richard. 'And William only has one arm. He cannot even write, let alone carry armfuls of green twigs around the abbey in the dead of night.'

'He manages very well with one hand,' said Alys. 'Do not discount him so readily.' She watched Richard tugging his tired horse from a particularly deep section of snow. 'What about John, the Visitor? Maybe he killed Pagan and tried to have us asphyxiated.'

Richard shook his head. 'John was not even in Kingswood when Pagan died and therefore could have no reason to want us dead.'

As he anticipated, the monks were not overjoyed to re-admit their reluctant guests. Hugh's face darkened ominously when he saw Richard leading his horses through the gate, and did not seem to believe that the roads were impassable. He drew himself up to his full height and regarded Richard with open dislike.

'I am abbot now, and I will not tolerate guests meddling in abbey affairs. Behave yourselves, or you will find yourselves evicted – heavy snows or no.'

'Take no notice,' said William, glowering at his new abbot's retreating back. 'The abbey will not turn anyone out in the snow, especially not a son of our noble benefactor.' He gave Richard a smile that was unpleasantly ingratiating, and Richard saw immediately what he was trying to do: William hoped Richard would express reservations to his father about Hugh's appointment, and, although abbey business was none of Lord Berkeley's affair, the Cistercian Order would want to retain good relations with its generous patron. If Hugh were discreetly removed from office, then William would be ready to take his place.

'That is reassuring,' said Richard shortly, not appreciating William's obsequious friendliness any more than Hugh's open hostility.

'Hugh was a poor choice as abbot,' said William, shaking

his jowls disapprovingly. He lowered his voice conspira-
torially. 'I believe you were right to be concerned about
the wine on which poor Pagan choked. Hugh was also the
last person to see Pagan alive – Eudo and I left when asked,
but Hugh stayed a few moments longer.'

'Why did you not mention this yesterday?' asked Richard,
uncertain how much was true, and how much was William's
thwarted ambition speaking.

'Yesterday we did not have a murderer as abbot,' said
William tartly. He turned quickly as Eudo approached, and
hurried away.

The usually friendly Eudo was almost as unwelcoming as
Hugh. 'I hope you have not returned to make more nasty
accusations,' he said as he escorted them to the guest house.
'I appreciate you were fond of Pagan, but we cannot allow
your grief to sully the abbey's good name.'

'When Pagan dismissed William, Hugh and you from his
chamber the night he died, did you all leave at the same
time?' asked Richard, bothered by William's claims despite
his scepticism.

'I suppose William told you Hugh lingered,' said Eudo
heavily. 'Well, he did, but only for a few moments. I saw
him leave Pagan's room before I had walked as far as the
infirmary – a short distance as you know. No matter what
William might say, Hugh had no time for foul play.'

'Not even for smothering with a cushion?' asked Richard.

Eudo regarded him expressionlessly. 'I thought you were
fixed on poison.'

'I am fixed on nothing,' said Richard. 'But was there time
for Pagan to have been suffocated? It would leave no marks
and would make a death seem natural.'

Eudo gestured for him to enter the guest house and then
strode away without answering.

Richard attended sext at noon, bored with being confined in
the guest house, although Alys, reassured by the presence of

a burly lay-brother who kept watch by the door – as much to prevent them from wandering as to protect them from would-be assassins – could not be persuaded to join him. In the church Richard watched the monks at prayer. None of them seemed to fear being struck down by divine anger for the murder of Pagan, but since there seemed to be a consensus that Pagan's time had come anyway – naturally or otherwise – Richard supposed he should not find a lack of remorse in Pagan's killer surprising.

After sext he lingered in the church alone, thinking about Pagan and mulling over all the claims and counter-claims the brothers had made concerning his death. A rustle of cloth made him spin round in alarm, fumbling to draw his dagger from its sheath. Father John of York walked softly towards him, holding up his empty hands as the weapon glinted in the dim light.

'Like you, I have come to say a few private prayers for Pagan,' he said, looking at the beaten earth that formed the floor of the chancel to select a spot that was less dirty than the rest. He found one and knelt, hands clasped and his thick cloak falling in elegant folds around him.

Richard relaxed and went to stand near him, sheathing his knife as he did so. 'My apologies, Father. My experience last night has made me nervous.'

'Quite understandable,' said John. 'I was appalled that someone would do such a terrible thing in an abbey. Unfortunately, Hugh does not seem disposed to look into the matter, and says he is more concerned with finding Cynan's murderer.' He sighed. 'Despite my prayers for guidance, I think I made a mistake in appointing a new abbot so soon. I confess I did not take your anxieties about Pagan's death seriously – until the incident last night proved you were right to be suspicious.'

Richard felt a great weight lifted from his shoulders: he and Alys were no longer alone. 'Do you have any ideas as to the identity of the culprit?'

John shook his head. 'Eudo is infirmarian and has access to poisons that might be difficult to detect but that kill quickly. Meanwhile, William is cellarer, and might have doctored Pagan's wine – since William serves the wine himself, it would be simple to use one jug for Pagan and another for everyone else. And further, William's claim that the bread was tainted is absurd – the abbey's bread comes in large loaves that are shared by all, and Hugh could never have managed to poison only the portion that Pagan took. Hugh seems to be the least likely suspect.'

'Is that why you appointed him over the others?' asked Richard. 'Because he seemed less likely to be a murderer than them? But William said Hugh lingered in Pagan's chamber after the others left. He could have harmed the old man then.'

'True, but I did not know that until William told me this morning.'

'So, what do you plan to do?'

John gazed into the gloom and sighed heavily. 'Pray for guidance again. And hope that this time, it is God and not the Devil who whispers the answer in my ear.'

Three days passed and the weather showed no sign of relenting. Richard grew restless in the guest house and longed to return to his own manor. One afternoon, he was in the conclave trying to read a beautiful Book of Hours that Pagan had composed, but found he could not concentrate and decided to visit the stables to ensure his horse had been properly looked after. Cynan, whatever the villagers thought about him, had been an excellent groom, and Richard did not trust the abbey's stable boys as he would have done Cynan.

He opened the stable door softly, so as not to alarm the horses within, and was about to walk to his own mount when he saw a dark shape moving stealthily up the ladder to the hayloft above. Curious, Richard followed, taking care not to let the wooden steps creak as he climbed. The figure was

Hugh, and Richard watched in growing confusion as the monk knelt next to a crudely crafted crate that represented Cynan's worldly goods. The box was locked, but Hugh prised it open with a knife and began to sort through its contents. He held something up to the light and Richard heard him take a sharp intake of breath before thrusting it inside his scrip.

At that moment, a gust of wind blew the stable door shut with a loud crash, and Hugh leapt to his feet. He saw Richard standing behind him and his face became a hard mask of fury. He snatched up the knife and advanced menacingly. Richard backed away and made a dive for the ladder. Hugh came after him, slashing violently at his head as he scrambled away and then seizing a bale of hay and throwing it in an attempt to dislodge his precarious hold on the rungs.

The heavy bundle caught Richard a glancing blow on the shoulder, and he felt himself begin to slip. Another slash of the knife made him flinch backwards, and then he was falling in earnest, landing with a bone-jarring thump on the floor below. For a moment he was too stunned to move, and Hugh clambered down the stairs and darted towards him, the knife flashing wickedly as it plunged downwards.

'No!'

Alys' agonised cry from the door made Hugh falter, and Richard was able to duck away from the weapon, grabbing Hugh's knees as he did so, so that the monk fell backwards and the blade went skittering from his hand. Richard leapt on top of him, trying to prevent the monk's groping fingers from reaching the knife. Hugh fought like the Devil himself, scratching and kicking so that Richard could do little more than parry the blows.

Just when Richard's strength was almost exhausted and a wild lunge finally secured Hugh the weapon, Eudo arrived, alerted by Alys' scream, with William, John and a number of others breathless behind him. Richard saw Hugh's arm muscles bunch as he prepared to strike the fatal blow, but Eudo bounded forward and knocked the weapon from Hugh's hand, while others dragged their abbot from his intended victim.

It was not long before Hugh's fury at being thwarted was spent, and he suddenly sagged exhausted in the arms of his captors. Richard climbed unsteadily to his feet and leaned on Alys for support.

'From our window I saw Hugh enter the stables,' she explained. 'Then I saw you follow so guilelessly and I sensed he would not appreciate being disturbed at whatever it was he was doing.'

'He was searching Cynan's belongings,' said Richard. 'And he attacked me with a knife when he saw he was caught.'

'Of course I was searching his belongings,' said Hugh, in control of himself again. 'Cynan was murdered on abbey soil. I wanted to see if the killer left any clues.'

'Then why did you attack me if your actions were honest?' demanded Richard.

'I did not attack you,' said Hugh indignantly. 'You attacked me – I was merely defending myself against a man so twisted with grief that he has become unbalanced.' He shrugged out of his captors' grip. 'Eudo, take this man to the infirmary at once, before he does any more harm.'

'You were going to stab him,' accused Alys, outraged by Hugh's lies. 'I saw you.'

'So, it was you who killed Pagan,' said John in wonderment. 'And I believed you the one most likely to be innocent.'

'I *am* innocent!' protested Hugh, outraged.

'He took something from Cynan's box and hid it in his scrip,' said Richard.

'I did nothing of the kind,' said Hugh, slapping away William's eager hand as it reached towards him.

'Show us your scrip, Hugh,' said John reasonably. 'If you are innocent, you have nothing to fear.'

'I will not be subject to such indignities on the claim of a madman,' hissed Hugh. But William had already torn the bag from Hugh's belt, and began to sort through it. Hugh tried to snatch it back, but the other monks moved forward at John's nod and held him again.

'It is a letter from Brother Pascal at L'Aumone Abbey in France, addressed to Pagan,' said William, reading it quickly. He handed it to John. 'It says Hugh was at L'Aumone before he came to Kingswood. When that abbot died, Hugh expected to be appointed in his place, but Pascal says the abbot's end was not natural. Although nothing could be proven, the brethren had their suspicions about Hugh, and he was sent back to England.'

John frowned as he scanned the document. 'I know Pascal; he would never make such an accusation unless he were sure of his ground. The rest of the letter warns Pagan to be on his guard against Hugh.' He handed it to Richard, who felt numb as he read the spidery scrawl of the French monk.

'Lies!' howled Hugh, struggling uselessly. 'I have killed no one! Pagan died from choking on William's sour wine. He was not poisoned!'

'But Pagan *was* poisoned,' said Eudo softly. He held up a Cistercian habit for all to see. 'This is the gown he was wearing when he died – we dressed him in his best one for burial, and I was given this to clean for a lay-brother to wear. But before I washed it, I found this.'

Everyone crowded round to see. There was a splatter of dark spots against the pale material, burned around the edges.

'So?' asked John, not understanding. 'How do these stains prove Pagan was poisoned?'

'I have a virulent substance in my infirmary that leaves stains like this if spilled,' said Eudo. 'I keep it for killing rats. And some of it is missing.'

'Why did you not mention this before?' asked John, appalled. 'You must have seen it was important.'

'Because I only noticed it was gone this morning,' said Eudo. 'I went to check it when I found these stains on Pagan's habit. That the robe is stained with this stuff implies that Pagan had been drinking it – and the splashing suggests to me that he did not do so willingly. Someone forced him to swallow it.'

'Hugh was alone with Pagan after you and I left,' said William thoughtfully. 'There was enough time for him to have forced Pagan to drink the poison and then left him to die.'

'No!' yelled Hugh frantically.

'Yes!' cried William. 'And Hugh has betrayed his murderous inclinations a second time – by trying to kill Richard with a knife.'

'But think!' shouted Hugh, struggling ineffectually against his captors. 'Why would Cynan have this letter? He could not read. Someone planted it there intending to incriminate me!'

'Cynan often acted as messenger because he was a good horseman,' said William. 'I do not find it surprising that he had a letter for the abbot among his possessions. Doubtless you killed Pagan before Cynan could deliver it, and so he kept it for the new abbot. But you, of course, killed Cynan before he delivered anything.'

'Take him away,' said John, regarding Hugh in disgust. Still protesting his innocence, Hugh was dragged from the stable to be locked in a cell until justice could be dispensed. 'It seems I made a grave error for which I will atone for the rest of my life. I hereby appoint William as the new abbot of Kingswood Abbey.'

Once the murderous Hugh was safely under lock and key, Richard and Alys began to relax and even enjoy their forced sojourn at the abbey. The new year was ushered in, bringing with it a warm spell that melted the snow. On the morning they were due to leave, Richard sought out William to thank him for his hospitality.

The door to the abbot's solar was open, and Richard could see William at his desk. He knocked and walked in, startled when William immediately became flustered and scrabbled around to conceal what he had been doing. In his haste, something fell to the floor. It was a quill and the abbot had been using it to write. Richard was puzzled to see William sweating heavily.

'I can just sign my name,' William gabbled in agitation. 'I cannot really write.'

Richard was perplexed, not understanding why the abbot should seek to hide a talent that would prove useful to him in his new position. And then he glimpsed the spidery writing on the document William had been scribing, and the reason for his secrecy became horrifyingly clear.

'*You* wrote the letter purporting to be from Pascal in France,' he said slowly. 'And you put it in Cynan's box so that everyone would assume Hugh killed Pagan.'

'No, I . . .' stuttered William, gazing about him with wild eyes. But he was not an accomplished liar, and he was unable to bluff his way out of his predicament under Richard's unwavering gaze.

'Tell the truth,' said Richard quietly. 'There has been too much deceit of late.'

William's shoulders slumped and he put his head in his hands. When he spoke, his voice was muffled. 'I did it for the abbey. The story about the Abbot of L'Aumone was true, as was the claim that Hugh left there under something of a cloud of suspicion – I had it all from Brother Pascal, who then swore me to secrecy. But you are right – I wrote that letter, not Pascal. I could not bear to think of my beloved abbey in the hands of a man who had murdered twice to satisfy his cravings for power.'

'So Hugh did kill Pagan?' asked Richard.

William nodded. 'The similarities between the deaths of the abbots of L'Aumone and Kingswood are too great to be mere coincidence. I did not know what to do – I promised Pascal I would never reveal what he had told me, but I could not let Hugh remain victorious. I put that letter in Cynan's chest because I thought John of York would investigate Cynan's death – I expected Father John, not Hugh, to discover it.'

'But how did Hugh know to look in Cynan's box for this letter?'

'He did not. He was telling the truth, and was hoping to find a clue to help him solve Cynan's murder, so he could show everyone what a caring and dedicated abbot he would make them. I imagine he was horrified to find Pascal's letter.'

Richard remembered Hugh's sharp gasp of horror and supposed William was right.

'I seldom write,' William continued, holding up his useless limb. 'And when I do, it is a painful and laborious process. But this time, it worked to my advantage: I write so rarely that I knew no one here would recognise my hand – or assume it was me who scribed Pascal's letter if things went wrong.'

'And was it you who attempted to suffocate us in the guest house?' asked Richard, regarding the abbot with disdain. 'I could see no reason why Pagan's killer wanted us dead, given that I had already made my suspicions public. Did you do it so that an attempt on our lives would reflect unfavourably on Hugh's abbotship?'

Richard expected vehement denials, but William simply nodded his head. 'I intended you no serious harm – it was me who raised the alarm that sent Eudo to the door with an axe. But I wanted John to see Hugh was not a good choice as abbot.'

'And you are?' asked Richard in disgust.

He was about to turn on his heel and leave, revolted by William's behaviour, when he saw that John stood in the doorway and had plainly overheard every word. With a cry of anguish, William leapt from his chair. He tried to grab the Visitor's arm to force him to stay so that he could justify his actions, but John was as disgusted by him as was Richard. During a brief struggle, in which William clung to John's sleeve and John thrust him away impatiently, a bottle of ink was knocked over, leaving a dark stain on John's white habit. Furious at the damage to his expensive robe, John stalked from the chamber. Within moments, he was ringing the bell to summon the brothers to the conclave, so that he might appoint yet another abbot to take Pagan's place.

Later that day, Kingswood's latest abbot, Eudo, stood with Richard and John in the courtyard as John prepared to travel back to his own abbey at Tintern. Richard was satisfied with the way matters had resolved: the machinations of Hugh and William to secure power for themselves had been exposed, and the abbey Pagan had nurtured for thirty years was now under the rule of the jovial and tolerant Eudo.

John sat astride a lively horse that pawed at the ground in its eagerness to be away. He had changed his ink-splattered habit for an older one, and frayed cuffs poked incongruously from under his fine fur-lined cloak. He extended a friendly hand to Richard, who was about to grasp it to wish him farewell when a splattering of spots on the sleeve made him start backwards with a gasp of disbelief. Eudo saw the stains at the same time, and he and Richard gazed up at the Visitor in horror as the implications slowly dawned on them.

'Pagan refused to resign the abbotship to allow Hugh to take over,' said John with a careless shrug. 'Of course, now I know Hugh better, I can see exactly why Pagan declined to oblige me. But no matter. It all worked out well in the end.'

'But how could you be the killer?' asked Richard, scarcely believing what he heard. 'Pagan died before you arrived.'

'I was instructed to secure Abbot Pagan's resignation with the minimum of fuss, so I paid him a discreet visit after lauds one night. By coincidence it happened to be the night he choked over his supper and had been escorted to his chamber. Hugh and William were telling you the truth there – no wine or bread took the abbot's life. What killed him was a potion

I stole from the infirmary. It was fortunate for me he had dismissed everyone from his presence, and fortunate for him that his choking fit had left him frightened enough to make his last confession anyway.'

Richard could do nothing but stare at him in speechless dismay.

'Cynan caught me leaving the infirmary. We struck a bargain for his silence, but then I heard he had been spreading rumours that Pagan had not died as naturally as the monks were so keen to have us all believe. It was only a matter of time before he revealed what he had seen, so I killed him. I slit his throat rather than use poison, so that people would think some angry villager had done it.'

'So Hugh is innocent after all?' asked Richard, still bewildered. 'He killed no one?'

John smiled. 'No man is innocent, Richard, and it seems clear to me that Hugh played some role in the untimely death of the Abbot of L'Aumone. William, meanwhile, was guilty of almost suffocating you to have his rival dismissed, not to mention forging a document to have Hugh indicted for slaying Pagan.'

'I have been appointed abbot by a common murderer!' whispered Eudo, his face white with shock.

John gave a sudden grin as he gave his impatient horse its head to set it trotting across the courtyard towards the gate.

'But at least you did not inherit your position from one,' he called merrily over his shoulder as he rode away up the High Street.

Historical note

Kingswood Abbey was founded in 1131 as a Cistercian daughter house of L'Aumone in France, on land donated by Roger, Lord Berkeley. Pagan's name first appears in historical records in about 1149. Perhaps there were others in between, but the next recorded abbot is Hugh, who was deposed by

Visitors from the Cistercian Order in 1180. William, the next abbot, was deposed in 1181 and was succeeded by Eudo. Why Hugh and William were deposed is unclear, although it is more likely because they proved themselves to be inadequate businessmen than because they were involved in the murder of Pagan! John of York was abbot of the splendid Fountains Abbey in Yorkshire 1203–11, one of the biggest and most impressive Cistercian houses in the country.

For some writers distance is as important as closeness. When I walk along the street I don't notice a thing; yet my novels about Egypt are saturated with details remembered from my adolescence in the Middle East. I see them best at a time remove. If that is the kind of writer you are, I suspect you're naturally drawn to historical fictions.

But why history mystery? Obviously because one is interested in history and in mystery. The kind of history I'm interested in is the moments when the course of history might have been otherwise: Russia in the 1890s, for instance, when there was just a chance that a genuinely independent legal system might have taken off, with huge consequences for individual liberty; Egypt in the early 1900s with the rise of nationalism and the British trying to keep a lid on it. The kind of crime that I'm interested in is political crime – I see Gunpowder Plots exploding all about me! These things come together very neatly in the history mystery genre.

All this sounds more than a little earnest, but there's another thing that draws me to the genre: it's a marvellous genre for play. You can play with all the genre conventions: make the hero an anti-hero, locate the story in some extraordinary setting – a medieval monastery, for instance! – relate the story to all kinds of bizarre devices (a Catherine

Wheel, even) and generally lead the reader up the garden path.

Only so far. History mystery is an unusually reader-friendly genre. The writer gets enormous benefit from the reader's involvement in the story through the medium of the plot and the relationship must not be abused. You must not cheat.

One of the things that underpins the relationship is the use of historical details. The details have to be right, which is a matter of research, and they have to seem right, which is a matter of narrative skill. Ellis Peters understood both these things. She knew, too, how to use the details to create an entire believable world, which is in many respects the supreme requirement of the genre.

She did it by story. Care to read five hundred pages on the monastic rule? Gee, well, thanks; tomorrow, maybe? But if it's: 'There was this juicy murder, see, and this weird old monk' – well, now you're talking!

Michael Pearce

The Mamur Zapt and the
Catherine Wheel

Michael Pearce

'Sheep,' said the official.

'Goats,' said Owen.

The official drummed his fingers on the table.

'His Highness specifically mentioned sheep.'

'There aren't any sheep over there. What would they feed on? It's all desert.'

The official looked worried.

'His Highness had in mind a traditional Bedouin feast.'

'Eyeballs?'

'I beg your pardon?'

'That's what they eat.'

'No, I don't think so. A token one, perhaps. Or perhaps an imitation one. Sweet.' The official hesitated. 'I think, actually, His Highness would prefer lobster.'

'The Bedouin don't eat lobster.'

'That evening, perhaps?' said the official hopefully. 'At the monastery?'

When the trip to the monastery had been mooted, Owen had been doubtful.

'What does he want?' he had asked the Consul-General's aide-de-camp.

'To show goodwill to his Christian subjects.'

'Couldn't he show it back at home? In Cairo?'

This was a thought which was possibly occurring to His Highness himself as the cars toiled upwards through the rocks and crags of the Sinai peninsula. The cliffs trapped the heat and even with the car windows open and the resultant breeze the temperature was over 130. They had known it would be, of course, which was why they had planned a stop after passing through the Valley of the Turquoises and a picnic lunch (His Highness' 'Bedouin feast') in what the map said was the only oasis they would encounter on the journey.

The official peered through the window.

'Surely we should be there by now?'

'Why don't we stop here for a minute or two?' suggested Owen. 'Give the cars a chance to cool off. I'll take one of the smaller ones and go on ahead.'

The track, designed for camels not cars, ran precariously across the side of a cliff, made one or two impossible hairpin turns and then dipped down into an unlikely valley.

Which was full of sheep.

'What the hell are you doing here?' said Owen.

'We're on our way.'

It transpired that they were driving them from somewhere in the Hedjaz to the markets in Cairo.

After what he had said to the official, Owen did not like to find life contradicting him.

'Listen,' he said, 'in two minutes His Highness gets here. He is great and he is mighty and he has an enormous appetite. Any sheep found on this spot when he arrives will be seized and eaten.'

One minute later the valley was empty; except for some tents which were being hurriedly struck, a passing merchant with some camels and an unusually unhappy face, and a stunningly pretty girl standing at the entrance of one of the tents. Unlike the girls of the city, desert girls went unveiled and had a name for being bold. Even so, he was surprised to find that this one seemed almost, well, very nearly as if she was giving him the wink.

As evening approached, they turned left up a narrowing wadi and there ahead of them were the fortress-like grey walls and pointed cypresses of St Catherine's Monastery. They were not there yet, however. First they had to negotiate a steep, narrow ramp with a chillingly precipitous drop on one side. At this point, His Highness prudently got out and walked, leaving his harem, however, which he had insisted on having with him, in the cars. As the cars struggled, one, indeed, rolling back to the very bottom of the track, cries of alarm came from inside. Eventually, however, their attempts were successful and they arrived at the great entrance door of the monastery and clanged the old bell high up on the wall.

That evening they dined in the old refectory around the magnificent long table carved at intervals with the coats of arms of crusaders who had visited the spot centuries before. The food was somewhat plain for His Highness' taste but with Arab courtesy he concealed his disappointment and talked politely with the Abbot about the history of the monastery.

'Founded,' said the Abbot, 'in the sixth century by the Emperor Justinian in honour of St Catherine. You perhaps know the story?'

'Not sure I do.'

'Well, she was the young martyr who, according to tradition, stood up bravely to the Emperor Maximus; so bravely, in fact, that he ordered her to die bound to a wheel.'

His Highness was impressed.

'Drastic,' he said, 'but original. And this was how the monastery originally began?'

The Abbot nodded.

'A lesson to us all,' murmured His Highness.

They were led through thick-walled passages under low heavy

archways, round buttresses and past nail-studded ancient doors, until they emerged on to a verandah running round an internal courtyard. A number of small, whitewashed rooms, each with an iron bedstead, gave off the verandah. It was here that the visitors were to be housed. There were not enough rooms for all the party and Owen agreed to take his bedroll up on to the roof, which he might well have done in any case had he been still in Cairo. At this time of year the nights were so hot that you were glad of any chance of air. Here in the mountains, however, they were some six or seven thousand feet above sea level and the night was distinctly cold. He found it hard to get to sleep; and it was not made any easier by the hubbub in the rooms below him. How they did chatter! Eventually, however, the harem ladies got to sleep and soon afterwards he himself drifted off into an uneasy doze.

About halfway through the night he woke up sharply. The sky was frosty clear and the moon lit up the roofs and the turreted battlements as if it was day. He thought he heard a noise over towards the outer wall and sat up in his blankets to see what had made it.

Suddenly, he saw to his amazement what looked like a large fiery wheel rolling across the roofs. It came to the battlements, rocked and then plunged on straight over the wall. A moment later he heard it crashing down the slopes on the other side.

He leapt to his feet and ran across. By the time he got there the crashing had stopped and all was still again. The cliffs dropped away steeply at that point and even in the moonlight it wasn't possible to see where the wheel had fallen.

If it had fallen; and if, indeed, there had been a wheel at all. He looked around him. Everywhere was quiet. He was alone on the roof. It wasn't like him to imagine things, but . . .

He went back to his blankets. It wasn't like him to imagine things but what other explanation was there? Wheels, fiery or otherwise, did not normally run along roofs, not in Cairo, at any rate, and he could hardly feel that St Catherine's was different.

Perhaps it *had* been a mistake to go for that third bottle

of Montrachet. He had been persuaded into it by Prince Neri. He had been sitting next to the Prince, one of His Highness' many illegitimate sons, at dinner and the Prince, after surveying the prospects gloomily, had sent for his own refreshment. His Highness himself, a strict Muslim, at least in public, did not drink and although the monastery was able on occasion to offer wine to its guests, it was a thin and watery wine made locally. The Prince's own supplies were decidedly superior and he and Owen had passed a pleasant evening together. That third bottle, however, may well have been a mistake. Yes, decided Owen, drawing his blankets around him on the cold roof, almost certainly a mistake.

The cold awoke him early: either that or those bloody women again down below. He could hear the shrill voices raised once more in protest. You'd think His Highness would do something about it, send his harem master in, perhaps, that big Nubian eunuch, Zubair, or whatever his name was. Probably he did, for the noise stilled suddenly.

It was not yet sunrise, just the grey, indeterminable period before dawn, but he knew he would not get back to sleep again. He rolled up his mattress and went down to the kitchen to get some hot water for a shave. Already the kitchen was full of dark-eyed, sallow-skinned men who looked like Arabs but were not. The monastery servants were descended from some Wallachians who had been sent there centuries before from Rumania. They had lost their language and now spoke only Arabic; curiously, too, – even more curiously, considering where they were – they had lost their religion and now professed to be Muslims. One of them poured him some water and he shaved in a corner.

Afterwards, he went out into the courtyard. It was still in shadow but then, almost as he stepped into it, the shadows parted and a patch of sun appeared. Virtually at the same moment the muezzin began his call from somewhere high up on the roofs about him.

187

The muezzin? In a Christian monastery?

And then he realised. There before him, right next to the small church, was an even smaller mosque, there for the benefit of the monastery's Muslim servants. It was oddly comforting for Owen to see it there, co-existing amicably in the heart of one of Christianity's oldest places; for Owen was the Mamur Zapt, the man responsible for maintaining peace and order in Egypt, including the Sinai peninsula, and much of the threat to that order came from the tensions among the various ethnic and religious groups that made up the Khedive's subjects: Arabs and Copts, Italians and Nubians, Greeks and Jews, Christians and Muslims.

Soon, men began filing into the mosque, not just the monastery's servants but the visiting party, including His Highness. They began prostrating themselves.

Later, of course, there were the ordinary Christian services of the monastery, and it was not until mid-morning that the visitors were able to be shown the library and the monastery's treasures. It was an unromantic room lined with yellow pitchpine cupboards and chests smelling of old books, sandalwood and something else besides which Owen was not able to place. It was for all the world as if someone had been in the room wearing expensive Parisian perfume. Owen was no expert on monks but he thought this unlikely.

One by one the cupboards and chests were unlocked and the beautiful rare objects brought out and placed before them: marvellous old illustrated manuscripts, jewelled Bibles and rich icons, many of them the gifts of long-dead Tsars and Tsarinas, for the affinities of this monastery were with the Eastern, not the Western, church.

As they were leaving, Prince Neri came up to Owen and put his hand on his arm. 'My dear fellow,' he said.

'Yes?'

'There's been a spot of bother. At least, I think so. The fact is –' he hesitated – 'one of the women has disappeared.'

*   *   *

But when Owen went to the senior official, the man denied it.

'No, I don't think so.'

Politely, he consulted His Highness.

'One of the women? No, I don't think so. Though with such numbers it is easy to make a mistake. Go and count them.'

The official returned with the master of the harem.

'Anyone missing, Zubair?'

'There'd better not be,' said Zubair.

'Well, there you are, old chap,' said His Highness, turning to Owen. 'False report, apparently.'

Prince Neri, however, stuck doggedly to his guns, though he declined to be publicly quoted on the matter.

'But, my dear Prince,' remonstrated Owen, 'how do you expect me to proceed? If His Highness denies that anyone from his harem is missing, I can hardly challenge that statement without some independent evidence.'

'I'll bring you some,' promised the Prince.

He arranged a clandestine meeting with one of the ladies of the harem.

Clandestine it had to be; for her sake as well as for Owen's. It took place that afternoon when the heat, pressing down on the monastery like a great iron fist, had driven everyone else indoors. Eccentric Englishmen, however, might still wander, and Owen chose to wander, like others more poetically inclined before him, in a monastery garden. It was a surprising touch of green among the grey stone and the red rocks, not just one green but several, the dark green of cypresses, the pastel of olives, the lovely fresh green of almond trees just out of their spring foliage.

In a secluded corner of the garden there was a little white house and it was here that they had arranged to meet. Owen went in quietly, and received something of a shock. All around were rows and rows of human bones, neatly arranged, skulls, legs, arms all tidily together. It was, in

189

fact, the monastery's ossuary. Burial spaces were scarce in the hard red rock so after a while the body was exhumed and the remains placed in this quiet resting place.

Owen edged the door to behind him – and then received another shock. Just behind the door was a skeleton sitting on a chair. It was dressed in a monk's habit and held a rosary between its fingers.

Owen had not been there long when he heard quick, light feet approaching. The door was pushed open cautiously and a slim, veiled form slipped in.

'Jesus!' said an unmistakably Irish voice, as the woman caught sight of the skeleton.

Owen stepped forward. 'It's all right,' he said. 'It's just an ossuary.'

'Where they collect the bones?' The figure gave itself a shake. 'Well, they might have tucked it away somewhere!' Green eyes scrutinised Owen. 'You're the Mamur Zapt, are you?'

Owen nodded.

'Well, look, I can't stay long. That great beast has eyes everywhere. That's how he got to know about Nuala.'

'Nuala's the one who's disappeared?'

'That's right. He came in last night and tried to beat it out of her but the others wouldn't let him. Whether he came in again later, I don't know, but this morning she wasn't there.'

'Could she be somewhere else? In the women's quarters, I mean?'

'Not in the women's quarters,' said the woman positively.

'His Highness?'

She shook her head.

'When he wants to do his business, he comes into the harem.'

That was all she had to tell him.

He asked a few more questions but all the time she was looking round nervously.

190

'I must go,' she said.

'Okay.' He held the door open for her.

But then she hung back.

'Nuala was nice,' she said. 'I hate to think that something has happened to her.'

'Maybe nothing has happened to her.'

She shook her head definitely.

'Oh, no,' she said. 'It's happened to her, all right. They never let you get away with anything like that.'

'Like what?'

She regarded him coolly.

'What do you think?' she said.

'Prince Neri?'

'There are lots who keep trying,' she said, 'but they never get anywhere.'

A little pink bird hopped in at the doorway. From its curiosity and its colouring, Owen thought for a moment that it might be a robin, but it was pink, not red, the pink of the surrounding rocks, and there were no robins here. It must be the Sinai rose finch. It stood there for a few seconds looking dubiously up at the skeleton, then flew away.

'It's all right for some,' said the woman from the harem.

But how would one dispose of a body here? Owen asked himself, as he wandered back through the garden. On the evidence of the ossuary, even the monks who lived here found that difficult. Bury it? But the soil here was thin and one soon encountered the rock. What kept the garden green was not the depth of its soil but the water running through it. A well, then? But wells here were important and one did not idly throw things in them. Not bury, then, but somehow hide? There were plenty of rarely used rooms here, it was true, with thick doors and heavy bolts: but wherever a body was put, above ground, in this heat it would soon declare itself. How far, how quickly, would a smell in a place like the monastery declare itself? To reason thus was perhaps to reason too curiously; but it would not be long. So what would one do if one had an unwanted body to dispose of? Pitch it over the wall, probably, as one would, in Egypt, any other old rubbish. Pitch it over the wall?

The drop was steep and precipitous and Owen was certainly not going down without a rope. He got one of the gardeners to lend him one. He fastened it securely to a rock, described in impressive detail to the onlookers the mutilations they would suffer should the rope be interfered with, and lowered himself down the slope.

The rock was hard and grey and there was no vegetation to soften it. When he put his hand on it, it was so hot that it almost burned his palm. For the most part he did not need to do that. He was able to lean outward from the face and use his feet. The problem, he knew, would be coming back.

It was a problem that loomed larger as the descent went on. From the top the drop had seemed huge; close to it was even huger. He stopped to rest. A yard away a small rock on the cliff-face moved suddenly; moved, and declared itself to be not a rock after all but a lizard, so protectively coloured that he had taken it for the stone it lay on.

After a moment or two he scrambled on, taking care not to look down: and so was astonished when he at last reached the ground to find a young woman sitting there waiting patiently for him.

'You're not – you can't be!'

She was not. For there, a few feet away, was Nuala herself, or the remains of her, tied to what was left of the wheel, scorched black, probably unrecognisably, by the flame.

'Why did they have to burn her?' complained the lady sitting opposite him. 'It left nothing worth taking.'

There was something familiar about her; familiar in all senses. Then he remembered: as familiar as she had struck him the day before when he had seen her looking out of the tent at the shepherd's encampment.

'What's your name?'

'Dalila,' she said.

'How did you get here?'

She pointed to a broad, easy track which came round the bottom of the mountain.

'Why did you come down the cliff?' she asked curiously.

'Because I was following her,' said Owen.

The girl nodded.

'That must be because you are the Mamur Zapt,' she said. 'The men were talking about you.'

'Have you taken anything from the body?'

'Nothing to take.'

'How did you know it was there?'

'One of the watchmen saw it. He said it was like a fiery angel descending. He ran back to the camp in fear. Then everyone was afraid, for they thought God must have sent it as a sign. But I did not think God had sent it, for why would he want to send anything to shit like that lot? So I said we should go and see what it was. But no one would come with me. And now really, I'm sorry I came, for there was nothing worth taking. Except you, perhaps,' she said, considering.

'Well, thank you. However, not just now. For I have to get the body back up the cliff. And how the hell I'm going to do that, I don't know.'

'You could ask the Christians to lend you their basket,' suggested Dalila.

'Basket?'

'The one they use to lower bread.'

Owen remembered seeing it now, attached to the top of the wall: a basket large enough not just to lower bread in but also to raise people in time of emergency. And wasn't there some kind of windlass?

'Thanks, Dalila. Your ideas fly far ahead of those of humble men.'

'I've always thought so.'

She agreed to show him a path up to the monastery from

the track she had come on. At the last moment before setting out, however, she lingered.

'How about tonight, then? Where do you sleep?'

'On the roof, as it happens. However—'

'That's all right, then.'

'All right?'

But Dalila had already set out. As she left she gave one last glance over her shoulder at the burnt remains adhering to the wheel and shook her head.

'The things these Christians do,' she said, 'when they've worn you out and got no further use for you!'

'Zubair,' said His Highness severely, 'I am displeased with you; you can't count.'

Zubair said he was sorry about that but that sometimes the numbers were a bit big for him.

'Well, I know, but you should have taken more care. You've caused the Mamur Zapt a lot of trouble.'

The eunuch said he was sorry about that, too. His expression, however, conveyed the reverse. Probably thinking about wheels, thought Owen.

'Your Highness, I'm afraid it's not just a question of counting: it's a question of murder.'

'Murder? Surely not. Suicide, perhaps.'

'Suicide? Tie yourself to a wheel, set fire to yourself, and then roll yourself over the top of a wall?'

'There's no length some of those girls won't go to,' said His Highness fondly, 'for kicks.'

'You're going to have to tell me more,' said Owen.

'I don't know any more,' said Prince Neri hopelessly. 'She was there, then she was not.'

'You knew her, of course.'

'I knew her before she went into his harem.'

'She was a wife? Or a concubine?'

'Concubine. I saw her before she was purchased.'

'Where was that?'

'In the slave market of Istanbul. She was very beautiful. Many men wanted to possess her and would have paid a high price. I would have paid a high price, too, anything! Then one day she was taken out of the market and I learned – I learned it was him. I could not give her up. It was what she wanted too, I am sure. He was too old for her. She wanted youth, love. I would have given it to her.'

'Did you offer it her? After she had gone into his harem?'

'I never got the chance. His eunuch was always there. Oh, I bribed slaves, I bribed the other women and sent messages. But I never knew whether they got there. Some of them I think he must have intercepted, for he often upbraided her. As he did that night.'

'You had sent her a message?'

'Yes. I thought it was my chance. They were in several rooms, you see, there were so many of them, and it was hard for Zubair to keep an eye on them. I arranged to meet her.'

'Where?'

'In the library. I thought that no one would be there at that time of night. But someone was there. I saw a candle. I couldn't think what to do. I said to myself: suppose she comes? So I hung about outside the door.'

'And did she come?'

'No. I stayed there until a man came out. It was one of those servants, you know, the Wallachians. He left the candle lit, and I thought that perhaps there was a monk still there whom he had been seeing. So when he went away, I did not go in but stayed outside the door, behind an arch. For I thought she might still come. But then I heard the Wallachian coming back and ran to the other end of the corridor and hid there, for I thought that perhaps he had come to fetch his master and I did not know which way they would go when they came out. But perhaps there was no master, for this time, when he left, he blew the candle out and all was dark and I could hear him sighing as he went away along the corridor.'

'And did you then abandon your watch?'

'No, I stayed there. I thought she might come again.'

'Again?'

The Prince hesitated.

'When I put my head in at the library I smelled a strong smell of perfume. And I thought that perhaps it was hers and that she had been and that perhaps hearing footsteps, the servant maybe, she had fled. I thought that if that was so, perhaps she could come back.'

'And did she?'

'No. I stayed there until it was nearly dawn, hoping that she would come. And I thought, perhaps she has not been here at all, perhaps she does not care for me. But then, as I went back to my room, I heard the women crying and thought that perhaps she *had* tried to come but that Zubair had caught her.'

'O, Zubair,' said Owen, 'master of the harem. Do your duties hang heavy on you or do they hang light?'

'They hang light; or perhaps they are heavy and I carry them lightly.'

'Have they weighed more heavily since you came to this place?'

'Why should they? A place is just a place.'

'But when the place is different, the ordering of things is different.'

'That is true.'

'And perhaps people themselves do differently.'

'It is possible. What are you thinking of?'

'That woman. Did she do differently that night?'

'She must have done.'

'You are the all-seeing eye, Zubair. Did you know she had done differently?'

The big eunuch hesitated.

'Or would, perhaps, have done differently had she been able? Had you not prevented her, Zubair?'

'I did not see her that night. Or, rather, I did see her when she went to her chamber, for the ordering was different that night, as you say, and I wanted to be sure that all were safely in their appointed places. I marked her when she went in. But after that I neither saw her nor spoke with her nor had anything to do with her.'

'And in the morning you found that she had gone?'

'I heard the women. And I thought, this is a fine to-do when we are guests in another's house, and went in to admonish them. And then they told me she was not there.'

'So what did you do?'

Zubair looked him in the face. 'I went to the room of Prince Neri.'

'And found him?'

'That is so.'

'But not the girl?'

'Not the girl.' The eunuch hesitated. 'Effendi, the Prince had but newly returned to his room. And therefore I think it is to him that you must address your questions if you wish to find out what happened to the girl after she left her room that night.'

A traveller had come into the courtyard and was making his camel kneel. As he was swinging his leg over the horn of the saddle, he caught sight of Owen; and after he had dismounted he came across to him.

'Effendi, this is a fortunate meeting.'

'How so?'

'Effendi, I need help.'

'Why should that be?'

The man squatted down. Owen fell into a squat beside him. This was clearly going to be a long story.

'Effendi, I saw you the other day when you rode into that den of thieves and bade them remove their sheep.'

'Ah, yes. And I saw you.' He recognised him now. It was

the merchant who had been there with his camels among the tents. 'What help is it you need?'

'Effendi, you will be returning soon to the place from which you come. I would like to return with you.'

'But we travel by car and you by camel.'

'Effendi, I would leave my camels. They could be fetched later. Just let me come with you in your car.'

'This is a caravan of consequence, friend.'

'I can see that,' said the merchant, with a worried look. 'My need is great, however. Even the smallest place would do.'

'Why is your need so great?'

The man hesitated. 'Effendi, while I was with those villains, I was a fool. There was a girl and she tempted me into her tent. I went willingly, because I thought: the Bedouin women are free with their favours. But afterwards her men came and said: "You have defiled a virgin and must pay the consequences."'

'I think it unlikely that she was a virgin.'

'So do I. But they said: "Either you must marry her or you must pay her family compensation."'

'Pay; that would be wisest.'

'I would, Effendi, but – but I have not yet made my trade.'

'What is your trade?'

'I am a traveller in turquoises.'

'A traveller in turquoises? In these mountains?'

He remembered now. Hadn't there once been workings somewhere over here? But that was long ago, in the Pharaohs' time. Surely they weren't still being worked! And, anyway, now he came to think of it, the Valley of the Turquoises lay behind them, on the route back. What was the merchant doing here?

'What brings you this far, then, my friend?'

'I come to pick up a package for another merchant.'

It was quite possible. Merchants were always doing each other favours in this way.

'So what is it you seek?'

'To ride with you. So that those bad men will not seize me and do evil things to me.'

'Well, I will see what I can do. But if you flee, having made no settlement with these people, you will not be able to travel in these mountains again.'

'That I can endure,' said the merchant, looking round him at the hard, red mountains that rose on every side.

Although he had taken the precaution of acquiring an extra blanket, it was still cold up on the roof. He was sleeping lightly and that was why, perhaps, he heard the footsteps. They were very faint, almost inaudible, the sort made by bare feet. Whoever it was paused uncertainly and then made straight towards him. As they bent over him, he reached up and caught them by arm and neck, twisted and threw them down on the roof beside him.

'Oh!' said Dalila.

Owen released her. 'What the hell are you doing here?'

'Coming to see you,' said Dalila, creeping under the blankets beside him.

Later, warm now and with Dalila's soft body snuggled against him, he lay on his back and looked up at the stars. The turrets were dark against the sky, their edges, though, clear in the moonlight.

'How did you get up here?' demanded Owen.

'Came up in the basket.'

There was something wrong with the security arrangements in this place.

'I heard your steps,' said Owen.

'I didn't come up here straight away,' said Dalila. 'I thought I would take a look around. And do you know what I saw? That bastard of a merchant!'

'Yes, he arrived this afternoon. He wants me to give him a lift. Apparently there was a woman who . . . Dalila! It wasn't you?'

199

'I may have had something to do with it,' she said modestly.

'He'll try to get away without marrying you!' Owen warned.

'Marrying?' said Dalila, aghast. 'Who said anything about marrying?'

'You did. Or . . . at least, your men did. Marry or pay, they said.'

'Oh, that's all right. He'll pay, won't he?'

'He says he hasn't got any money.'

'That old money-bags?' Dalila scoffed. 'He's got plenty. We know him of old up here in the mountains. Always up to something. And he was up to something just now, I'll be bound. Meeting someone in the middle of the night? Being slipped a package? That's something he wanted to keep quiet, you can bet!'

'What's this about a package?'

'Someone was giving him one.'

'A monk?'

'No, one of those creepy servants they have here. They look like Arabs but they're not Arabs. Wouldn't trust them an inch. Nor him, either,' said Dalila darkly, 'that bastard of a merchant.'

'So, friend, you have made your trade, then?' said Owen.

'Trade?' The merchant looked startled. 'No, not yet.'

'Picked up the package, then.'

'Package?'

'You were going to pick up a package for another merchant, remember?'

'Oh, yes.'

'Were you thinking of bringing it with you? When you leave with us?'

'I was.'

'It is a package of importance, then?'

'Not very. A few knick-knacks.'

'It seems a long way to come for a few knick-knacks.

200

Perhaps it does not contain knick-knacks at all but something more precious? Turquoises, perhaps, for are you not a traveller in turquoises?'

'It does not contain turquoises.'

'What does it contain? I would like to see.' Owen waited. 'I would need to see,' he pressed gently, 'before I could allow such a package to come on our caravan.'

'Perhaps I will not come with you after all,' said the merchant.

'No? That is a pity. For I noted this morning that your enemies await you outside the gate, and ours is a strong caravan. There will not be another such.'

The merchant began to perspire. 'The package is of no consequence,' he muttered.

'Then let me see it. Let me see it,' repeated Owen, his voice hardening. 'It is the Mamur Zapt who speaks.'

Unwillingly, the merchant unwrapped the parcel. Inside was a beautiful old chalice, its rim sparkling with precious stones.

'Knick-knacks?'

The merchant swallowed. 'I had to say that,' he pleaded, 'for I was bound to silence.'

'Who bound you?'

'Those who gave me the package.'

'And who were they?'

'The . . . the . . .' The man had dried up. 'The monks,' he said, with sudden inspiration. 'Yes, it was the monks who gave it to me.'

'Beware!' warned Owen. 'For I shall ask them.'

'They will not say. For it is a private matter, you see, between the monastery and Great Ones in Cairo, and they would not wish it to be known.'

'And so they gave it to you,' said Owen sceptically, 'in secret, at dead of night?'

'So that no one would know,' insisted the merchant.

'Tell me: who put it into your hands?'

'The monks, I do not know—'

'His name!' said Owen.

'So tell me, Robert,' said Owen, 'where was the chalice kept?'

The brown eyes looked at him unfalteringly.

'In the library. That is where they keep their treasures.'

'I have seen the library. Are not the treasures kept in strong chests?'

'They are.'

'And are not the chests locked?'

'They are; but I have a key. I took an impression once in beeswax and gave it to the merchant so that he could have a key made.'

'You have, then, stolen from the monastery before?'

The servant was silent.

'No matter. There are other things I wish to know. When, for instance, was it that you went to the library and took the chalice?'

The man closed his lips firmly.

'I can tell you,' said Owen: 'the night before last. It is useless to try to hide these things, for you were seen.'

The man shrugged. 'Well, then, I was seen.' He seemed shaken, however.

'Tell me,' said Owen.

'It was the night His Highness came,' said the man reluctantly. 'I thought it would be a good time, for in his arrival there was much confusion.'

'You went to the library. It was dark in there and you lit a candle. You opened the chest and took out the chalice. Now,' said Owen, 'what I want to know is this: at what point did the girl come?'

'Girl?'

'Did she come when you were taking out the chalice?'

'How did you know there was a girl there?'

'You were seen and she was smelt.'

Robert was silent for a long time.

'Yes,' he said at last. 'It was the smell. She smelt of rosewater and musk. It disturbed me.'

'She was expecting to see someone else,' said Owen. 'Instead, she saw you.'

'She was surprised, and would have cried out, but I took her by the throat. She pleaded with me, she thought I was a Christian. "I am no Christian," I said, "and I know what to do with sluts."'

'Especially when they catch you stealing.'

Robert shrugged. 'A man has to live,' he said.

'So does a girl. Why did you bind her to the wheel?'

'I could not think what to do with her. There is no place in the monastery where a body could stay for long undetected. There is no ground in which to bury. If I threw her over the wall they would find her the next morning.'

He looked down at his feet.

'It was something she said. "This is a holy place," she said, "if you do wrong in it, God will punish you the harder." "You did not choose this place," I said, "and nor did I."'

'She said: "It is named after a holy woman and if you do a woman a wrong in it, the place itself will take revenge." But I hardened my heart, for if I let her go, I would be discovered. And then the thought came to me: to bind her to a wheel, as they had Saint Catherine. For would not the body roll further, even; perhaps over the cliff? And if they see it, will they not think it a miracle and that it is God's work and not man's?'

'A very happy outcome!' said His Highness warmly, as they were driving back through the mountains the next day. 'To restore the chalice to them even before they had realised it was missing – that's what I call service! It just shows how I look after my Christian subjects.'

Owen turned round and peered back at the caravan behind them. The merchant was not in it. His Highness had had him flogged, confiscated his camels and turned him loose to find his own way back through the mountains on foot. If he could; and if his acquaintances would let him.

Dalila was not much interested.

'See you in Cairo!' she said to Owen.

Owen was pretty sure she would.

But where was Robert? Owen had ordered him to be punished and put in one of the cars.

'Oh, he's back at the monastery,' said His Highness, 'with Zubair. Zubair has one or two little things to attend to. Something to do with wheels. I believe.'

Edith Pargeter was always most generous in encouraging newer writers and her kind encomiums appeared on the back covers of many early books of authors who have now established themselves in the historical mystery field.

In her spirit, I felt it would be only fitting to feature a first-time writer in this anthology, and a competition was organised with *Crime Time* magazine. David Howard's 'The Great Brogonye' is the winning entry as selected by the editors of *Crime Time* and myself, and we hope it will prove the beginning of a new mystery career. The runner-up, which we sadly do not have space for here, was Christina Lynn Vaun's 'Let Them Swing'.

I am confident Ellis Peters would have approved of both.

(Maxim Jakubowski)

The Great Brogonye

David Howard

Above the vineyards the grey walls of the castle rose to announce that the Brogonye family had risen to prominence in the town.

I was Wilhelm Brogonye. No longer a prominent member of the family, and tomorrow I would be even less prominent.

I would be hung by the neck. Dead.

Marietzburg is a small Bavarian town of little importance. The nearby Marietzburg Falls were spectacular, it is true. But they were not enough to persuade most people to remain in the town. So in 1904 my brother and I left.

Ralf was destined for America. A part mythological country which was pronounced with a breathless awe by the inhabitants of Marietzburg.

A magic land where everything was possible they said.

'And what of you, Wilhelm,' they asked, 'where are you bound for?'

'India,' I replied. Silence. 'They have need of doctors out there,' I added by means of further explanation, but I could see that I had already lost their attention.

'America,' they muttered. 'No one has ever gone to America before.'

America was like Marietzburg, but much, much better.

It wasn't long before news about Ralf began to reach Marietzburg. He'd joined a circus troop travelling the southern States. Found himself a wife in a town called Cincinnati. And ended every circus performance by mesmerising audiences with what he called 'a death-defying high-wire act'.

'And what news of Wilhelm?' they asked my father in the market square of Marietzburg.

'Oh, he's still in Calcutta,' my father replied. 'Helping the sick. He's a good boy.'

Yes, they agreed, Wilhelm was a good boy.

But America, what a place.

Ralf's letters home now had a Manhattan postmark. He'd left the circus, and his wife. Hadn't there been children too?

Me? I hardly wrote at all. After all, what interest were malaria, typhus and leprosy compared to the temptations of America?

Soon Ralf's letters began to be accompanied by clippings from the New York newspapers.

'That can't be my son,' my father exclaimed, pulling the front page of the *New York Times* from the latest envelope. 'It's not true, Mimi, tell me this is impossible.' He pushed the newspaper across to my mother's side of the table.

She took one look at it and muttered something incomprehensible in Russian, her native tongue.

'Heaven help us,' she declared moments later, 'he's even calling himself The Great Brogonye.'

It wasn't often the people of Marietzburg were lost for words, but when the newspaper photograph was passed among them . . .

Well. A circus act they could understand, but this! A high-wire walk between two New York skyscrapers. It was madness. Whatever next, they said.

*   *   *

207

Next was an even higher walk between two different buildings; followed by a walk across some famous falls; and an escape from a sealed metal coffin thrown into the Hudson River.

When The Great Brogonye was presented before President Theodore Roosevelt, the photograph even reached the front page of Bavaria's own newspaper. Now the people of Marietzburg could read for themselves about the latest exploits of The Great Brogonye.

But their eyes would always alight on the same word.

That word was 'millionaire'.

'And what news of Wilhelm?'

The question was asked less and less in the narrow cobbled streets of Marietzburg.

And not often in the castle above the town either.

Here, I must partly share the blame.

I see that now.

My journeys home – and they were few – were not without motive.

The Mission in Calcutta was not thriving.

At first my father was generous. But as my requests grew larger his excuses grew ever more fanciful.

He had to buy more vineyards to expand the business; the castle needed expensive repairs; the river barges were old and must be replaced.

'Why don't you ask The Great Brogonye?' he suggested dismissively one night on the eve of my return to India.

It was only then that I realised that to my father Ralf no longer existed.

He was now The Great Brogonye.

At first my letters to Ralf received no reply. The situation at the Mission was now becoming critical. We had run out of quinine and were short of many other essential drugs.

On top of that the Mission building itself was in disrepair.

I now spent several hours a day engaged in repairs when I should have been inside caring for the sick.

In despair, I wrote again to my father. It was nothing less than a begging letter and didn't deserve the generous response it received. A small cheque. Enough to keep the Mission going for a month at least.

But from Ralf there was nothing.

Then one day a letter arrived via my bank in Calcutta. Noting the New York postmark, I ripped the pages from the envelope and hastily read the contents.

Dear Wilhelm,

Please do not send any more of your unpleasant letters. I receive many requests for money every week and cannot possibly choose between one so-called charitable institution and another.

In such circumstances I have refused all such requests, and must also decline yours.

Ralf. The Great Brogonye.

I could scarcely believe what I had just read and can remember very little of the events of the next week.

My anger was only broken by an unexpected letter from my father.

Ralf had been injured in an accident. He knew few details, except that one of Ralf's performances had gone badly wrong and he was now in hospital with extensive burns to his face and arms.

Although I was shocked by the news, my lack of compassion for Ralf was only slightly less surprising than the knowledge that my parents were going to visit him in New York – it was the first time I had ever known them leave Germany.

The plans were already set. They would travel to France where they would board a new ship of the British White Star Line.

That ship was the SS *Titanic*.

The news of the *Titanic* took several weeks to reach Calcutta. By that time Ralf, not as critically injured as it first appeared – although his facial injuries were such that he now wore his performing mask in public – had already returned to the family castle at Marietzburg.

In my absence, Ralf had quickly assumed control of the family wine business. A situation which soon became official in the eyes of the state of Bavaria.

I was in bed with malaria when a copy of my parents' will arrived from the family lawyer.

For a man fighting for his life, the news of his disinheritance is at first laughably unimportant. It was only when the fever broke that the depths of betrayal began to darken my already weakened thoughts.

I cannot now blame the malaria for the plan that began to congeal in my mind.

I've heard it said that we all have a darker side. It was then that I discovered mine.

The next day I was up early. I felt curiously elated as I greeted my staff at the Mission, who were as surprised to see me as they were curious about my renewed vigour.

Hope is as infectious as any disease, and hope is what I now had for the survival of the Mission. But first I had to put several events in motion.

That night I wrote a letter home to Bavaria. The following morning I asked Gitsa, one of my nurses, to write out two copies of the letter and address them to my brother in Marietzburg and our family lawyer in the nearby town of Umsdorf. Gitsa, who speaks no German, diligently reproduced the letters in her own hand and gave them to me without question.

Not many of us have the chance to announce our own deaths, but that's what I did when I posted those two envelopes. Although I hated leaving the Mission in the care of my staff, I could see no other alternative.

I now worked my passage by ship to Venice, and then made my way north through the Swiss valleys until I reached Bavaria. I avoided all towns where I had acquaintances, although with my hair now drooping over my shoulders, and a beard which wouldn't shame a pirate, I hardly even recognised myself.

I took lodgings in Umsdorf, a town half a mile downstream from the Marietzburg Falls. Although Umsdorf was the last navigable town on the river, some barges travelled further upstream to a small private quay my father had built for his business just below the falls.

It was here that I now passed on my way into Marietzburg.

Darkness had fallen some hours before but as I entered the market square I still kept my face to the cobbled ground. I had many friends in the town but I quickly grew confident that my disguise together with my absence from the town for most of the previous eight years would protect my identity.

For my purposes, it was the ideal time to return to Marietzburg. The grape harvest had brought the usual ragbag of workers into the town, and soon I was sitting between a pair of them in an ill-lit tavern.

I was seeking confirmation of what I had first heard in Calcutta and I quickly guided the conversation in the direction of the castle and its new occupant.

'The Great Brogonye is not so great now, my friend,' one of them declared, lifting the beer I had just bought him to his rugged, sunburnt face. 'Even Rudi here would have more luck with women if he wore a mask all the time like The Great Brogonye.' He laughed, waved his hand in the general direction of his companion, and spilled beer down his beard. Noting the surprise on my face he now turned fully to me.

'Where have you been not to hear all about The Great Brogonye,' he muttered disdainfully. 'Maybe he's worried if he takes his mask off he'll crack a mirror, eh . . . and now this, more foolishness.' He pointed towards a large placard barely visible through the grimy window of the tavern.

Finally outside in the cool air, I found it difficult at first to believe the information the placard conveyed. To celebrate the wine harvest and the fiftieth anniversary of the Brogonye Wine Company The Great Brogonye would perform a feat so unusual and so dangerous that he had attempted it only once before – at the famous falls at Niagara. The Great Brogonye was going to go over the Marietzburg Falls in a wine barrel.

The stark outline of the castle's turrets stood like sentinels guarding the town below. It was a week later and my plans were almost complete. I'd waited in the woods all day watching the final preparations for The Great Brogonye's jump the following morning.

Night had now fallen and the castle workshop pressed into service to make the specially strengthened barrel for the jump was now deserted.

Waiting for cloud to conceal the moonlight, I left the shadow of the woodland and silently crossed the cobbled courtyard. The large barn doors of the workshop were closed, but as I knew from my childhood at the castle, entry was easy. I pulled both ill-fitting doors towards me and eased myself through the gap created by decades of wear in the mechanism.

Once inside, the wooden barrel loaded on to the cart for its journey to the falls was immediately visible. I pushed grain sacks into the gaps between the barn doors and the frame, and satisfied that no light would be visible from outside, lit the oil lamp. I now jumped on the cart and inspected the wooden barrel. I needed to work quickly. Taking a hand-drill from one of the workbenches, I drilled quarter-inch holes through all the knots in the wood – well over fifty in all. I then re-filled the holes with a mixture I had made earlier in the day and disguised my handiwork inside and out with a mixture of Indian ink and water.

Removing the sacking from the bottom of the barrel, where it had been placed to protect The Great Brogonye from the impact of the fall, I now tipped a mortar mixture bought in Umsdorf into the base of the barrel to a depth of four or five inches.

I then sawed a piece of wood to exact dimensions and secured it firmly into position to form a false base to the barrel just above the mortar mix.

With the sacking now returned to the base of the barrel, I inspected my work, moving the oil lamp around the barrel inside and out before I was satisfied that all was well.

Outside again, I made my way across the courtyard to the cooper's workshop. From several dozen I chose a barrel as near as possible to the one I had just been working on – for my purposes it would not have to be so strong. And using sacking to smother the noise of the cobbled courtyard, rolled the barrel to the woodland I had emerged from three hours before.

From there it was all downhill – literally. Until I eventually emerged from the woods at the bottom of the grass track and set off in the direction of the Marietzburg Falls. It was past midnight before I was able to conceal the barrel beneath bracken and branches at the bottom of the falls.

I now had one more task to perform. Slowly I took the phial of hydrochloric acid from my tunic pocket.

Taking care to remove all traces of my stay, I left my lodgings early next morning and vanished into the charcoal-grey of first light. My reappearance at the Marietzburg Falls a while later coincided with the first shafts of sunlight broaching the trees on the far bank.

Feeling vulnerable in the open, I quickly changed into the passable replica of The Great Brogonye's costume I had stitched together during the past week. Necessity had taught me to sew in Calcutta, and with a rudimentary knowledge of chemical dyes learnt from medical school, I was able to reproduce the bright red and yellow colours of The Great Brogonye's costume.

Retaining nothing except a six-foot length of rope and the black leather face-mask which completed the Brogonye's costume, I bundled my discarded clothes into my leather hold-all, piled it full of rocks and flung it into the river. Within seconds the treacherous waters beneath the falls had consumed it within their twenty-foot depths. Retrieving the barrel from beneath its camouflage, I rolled it down the grass slope until it slid into the water. At first the power of the torrent tried to rip the barrel from my grasp. I clung hold, forcing the barrel several yards upstream to where the flow ebbed.

I was now within touching distance of the fifty-foot-high wall of thunderous water that was the Marietzburg Falls. Already soaked, I now had no choice but to plunge into the alpine meltwater myself. It was breathtakingly cold, but to my relief I was still able to touch the riverbed.

Hanging on to the rock outcrops on the riverbank with one hand and the barrel with the other, I hauled myself through the barrage of cascading water and up on to one of the boulders that littered the base of the hollowed-out rockface beyond. Exhausted, I sat for several minutes, my eyes closed to the new world I had just entered.

From my position inside the falls it was impossible to see anything beyond the impenetrable wall of water before me.

I waited patiently for several hours and it was only the approaching sound of a brass band that made me aware that a large crowd was gathering on either side of the falls. Taking my timepiece from its waterproof pouch, I saw that it was only minutes before The Great Brogonye was to make his jump.

My pulse pumping in my temples, I quickly tied one end of the rope to the rockface, pulled on my face-mask and lifted the barrel into the swirling water. With some difficulty I hunkered myself down into the barrel, my firm grasp of the rope keeping me from leaving the rockface too early.

Above the roar of the waterfall, it was still surprisingly easy to discern what was happening in the bright sunlight outside. The crowd cheered when The Great Brogonye first entered his barrel; they applauded as he rolled into the swirling water; and now, as The Great Brogonye raced towards the fifty-foot drop, the cheering and clapping diminished to nothing.

Wiping the water continuously from my eyes, I scanned the cascading torrent, searching for the Brogonye's barrel as it fell.

Then suddenly it was there, the weight of the barrel spinning and cutting through the wall of water as it came fully into view right above me. If I hadn't moved quickly the barrel would have smashed on top of me. Instead it plummeted into the swirling water beyond and disappeared from view.

It all happened too quickly for me to see properly. But the knot holes in the barrel that I'd filled with clay would have dissolved by now, sucking the water into the Brogonye's barrel where it would be absorbed by the mortar, dragging them both to the riverbed twenty feet below.

I now let go of the rope, fixed the lid of the barrel into place and braced myself as the weight of the falling water took us under and into the white water beyond.

I had padded the inside of the barrel but nothing could prepare me for the pummelling I now received. In the space of seconds, I was rolled a dozen times and tipped upside-down so that my head was smashed continuously against the top of the barrel. I lost consciousness for a few seconds. Not long enough. The barrel now smashed against a rock, splitting the wood, allowing water to seep inside. Still the barrel kept tumbling, the inflowing water choking the breath from my lungs.

Then suddenly all was still. The power had been drained from the river and I was just floating along.

I pushed against the lid, and suddenly the vacuum of the barrel was filled not only with sunlight but a swelling applause.

A barge which was delivering wine for the festival was diverted to pluck me from the barrel and convey me safely to the shore.

From there I was hauled on to a cart draped with the yellow and red of The Great Brogonye and conveyed into town. I used my elevated position to search the river for the other barrel. Nothing.

The Great Brogonye was dead.

I was paraded in the market square, lauded over by all, and slapped on the back so many times my shoulders ached. Despite my protestations, I was persuaded to say a few words.

I spoke falteringly about my parents: my father who had asked me to 'perform something memorable for the wine festival'; and my mother who had 'always tried to put a stop to such foolishness'. That met with a peal of laughter from the crowd because my words echoed their own memories of my parents.

My confidence grew.

'I would also like to pay tribute to the dedication of my brother, Wilhelm, who gave his life for the sick of Calcutta.' I was tempted to continue, but I was surprised how easy it was to speak about myself like this. It was as if now I'd slipped into The Great Brogonye's costume, Dr Wilhelm Brogonye had ceased to exist.

Wisely, perhaps, I resisted the temptation to ask for donations to the Mission. Best not to push my luck. After all, now I had become The Great Brogonye, heir to the Brogonye Wine Company, the Mission would never be short of money again.

'And now, ladies and gentlemen, I have one final announcement to make.' I paused for effect before continuing. 'What you have witnessed here today was the last ever performance by The Great Brogonye.' And with a flourish I frankly enjoyed, I removed my black leather face-mask.

At first there was silence as they absorbed the blood-red

burns melted into the side of my face. In truth, the dilute hydrochloric acid burns I had inflicted the previous night were more impressive than they would be longlasting. And besides, sympathy would be the perfect cover for any doubts that I really was The Great Brogonye.

'And now, friends,' I continued, 'although I cannot recommend dropping over a waterfall to give you much of an appetite, let the feast begin.' I now raised my goblet to the air expecting it to be full of wine. It was empty.

'It seems we're the only wine festival in Bavaria with no wine,' I declared.

It was then that I was told about the accident at the jetty. The crew of the barge delivering the wine – I now damn them to hell! – had been distracted from their duties by the jump of The Great Brogonye. The six barrels of wine had fallen from the barge into the river.

I was just about to announce the delay when the cart carrying the wine rattled into the market square. The crowd, already excitable, cheered ever more loudly.

Except for me.

I'd just realised there were seven barrels on the cart and one of them wasn't silent.

Kate Ross was a trial lawyer with a prominent Boston law firm and the creator of a wonderful historical sleuth, Julian Kestrel. Her character was a Regency dandy irresistibly drawn to baffling cases in the colourful setting of mid-nineteenth-century Europe. He appeared in four novels, *Cut to the Quick*, *A Broken Vessel*, *Whom the Gods Love* and *The Devil in Music*.

When approached to contribute to this anthology, Kate chose to create a new female character, who she hoped would become the linchpin of a new series set a quarter of a century earlier. 'The Unkindest Cut' is the first story featuring Harriette Wilson, and she proves to be a particularly unusual and endearing heroine. Sadly it will also be the last Harriette Wilson story.

Kate Ross died of cancer at the age of only forty-one shortly after completing the story. She will be as sorely missed as Edith Pargeter.

(Maxim Jakubowski)

The Unkindest Cut

Kate Ross

O nce one begins on 'ought not to haves' and 'if onlys', there is no end to it. I ought not to have left my father's house at fifteen to live with the Earl of Craven. Having once done so, and knowing as I did that my father would never take me back under his roof, I ought to have cleaved to the noble lord for his wealth and his consequence, and taught myself to endure his hideous cotton nightcaps and his unending stories of battles fought among cocoa trees in the West Indies. Most certainly, I ought not to have become such friends with the Honourable Frederick Lamb that Lord Craven saw fit to cast me off, although I call heaven to witness I had never deceived him, but had always held fast to the principle that a girl ought to love only one man – or, if she cannot, only one at a time. And finally, on finding myself alone in the world, I ought not to have thrown in my lot with Fred Lamb, who certainly loved me to distraction, but who was an impecunious younger son without the means or the inclination to provide me with even the minimal comforts of life. Having made all these mistakes, I perhaps had no right to complain when I found myself ensconced in a cramped little lodging in Somers-town, with a dead man on my sofa.

At the time Lord Astrey first arrived at my house, he had nothing in particular wrong with him except that Fred had shot him. The quarrel had come about in Hyde Park the previous morning, when Fred was out riding, and Astrey was driving his curricle. The two had a near collision, resulting in rearing horses, tangled traces, and trampled hats. There was a good deal of cursing and mutual recrimination, in the course of which Fred told Astrey he might as well have given over the reins to a monkey. Astrey was sensitive about his driving, having come to grief a year or two earlier when his phaeton had had the impertinence to overturn, notwithstanding that the perch was no more than ten feet off the ground, and he had had at least a finger or two on the reins. At all events, he demanded that Fred take back the words, and on Fred's refusing, a meeting was appointed at Primrose Hill. I knew naught of the matter till Fred appeared on my doorstep at seven in the morning, with his late antagonist, the two seconds, and their surgeon in tow.

'But wouldn't Lord Astrey be better off in his own house?' I whispered to Fred, who had whisked me into the parlour for a quick kiss while the others were taking off hats and gloves in the hall.

'Not a bit of it,' said he. 'His wound is only a scratch. My ball just grazed his chest. The surgeon has dressed it and pronounces it will do very well. Honour being satisfied, I could take back the words I spoke in haste, and Astrey and I are quite friends again. And as your house is on the way back to town, I brought the whole party here for a bit of refreshment – and of course to show you off, dearest Harry.'

'But Mrs Osgood is away,' I protested, she being my old nurse, with whom I lodged.

'Well, what of that?' laughed Fred. 'You are a little beyond any need for a duenna, my love!'

I bit my lip. He mistook the cause of my distress. 'Do not fret,' said he, kissing me again. 'I am quite unscathed.'

This I could well see. All six feet of him was as healthful and handsome as ever. But how could he bring all these visitors to my house to eat and drink their heads off, when he must know full well that I was nearly at the end of my resources? He provided me so little to live on that of late I had been obliged to part with such money and trinkets as Lord Craven had given me, merely to keep myself in tea and stockings. Yet I was loath to put him in a temper. I remembered all too well my father's violent rages when approached about money – or any other subject he was not in a humour to discuss.

'I've only cold mutton and a little Dutch cheese in the larder,' I began.

'No matter,' said he, gaily, 'we shall make do. I am sure my dearest little wife will manage famously.' He often called me this when he was in a good temper; and indeed, nothing can exceed the tenderness of gentlemen for these wives in watercolours, from whom they may be divorced tomorrow, through their own caprice or the lady's inconstancy.

He poked his head into the hall and called, 'Come in, gentlemen, and be introduced to Miss Harriette Wilson.'

I duly made the acquaintance of Lord Astrey, a gentleman of about two-and-twenty, with blue eyes and a baby's face – round, rosy, and crowned with golden curls. Fred's ball had slashed his coat, waistcoat, and shirt across the front, so that the neat lint dressing on his breast showed through. He was up and about and in tolerable spirits, but drowsy, and though the May morning was cool, he kept mopping his brow with his handkerchief.

Lord Astrey's second was his cousin, Mr Edward Bingham, who was about thirty and educated for a barrister, though I gathered he had felt no urgent call to practise his profession. Fred's second I knew already, to my cost. He was Captain James Farrell, of the Royal Horse Guards, who fancied himself a great conqueror of ladies' hearts, and who, from the time Fred had been so unwise as to introduce us, had made a dead set at winning me away from his friend.

'And this is the famous Goff,' Fred announced, clapping the surgeon upon the shoulder, 'surgeon to the ring and the turf. It was he who saved Astrey's life when his phaeton overturned last year, and since then nothing will do but to have Goff attend at race meetings, prize fights, and affairs of honour.'

The famous Goff was in his forties, short, snub-nosed, and broad about the middle. His costly clothing and immense gold watch attested to the fortune to be made from patching up boxers, jockeys, and reckless young gentlemen of means.

'I vow,' said Lord Astrey, 'I cannot keep my eyes open another moment.'

'He probably didn't sleep a wink last night in anticipation of our meeting,' Fred whispered to me complacently. He himself had clearly slept very well.

'You ought to lie down and rest, my lord,' advised Goff. 'Pray, Miss Wilson, is there some quiet, out-of-the-way place where His Lordship might sleep for a while?'

I thought this over. I lived in a little brick house in Dukes Row, Somers-town. Everything was on doll's-house scale: tiny kitchen, pocket-handkerchief-sized scullery, wine cellar consisting of an oven-shaped nook in the wall. The dining room would seat half a dozen, provided no two on opposite sides of the table were so rash as to push out their chairs at the same time. The kitchen and scullery were in the basement. The ground floor had Mrs Osgood's parlour in front and her bedroom in back. The first-floor front was the drawing room; the back was the dining room. The second floor had my sitting room in front, my bedchamber in back. My maid, Ellen, slept in the attic.

I decided to offer Lord Astrey my sitting-room sofa, if he could walk up the two flights of stairs to it. He assured me that he could, and Mr Goff and I accompanied him thither. We saw him settled face up on the sofa, with ample cushions beneath his head and feet. Goff took his pulse and felt his brow with pudgy little hands that were unexpectedly quick and agile. I drew the blinds, and Goff and I went out.

'He is in a great perspiration,' said I, frowning.

'That is his body striving to heal itself,' the surgeon explained. 'His brow is quite cool, and there are no signs of fever about him.'

'Then we may safely leave him?'

'To be sure,' said he. 'Else I should not do so.'

With Lord Astrey disposed for the present, the other men took over the drawing room and dining room. Ellen and I were at our wits' end to find meat and drink enough for them. I was obliged to send to a public house for veal pies, roasted fowls, hock, and claret, all which expense Fred promised to repay, then promptly forgot about.

Mr Bingham held forth in the drawing room on a variety of subjects. He was a man of considerable address and learning, though rather too aware of his own gifts and unable quite to keep his veil of modesty in place. His person was fairly agreeable: thin and sleek, with fair, straight hair that lay smoothly against his head in defiance of the fashion for curls. His nose was rather long, his skin white and delicate as a woman's.

He explained to us why the peace with Bonaparte would not last, how the smallpox vaccination worked, and what was the jurisdiction of the various law courts. I was willing to sit through Bonaparte and even vaccination, though the talk of scratching people with lancets to infect them with cowpox made me a bit green about the gills. But the law courts were a dead bore. I slipped away and went to look in on Lord Astrey. He was sleeping, but woke when I came in. 'Is that you, Miss Wilson?' he croaked.

'Yes,' said I. 'Are you quite comfortable, my lord? Is there anything you need?'

'My mouth is confoundedly dry,' he replied. 'I should be glad of a drink of water. Otherwise I'm well enough, though I've been having the most extraordinary dreams. First I thought I could fly, then I felt myself in a great whirlpool, spinning round and round, and unable to get free.'

I felt his brow. It was cool but moist. Then I gazed in surprise at his eyes. Though the room was dimmed by the closed blinds, his pupils were shrunk to pinpoints, as if he were in a bright light.

I thought it would be well if Goff examined him again, but I did not wish to alarm him and so merely said, 'Shall I fetch you some water, my lord?'

'I should be very grateful.' He smiled a weak, sweet smile. 'Lamb said you were an awfully good fellow.'

'Not so good as that comes to,' said I, 'else I shouldn't be here.'

I ran down to the dining room for a glass of water, but when I returned with it, Lord Astrey was sleeping more soundly than before. I left it on a table by his sofa and went downstairs.

Captain Farrell was lying in wait for me on the landing outside the drawing and dining rooms. I had lifted my skirt a little in order to descend the stairs, and his eyes went straight to my ankles.

Now, even were I disposed to intrigue behind Fred's back, Captain Farrell was the last man to attach me. I have ever admired fair complexions, blue eyes, and graceful hands and feet. Captain Farrell was a big, ruddy man with fierce black side whiskers, hands like sides of beef, and feet so immense that the tassels on his Hessian boots were like pennons atop a barge. I had acquainted him time and time again that his suit was hopeless, but so great was his vainglory that no amount of quizzing or rejection discouraged him.

'I've been waiting to catch you alone,' said he, attempting to lay hold of my hand.

I put both hands behind me and tried to get into the drawing room. He blocked my way. 'It won't do, Captain Farrell,' I warned. 'You may keep me cooling my heels, but you won't warm my feelings. *L'amour ne se commande pas.*' I was educated in a French convent. Even a French convent will occasionally turn out a mistake.

'You are so deuced hard on me,' he complained. 'I've never been put to such trouble over a girl.'

'Then you had much better give me up, hadn't you?' I replied. 'Hasn't your military training taught you to lift a siege when it is quite hopeless?'

'Not when the prize is so great as this,' he smirked, as if inviting the gallery to applaud him. 'You are really too nice in your scruples, Harriette. You owe Lamb nothing. He stints you of pocket money, and leaves you alone five nights out of seven. What is he to you?'

The truth was, I had no reason for remaining with Fred Lamb except that he was handsome, I liked no man better, and it seemed both disloyal to him and dangerous to myself to leave him and try my luck in the wide world. But none of this was for Captain Farrell's ears.

'When is your birthday, my dear sir?' I asked. 'I shall buy you an ear trumpet, since it seems you hear nothing I tell you. If there were no such person in the world as Frederick Lamb, you would never succeed with me.'

His face grew, if possible, redder, and he ground out, 'I can't see much to choose between one man and another, to a girl of your sort.'

'You are confusing virtue with taste,' said I. 'A girl who has forfeited the one may still lay claim to the other.' And with that I darted under his arm and obtained the drawing room.

'How pink you are, Harry!' observed Fred, who was standing near the door.

'I've been taking exercise,' I told him, 'fending off your friend Farrell.'

'Still dangling after you, is he?' Fred crowed. 'It does you credit, dear Harry! Make him sigh for you a twelvemonth, if you can. It is such good fun!'

I saw that he would be no help at all. It delighted him to have a mistress whom his swaggering friend Farrell coveted in vain. 'You would be well served if I went off with him,' I remarked.

'Fiddlestick!' said he, squeezing my hand. 'I know that I can trust my little wife with anyone.'

This, observe, is what comes of adhering to principles. Because I had held Fred at arm's length as long as I remained under Lord Craven's protection, he now felt secure enough of my affections to dangle me before his friends.

'Where is Mr Goff?' I inquired, not seeing him in the drawing room.

'In there, I expect,' said Fred, motioning with his head toward the dining-room door.

'I wish him to examine Lord Astrey,' said I. 'I don't at all like the look of him.'

'You are making a great fuss about nothing. Astrey will be right as a trivet in no time.'

I did not stop to argue with him, but passed into the drawing room. The great Goff was at table, absently picking at the remains of a roasted capon. He got to his feet when I entered. I told him my errand, and he agreed to go up and see his patient. I accompanied him out of a vague sense of unease, which Fred would no doubt have ascribed to women's megrims.

We found Lord Astrey lying as I had left him. But though I threw up the blinds, and Goff said heartily, 'How now, my lord?' the young man remained insensible.

Goff took him by the wrist to feel his pulse. The next moment I saw the surgeon's mouth drop open, and his eyes get very round. He hastened to feel Lord Astrey's neck and put his ear to his breast. When he lifted his head once more, his face was ashen. 'Miss Wilson, he is dead!'

'Dead!' I cried. 'How can he be?'

'I do not know. I did not think his wound so serious.'

Goff unbuttoned Astrey's torn shirt and waistcoat and lifted a corner of the bandage on his breast. I shrank back and half-turned my eyes away, hardly knowing what dreadful signs of mortification I might see about the wound. But it was a simple scratch, albeit a long one, the blood dried upon it, the flesh around it fair and wholesome.

Fred, Captain Farrell, and Mr Bingham appeared in the doorway. 'Is all well?' Bingham asked me. 'Lamb tells me you brought Goff up to see my cousin.'

'I am afraid, sir, your cousin is dead,' stammered the surgeon.

They all exclaimed at once. Goff wrung his trembling hands and assured them there was no mistake. I quietly closed the poor young man's eyes and smoothed the damp gold curls from his brow. In the midst of all this, Ellen came up to see what the rumpus was, and on learning Lord Astrey's fate, sat down plump on the floor, threw her apron over her head, and began shrieking.

I was at some pains to quieten her and help her downstairs. When I returned, the learned Mr Bingham had recovered himself sufficiently to take a practical view of his cousin's untimely death. 'We are all in a most delicate position,' he pointed out. 'When a gentleman perishes as a result of a duel, the law regards both his opponent and the seconds as principals in his murder, and the attending surgeon as having assisted in it.'

'But he can't have died as a result of the duel!' exclaimed Fred. 'I barely grazed him!'

'You shot him not four hours ago,' coldly answered Bingham, 'and now he is dead. And since nothing can be done for him, I must advise that we all put a distance between him and ourselves.'

'You cannot mean to leave him here!' I exclaimed.

'She's right,' said Farrell. 'We ought to take him back to the duelling ground.'

'It's too late in the morning now,' said Bingham. 'We would be seen.'

'We could hide him here until nightfall,' Farrell proposed.

*   *   *

'That you could *not*!' said I.

'Steady now,' said Farrell. 'No need for us all to get into a taking. The only one of us in real danger is Lamb. It was he who fired the shot, and a good many people saw him and Astrey get into a row yesterday morning. Lamb, you'll have to quit the country as quick as may be. The rest of us will find some way to make Astrey's death known without getting ourselves into hot water.'

'But I don't want to quit the country!' Fred expostulated. 'And I oughtn't to have to. I barely grazed him! He did not, *could* not, die of such a flea bite as that!'

Goff slipped out of the room, his brown leather medical case in his hand. I followed, and saw him descending the stairs as fast as his short, stout legs would carry him. I flew in pursuit, and just as he reached the first-floor landing, caught him by the tail of his coat.

'M-Miss Wilson, I really must go!' he pleaded.

'Pray, Mr Goff, stay a moment and speak with me. Fred's life may depend upon it! *Could* Lord Astrey have died of the wound Fred gave him?'

Goff turned up his eyes solemnly. 'The human body is mysterious. Some of its workings defy understanding.'

'That is no sort of answer!' I cried impatiently; then, mindful that I must not make an enemy of the one man whose knowledge might serve me, I sweetened my tone – still, however, keeping a firm hold on his coat-tail. 'Mr Goff, you are the most esteemed surgeon in London. I am sure no man's understanding of bones, blood, and sinew rivals yours. If any man may dare pronounce upon the cause of so unexpected a death as Lord Astrey's, it is you.'

While Goff dithered, shifting from one foot to the other, Mr Bingham came down the stairs and joined us. He had evidently overheard my question to the surgeon and was listening with cool, scientific interest for the answer.

Goff looked from one to the other of us and said at last, 'I must admit that such a shallow wound, with no sign of mortification, would have been highly unlikely to kill a young man of Lord Astrey's constitution.'

'Then how did he die?' I wondered.

'Perhaps his heart failed him,' said Goff.

'Could not you tell everyone so?' I begged. 'Then Fred and the rest of you would not be blamed for his death.'

'The law might not take Goff's word for that,' pointed out Bingham. 'After all, it is in his interest to say that my cousin died of natural causes. In any event, if it was the duel that caused Astrey's heart to fail, we might all still be held responsible.'

I pressed a hand to my brow. It was all too difficult. Everything was happening too fast. I wanted these men to be gone so that I might think. I wanted Lord Astrey to come down the stairs alive and laughing at how he had quizzed us. I wanted my mother.

'Mr Goff,' I said, thinking back feverishly, 'when Lord Astrey arrived here he was drowsy and kept mopping his face with his handkerchief. When I looked in on him a few hours later, he complained that his mouth was dry, and told me he'd been afflicted with strange dreams of flying and of being sucked down into a whirlpool. He was still perspiring, and the pupils of his eyes were shrunk to pinpricks. Mr Goff, if he had not fought a duel at all, but had looked and behaved as he did, what would you think?'

Goff wet his lips. 'I should think – I should think—'

'Yes?' I prompted eagerly.

'I should wonder, Miss Wilson, if Lord Astrey had taken laudanum within a few hours before his death.'

'Laudanum?' said I, staring.

'Tincture of opium,' explained Mr Bingham, as if I lived on some distant star where all the world and his wife did not keep a bottle of laudanum about for the relief of pain. 'Goff apparently thinks my cousin showed signs of opium poisoning.'

'Did you give him laudanum for the pain after he was wounded?' I asked Goff.

'I offered it,' said Goff, 'but he would not take it. Surely you recall, Mr Bingham,' the poor man pleaded, pressing his hands together, 'he would not take it!'

'I do recall,' Bingham said calmly. 'If he had taken it, I should have been astonished. He loathed taking medication of any kind. I cannot see that you are at fault in the matter. Even if you had given him laudanum, he could not have died of an ordinary dose. He would have had to take a very great quantity – either that, or a more highly concentrated form of the drug.'

'How might he have done that?' I queried.

Mr Bingham seized upon this chance to display his knowledge. 'Opium is available in all manner of strengths, from the brown syrup that is the crudest form of the drug, to laudanum, which contains a very low ratio of opium to alcohol. But all this is of no consequence. My cousin had no opportunity to ingest the drug in any form without being observed.'

'When would he have had to take the opium in order to have died when he did?' I asked Goff.

'No less than two hours before,' said the surgeon unhappily, 'and no more than four.'

Bingham looked at his watch. 'It's a little after nine. I was with my cousin four hours ago, on our way to the duelling ground. If Astrey had taken opium in any form, I should have seen it. Captain Farrell is right: the best course is to return Astrey's body to the duelling ground and let investigation take its course. It will easily be guessed that he and Lamb engaged in an affair of honour, but Lamb can abscond, and the rest of us will keep our own counsel about the matter. The authorities may be puzzled by the inconsequence of Astrey's wound, but most probably his death will nevertheless be attributed to the duel.'

'But Fred doesn't wish to abscond,' I objected. 'And he

ought not to have to leave his country – perhaps for years, perhaps for the rest of his life! – on account of a murder he never committed!'

'It would be an injustice, perhaps,' Bingham acknowledged. 'But to stay and risk prosecution would be nothing short of madness.'

He walked past us into the drawing room. I looked after him, thinking that he seemed unlikely to perish of grief at his cousin's demise.

'I must go now, Miss Wilson,' said Goff, shuffling toward the stairs again.

I clutched his coat-tail with both hands and resolutely dug my heels into the carpet. 'Do not go yet, Mr Goff! Fred and I cannot do without your medical knowledge, if we are to make sense of how Lord Astrey died.'

'I've told you all I can,' said he, quaking. 'Now I must ask you to leave go of my coat, and let me go!'

I still held on, and we played tug-of-war, so that I was nearly dragged off my feet. 'Surely it is to your advantage to help us!' I panted. 'If Lord Astrey was poisoned, then no blame can attach to you for his death, whereas if he is held to have been killed in the duel, Mr Bingham says you could be taken up for assisting in his murder!'

Goff plucked up courage. 'Mr Bingham, Mr Lamb, and Captain Farrell are gentlemen. They will not reveal I had anything to do with the duel.'

'*I* am not a gentleman,' said I.

His jaw dropped, and he stopped tugging so suddenly that I almost fell backward. 'You – you don't mean to say you would turn informer against me?'

'Of course not,' said I, 'any more than you would leave me in the lurch when I need your help.'

'Very well, Miss Wilson,' he said heavily. 'I will stay.'

'Thank you, Mr Goff! Now I must talk to Fred.'

I ran up the stairs, and met Captain Farrell coming out of the sitting room where I had left him, Fred, and poor Lord

Astrey. 'Harry,' he accosted me, 'you must persuade Lamb to fly the country.'

'But that will be as good as his admitting Lord Astrey died by his hand.'

'He did,' said Farrell, 'or as nearly as makes no odds. But don't worry, dear little Harry,' he said smugly, 'I'll take care of you when Lamb is gone.'

'If Fred goes into exile, I shall go with him!' I proclaimed. But inwardly my heart sank. Fred had taken little enough care of me in England. How could I entrust myself to him on the Continent, where I had no family, no friends who would care a fig for my welfare, no old nurse to lodge with?

'I am sure you won't do anything so crack-brained,' he said comfortably. 'But you had better talk sense to Lamb. He hasn't much time.'

He clumped downstairs and I went into my sitting room. Fred was standing by a window, and spun around to face me. 'Harry, I barely grazed him!'

'For heaven's sake, Fred,' I exclaimed, 'you are like a music box that plays only one tune!' I skirted the sofa, where someone had had the grace to throw a blanket over Lord Astrey, and joined Fred at the window. 'I've been talking to Goff and Mr Bingham. It seems possible that Lord Astrey died of opium poisoning, and not of his wound.' I quickly explained how we had come at this idea. 'Mr Bingham says Lord Astrey had no opportunity to swallow any opium within four hours before his death. But—' Here I came up short. The direction of my thoughts caught me by surprise. I said slowly, 'The question is, might Lord Astrey have taken opium without knowing it – because somebody wished him to?'

Fred goggled. 'Do you mean to say you think he was poisoned?'

'If he didn't take the drug of his own accord, it must have been given to him on the sly,' I reasoned.

'It all sounds deucedly like something one would see on the stage at Drury Lane,' Fred grumbled.

'Either Lord Astrey was poisoned,' I put it succinctly, 'or you killed him, Fred.'

'I did not kill him!' he shouted.

'Then he was poisoned. That is how and about it. Now.' I sat down at a table in my favourite attitude, my head resting on my forefinger, my thick, dark curls falling over my hand. 'Tell me everything you can about what Lord Astrey said and did this morning before you all came here.'

He walked back and forth before the window, his hands clasped behind him. 'Farrell and I set out for Primrose Hill about four o'clock this morning. Farrell drove us in his curricle. We arrived on the ground a little before five, then Farrell went to an inn nearby where he had arranged to meet Astrey and Bingham, and they all returned together. Goff joined us soon after. Astrey and I kept apart while Farrell and Bingham marked out the ground and loaded the pistols. We took our ground, the seconds and Goff withdrew from the line of fire, and on the signal we discharged our pistols. Astrey fired wide; I grazed his chest, as you saw. Goff probed the wound with a lancet, feeling for bone fragments, then dressed it. Astrey and I made up our quarrel, and we all came here.'

'Think back,' I urged. 'Did you see Lord Astrey eat or drink anything?'

'By Jove, I did!' Fred stopped walking. 'Farrell had a flask of brandy with him, and though Astrey wouldn't take laudanum when Goff offered it, he did quaff some brandy from Farrell's flask.'

'Did anyone else drink from the flask?' I asked.

'I didn't,' said he. 'But what does that signify? You can't suppose Farrell poisoned Astrey. Why the devil should he have done so?'

'He wanted me for himself,' I said. 'He could have put opium into a flask of brandy and brought it to the duelling ground to give to whichever of you was wounded.'

'How could he know which of us that would be?'

'It didn't matter,' said I, triumphantly. 'If you it were you, he could poison you, and if it were Astrey, he could make you out a murderer. Either way, he would be rid of you.'

'Supposing neither of us was hit?' he wanted to know.

'Then he could simply pocket the flask, with no one the wiser.'

'But look here,' Fred objected, 'aren't you creeping into favour with yourself a bit, thinking Farrell would murder a man on your account?'

I was dashed. In my pleasure at perceiving a possible explanation for Lord Astrey's death, I had not stopped to consider its inherent absurdity. It required more vanity than I was mistress of to believe Captain Farrell would poison a man with whom he had not the slightest quarrel in the world, for the sake of my *beaux yeux*. If nothing else, he could be by no means certain I would not follow Fred into exile, wretched though our existence might be.

'Had Captain Farrell any other quarrel with Lord Astrey?' I asked hopefully.

'Not that I ever heard of,' said Fred.

I pondered. 'What about Mr Bingham? Was there bad blood between him and Lord Astrey?'

'I don't believe so. They were cousins and had known each other from boyhood.'

'Cousins,' I repeated thoughtfully. 'Did Mr Bingham stand to gain anything by Lord Astrey's death?'

'He stood to gain everything,' said Fred. 'He is Astrey's heir.'

'And Lord Astrey was very rich, was he not?' I exclaimed eagerly.

'I expect he'll cut up large.' Fred nodded. 'And of course there's the title – that will go to Bingham as well. But even supposing Bingham would kill Astrey for such a reason, how will you ever prove that he actually did so? He won't admit it, and Astrey can tell us nothing.'

I knit my brows. 'You said Captain Farrell went to meet

Lord Astrey and Mr Bingham at an inn before the duel. Perhaps he observed something of importance there. Besides which, I should like to find out more about that brandy flask of his.'

'How are you proposing to do that?' Fred demanded. 'You can't very well ask him if he has taken up poisoning people.'

'I wasn't going to,' said I, loftily. 'I have an idea. Wait here!'

I ran to the door. There I had a new thought and looked around again. 'I suppose it is quite out of the question that Lord Astrey meant to make away with himself?'

'I should be absolutely floored if he did,' said Fred. 'He was in spirits. He was going to be married to a girl he was dead smit with.'

'Ah!' said I.

'Now you look like the cat that swallowed the cream,' he told me. 'What are you playing at?'

'I'll tell you presently,' I said, and darted out.

I sped downstairs and looked about for Captain Farrell. He was in the dining room, seated at the table drinking claret. When I came in he lumbered to his feet.

'Oh, Captain Farrell,' I breathed, putting a hand to my brow, 'I am absolutely done up – *frappée en mort*! I should like nothing so much as a drop of brandy, but there is none in the house! Fred told me you had a flask with you. May I trouble you to give me a drink from it?'

'I should have to go downstairs to get it,' objected this pattern of chivalry. 'Won't claret do as well?'

'I thought you had been willing to take a little trouble on my account,' I said reproachfully.

'Of course, of course!' He summoned up his elephantine gallantry. 'I left it on the hall table. I'll be back with it like a shot!'

While he was gone, I flew to the sideboard, removed the bottle of brandy I knew it contained, and hid it behind the

236

window curtains, so that he should not discover I had been fibbing. When he returned, I was sitting in the window seat looking as faint and wan as possible.

He presented the flask to me with a florid bow. I regarded it in sudden dismay. I had been assuming that his ready production of it would mean there was nothing wrong about the brandy it contained. But suppose he had decided to make away with me, because he thought me suspicious of him? If Lord Astrey could die of poisoning under my roof, what might not happen next?

I brought the flask to my lips with an unsteady hand. But my fears were assuaged, though my curiosity (not to mention my thirst) was left unslaked, when I discovered it was empty.

'I must have drunk the rest of it myself,' said Farrell carelessly. 'Bad luck! Take some claret instead.'

He poured me a glass and came around behind me, putting his arm about my shoulders as he offered me the glass. 'I'm afraid you are in a bad way, poor little Harry, and need supporting.'

'There is no need for that, Captain Farrell,' said I, wriggling out from under his arm. 'I can stand perfectly well.'

He shrugged up his shoulders and seated himself at the table again. 'Have you had any luck persuading Lamb to leave England?'

I did not reply. I was racking my brains for some new stratagem. All at once inspiration struck. I sat down beside him and conquered my repulsion to his person sufficiently to touch his hand with my fingertips. 'Captain Farrell, I entreat you to help me! You are the only person I can turn to. Fred is in too much distress to be of service to himself or me.'

The captain's eyes lit up. 'Why, what can I do for you?'

'I am speaking to you in greatest confidence, because you are the only one I trust. I believe that Lord Astrey was poisoned, and that Mr Bingham is the culprit!'

'What?'

I explained rapidly what cause there was to believe that Astrey had died of a surfeit of opium. 'Mr Bingham was with him this morning before the duel. He stood to gain a peerage and a fortune by his death. He is clever, probably ambitious, and might well have thought he could make better use of the family title and wealth than a rattle-pate like Astrey. And finally – Lord Astrey was about to be married, and might soon sire heirs who would cut Mr Bingham out!'

'It seems fantastic,' said Farrell, shaking his head.

'The one mystery,' I pressed on, 'is, when and how might Mr Bingham have given the poison? Pray, Captain Farrell, can you throw any light on that?'

He eyed me with ill-concealed calculation. I saw that he was trying to decide between telling me this idea of poisoning was all my fancy, and winning my gratitude and admiration by making common cause with me. I held my breath. At last he said, 'I do have knowledge that might serve your turn. Astrey and Bingham breakfasted together at the inn where I met them before the duel. Astrey mentioned he'd taken nothing but coffee with brandy. And now I come to think of it, he said he hadn't fancied the taste of it.'

This was more than I had dared hope for. 'Oh, thank you, Captain Farrell! How kind you are, and how clever!'

'Tut! – there's nothing I wouldn't do for you!' He bent towards me, his lips aiming for mine. But I was out of my chair and running to the door. I kissed my hand to him and sped out.

Now I must find Mr Bingham. He was not in the drawing room. I descended to the ground floor. Noticing Ellen in the hall, I asked, 'Have you seen Mr Bingham?'

'I think he's in the parlour, miss.'

'You seem to have recovered from your fright,' I observed.

'Oh, yes, miss,' she said, and giggled, then put both hands to her mouth.

I looked at her narrowly. It was not like her to be laughing and giddy, with a man lying dead upstairs. I supposed it was some new form of hysterics. As it seemed fairly harmless and I was in haste, I left her and went into the parlour.

Mr Bingham was sitting at a table reading a newspaper. When he saw me he rose in his cold, polite fashion. 'Are you looking for me, Miss Wilson?'

I stood with my back up against the door, my eyes round and fixed on his face. What was I to say? I needed another inspiration. When it came, I obeyed it blindly. 'Mr Bingham, I am sorry to disturb you, but I must talk to you. You are the only person I can turn to! You have such a level head, and your knowledge of law and medicine and all worldly matters is so great. If you will not help me, I know not what I shall do!'

Bingham thawed a little – whether from compassion or gratified vanity I did not know. 'If it is in my power to serve you, Miss Wilson, you may command me.'

'Mr Bingham.' I came closer, sinking my voice and trying to give it the throb I had heard Mrs Siddons use in a wrought-up moment in *Macbeth*. 'I believe that your cousin *was* poisoned, and that Captain Farrell killed him. You may remember that, after Lord Astrey was wounded, Captain Farrell gave him a drink from a flask of brandy. A man of your perceptions will have noticed, too –' here I lowered my eyes and looked at him modestly but becomingly through my lashes – 'that Captain Farrell was not indifferent to me.' I explained how, by poisoning either combatant in the duel, Farrell could have separated me from Fred. 'Of course, you will think me monstrous vain, supposing myself to be the cause of such a dreadful crime.'

'No,' said he, thoughtfully, 'not when one considers the money Farrell had at stake.'

'The money?' I gaped like a schoolgirl, quite forgetting to be Mrs Siddons.

'Did you not know about the wager?' he asked. 'Farrell bet a brother officer five hundred pounds he could take you from Lamb within a month. I saw it entered in the betting book at

239

White's. That was several weeks ago – I daresay the month has nearly run.'

'Good heavens!' This put quite a different complexion on things. My accusation against Farrell, which I had intended merely as a means of starting my fox, Bingham, from his hole, now began to have a ring of truth. Five hundred pounds was a great deal of money, and Farrell was not rich.

I asked, 'Did you drink from Captain Farrell's flask?'

'No,' said Bingham. 'And I can't recollect to have seen anyone else drink from it, except my cousin. What has become of it?'

'It's empty,' said I. 'Captain Farrell says he drank off the rest of the brandy, but of course he might as easily have poured it out when no one was looking. Still –' I put on a scrupulous face. 'I suppose in fairness to the captain, we ought to consider whether Lord Astrey might have been given opium at some other time, by some other means.'

'Goff said he had to have been given it no more than four hours before his death,' Mr Bingham reminded me. 'As I told you, I was with Astrey all that time – first on our way to Primrose Hill, then at breakfast at an inn, and finally on the ground where Astrey and Lamb exchanged shots. If Astrey had taken opium in any form, I should have seen it.'

'You mentioned that the two of you breakfasted together,' I observed delicately. 'Is it possible opium might have been put into something he ate or drank?'

'It is quite impossible,' he pronounced. 'Astrey took nothing but coffee with brandy. I drank coffee from the same pot and brandy from the same bottle, and suffered no ill effects. If you doubt my powers of observation –' his tone suggested that I would then be a little fool unworthy of his further notice – 'you may enquire of the waiter who attended us and who poured the coffee and brandy.'

'I should not dream of doubting you, Mr Bingham,' I assured him. 'Thank you a thousand times for your help.

240

It is of such importance to me to prove Fred innocent of Lord Astrey's death!'

I hastened out. Where ought I to go now? Back to Farrell, I decided, and ran up the stairs. Then I bethought me that I had better prime myself to engage the captain's sympathies. I went into the drawing room and stood before the looking glass, arranging my cascade of curls about my shoulders and pinching my cheeks to bring up the colour.

'What the deuce are you about?' Fred demanded from the doorway. 'You bade me wait for you in that infernal sitting room, with Astrey's corpse for company, and you never returned.'

'I've been talking to Captain Farrell and Mr Bingham,' said I. 'I hope to prove that one or the other of them poisoned Lord Astrey. At present it looks a deal more like Captain Farrell.'

'And in order to question them, you must needs primp before a looking glass?' he jeered.

'What are you implying?' I asked.

'I believe you think I shall be obliged to flee the country, and have not even bundled me out of the door before you've begun to scout for a new protector. I advise you to choose Bingham. His inheritance will enable him to keep you in far greater luxury than either Farrell or I could do.'

'How can you?' I exclaimed, and burst into tears.

'Now, Harry,' said he, shifting from one foot to the other, 'don't take on.'

'Don't take on? A poor young man who never did harm to anyone but himself is lying dead in my sitting room, and his murderer is somewhere in my house! I am over head and ears in brandy flasks and breakfasts, gunshots and opium! And now you, for whose sake I've been playing at conundrums with possible poisoners, accuse me of betraying and abandoning you! I am quite finished with you, Fred Lamb! Henceforth you may get yourself out of this scrape!'

I tried to quit the room, but he held me back. 'Have you found out anything?' he asked.

'A great deal,' said I. 'But it won't do you any good, because I am leaving the house.'

'Wait!' he pleaded. 'How am I to get to the bottom of this without you?'

'You ought to have thought of that before you pitched into me as you did. Stand out of my way, Fred Lamb! I *will* go!'

'Harry, please!' Against my will he steered me to the sofa and put his handkerchief into my hand. 'Dry your eyes,' he cajoled, dropping on one knee beside me. 'I beg your pardon, dearest Harry, with all my heart. What with Astrey's dropping off the perch like that, and my having to fly the country, when I know I am no more responsible for his death than the man in the moon, I'm so knocked I hardly know what I'm saying. And of course the thought of losing you was in a fair way to driving me mad. Say that you forgive me and won't forsake me! I couldn't do without my sweetest little wife at such a time.'

He could not do without the information I possessed, and might still obtain, about Lord Astrey's death. I was sorely tempted to run away and give over the whole dreadful business, even if it meant taking refuge with my mother and braving my father's wrath. But then, the thought that Fred and I would have been done over by an evil man who had killed Lord Astrey and would laugh up his sleeve at us and all the world! Besides, I did believe Fred loved me, in his way, and I had not the heart to abandon him when he was in such trouble.

'If I stay and continue trying to find out who really killed Lord Astrey, will you give me a free hand and not cross-question or accuse me?' I asked.

'I swear it!' said he, laying his hand on his heart. 'Is there any way I can be of help to you?'

'Keep out of the way for present,' I instructed.

'Very well,' he said reluctantly. 'But I shall be at hand if you need me.'

He went out. I was going to bathe my eyes in cold water

– then I decided that my tears might make me a yet more interesting object to Captain Farrell. I held Fred's handkerchief delicately in my hand, the end trailing, and went into the dining room.

Farrell was seated at the table, but came over to join me. 'Fore gad, you look blue-devilled! What's the matter?'

'Captain Farrell, you will hardly believe what a cunning villain Mr Bingham is! He has actually tried to throw the blame for Lord Astrey's death on you. He says you gave Lord Astrey brandy from your flask, and no one else was seen to drink from it.'

'Does he, by heaven?' Farrell thundered. 'We'll see if he dares to speak so to my face!'

He started toward the door. I darted in front of him. 'No, no, Captain Farrell! I don't want him to know I am telling you everything he says! My only hope is to win his trust and trick him into betraying himself.'

'Well, I'll give you a little time with him,' he allowed. 'But if he still persists in accusing me, I'll have satisfaction. Fire and fury! Kill Astrey? Why the devil would I do that?'

'You would doom Fred to fly the country,' I pointed out delicately. 'And Mr Bingham says you wagered five hundred pounds that you could separate Fred and me.'

'I'd never have committed murder on that account! To be sure,' he added gallantly, 'there's not much I wouldn't do to win you. But I wouldn't be much good to you dangling from a gallows.' His brow darkened again. 'A pox on Bingham for putting his oar in! What does he say about that coffee and brandy Astrey drank with him this morning?'

'He says he drank coffee from the same pot and brandy from the same bottle.'

Farrell tramped back and forth, hands clasped behind him, head bent bullishly. All at once he stopped. 'I have it! Look here – suppose Bingham were in the habit of taking laudanum? People who are used to it can tolerate whacking

243

great doses. I know a fellow who's been taking it for years, and he can swallow a dose that would kill a horse.'

'So he could have put enough laudanum into the coffee or brandy to kill Lord Astrey, without any danger to himself!' I perceived. 'How clever you are, Captain Farrell! I should never have thought of such a thing.'

I saw by his eyes that he felt entitled to some reward, and prudently stepped out of his reach. 'Harry –' he coaxed.

'I must go to Mr Bingham. I believe we have him now, Captain Farrell! I shall come back and tell you what happens.'

I ran out, and flew downstairs to the parlour where I had left Bingham. On the way it crossed my mind that Farrell's having a friend who took opium might have given him the idea of poisoning Astrey with it. But that did not prove he had done so.

I went into the parlour and found Bingham still there. I closed the door portentously and looked at him in grief and horror. 'Mr Bingham,' said I in my Siddons voice, 'Captain Farrell is far more wicked than I had any idea. In his desperation to avert suspicion from himself, he has dared to accuse *you* of poisoning Lord Astrey!'

'That is absurd,' he said scornfully. 'Did you not tell him I drank the same coffee and brandy as my cousin did?'

'To be sure,' said I. 'But he insinuated that you might be an habitual opium eater, and could tolerate a dose that would have killed Lord Astrey.'

His lip curled. 'If that were so, I should not be able to do without the drug for more than a matter of hours without becoming violently ill. As it happens, I can do without it quite well, as anyone who cares to observe me for an extended period can attest.'

'Then there can be no question that Captain Farrell killed your cousin.' It was, I thought, the only possibility left.

'I can't see how one would prove it to the satisfaction of a jury,' Bingham remarked.

'I know nothing of juries,' said I. 'I suppose he will have to be made to confess.'

'I shouldn't think he would do that,' he said, seating himself and crossing one leg comfortably over the other.

I marvelled at his cold-bloodedness. But what was it to him whether Fred or Farrell were blamed for his cousin's death, as long as he had the enjoyment of Astrey's title and fortune? He had obviously borne no great love to his cousin, and being a lawyer, he cared but little for the truth. He would be of no further help to me.

I left him. Now I must have another try at Captain Farrell, but I had no notion how to go about it. As I stood pondering, Ellen came up the stairs from the basement. Her cap was askew, and she was crooning under her breath. I realised that the odd behaviour I noted in her earlier was not due to hysterics at all. She was, quite simply, drunk as a lord. I felt rather cross. 'How on earth did you get into this state?'

'Oh, miss!' Her face crumpled. 'I didn't mean any harm, and I know I oughtn't to have done it, but I was in such a pucker about the poor young lord's death, and so afeard we should all get into trouble and be hauled off to Bow Street. I only meant to take a sip, but the brandy did taste so good, and made me feel so much better!'

'Brandy?' I said quickly. 'What brandy?'

She swayed. I helped her over to the stairs and sat her down beside me. 'It was in a flask, there,' she hiccoughed, pointing to the hall table. 'I think it was Captain Farrell's. You won't tell him, will you, miss?'

'No, I won't,' said I, 'but you must answer a question for me. It is of the greatest importance. How much brandy did you drink from Captain Farrell's flask?'

'Are you going to take it out of my wages, miss?' she asked, shrinking.

'No. I'm sure Captain Farrell can spare it. But I must know how much it was.'

She blinked, searching back through her spirit-soaked brain. 'The flask was about half-full, miss.'

'Are you certain?' I pressed her.

'Quite certain, miss.'

That meant Ellen had drunk at least as much as Lord Astrey. I peered into her eyes. Her pupils were not shrunken. She showed none of the symptoms Lord Astrey had. But perhaps she was one of those people Captain Farrell had spoken of, who were accustomed to taking opium. 'Ellen, have you ever taken laudanum?'

'I did once, miss, for a toothache that hurt very bad.'

I shook my head dazedly. 'You had better go downstairs again,' I told her, 'till you feel more the thing.'

'Yes, miss.' She got to her feet unsteadily and started down the stairs. I watched to be sure she would not lose her footing, then sat puzzling, my head resting on my hand. Bingham did not poison Astrey at breakfast. Farrell did not poison him with the brandy. No one saw him eat or drink anything else, and he had not been out of anybody's sight long enough to have done so. Was all this notion of his having been poisoned moonshine? Did he die of his wound, after all?

I had only one hope left, and it was a forlorn one. I recollected that Goff had offered Astrey laudanum after he was wounded – that must mean Goff had a bottle of the stuff in that medical case he carried about. I wondered if anyone could have secretly taken some of it and fed it to Astrey when no one was watching. How this might have been done, I could not conceive, but I thought it worth taking a look at the bottle for whatever clues it might offer.

I did not know where Goff was, but having spent the last hour dashing in and out of almost every room in the house, I had quite a good idea of where he was *not*. I concluded he must be in Mrs Osgood's bedroom at the back of the ground floor, and went to have a look.

Goff was not there, but that he had been very lately was attested by the deep depression his ample form had left in an easy chair, and by the very medical case I sought, pushed behind the washstand in a corner of the room. I dragged it out and set it on a table, mindful that I ought to ask the surgeon's leave to look inside it, but too curious to await his return.

I lifted the lid and found an array of shining lancets, strips of lint, and pill boxes, neatly confined by leather straps or lodged in pouches. Seeing the lancets made me think of Goff probing for bone fragments in Lord Astrey's wound, and of Bingham's gruesome account of how lancets were used to insert cowpox under the skin in vaccination. I shuddered and concentrated on my search for laudanum.

I soon unearthed a bottle of the ruby-red liquid. The label tied to the cork read 'Laudanum', and beneath that, 'POISON'. The bottle was full to the brim, the cork firmly in place. No one could have extracted enough of the drug from this bottle to kill Lord Astrey. My last hope had gone down the wind. Fred and I were all to pieces.

Just then I noticed a bulge in the felt lining at the bottom of the case. I absently tried to smooth it out, but could not. There was something shoved inside. With an effort, I got my fingers under the lining, which was coming unglued at the edge. Working my fore and middle fingers like pincers, I contrived to grab hold of the object and pull it out.

It was a piece of oiled paper, folded into quarters. I unfolded it and found it contained a thick, brown, glutinous substance. I had never seen anything like it before, yet I felt that I ought to know what it was – that I had heard about it only just lately.

A gasp from the doorway caused me to look up quickly. Goff was staring at the object I held in my hand. I had never seen such horror, guilt, and terror on a human face. I knew then what I had found. I recalled how the all-knowing Mr Bingham had spoken of opium in its crudest form as *a brown syrup*.

'*You* gave Lord Astrey the opium,' I divined. 'But how?

When? He would not have taken it. He hated taking medicine. If he did not swallow it, then how could it have killed him? How else could poison enter a man's body—' I drew in my breath suddenly. 'Vaccination,' I whispered.

Goff began trembling violently.

'If coxpox can be introduced into a scratch,' I went on breathlessly, 'could not opium be administered in the same way? When you probed Lord Astrey's wound with a lancet, could you not have introduced some of this syrup inside?'

'That is absurd, Miss Wilson.' Goff edged toward me, his voice soft and reasonable, his face ghastly. 'You do not understand such matters. What could a chit of a girl like you know of medicine?'

'Naught,' I admitted. 'But if I am talking nonsense, then why are you so frightened?'

'I would never do such a thing,' he urged, creeping closer. 'I'm a medical man.'

'That is how you would know how to do it,' said I.

'For God's sake, Miss Wilson – I saved Lord Astrey's life only last year!'

'He was beholden to you,' I realised. 'Did he leave you money in his will?'

He let out a hoarse cry and lunged, seizing me around the waist with one hand, and a lancet from his medical case with the other. I shrieked, kicked out at him, bent backwards over his arm in a desperate effort to keep away from that evil blade.

Suddenly Fred, Bingham, and Farrell burst in. Bingham and Farrell seized Goff, while Fred pulled me to safety. I clasped Fred tightly, hardly able to believe that the previous moments had not been my last.

The fight went out of Goff after that. Bingham and Farrell bound him with curtain cords (for want of ropes), and Bingham subjected him to a rigorous cross-examination. The unfortunate surgeon broke down and admitted that his constant attendance at race meetings and prize fights had drawn him fatally into gambling, that he was deep in debt to the cent-per-cents, and that Lord Astrey had bequeathed him one thousand pounds – which in the event, said Bingham, he would not be able to collect, the law looking askance at legatees who attempt to hurry along their inheritances. At length Bingham and Farrell bore him off to the Bow Street Magistrates' Court. Fred remained behind to bear me company.

He put his arms about me. 'I feel as if I had not been alone with you this twelvemonth. Should you not like—' His voice trailed off insinuatingly.

'Of course it is what I should like above all things, having nearly been killed minutes ago.'

'You needn't claw a fellow off like that,' he grumbled, letting me go. He added after a pause, 'I suppose I ought to thank you for helping me as you did.'

'I suppose you ought,' I agreed.

'You are become very saucy,' he remarked.

It was true, and the reason was not far to seek. I had saved Fred Lamb from exile, but at the same time, I had taught myself that I could do without him. No ordeal I might face henceforth could be more terrifying than Goff and the lancet; no riddle I might be called upon to solve could be harder to fathom than Lord Astrey's death. Yet I had got through it all. The wide world no longer seemed so daunting. I began to think I might be a match for it, after all.

I magine waking up tomorrow morning beside the body of a total stranger. You can't ring 999; there's no telephone and in any case no police force in existence. You're scared, you don't know what to do, and just as you're wondering how come the corpse is covered with stab wounds and there's a bloodstained dagger underneath your bed, a group of soldiers bursts in, ready to kill you if you so much as struggle.

You're taken away. Manhandled. Thrown into a cell stinking of sewage, the walls running with slime. You've told them you're innocent, that you've been framed for murder, but what happened? A cudgel to the head's what happened!

No one listens to your story. No one believes your denials.

There's no forensics team able to prove the person had been killed elsewhere and dumped, no pathologist to say 'actually, chaps, the cause of death was coronary, the blood is from a rabbit, all wounds were made long after death'.

Hence the judge has no qualms about pronouncing you guilty. And your final thoughts, as you mount the scaffold, are: 'Why will no one help me?'

Well . . . Ellis Peters redressed that imbalance.

Through Brother Cadfael, not only was Shrewsbury brought vividly to life, murderers were brought to book

251

using the simple tools of observation and an understanding of human behaviour. Our own wits were pitted against those of the killer, yet still our eyes were not so sharp, our reading of characters not half as astute as that one mild-mannered monk.

So I say, let's all raise a glass to the memory of Ellis Peters – and then another one to the future of historical crime!

Marilyn Todd

Girl Talk

Marilyn Todd

Sometimes, when Destiny calls, it's best to pretend to be out.

This was, after all, the Circus Maximus – and amid pulsating excitement and a frantic rush for seats, what was one more silly rumour? Ignore it, Claudia told herself. Rumours are like fires, they fizzle out unless you poke and prod them.

But instead of moving on down the steps and bagging a seat near the racetrack, Claudia Seferius found herself edging that little bit closer . . .

Two minutes later, she'd cleaved a path through the surge of humanity and was elbowing her way out the turreted entrance which, despite mid-morning, lay deep in shade from the Palatine Hill.

'Alms?' A grubby hand with bitten-down nails thrust a container towards her and rattled it. 'Alms for a one-legged warrior?'

'Unless you wish to wear your nose on the back of your lice-ridden head, I suggest you move out of my way.'

Skewered by her glare, the beggar, whose sole brush with the army had been to doss in the lee of the barracks, forgot his sham disabilities and hopped smartly aside, and when he looked in his bowl, he could have sworn he was two asses down. Bugger! He'd planned to buy a pie off the vendor with that!

Claudia bit deep into the hot crumbly pastry as she marched beneath the steep escarpment. How dare he! How bloody dare Hector Polemo spread vicious gossip, insinuating she watered down the wine she sold! Claudia glowered at the flagstones which sped beneath her feet. That's where he belongs, Polemo. In the sewer which runs below these wretched cobbles! And that, by all the gods, is where I'll have him crawling.

The street being narrow, she ducked into the spice-seller's to avoid a braying donkey, its panniers bursting with melons, dates and pomegranates, and took the opportunity to sneak a pinch of pepper on her pie. Holy Jupiter, wasn't she having enough trouble keeping the business afloat without some reptile spreading lies? I mean, it's all fine and dandy people calling you lucky, just because that ageing lardball you married popped his clogs years before expected, what do they know? Rich, wasn't he, the old wine merchant? Huh! It was only *after* the funeral feast had been cleared away that Claudia discovered her luscious inheritance was tied up in stock and trusts and property – and you just try spending an apartment block in Naples or half a brickworks on the Via Tiburtina!

Claudia tossed the last corner of her pie to the hopeful mongrel who'd been pattering behind and brushed her hands together. Offers to buy the business had come flooding in, including one from Polemo so tempting that Claudia had almost drawn up the contract. Until, that is, she discovered profit margins on wine were virtually double that of any other business! Goddammit, she'd be a fool to cash that in. Why not take a chance and break out on her own?

The street veered left, a bustle of shops and shoppers concerned exclusively with luxuries – perfumes, emeralds, books of vellum, tunics woven with wool spun as fine as babies' hair.

Why not? Because the Guild refused to deal with women, that's why not. Unheard of, don't y'know. A woman's place was in the bedroom, ha-ha-ha, and the proposals, which had at first been oh-so-fair, became hard-nosed ultimatums, until finally they petered out – and it was at this point Polemo revealed himself to be a pirate in commercial waters.

'Take what you want by whatever means you can, that's my motto,' he had laughed in that distinctive boom of his. 'Sooner or later you'll have to sell and when you do, my pretty widow, I'll be the one who's mopping up the spills.'

He'd had the gall to approach her during the very parade in which her husband, had he lived, would have been at the fore. Polemo and that stuck-up bitch he married – what was her name? Selina, that's right. Selina, with her predatory green eyes and flawless skin.

'My family's produced wine for generations,' he said, unmoved by shining breastplates and caparisoned white horses. 'When we set out to expand, we expand and nobody – I mean nobody – stands in our way.' He smiled a lizard smile to emphasise his point. 'So why don't you reflect on that?'

Auburn-haired Selina was standing at his shoulder.

'I don't need to,' Claudia had replied, keeping her gaze fixed on the swords held aloft by purple-robed riders. 'Your threats don't frighten me, Polemo, and my response remains a raspberry.'

Selina slipped in front of her husband, and Claudia had been able to smell her expensive perfume above the acid tang of horseflesh and leather and dung. 'You'd be wise not to cross us,' she purred. 'Hector always gets his way in the end.'

For the first time, Claudia wrenched her eyes away from the dazzling display of weaponry and armour. 'Not only am I immune to bullying,' she replied, 'I won't be *cowed* either!'

Selina's breath came out in a hiss, but Hector's restraining hand on her shoulder had cut short retaliation. Well, that little interchange had taken place exactly one month ago today, and clearly Polemo wasn't a man to let the grass grow beneath his finely tooled sandals. Already the rumour-mongers were putting it about that Claudia Seferius watered her wine – what a cheek! The thought never entered her head! Not while she was palming it off as eight-year-old vintage . . .

On the corner by the basilica, a score of male prostitutes draped themselves against the columns and the walls, kohl-eyed and preening, but Claudia paid scant attention as she swept into a Forum ablaze with late summer sunshine and seething with advocates and acrobats, charlatans and hucksters, with slaves pushing handcarts and porters balancing amphorae of sweet olive oil. Pungent aromas exploded all around. Sausages sizzling on a spit, incense from the temples, fragrant roots from the herbalist.

'The sun's high in Libra,' an astrologer said. 'Would the lady like me to draw up her horoscope?'

His scrolls scattered across the travertine flags as the whirlwind blazed on. She half-expected to see Polemo striding towards her any minute, mastiff at his side, lackeys at his heels, brushing his hand through the air as he waved interruptions and issues aside. By the gods, Claudia fumed, I'll choke you with your chitterlings for this! Influential he might be, but Hector Polemo wasn't above being knocked off his perch and exposed for the worm he truly was.

Handsome enough, though, she conceded. Knocking forty with a thatch of hair envied by many half his age and, to be honest, they made a handsome couple, him and his foxy-faced wife. There was a teenage daughter, too. Lotis, wasn't it? Though rumour had it that raising children was a job for nannies and for nursemaids as far as those two were concerned.

The house lay just off the Via Sacra. A respectable house, in a respectable neighbourhood, with a respectable white cat washing on the window edge until the clatter on the knocker sent it diving under the laurels.

'Where are they?' With the flat of her hand, Claudia barged the doorman aside. 'That slimeball Polemo and his poisonous wife. Where are they?'

'Who . . . ?' The elderly janitor strove to keep up as Claudia flounced through the vestibule and into the bright, airy atrium. 'Who . . . ?'

'What are you?' she asked, throwing up her hands. 'An owl?'

'I believe,' a deep voice intercepted from the corner, 'the janitor is enquiring after your own name.'

I don't believe this! Holy Jupiter, Destiny must be doubled up with laughter!

Ignoring the baritone, Claudia instructed the janitor to fetch that lowlife weasel, Hector, and be bloody quick about it. Rheumy eyes darted to the corner and back again, but the doorman didn't move.

'The lowlife weasel's out.' The baritone made no attempt to eliminate the amusement from its vocal cords. 'Or so everyone surmises. He's not been seen since last night.'

Down in the Circus Maximus grim-faced competitors would be racing each other on thickly greased hides, much to the delight of the crowd, while here, finches in an aviary chirruped and sang as though this was the happiest day of their lives. Shit! Claudia ground her heel into the nose of a mosaic dolphin and was damned if she'd turn around.

'In that case –' Claudia's eyes bored so hard into the old man's, his began to water – 'you can wheel out the frosty-faced old haddock that he married.'

Wouldn't you just know the poor janitor would be pipped to the answering post!

'Selina,' the baritone pronounced, 'is still in bed.'

The fountain in the pool juggled droplets of water in sunshine which turned bronze ancestral busts to gold.

'Orbilio,' Claudia said wearily. 'Why do you persist in bugging me?'

She really did not need this. Not here. Not some ferreting investigator snooping around to rattle the bones in her closet. And sod's law meant it was Marcus Cornelius Orbilio she had to bump into! The only man in Rome who knew the dark side of her past! Not, of course, that it was her past which was the problem at the moment. For reasons best known to themselves, the Security Police were attracted to offences which resulted in things like exile. And when it came to sniffing out crime, Orbilio had the snout of a trufflehound.

'Me?' The wool of his toga squeaked as he slid off the polished table he'd perched against and Claudia caught a faint whiff of his sandalwood unguent. 'I was under the impression it was the other way around.'

Claudia heard a grinding sound and, in the absence of any quernstones in the atrium, concluded it was the gnashing of her teeth.

'After all,' he continued mildly, 'I got here first, remember?'

Crossing her arms, Claudia stared at the sky through the opening in the roof and wished something would happen up there to break the blue monotony. Nothing did, of course. No honking geese, no passing butterfly, not even one tiny puff of cloud. Though for a busy household, it seemed odd that she could hear only the thumping of her heart against her ribcage.

'Perhaps,' he suggested, and she could feel the twinkle in his eyes boring deep into her shoulder-blades, 'you would care to join the treasure hunt?'

He came into view then, casting his tall, broad shadow over the pool and for half a second Claudia allowed herself the hope that maybe, just maybe, he was here on a social visit, patrician to patrician and all that.

'Are we,' she enquired, 'talking cryptic clues on scraps of parchment?'

'N-not exactly.' Bugger. 'The hunt is for one Justus Capella.'

'Oh, and what might the Security Police be fitting this poor sod up with?'

Dark eyes crinkled at the corners. 'Strange as it may seem,' he said, 'we have a preference for villains.' He leaned his weight against a marble podium, and Claudia watched a pulse beat in his neck. 'Prosecutions tend to stick more easily, although in Capella's case we'll have no problem. His attempt to kill the Emperor was quite blatant.'

Assassination! Curious, despite herself, Claudia trawled her memory. Capella. Capella. She knew that name, surely? Ah, yes. The half-baked revolutionary! Like father, like son, so they said, and whilst his father might have died fighting at Mark Antony's side, Justus had retained his father's papers, met with his father's friends and still found time to whip up sympathisers of his own.

All very noble, Claudia supposed, all very idealistic – had it not been for the fact that the Antony rebellion had been quashed twenty years ago!

Mind, she'd seen Justus in action on the Rostrum, and not only were his tones persuasive, he was a head-turner, too. Small wonder most of his devotees were women, but then women always did go for dimples in the chin. Makes even brutes seem somehow vulnerable.

'Let me get this straight,' she said, running her fingers lightly back and forth across the aviary. 'Justus Capella takes a pop at the Emperor and you come here to arrest him on your own. My hero.'

'More hack than hero,' Orbilio said wistfully. 'Capella's disappeared and while the army gets the glory, searching every crevice and shaking down every cart, your champion is reduced to tramping round the city, questioning the man's associates.'

'Or not questioning them, as the case may be,' Claudia corrected cheerfully.

'Did I say it was easy being a hero?'

His fingers closed round the bars of the birdcage; she could see the short dark hairs on the back of his hand, smelled the rosemary in which his tunic had been rinsed . . . She forced her mind back to business.

'Is Hector involved in the assassination plot?' Two birds with one stone and all that!

'Who knows. Capella called yesterday and there was one humdinger of a row between Hector and his wife, though the slaves couldn't hear what it was about. Unfortunately, since Selina has left explicit orders not to be disturbed –' the fingers released the wooden bars and spiked their way through his curls – 'I'm forced to wait for Lotis to return, in the hope she can shed light on the whereabouts of either her father or, better still, Capella. Patience –' he released a weary grin and Claudia's heart seemed to bump that little bit harder (proximity of the law, of course. What else?) – 'is but one of my many virtues.'

'Patience,' she said, marching towards the bed chambers, 'is a damned good waste of drinking time.'

As her footsteps echoed down the corridor, Claudia was again struck by the opulence of Hector's house – Parian marbles, painted frescoes, gilded stucco ceilings – and her resolve hardened. Polemo might be an aristocrat whose family tree had its roots intertwined with the vine, but the moral was clear. Stick at it, girl, and you too will be rolling!

'Upsy-dupsy, Selina,' she trilled, flinging wide the bedroom door. 'It's time we girls had a little chat.'

Claudia had not taken three paces before she pulled up sharp, clamping her hand over her mouth. Selina was indeed still in bed. Her lush auburn hair streamed across the damask pillow, her emerald eyes wide and lovely, even in death.

And make no mistake, Selina was dead. Her head had been neatly detached from her body.

That, though, wasn't why Claudia reeled out of the room. She'd seen enough blood spilled in the arena not to be squeamish. No, it was more the fact that the body upon which the head had been placed did not belong to Selina.

The torso belonged to a man.

Marcus Cornelius Orbilio stared at the bed for several minutes without so much as blinking. Through his current work and during his stint as a tribune in the army, he'd seen death in all its guises and it rarely, if ever, fazed him. He'd seen men writhing on the battlefield, whores stabbed in alleyways, vagrants with their throats cut, and whilst he'd been saddened by it, in turns angered and debased, one thing Orbilio never underestimated was man's capacity to savage his fellow human being.

Thus, anyone watching now, as the sun dazzled the eyes of a mosaic lion, would have been surprised to see him standing motionless, his face set solid, apparently in shock at the grotesque arrangement on the couch.

Orbilio would have been flattered, since his introspection was considerably baser than concern for Selina or Polemo, or even tracking zealous revolutionaries. All that mattered, as far as he could see, was that fate had catapulted Claudia Seferius – the woman who broke laws the way a trainer breaks horses – back into his orbit . . . and this time she would not slip through his grasp!

And slip she would, given half a chance; she had more tricks up her sleeve than Circe, the enchantress who had bewitched Odysseus on his return from the Trojan War. Take this morning, for example. What magic inspired such passion, such lust inside him that, even when she stumbled into the atrium, whey-faced and shaking and any fool could sense something was seriously amiss, his sole impulse had been to take her on the spot, there and then! Orbilio closed his eyes and inhaled the memory of her spicy, Judaean perfume. Mother of Tarquin, how he yearned to watch the pale blue cotton of her tunic slither to her ankles, to loosen her breast band and feel the—

'So.'

Her voice in his ear sent colour rushing to his cheeks. She could read minds now? He wouldn't put it past her!

'Double suicide?'

'Undoubtedly.' He grinned back, and felt something lurch in his gut when he looked at her. 'What else could it be?'

Then he glanced down at the body/bodies and the storm inside him subsided. At last he understood why they called it the Security Police, because that's how his emotions were now his brain was centred again. Secure and in control. Oh yes, a chap knows where he is with a maniac running wild . . . He heard the door click as she closed it behind her.

'I gather,' she said, 'from the routine hum of housework, that this is still our little secret?'

Secrets, Claudia? With you? The prospect brought a tightness to his chest, but he forced himself to focus on her words. Strange how the instant he'd read the horror in her eyes, he'd dismissed the janitor. Pure instinct, but that selfsame instinct had been quickly vindicated, because the last thing he needed was a houseful of panic-stricken slaves screaming their heads off and trampling any evidence the murderer may have left in his wake.

'They were killed elsewhere,' he said needlessly. She knew as well as he there was barely one drop of blood on the sheets. 'And positioned here later.'

But why?

'Do we have a madman on the loose?' Claudia turned to examine an onyx flask as Orbilio pressed the back of his fingers against Selina's alabaster-white skin.

'Not in the sense you mean, no.'

The sun reflected ripples from the washbasin in lines against the wall, and he noticed her gaze was fixed on these as he drew down the shutters on Selina's emerald eyes.

'I don't, for instance, envisage a killer on the rampage, mismatching wives to husbands.' He heaved Hector's body on to its front. No marks. He rolled the body back again – it seemed proper, somehow, to align it with the head. 'On the other hand, however many enemies they made, these two –' he shot Claudia a sharp glance – 'this doesn't seem the work of a sane and balanced mind.'

Orbilio straightened up and wiped his hands on the counterpane.

In fact, unless he missed his guess, Selina's body and Hector's head would be lying next door in Hector's bedroom.

Life is rarely as we plan it, otherwise we'd all be millionaires with perfect figures, perfect marriages and a deep all-over tan. Clicking her fingers, Claudia marched up and down the atrium. By rights she ought to be ensconced in her seat at the Capitoline Games, cheering the competitors and making furtive bets as she nibbled honeycombs and winecakes. Ought, though, was the operative word! Supersnoop had spoken and she was grounded, stuck not with wrestlers and racers, but with a couple butchered in their beds. Destiny must have a stitch in her side!

'Sorry,' Orbilio had said, looking as contrite as a puppy with a slipper. 'I need you as a material witness.'

Material witness be buggered, he was on to her! Claudia slapped her palm against her forehead. What an idiot she'd been! The instant she found him here, in Polemo's townhouse, she should have spun on her heel and to hell with rumours about diluting wine!

She plumped down in a chair and stuffed a cushion into the small of her back. What was that word, when you pass one thing off as another? A five-letter word, was it not? Starting with F, ending with D, and didn't it have an R and an A and a U in between?

She bounced out of the chair and resumed her pacing. Think you're clever, do you, Marcus Trufflehound Orbilio? Think that by keeping me hanging round the murder scene

I might let something slip and you can lure me into a confession? You can forget those slugslime tactics. Find yourself another mug!

Claudia pulled up short at the family shrine. Hang on. There might just be a way out of this . . .

Orbilio was in Hector's bedroom and the furrows in his brow could have been left by a ploughshare, they were that deep. But there was disappointment, as well as perplexity, etched on his face.

The room was a mess. A bloody mess, in fact, with the counterpane strewn across the floor, the rug crumpled in a corner, feathers bursting out of the bolster. Unfortunately for Hotshot's investigative prowess, it was a room in which someone had lost their temper rather than committed double murder. Not a cadaver in sight, leaving Claudia torn between relief and reservation.

Relief, because she didn't have to confront the grisly spectacle he had predicted.

Reservation, because without the bodies she was stuck with this cocky patrician who might, if the gods sided with him, solve three cases in as many hours – and if nailing an assassin, exposing a murderer and catching a fraudster didn't hasten his path to the Senate, what would?

Claudia's objective was to persuade the gods to settle for two out of three.

An overturned lampstand had left pools of olive oil and Orbilio trod carefully as he searched the rare wood caskets and probed the heavy clothes chests. In contrast to Selina's taste for greens and gold, Hector had chosen earthy colours for his room. Wars were fought on walls and floor, visceral and vivid. Horses reared, shields rolled, javelins rained from the sky and Claudia decided that if murder hadn't actually been committed here, it damned well should have! The room *was* Hector. Brutal, domineering, riding roughshod to achieve his own ends and it was hardly surprising he'd met with such a violent end.

'As I thought!' Orbilio waved rolls of parchment in triumph. 'Confirmation that Polemo was financing Capella's operation!'

Claudia chewed her lower lip. 'You think this is an execution?'

'Quite possibly,' he said, leafing through the sheaves of paper. 'Augustus has followers so devoted, so fanatical they would kill without conscience to protect the emerging concept of Empire, the same way Justus would kill to have it revert.'

True. Thirty years might have passed since the Roman world had been wrenched in two, Augustus taking control of the West, Mark Antony running the East, but old wounds still festered and grievances passed down. Even now, philosophers debated the case around the Rostrum.

Mark Antony, the neutrals argued, was no less a patriot, but had he been wise to ally himself with the Egyptian whore, Cleopatra? She who'd already tried – and failed – to ensnare Julius Caesar?

Some said yes, definitely. Antony (unlike others they could mention) would not have stopped at the Danube but pressed on to annexe Germany and the Belgica tribes, perhaps even Britannica, and by making Alexandria his capital, almost certainly Arabia and the Orient would be ours.

Bollocks, others scoffed. For ten years Antony had ample chance to change things. Instead, he waged continued civil war; he'd never have given us half what the Emperor has. Look around! We have peace and prosperity, food in our bellies, gold in our temples – and moreover, our sons don't lie dead on the battlefield.

Oh yes, thought Claudia. To retain such stability, men would kill gladly – but did Hector pose such a threat? A few sesterces thrown to Capella's cause was probably more of an insurance policy, should the political scene change in the future.

'Wouldn't the executioners want to leave a clear message?'

she asked. A warning to others sympathetic to rebellious causes?

'This isn't clear?'

Hmm. Since Supersnoop had already checked the bedrooms for bodies, it was with curiosity as opposed to trepidation that Claudia left him to his scrutiny and slipped into Lotis' chamber. Usually a fifteen-year-old surrounds herself with clutter bridging infancy and womanhood – the latest robes, pots of perfume, new cosmetics alongside her cracked miniature tea set and a ragged knitted doll. Because by now she'd be affianced, there should be tokens from her future husband, too – a fan, perhaps a parrot. This could pass for a guest room, it was so bare!

A stone dropped in Claudia's stomach and suddenly she felt considerably less sympathy for Hector and Selina, dedicating themselves to the pursuit of pleasure and ambition with not a thought to little Lotis. Fumbling in vain for a ragdoll tucked inside the bedclothes, her vision clouded as she pictured a small child with a light in her eyes and a laugh in her voice rushing up to show Mummy her new tambourine, her gown, her brand-new whistle, only to be coldly turned away. Little Lotis would not have sat on Daddy's knee, pulling at his ears, or had him rolling on the floor as they played knucklebones together – and the tragedy was, Lotis would have known what she was missing. Growing up in a house full of slave children, chortling and happy as they bounced balls off cellar walls and played piggy-in-the-middle, her isolation would have been complete.

With a lump in her throat, Claudia left the dismal void of Lotis' bed chamber and passed into the peristyle. Orbilio was browsing through the ledgers in Hector's office and without him noticing her, she approached the bathroom door.

'Sorry, ma'am, the mistress says you can't go in.' A dumpy kitchen maid scurrying past with a brace of duck and a skillet tucked under her arm paused to admonish the visitor.

The visitor saw no point in mentioning the mistress was

in no position to countermand the order. 'Why's that?' she asked.

The girl giggled, before remembering herself. 'Well, she likes her privacy, does Miss Selina.'

Claudia considered the implications. Selina had been dead some hours, probably since last night . . .

'When did Miss Selina give this order?' she enquired.

'Ooh.' The wench thought back. 'Yesterday afternoon, it would have been, when—' She stopped short, her cheeks aflame, and by somehow indicating that the duck were so urgently required by the cook that to delay might cause reverberations right across the Empire, she scampered out of sight.

Claudia opened the door to the bathroom and peered in. 'Hey, Trufflehound,' she called out. 'There's something here which might interest you.'

Marcus Cornelius Orbilio heard, rather than observed, Claudia pass behind the office and he was intrigued. When he'd informed her she was required to stay as a material witness, he'd been prepared for a battle – and found instead compliance!

He bit his lip. She was up to something; he could smell it. Ask her to hang around a murder scene when the dead are virtual strangers and the Capitoline Games are in full swing, and you don't expect her to shout 'yippee'. At best he'd have envisaged her sprawled across a couch, one long leg swinging with an air of nonchalance as she maybe read a spot of Virgil or nibbled chestnut bread, but never in his wildest dreams (correction, nightmares) did he imagine her assisting his investigations on a voluntary basis.

She was digging a pit for him to fall into.

All he had to do was to spot it.

Vaguely uneasy, but unable to say why, Marcus was checking Polemo's accounts when he heard Claudia call out. The grim set of her face said it all, and through the open doorway his eyes scanned the sunken floor and frescoes of winged cupids. Blast! While he'd been chasing rabbits, she'd stumbled on the bodies . . .

He ran along the peristyle and skidded to a halt inside the doorway. There were no windows to the room. Illumination came from two bronze lampstands each supporting six small hanging lanterns – ample light to reveal the painted waterfall under which two painted nymphs cavorted with a painted satyr and the cleaver propped against the rocks. Except the cleaver wasn't art. Blue steel glittered in the lamplight, flickering and wicked, its handle in a pool of dark brown sludge.

Orbilio swore under his breath. Bloodstains by the bucketload where the bodies had been chopped up – but no trace of the remains! Where the *hell* could they be? A prolonged and penetrating scream cut short his musings. Damn! He sprinted back along the corridor. He'd given explicit orders to keep clear of Selina's room –

Oh, shit. Orbilio passed his hand over his eyes and experienced a wave of nauseous shame. In his efforts to link Polemo with the plot against the Emperor, he'd completely overlooked the fact that he'd originally been waiting for the daughter, Lotis.

Who'd now returned – and paid a call upon her mother!

Morning turned to afternoon to evening and the smell of scapegoat hung rank in the air.

Between them, the slaves travelled every single gamut of emotion and as the shadows lengthened and the air cooled down, they retreated into silent huddles, terrified and stiff. Unless the killer was unmasked and quickly the entire contingent faced execution on the grounds that the murderer must, by default, be one amongst them.

Not all the gods they prayed to were Roman.

Not all the gods they prayed to were listening.

*   *   *

Undertakers came and went, military boots left mud on fine mosaics, metal styluses etched notes in wax tablets and the atrium became lit, not by sunshine, but by the golden glow of lamplight as the finches in the aviary tucked heads under jewel-coloured wings.

Claudia, amusing a family of kittens with a lengthy skein of wool, reflected that the Circus would be swept clean of litter and in darkness, while exhausted competitors rehydrated in taverns thronging to the rafters as spectators walked home girls they'd met at the racetrack.

She sighed as she twirled the tail of wool. By rights she should be revelling, too, but she'd got herself into this mess and now she had to get out. Preferably without the word 'exile' bandied about, even in jest! Unfurling her legs and leaving the kittens mauling a sardine apiece, she wandered into the garden. Waterlilies bobbed luminous and silent on the dark, still waters of the fishpond and a tabby coiled its lazy limbs beneath a hibiscus, alert for careless moths. Someone had been collecting herbs; the air was redolent with borage, mint and thyme, and the moon was not yet up. Such was Polemo's wealth, street sounds – drovers, carters and carousers – were muffled by high walls faced off with honey-coloured travertine. Only a subdued clatter from the kitchens and ragged sobs from deep inside the building disturbed this oasis of tranquillity.

'Still here?' Orbilio's eyebrows lifted off their launchpads as he emerged from the body of the house, and Claudia thought she caught something other than surprise in his eyes.

'Someone has to solve the crime,' she said cheerfully.

'Silly me,' he murmured. 'Here I was thinking you didn't give a damn who killed Polemo and his wife, them being an unscrupulous couple who attracted enemies like flies in their ruthless quest for power – yet here you are, competing with me for a job.'

Claudia smiled ingenuously and tried not to think of sixty

chained slaves thrown into an arena howling for justice and for blood. 'How's Lotis?'

If her change in tactics threw him, he didn't let it show. 'A real chip off the Polemo block,' he said, plucking petals from a purple aster. 'As the undertakers wheeled the . . . bodies away, she stood by, white-lipped, clench-fisted, but none of the wild hysterics you might expect.'

You might expect, thought Claudia. Not me! The instant that girl sees emotion, she wrestles it to the ground and sits firmly on its chest to show who's boss. Although, in this case, Lotis could be forgiven for breaking down, poor cow. Tradition decrees that, for the nobility especially, the body lies in state for several days, feet towards the door with torches burning at each corner and cypress laid around. In Hector's case, of course, there was no head to decorate with wreathes of oak and to say it would be in poor taste to display Selina's bonce on its own was an understatement! No doubt something would be worked out before the funeral, but in the meantime the undertakers had collected the remains and Lotis had stood stoical throughout. This before her sixteenth birthday!

Absently Claudia drummed her fingernails against a bronze Apollo. 'Suppose,' she said, 'I'm in a position to have you fêted by your peers and cited for your – Orbilio? Are you listening?'

His pupils were dilated, his expression distant. Claudia blamed the twilight, and thought she heard him mumble, 'Circe.'

'Circe?' she frowned. 'Circe was an enchantress!'

'And how.' He gave a strange and distant smile. 'She turned men into swine.'

'That's not magic, Orbilio, that's human nature. Now are you ready for my proposition?'

'Always, Claudia,' he muttered, and she wondered whether he'd been sniffing hemp seeds on the quiet. His eyes were raking hers intently, and any other time she might have thought he was . . .

'Right.' She settled herself on a marble bench and wondered why his sandalwood unguent seemed so fresh after such a full and busy day. 'My proposition is simple. In return for delivering a killer, you overlook my little scam. Is it a deal?'

'Hmmph.'

Claudia spun round. The poor chap seemed to be having a coughing fit in his handkerchief; his shoulders were shaking, his eyes watering, though for one ridiculous moment, she mistook the bout for laughter.

'I'll take that as an affirmative,' she snapped.

The moon, rising now, reflected whiter than the lilies in the fishpond and it was in this dark mirror she watched her tall protagonist settle his weight against a scarlet fluted pillar.

'While you were playing Centurions and Soldiers, I've been collating information. One.' Crisply Claudia ticked the points off on her fingers. 'Capella and Polemo were in fact the best of friends. Hector, being a dyed-in-the-wool expansionist –' (she should have guessed!) – 'held similar political beliefs.'

Polemo, dear soul, being power mad, also believed Augustus wrong in consolidating the Empire when he could be conquering the East and subduing half of Dacia.

'So friends they were. Point two.'

She swivelled round to check she had Supersleuth's attention and, finding the wicked glint in his eye offputting to say the least, swivelled back again.

'Selina and Capella were embroiled in a passionate affair. It began eight, ten weeks ago and in the beginning, when their furtive assignations took place up in the hills, only Selina's maid knew anything about it. Then the unimaginable happened. Selina – hard, ambitious, cold Selina – fell in love!'

And who could blame her, really? Justus Capella was, what, six years younger than her workaholic husband; he was handsome, dashing, charismatic; he simply swept her off her feet. Lately they'd meet here, making love in the bathroom, in the garden, in the bedroom, until—

'Yesterday,' Claudia ticked another finger, 'and I confess

it's guesswork from now on, Selina announced she was leaving.'

Across the garden, the tabbycat stretched, yawned and decided that, moths or no moths, she really ought not to abandon her kittens. Tail crooked, she padded back to the house.

'Hector went ballistic,' Claudia continued. 'Never, he said, had he imagined such treachery, an adulteress under his own roof, cavorting with a man he trusted. He shamed her, blamed her, threatened to disown her—'

'Ah, but did he threaten to kill her in this hypothetical scenario?'

Claudia ignored the interruption. 'In fact, Hector was on the very point of throwing her into the gutter, when Guess Who turns up? Well, Polemo, being as mad as a dog with its nose in a wasps' nest—'

'Threatens to shop Capella?'

Claudia's lips pursed. Fine. Cleverclogs arrived at the same conclusion by himself, so what? A deal's a deal, and he had given his word. (All right, if you're going to be pedantic, he'd actually given his cough, but when fraud was the issue, a girl can't afford to be fussy!) Now where was she? Oh yes, Hector was on the brink of exposing Capella.

'When Justus realises his friend is serious, he brains him with a statuette – that's why Hector's head is missing. Selina, of course, is witness to the act, and the gal is horrified. Leaving Hector is one thing, but she'd been married to the man for twenty years and not without affection, and suddenly not only is she a widow, her lover is his murderer. Maybe she attacks him; perhaps she, too, threatens to call the army out, but whatever the circumstance, by now Capella is a desperate man. Drawing his dagger, he runs her through – hence Selina's body also has to be disposed of.'

'Hm.' Stroking his jaw, Marcus began to pace the path which criss-crossed the peristyle. Something was clearly bothering him, presumably the issue of why Capella would need to hide the evidence of his atrocities.

'Because,' Claudia explained, without waiting for him to ask, 'Justus needed time to make good his escape. By laying the two – er, pieces together in bed, he could make it appear as though there was some maniac on the loose. So!' She paused for effect. 'Am I brilliant, or what?'

Time passed. A chilly breeze capered round the peristyle, wafting late summer roses and heliotrope into the air. Claudia drew her wrap tighter round her shoulders. She had expected applause, though bouquets at her feet would be nice, a standing ovation even better. Instead he kept loping up and down the path like a cheetah in a cage. Oh, well. You can't rush fraud . . .

Eventually the pacing stopped and Marcus scratched his chin. 'Plausible,' he muttered, 'apart from—'

'Plausible!' she gasped. 'Is that all you can bring yourself to say? Goddammit, Orbilio, you have a dangerous, devious killer on the—' She broke off, as the impact of his words sunk in. 'Apart from what?'

'Apart from the fact you may be wrong,' he said, so quietly she had to strain to catch the words.

'I may be many things, Orbilio, but I am never wrong.' She sniffed. 'And if I read Capella correctly, he won't run before he's had another pop at Augustus. If I were you, I'd stop haunting this place like a lovelorn ghost and start looking for him in—'

'Oh, I know where Capella is,' Orbilio said, sucking in his cheeks.

'*What?*' He had the assassin banged up all along? Double-duplicitous, vermin-tongued skunk! He'd been winding her up . . . and enjoying every single minute! Claudia managed to turn her indignant 'What?' into a mildly curious 'Where?'

'Lotis, you see, was quite adamant,' Marcus said, and clearly Claudia hadn't explained herself. He was rambling along at a tangent.

'Orbilio, you deaf clod, I'm asking what you've done with Capella.'

'And I'm telling you.' He grinned, and she was tempted to mash his nose with her fist. 'You see, Lotis stumbled in on her mother, and shocked as she was at finding her dead, as I say, she was one hundred per cent certain.'

A strange sensation crept over Claudia. 'One hundred per cent certain of what?'

'That the torso was not that of her father,' Orbilio said with a sad, lopsided smile. 'Which means—'

Claudia nodded in weary understanding. 'The man in the bed was Capella.'

Confirmation arrived within the hour.

The marble merchant whose house backed on to the public gardens on the Esquiline Hill had despatched his steward with a doughty club to silence the mutt which had been howling for the past two hours and the man reported back, not with tales of a rabid dog terrorising the neighbourhood, but of a nobleman hanging from an oak, his mastiff baying at his feet. Despite the suffused face and black, protruding tongue, the steward believed he recognised the man as one Hector Polemo, regular guest at the marble merchant's table.

Lotis, orphaned now in earnest, responded by listening carefully to the legionary's report then calling for a scribe and parchment. To the astonishment of both Claudia and Orbilio, she then proceeded to dictate a letter to her fiancé, informing him that, now she had inherited the empire from her father, the marriage contract would be terminated.

There was no mention of regret.

As the breeze grew cooler and bright stars appeared, Claudia's eyes scanned walls dripping not with opulence, but with undiluted hatred. She shivered, and not from the cold.

The army had moved in, clodhopping over every room as they tried to decide whether Hector had committed suicide out of remorse or fear of public execution and searching for some hint of where he'd left his wife's torso and his arch-rival's head. Would they, for instance, when dawn had broken on another glorious late-summer day, find the star-crossed lovers laid out in another ghoulish embrace?

In the atrium, Orbilio debriefed a tired centurion as soldiers trickled back and forth and the kitchens filled with smoke in an effort to feed the uniformed invasion. The silence from Lotis' room was electrifying. Claudia shuddered. The venom in this house was cloying. Contaminating. It gripped you by the throat and by the heart and refused to let you go, and she was sickened by the whole damned sordid business. She had to get away. To think. To maintain some balance of perspective!

Find a place well clear of scheming, plots and lies, where the air was fresh and uncontaminated by treason, spite or murder . . .

Without a word, Claudia slipped through a side door, where the night quickly swallowed her up.

The little road coiled its way up the hillside like a cobra, and with every rumble of the wheels the trackway narrowed that bit further. Weeds grew waist-high along the roadside, potholes were frequent, and the greenery encroached lower by the cubit – hawthorn, oak and juniper.

'Are you sure this is where you want to go?' the driver enquired, and Claudia nodded, picturing the ancient temple cut into the rock high upon the hill, far (so far!) from the viper's nest which formed Polemo's house. A place of solitude and peace, where air was fresh and birds warbled from the treetops, where the wind would tug your hair and tease your skirts. Oh yes. This was the place, all right! Shunned by locals scared of ghosts who bent knees to ancient gods and who, while doing so, painted their bodies red like blood, the only worshippers today were lizards scuttling over fallen columns and swallows nesting in the crumbling eaves. Across the wooded valley, wide and distant, a buzzard mewed and circled.

'We can't go no further, ma'am.' The driver indicated the weed-choked road.

'Then wait here,' she instructed, jumping down. 'I shan't be long.'

The ascent was steep. Tendrils of ivy laid snares across the stony path and from time to time Claudia had to duck beneath an overhanging branch. Who cared, she thought, if her wrap snagged on a bramble? Anything to get away from the bitter atmosphere in that house just off the Via Sacra – but at least with Polemo dead, there'd be no more ugly rumours to contend with! Had, though, had she pulled it off? Had she done enough to make Supersnoop keep his bargain? Idly, she wondered what progress he and the military might be making.

Panting from the climb, Claudia approached the decaying temple, its stone now pitted by the elements, its grandeur and its elegance eroded by the forest closing in. Faint traces of paint remained – a figure dancing, a leopard in mid-leap – but only rats made their devotions at the altar and these days rainwater poured the only libation. What was that? A scuffle from the hillside, a flash of—

'Stay where you are!' a voice commanded.

Claudia jumped, and despite the heat, her blood turned glacial-cold. From the bushes to her left a bow protruded, its string pulled taut.

The arrowhead aimed directly at her heart.

Like a coney caught in torchlight, Claudia stood mesmerised by the tiny sliver of wood which could, with one brief twang, cut short the thread of life. Her tongue was dry, her legs had turned to granite. This can't be happening! It has to be a dream. A dream. I'll wake up any second . . .

But the sun beat down upon her back, the buzzard mewed and, high in the canopy, a squirrel pulled seeds from a pine cone. The bow flexed backwards in an arc, the knuckles drawing it white from the effort. Fear curdled Claudia's stomach; her head swam. Sweet Jupiter, don't let this happen. Not here. Not to me. In a spot so isolated, wolves would tear the flesh from my corpse, ants would devour my bones.

'I—' A dormouse could have squeaked louder. She cleared her throat and started again. 'I know what happened at the house,' she said, and this time there was no quaver in her voice. Like Lotis, Claudia was also well-versed in concealing emotion.

'Do you really?' The voice, from deep within the bushes, was heavy with sarcasm.

'Why do you think I'm here?' she said. 'To gather huckleberries?'

She knew now why the bodies were mismatched. Why it was so important the missing parts should not be found.

'What did you expect to achieve?' the arrow sneered. 'A confession?'

Claudia caught a movement down the path. Brown. The driver's leather jerkin?

The eyes behind the bow followed the direction of her glance. 'If you're looking for the young man who brought you, you're looking in the wrong direction. Try over your shoulder!'

An eagle clawed at Claudia's heart. Oh, no! Mighty Juno, say it's not true . . . With a neck made of wood, she forced herself to look down. From this dizzy vantage point, one could see clearly the dappled mare chomping on the grass which had finally impeded their progress. The horse seemed unaware of the driver slumped face forwards with an arrow in his spine . . .

Claudia blinked back the tears and tried not to remember how he'd boasted all the way from Rome about his new-born son and pretty wife and the impending birthday celebrations for his daughter—

The bowstring. Surely the arm must be tiring? Somewhere

in the recess of her mind, she remembered that killers are supposed to brag about their crimes, about how easy it was to fool the authorities.

'You'll never get away with it,' she taunted. 'If I, a mere civilian, can find you—'

'The army can? I doubt it!' The figure in the bushes laughed. 'I know your sort,' it scoffed. 'In fact, we're not so very unalike when it boils down to it. You came here to satisfy yourself that you were right, to crow a bit, perhaps gain credit with the army, and you never once considered failure. I admire that.'

The analysis was closer to the mark than Claudia cared to acknowledge. 'Good.' She drew a deep breath. 'Because I didn't trek up to this godforsaken rat hole to get killed. I thought you might care to hear a proposition.'

A long silence came from the bushes and Claudia wondered whether her last view of the world would be a broad valley with leaves just turning for autumn and paint flaking from columns. Her nails bit deep into the palms of her hands, and she felt a small dribble of blood run down her thumb.

'What put you on to me?' the voice asked, and in her mind Claudia punched the air and thought *yes!* The killer's ego had triumphed!

'It was,' she said, with a studied air of nonchalance, 'the body hanging from the oak.'

The shrubbery rustled with undisguised curiosity. 'Go on.'

'It occurred to me that Hector might use many methods – violence, blackmail, extortion – to achieve his ends.' Results meant more to him than methods. 'But at heart he was a self-serving son-of-a-bitch. Men like him,' she said pointedly, 'don't kill themselves.' They have an unerring belief that they can get away with it!

The arrowhead drooped as laughter boomed out of the bushes. 'Brains as well as beauty, eh! And courage – coming here alone!'

Courage? We shall see. For here, at last, was the moment of truth. Claudia drew herself up to her full height and stared straight at where she imagined the eyes in the shrubbery to be. Her mouth dry, her knees like aspic, she forced her voice to be even.

'That left two possible conclusions,' she said. 'Either someone was dressed up to look like Hector. Or Hector had been murdered. I asked myself who, then, had a motive – and the answer, of course, was you. So I suggest we stop playing hide-and-seek, and if you do intend to fire –' the nails bit deeper into her hands as she glanced around the temple – 'you can bloody well look me in the eye.'

Slowly the figure emerged from the thicket. 'Ballsy little creature, aren't you?'

Even with the bow and quiver, he still looked dashing. Floppy sandy hair made him look younger than his years. As did that distinctive dimple in his chin. Justus Capella moved into a single shaft of sunlight. 'Care to tell me how you worked it out?'

Funny how the memory plays tricks. Had Claudia not passed the basilica yesterday morning, with the rent boys preening on its corner, she might not have put two and two together.

Or in this case, two and one, for three murders had been committed yesterday. Clever, really. Because who, under such horrific circumstances, would notice a few superficial differences between Justus and the body in the bed? Same age, same height, same build – but, ah, the head, the tell-tale head! Capella had to stage his disappearance, and how better? Identifying Selina was straightforward – it was but a short leap to connect the torso with her lover.

The blame would fall on Hector, but Capella had already strangled him. All it required was to hang up the body under cover of darkness and let his mastiff raise the alarm.

'What did you do with the head of the boy you killed

279

and left in your place?' Claudia asked. 'Where's the rest of Selina?'

'Jackal bait.' He shrugged, and Claudia feared she might throw up any second. For gods' sake, Selina loved this man! Had he *no* compassion?

'How many times did you and Selina make love here, with the sun warming your naked backs?' she asked. 'Did you feel nothing for her, knowing how you intended to use her, should your attempt on the Emperor's life fail?'

'Selina?' He frowned, as though the name was unfamiliar. 'She was like a bitch on heat, played right into my hands. But you.' He edged forward. 'You are an altogether different woman.'

Claudia realised she was supposed to feel flattered, and the queasiness inside her increased. 'Then suppose I tell you we share the same cause?' she said. 'That I, too, believe Mark Antony to be a daring visionary who saw a dazzling future for our people in the East, not merely consolidating what we have, but pushing out?'

'You?' Capella's eyes travelled over her breasts.

'Don't flatter yourself –' Claudia tossed back her curls – 'that you're alone in fearing Augustus has weakened Rome by reducing our soldiers to a mere peace-keeping force.'

'Well, well, well.' Capella nodded in grudging admiration. 'Let's hear your proposition, then.'

Claudia felt her breath come out in one loud blast. She hadn't realised, until then, she'd been holding it. 'I'm rich,' she explained. 'I want to continue where Hector left off.' Through her mind flashed the image of the driver and her stomach flipped. But man, alas, cannot turn back time—

'Croesus, we need people like you!' he said, passion firing his features. 'People with courage, guts and spirit prepared to make whatever sacrifice is necessary to get that pretender, Augustus, out the way. And I shall, you know. Tomorrow I'll complete my task, we'll have a true democracy once more.'

'Long live the Republic!' she cried.

He grinned. 'Exactly. Do you have a coin?'

Excuse me?

'You do see, don't you,' he said sombrely, 'that the cause is greater than the man?'

Oh, no! Scarcely able to believe her eyes, Claudia stared at the weapon in his hands. Suddenly the arrow was pointing once more directly at its target, and she wondered whether Capella could hear the frantic pounding as her heart wriggled to escape its fate.

'So close am I to achieving my goals –' he shrugged – 'I can afford to leave nothing to chance. Although if there is any consolation in your death –' the bastard even sounded as though he might have meant it – 'it's knowing I take no pleasure in the act. The coin, now, if you please.'

Claudia did not recollect fishing the bronze from her purse, but she recalled it glinting in the sunshine.

'Put it in your mouth,' Capella instructed. 'You'll need to pay the ferryman to cross the River Styx.'

'Sorry.' Claudia tossed the coin so it landed at his feet. 'I get seasick.'

She watched his jaw drop open in amazement.

'But you'll need it, you callous little turd, and your crossing will be rough! Publicly and in disgrace, you'll die a lingering traitor's death in the arena, mocked and jeered by the very people you sought to save – and I tell you, Capella, I'll be in the front row, relishing every single second that you suffer!'

'Bitch,' he snarled, pulling back the bowstring. 'I was right not to risk my trust on you! Say "hello" to Hades.'

'You say "hello",' a deep voice growled, as thirty men stepped out from under cover. Some brandished spears, some lances, and at least a dozen bowmen aimed at Justus.

The revolutionary's eyes bored into Claudia's. 'You set a trap, you bitch! You kept me talking—' He made no effort to finish, as he released the bowstring.

There was a whoosh of air. A twang. Claudia spun through space. She heard a scream. A thud. And then came blackness.

Nothing else but blackness . . .

'Next time I throw myself on top of you,' said a disembodied baritone, 'the least you could do is struggle.'

'Mmffff!' Claudia's protest, she thought, might have been more forceful were it not for the greenery wedged in her mouth. She spat the thistle out and rubbed grit from her eyes. 'Orbilio, if you ever, *ever*—'

She broke off, because he'd trotted off to supervise the arrest to which Capella, it would appear, had not taken lightly. Blood gushed from his temple as well as his knuckles; his clothes were in total disarray. Claudia picked herself off the ground, shook the dust from her skirts and wondered why sandalwood outweighed the smell of dank weeds.

Embedded in a silver birch behind her, an arrow quivered.

'You were saying?' Marcus grinned, taking the temple steps two at a time.

Claudia's response was a stinging slap across his face. 'You took your bloody time!' she spat. 'Because of your pathetic dithering, that poor sod –' she jerked her thumb towards the driver – 'took an arrow in the back!'

A red mark flared down the side of his cheek, but the twinkle in his eyes flared brighter. 'He was one of ours,' he said. 'We had him padded out with leather and a man hidden from the rig to warn him when and what would happen. In fact –' Orbilio sniffed miserably – 'we'll probably lose him to the theatre after this.'

He deftly ducked the chunk of masonry which whizzed past his ear.

'So I was not in any danger?'

'None,' Orbilio said, swerving the branch of blackthorn she was brandishing. 'While you were diverting Capella's attention by making your ascent, our men were circling from behind—'

'I was scared witless!'

'Which is why Capella was so completely taken in,' Marcus said. 'In fact, your performance was even more convincing than the driver's.'

'That,' Claudia said haughtily, 'is because I never, ever fake it!'

His laughter echoed round the crumbling temple. 'Can I give you a lift back to Rome?' he asked.

'Never in your life,' she snapped. 'We're quits, remember?'

Marcus bounded down the path behind her. 'Yes, about that little scam you wanted me to overlook?'

'Hm?'

Her mind had already dismissed her role in coercing a confession from Capella. Life moves on, not backwards, and Claudia had a call to pay on little Lotis. Fifteen years of age? Far too young to cope with Polemo's massive empire – my, my, if ever a child needed a friend, it's now! Someone she can lean on, someone she can trust, can let her feelings go with. And who better than an expert in the trade?

Orbilio paused to examine the bark of a wild pear tree and his shoulders, from the back, appeared to be shaking. 'I don't suppose you'd care to tell me what that scam was, by any chance?'

Claudia gazed back at the ancient temple which had been gouged so painstakingly out of the rock and which had now virtually been reclaimed by the land. What more perfect spot, she wondered, in which to hide a body? Especially that of a tall, dark, handsome investigator.

'Marcus,' she said artlessly. 'Why don't you take my arm, dear?'

It may come as no surprise that, under my own name – which, very coincidentally, is Peter Berresford Ellis – I am a Celtic scholar. It was as a Celticist that I first started to read Edith Pargeter's novels of medieval Wales as dramatic and magnificent entertainments. Also, as a long-time devotee of crime fiction, I was delighted when, in August 1977, a literary editor of a national weekly asked me to review a crime novel featuring a Welsh monk and written by Ellis Peters whose real name was Edith Pargeter.

I reviewed *A Morbid Taste for Bones*, the first Cadfael novel, as 'Peter Tremayne' in case readers might think Ellis Peters was merely a reversal of my name.

I accept that Cadfael might, in some ways, be the 'father' of Sister Fidelma, although my own religious sleuth lived eight hundred years before Cadfael's time and in a different culture and law system.

Sister Fidelma, a seventh-century Irish religieuse who is also a qualified advocate of the ancient Brehon Law courts of Ireland, first made her appearance in four short stories published in various anthologies in the autumn of 1993.

She was born when I was lecturing on the ancient Brehon Law at a Canadian university. Attempting to explain the laws and the advanced position of women in ancient Ireland – that they could be judges and advocates – one student suggested that a painless and enjoyable way of instruction would be to write murder mysteries showing how things worked 'like the Cadfael tales'. That is what I did.

Since 1993 Fidelma has appeared in a dozen short stories and six full-length novels.

Without the popularity of Cadfael, which inspired my student to suggest I create a female Brehon, Fidelma might never have emerged out of the old law texts nor the lecture room. This is my tribute to Edith, my 'reverse namesake'.

Peter Tremayne

Invitation to a Poisoning

A Sister Fidelma Mystery

Peter Tremayne

The meal had been eaten in an atmosphere of forced politeness. There was a strained, chilly mood among the diners. There were seven guests at the table of Nechtan, chieftain of the Múscraige. Sister Fidelma had noticed the unlucky number immediately she had been ushered into the feasting hall for she had been the last to arrive and take her seat, having been delayed by the lure of a hot bath before the meal. She had inwardly groaned as she registered that seven guests plus Nechtan himself made the unfavourable number of eight seated at the circular table. Almost at once she had silently chided herself for clinging to old superstitions. Nevertheless she conceded that an oppressive atmosphere permeated the hall.

Everyone at the table that evening had cause to hate Nechtan.

Sister Fidelma was not one to use words lightly for, as an advocate of the law courts of the five kingdoms as well as a religieuse, she used language carefully, sparingly and with as much precision in meaning as she could. But she could think of no other description for the emotion which Nechtan aroused other than an intense dislike.

Like the others seated around the table, Fidelma had good cause to feel great animosity towards the chieftain of the Múscraige.

Why, then, had she accepted the invitation to this bizarre feast with Nechtan? Why had her fellow guests also agreed to attend this gathering?

Fidelma could only account for her own acceptance. In truth, she would have refused the invitation had Nechtan's plea for her attendance not found her passing, albeit unwillingly, through his territory on a mission to Sliabh Luachra, whose chieftain had sent for her to come and judge a case of theft. As one qualified in the laws of the Brehons to the level of *anruth*, only one degree below the highest grade obtainable, Fidelma was well able to act as judge when the occasion necessitated it.

As it turned out, Daolgar of Sliabh Luachra, who also had cause to dislike Nechtan, had similarly received an invitation to the meal and so they had both decided to accompany one another to the fortress of Nechtan.

Yet perhaps there was another reason behind Fidelma's half-hearted acceptance of the invitation, a more pertinent reason; it was that Nechtan's invitation had been couched in very persuasive language. He begged her forgiveness for the harm that he had done her in the past. Nechtan claimed that he sought absolution for his misdeeds and, hearing that she was passing through his territory, he had chosen this opportune moment to invite her, as well as several of those whom he had injured, to make reparation to them by asking them to feast with him so that, before all, he could make public and contrite apology. The handsomeness of the language was such that Fidelma had felt unable to refuse. Indeed, to refuse an enemy who makes such an apology would have been against the very teachings of the Christ. Had not the Apostle Luke reported that the Christ had instructed: 'Love your enemies, do good to them which hate you, bless them that curse you, and pray for them which despitefully use you, and unto him that smiteth thee on the one cheek offer also the other . . . '?

Where would Fidelma stand with the Faith if she refused to obey its cardinal rule; that of forgiveness of those who had wronged her?

Now, as she sat at Nechtan's feasting table, she observed that her dislike of Nechtan was shared by all her fellow guests. At least she had made a Christian effort to accommodate Nechtan's desire to be forgiven but, from the looks and glances of those around her, from the stilted and awkward conversation, and from the chilly atmosphere and tension, the idea of forgiveness was not the burning desire in the hearts of those who sat there. A different desire seemed to consume their thoughts.

The meal was drawing to a close when Nechtan rose to his feet. He was a middle-aged man. At first glance one might have been forgiven for thinking of him as a jolly and kindly man. He was short and plump, his skin shone with a child-like pinkness, though his fleshy face sagged a little around the jowls. His hair was long, and silver in colour, but combed meticulously back from his face. His lips were thin and ruddy. Generally, the features were pleasant enough but hid the cruel strength of character which had marked his leadership of the Múscraige. It was when one stared directly into his ice-blue eyes that one realised the cold ruthlessness of the man. They were pale, dead eyes. The eyes of a man without feeling.

Nechtan motioned to the solitary attendant, who had been serving wine to the company, to refill his goblet from the pitcher which stood on a side table. The young man filled his vessel and then said quietly: 'The wine is nearly gone. Shall I have the pitcher refilled?' But Nechtan shook his head and dismissed him with a curt gesture so that he was alone with his guests.

Fidelma inwardly groaned again. The meal had been

embarrassing enough without the added awkwardness of a speech from Nechtan.

'My friends,' Nechtan began. His voice was soft, almost cajoling, as he gazed without warmth around him. 'I hope I may now call you thus, for it has long been in my heart to seek you all out and make reparation to each of you for the wrong which you have suffered at my hands.'

He paused, looking expectantly around, but met only with embarrassed silence. Indeed, Fidelma seemed to be the only one to raise her head to meet his dead eyes. The others stared awkwardly at the remains of the meal on their plates before them.

'I am in your hands tonight,' went on Nechtan, as if oblivious to the tension around the table. 'I have wronged you all . . .'

He turned to the silent, elderly, nervous-looking man who was seated immediately to his left. The man had a habit of restively chewing his nails, a habit which Fidelma thought disgusting. It was a fact that, among the professional classes of society, well-formed hands and slender tapering fingers were considered a mark of beauty. Fingernails were usually carefully cut and rounded and most women put crimson stain on them. It was also considered shameful for a professional man to have unkempt nails.

Fidelma knew that the elderly man was Nechtan's own physician which made his untidy and neglected hands twice as outrageous and offensive in her eyes.

Nechtan smiled at the man. It was a smile, Fidelma thought, which was merely the rearrangement of facial muscles and had nothing to do with feeling.

'I have wronged you, Gerróc, my physician. I have regularly cheated you of your fees and taken advantage of your services.'

The elderly man stirred uncomfortably in his seat but then shrugged indifferently.

'You are my chieftain,' he replied stiffly.

Nechtan grimaced, as if amused by the response, and turned to the fleshly but still handsome middle-aged woman who sat next to Gerróc. She was the only other female at the table.

'And you, Ess, you were my first wife. I divorced you and drove you from my house by false claims of infidelity when all I sought was the arms of another younger and more attractive woman who took my fancy. By seeking to convict you of adultery I unlawfully stole your dowry and inheritance. In this, I wronged you before our people.'

Ess sat stony-faced; only a casual blink of her eyes denoted that she had even heard Nechtan's remark.

'And seated next to you,' Nechtan went on, still turning sunwise around the circle of the table, 'is my son, *our* son, Dathó. Through injustice to your mother, Dathó, I have also wronged you, my son. I have denied you your rightful place in this territory of the Múscraige.'

Dathó was a slim young man of twenty; his face was graven but his eyes – he had his mother's eyes and not the grey, cold eyes of his father – flashed with hatred at Nechtan. He opened his mouth as though to speak harsh words but Fidelma saw that his mother, Ess, laid a restraining hand on his arm and so he simply sniffed, thrust out his jaw pugnaciously but made no reply. It was clear that Nechtan would receive no forgiveness from his son nor his former wife.

Yet Nechtan appeared unperturbed at the reactions. He seemed to take some form of satisfaction in them.

Another of the guests, who was seated opposite Ess – Fidelma knew him as a young artist named Cuill – nervously rose from his seat and walked round the table, behind Nechtan, to where the pitcher of wine stood and filled his goblet, apparently emptying the jug, before returning to his seat.

Nechtan did not seem to notice him. Fidelma only half-registered the action. She continued to meet Nechtan's cold eyes steadily with her stormy green ones, and raised a hand to thrust back the rebellious strands of red hair which fell from under her head-dress.

'And you, Fidelma of Cashel, sister of our king Colgú . . .' Nechtan spread his hands in a gesture which seemed designed to extend his remorse. 'You were a young novice when you came to this territory as one of the retinue of the great Brehon Morann, chief of the judges of the five kingdoms. I was enamoured by your youth and beauty; what man would not be? I sought you out in your chamber at night, abusing all laws of hospitality, and tried to seduce you . . .'

Fidelma raised her jaw; a tinge of red showed on her cheeks as she recalled the incident vividly.

'Seduce?' Her voice was icy. The term which Nechtan had used was a legal one – *sleth* – which denoted an attempted intercourse by stealth. 'Your unsuccessful attempt was more one of *forcor*.'

Nechtan blinked rapidly and for a moment his face dissolved into a mask of irritation before reassuming its pale, placid expression. *Forcor* was a forcible rape, a crime of a violent nature, and had Fidelma not, even at that early age, been accomplished in the art of the *troid-sciathagid*, the ancient form of unarmed combat, then rape might well have resulted from Nechtan's unwelcome attention. As it was, Nechtan was forced to lie indisposed for three days after his nocturnal visit and bearing the bruises of Fidelma's defensive measures.

Nechtan bowed his head, as if contritely.

'It was a wrong, good Sister,' he acknowledged, 'and I can only admit my actions and plead for your forgiveness.'

Fidelma, in spite of her internal struggle, reflecting on the teachings of the Faith, could not bring herself to indicate any forgiveness on her part. She remained silent, staring at Nechtan in ill-concealed disgust. A firm suspicion was now entering her mind that Nechtan, this evening, was performing some drama for his own end. Yet for what purpose?

Nechtan's mouth quirked in a fleeting gesture of amusement, as if he knew her angry silence would be all the response that he would receive from her.

He paused a moment before turning to the fiery, red-haired man seated on her left. Daolgar, as Fidelma knew, was a man of fierce temper, given to action rather than reflection. He was quick to take offence but equally quick to forgive. Fidelma knew him as a warm-hearted, generous man.

'Daolgar, chieftain of Sliabh Luachra and my good neighbour,' Nechtan greeted him, but there seemed irony in his tone. 'I have wronged you by encouraging the young men of my clan to constantly raid your territory, to harass your people in order to increase our lands and to steal your cattle herds.'

Daolgar gave a long, inward sniff through his nostrils. It was an angry sound. His muscular body was poised as if he were about to spring forward.

'That you admit this thing, a matter known to my people, is a step in the right direction towards reconciliation, Nechtan. I will not let personal enmity stand in the way of a truce between us. All I ask is that such a truce should be supervised by an impartial Brehon. Needless to say, on behalf of my people, compensation for the lost cattle, the deaths in combat, must also be agreed . . .'

'Just so,' Nechtan interrupted curtly.

Nechtan now ignored Daolgar, turning to the young man who, having filled his goblet, had resumed his place.

'And now to you, Cuill, I have also made grievous injury, for our entire clan knows that I have seduced your wife and taken her to live in my house to the shame of your family before our people.'

The young, handsome man was sitting stiffly on the other side of Daolgar. He tried to keep his composure but his face was red with a mixture of mortification and a liberal amount of wine. Cuill was already known to Fidelma by reputation as a promising decorative artist whose talents had been sought by many a chieftain, bishop and abbot in order to create monuments of lasting beauty for them.

'She allowed herself to be seduced,' Cuill replied sullenly. 'Only in seeking to keep me ignorant of the affair was harm done to me. That matter was remedied when she left me and went to dwell in your house, forsaking her children. Infatuation is a terrible thing.'

'You do not say "love"?' queried Nechtan sharply. 'Then you do not concede that she loves me?'

'She was inspired with a foolish passion which deprived her of sound judgement. No. I do not call it love. I call it infatuation.'

'Yet you love her still.' Nechtan smiled thinly, as if purposely mocking Cuill. 'Even though she dwells in my house. Ah well, have no fear. After tonight I shall suggest that she returns to your house. I think my . . . infatuation . . . with her is ended.'

Nechtan seemed to take amusement from the young man's controlled anger. Cuill's knuckles showed white where he gripped the sides of his chair. But Nechtan seemed to tire of his ill-concealed enjoyment and now he turned to the last of the guests – the slim, dark-haired warrior at his right side.

'So to you, Marbán.'

Marbán was *tánaiste*, heir elect to Nechtan's chieftaincy. The warrior stirred uncomfortably.

'You have done me no wrong,' he interrupted with a tight, sullen voice.

Nechtan's plump face assumed a woebegone look.

'Yet I have. You are my *tánaiste*, my heir apparent. When I am gone, you will be chieftain in my stead.'

'A long time before that,' Marbán said, evasively. 'And no wrong done.'

'Yet I have wronged you,' insisted Nechtan. 'Ten years ago, when we both came together before the clan assembly so that the assembly could choose which of us was to be chief and which was to be *tánaiste*, it was you who the assembly favoured. You were the clear choice to be chieftain. I discovered this before the assembly met and so I paid bribes to many in order that I might be elected chieftain. So I came to office while you, by default, became the second choice. For ten years I have kept you at my side when you should have ruled in my place.'

Fidelma saw Marbán's face whiten but there was no registration of surprise on his features. Clearly the *tánaiste* already knew of Nechtan's wrongdoing. She saw the anger and hatred pass across his features even though he sought to control the emotions.

Fidelma felt that she had no option but to speak up and she broke the silence by clearing her throat. When all eyes were turned on her she said in a quiet, authoritative tone:

'Nechtan of the Múscraige, you have asked us here to forgive you certain wrongs which you have done to each of us. Some are a matter for simple Christian forgiveness. However, as a *dálaigh*, an advocate of the courts of this land, I have to point out to you that not all your misdeeds, which you have admitted freely at this table, can be dealt with that simply. You have confessed that you should not legally be chieftain of the Múscraige. You have confessed that, even if you were legally chieftain, you have indulged in activities which did not promote the commonwealth of your people, such as encouraging illegal cattle raids into the territory of Daolgar of Sliabh Luachra. This in itself is a serious crime for which you may have to appear before the assembly and my brother, Colgú, King of Cashel, and you could be dismissed from your office . . .'

Nechtan held up his plump hand and stayed her.

'You had ever the legal mind, Fidelma. And it is right that you should point out this aspect of the law to me. I accept your knowledge. But before the ramifications of this feast of forgiveness are felt, my main aim was to recognise before you all what I have done. Come what may, I concede this. And now I will raise my goblet to each and every one of you, acknowledging what I have done to you all. After that, your law may take its course and I will rest content in that knowledge.'

He reached forward, picked up his goblet and raised it in salutation to them.

'I drink to you all. I do so contritely and then you may have joy of your law.'

No one spoke. Sister Fidelma raised a cynical eyebrow at Nechtan's dramatic gesture. It was as if they were watching a bad play.

The chieftain swallowed loudly. Almost immediately the goblet fell from his hand and his pale eyes were suddenly wide and staring, his mouth was open and he was making a terrible gasping sound, one hand going up to his throat. Then, as if a violent seizure racked his body, he fell backwards, sending his chair flying as he crashed to the floor.

For a moment there was a deadly stillness in the feasting hall.

It was Gerróc, the chieftain's physician, who seemed to recover his wits first. He was on his knees by Nechtan in a moment. Yet it didn't need a physician's training to know that Nechtan was dead. The contorted features, staring dead eyes, and twisted limbs showed that death had claimed him.

Daolgar, next to Fidelma, grunted in satisfaction.

'God is just, after all,' he remarked evenly. 'If ever a man needed to be helped into the Otherworld, it was this man.' He glanced quickly at Fidelma and half-shrugged as he saw her look of reproach. 'You'll pardon me if I speak my mind, Sister? I am not truly a believer in the concept of forgiveness of sins. It depends much on the sins and the perpetrator of them.'

Fidelma's attention had been distracted by Daolgar but, as she was turning back towards Gerróc, she noticed that young Dathó was whispering anxiously to his mother Ess, who was shaking her head. Her hand seemed to be closed around a small shape hidden in her pocket.

Gerróc had risen to his feet and was glaring suspiciously at Daolgar.

'What do you mean "*helped* into the Otherworld", Daolgar?' he demanded, his tone tight with some suppressed emotion.

Daolgar gestured dispassionately.

'A figure of speech, physician. God has punished Nechtan in his own way with some seizure. A heart attack, or so it appears. That was help enough. And as for whether Nechtan deserved to be so stricken – why, who around this table would doubt it? He has wronged us all.'

Gerróc shook his head slowly.

'It was no seizure brought on by the whim of God,' he said quietly. Then he added: 'No one should touch any more of the wine.'

They were all regarding the physician with confusion, trying to comprehend his meaning.

Gerróc responded to their unarticulated question.

'Nechtan's cup was poisoned,' he said. 'He has been murdered.'

After a moment's silence, Fidelma rose slowly from her place and went to where Nechtan lay. There was a blue tinge to his lips, which were drawn back, revealing discoloured gums and teeth. The twisted features of his once cherubic face were enough for her to realise that his brief death agony had been induced in a violent form. She reached towards the fallen goblet. A little wine still lay in its bowl. She dipped her finger in it and sniffed at it suspiciously. There was a bitter-sweet fragrance which she could not identify.

She gazed up at the physician.

'Poison, you say?' She did not really need such confirmation.

He nodded quickly.

She drew herself up and gazed round at the disconcerted

297

faces of her fellow guests. Bewildered though they were, not one did she see there whose face reflected grief or anguish for the death of the chieftain of the Múscraige.

Everyone had risen uncertainly to their feet now, not knowing what to do.

It was Fidelma who spoke first in her quiet, firm tone.

'As an advocate of the court, I will take charge here. A crime has been committed. Each one in this room has a motive to kill Nechtan.'

'Including yourself,' pointed out young Dathó immediately. 'I object to being questioned by one who might well be the culprit. How do we know that you did not poison his cup?'

Fidelma raised her eyebrows in surprise at the young man's accusation. Then she considered it slowly for a moment before nodding in acceptance of the logic.

'You are quite right, Dathó. I also had a motive. And until we can discover how the poison came to be in this cup, I cannot prove that I did not have the means. Neither, for that matter, can anyone else in this room. For over an hour we have been at this table, each having a clear sight of one another, each drinking the same wine. We should be able to reason out how Nechtan was poisoned.'

Marbán was nodding rapidly in agreement.

'I agree. We should heed Sister Fidelma. I am now chieftain of the Múscraige. So I say we should let Fidelma sort this matter out.'

'You are chieftain unless it can be proved that you killed Nechtan,' interrupted Daolgar of Sliabh Luachra with scorn. 'After all, you were seated next to him. You had motive and opportunity.'

Marbán retorted angrily: 'I am now chieftain until the assembly says otherwise. And I say that Sister Fidelma also has authority until the assembly says otherwise. I suggest that we resume our places at the table and allow Fidelma to discover by what means Nechtan was poisoned.'

'I disagree,' snapped Dathó. 'If she is the guilty one then she may well attempt to lay the blame on one of us.'

'Why blame anyone? Nechtan deserved to die!' It was Ess, the former wife of the dead chieftain, who spoke sharply. 'Nechtan deserved to die,' she repeated emphatically. 'He deserved to die a thousand times over. No one in this room would more gladly see him dispatched to the Otherworld than I. And I would joyfully accept responsibility for the deed if I had done it. Little blame to whoever did this deed. They have rid the world of a vermin, a parasite who has caused much suffering and anguish. We, in this room, should be their witnesses that no crime was committed here, only natural justice. Let the one who did this deed admit to it and we will all support their cause.'

They all stared cautiously at one another. Certainly none appeared to disagree with Ess' emotional plea but none appeared willing to confess to the deed.

Fidelma pursed her lips as she considered the matter under law.

'In such a case, we would all need to testify to the wrongs enacted by Nechtan. Then the guilty one would go free simply on the payment of Nechtan's honour price to his family. That would be the sum of fourteen *cumal* . . .'

Ess' son, Dathó, interrupted with a bitter laugh.

'Perhaps some among us do not have a herd of forty-two milch cows to pay in compensation. What then? If compensation is not paid, the law exacts other punishment from the guilty.'

Marbán now smiled expansively.

'I would provide that much compensation merely to be rid of Nechtan,' he confessed without embarrassment. With Nechtan's death, Fidelma noticed, the usually taciturn warrior was suddenly more decisive in manner.

'Then,' Cuill, the young artist who had so far been silent, leant forward eagerly, 'then whoever did this deed, let them speak and admit it, and let us all contribute to exonerating them. I agree with Ess – Nechtan was an evil man who deserved to die.'

There was a silence while they examined each other's faces, waiting for someone to admit their guilt.

'Well?' demanded Daolgar, impatiently, after a while. 'Come forward whoever did this and let us resolve the matter and be away from this place.'

No one spoke.

It was Fidelma who broke the silence with a low sigh.

'Since no one will admit this deed . . .'

She did not finish for Marbán interrupted again.

'Better it was admitted.' His voice was almost cajoling. 'Whoever it was, my offer to stand behind them holds. Indeed, I will pay the entire compensation fee.'

Sister Fidelma saw Ess compressing her lips; her hand slid to the bulge on her thigh, her slender fingers wrapping themselves around the curiously shaped lump which reposed in her pocket. She had began to open her mouth to speak when her son, Dathó, thrust forward.

'Very well,' he said harshly. 'I will admit to the deed. I killed Nechtan, my father. I had more cause to hate him than any of you.'

There was a loud gasp of astonishment. It was from Ess. She was staring in surprise at her son. Fidelma saw that the others around the table had relaxed at his confession and seemed relieved.

Fidelma's eyes narrowed as she gazed directly into the face of the young man.

'Tell me how you gave him the poison?' she invited in a conversational voice.

The young man frowned in bewilderment.

'What matters? I admit the deed.'

'Admission must be supported by evidence,' Fidelma countered softly. 'Let us know how you did this.'

Dathó shrugged indifferently.

'I put poison into his cup of wine.'

'What type of poison?'

Dathó blinked rapidly. He hesitated a moment.

'Speak up!' prompted Fidelma irritably.

'Why . . . hemlock, of course.'

Sister Fidelma shifted her gaze to Ess. The woman's eyes had not left her son since his confession. She had been staring at him with a strained, whitened face.

'And is that a vial of hemlock which you have in your thigh pocket, Ess?' Fidelma snapped.

Ess gave a gasp and her hand went immediately to her pocket. She hesitated and then shrugged as if in surrender.

'What use in denying it?' she asked. 'How did you know I had the vial of hemlock?'

Dathó almost shouted: 'No. I asked her to hide it after I had done the deed. It has nothing to do—'

Fidelma raised a hand and motioned him to silence.

'Let me see it,' she pressed.

Ess took a small glass vial from her pocket and placed it on the table. Fidelma reached forward and picked it up. She took out the stopper and sniffed gently at the receptacle.

'Indeed, it is hemlock,' she confirmed. 'But the bottle is full.'

'My mother did not do this!' cried Dathó angrily. 'I did! I admit as much! The guilt is mine!'

Fidelma shook her head sadly at him.

'Sit down, Dathó. You are seeking to take the blame on yourself because your mother had a vial of hemlock on her person and you suspect that she killed your father. Is this not so?'

Dathó's face drained of colour and his shoulders dropped as he slumped back into his seat.

'Your fidelity is laudable,' went on Fidelma compassionately. 'However, I do not think that your mother, Ess, is the murderess. Especially since the vial is still full.'

Ess was staring blankly at Fidelma. Fidelma responded with a gentle smile.

'I believe that you came here tonight with the intention of trying to poison your former husband as a matter of vengeance. Dathó saw that you had the vial which you were attempting to hide after the deed was done. I saw the two of you arguing over it. However, you had no opportunity to place the hemlock in Nechtan's goblet. Importantly, it was not hemlock that killed him.'

She turned, almost sharply. 'Isn't that so, Gerróc?'

The elderly physician started and glanced quickly at her before answering.

'Hemlock, however strong the dose, does not act instantaneously,' he agreed pedantically. 'This poison was more virulent than hemlock.' He pointed to the goblet. 'You have already noticed the little crystalline deposits, Sister? It is realgar, what is called the "powder of the caves", used by those creating works of art as a colourant but, taken internally, it is a quick-acting poison.'

Fidelma nodded slowly as if he were simply confirming what she knew already and then she turned her gaze back to those around the table. However, their eyes were focused towards the young artist, Cuill.

Cuill's face was suddenly white and pinched.

'I hated him but I would never take a life,' he stammered. 'I uphold the old ways, the sanctity of life, however evil it is.'

'Yet this poison is used as a tool by artists like yourself,' Marbán pointed out. 'Who among us would know this other than Gerróc and yourself? Why deny it if you did kill him? Have we not said that we would support one another in this? I have already promised to pay the compensation on behalf of the person who did the deed.'

'What opportunity had I to put it in Nechtan's goblet?' demanded Cuill. 'You had as much opportunity as I had.'

Fidelma raised a hand to quell the sudden hubbub of accusation and counter-accusation.

'Cuill has put his finger on the all-important question,' she said calmly but firmly enough to silence them. They had all risen again and so she instructed: 'Be seated.'

Slowly, almost unwillingly, they obeyed.

Fidelma stood at the spot in which Nechtan had sat.

'Let us consider the facts,' she began. 'The poison was in the wine goblet. Therefore, it is natural enough to assume that it was in the wine. The wine is contained in that pitcher there.'

She pointed to where the attendant had left the wine pitcher on a side table.

'Marbán, call in the attendant, for it was he who filled Nechtan's goblet.'

Marbán did so.

The attendant was a young man named Ciar, a dark-haired and nervous young man. He seemed to have great trouble in speaking when he saw what had happened in the room and he kept clearing his throat nervously.

'You served the wine this evening, didn't you, Ciar?' demanded Fidelma.

The young man nodded briefly. 'You all saw me do so,' he confirmed, pointing out the obvious.

'Where did the wine come from? Was it a special wine?'

'No. It was bought a week ago from a Gaulish merchant.'

'And did Nechtan drink the same wine as was served to his guests?'

'Yes. Everyone drank the same wine.'

'From the same pitcher?'

'Yes. Everyone had wine from the same pitcher during the evening,' Ciar confirmed. 'Nechtan was the last to ask for more wine from the pitcher and I noticed that it was nearly empty after I filled his goblet. I asked him if I should refill it but he sent me away.'

Marbán pursed his lips, reflectively.

'This is true, Fidelma. We were all a witness to that.'

'But Nechtan was not the last to drink wine from that pitcher,' replied Fidelma. 'It was Cuill.'

Daolgar exclaimed and turned to Cuill.

'Fidelma is right. After Ciar filled Nechtan's goblet and left, and while Nechtan was talking to Dathó, Cuill rose from his seat and walked around Nechtan to fill his goblet from the pitcher of wine. We were all concentrating on what Nechtan had to say; no one would have noticed if Cuill had slipped the poison into Nechtan's goblet. Cuill not only had the motive, but the means and the opportunity.'

Cuill flushed. 'It is a lie!' he responded.

But Marbán was nodding eagerly in agreement.

'We have heard that this poison is of the same material as used by artists for colouring their works. Isn't Cuill an artist? And he hated Nechtan for running off with his wife. Isn't that motive enough?'

'There is one flaw to the argument,' Sister Fidelma said quickly.

'Which is?' demanded Dathó.

'I was watching Nechtan as he made his curious speech asking forgiveness. But I observed Cuill pass behind Nechtan and he did not interfere with Nechtan's goblet. He merely helped himself to what remained of the wine from the pitcher, which he then drank, thus confirming, incidentally, that the poison was placed in Nechtan's goblet and not the wine.'

Marbán was looking at her without conviction.

'Give me the pitcher and a new goblet,' instructed Fidelma, irritably.

When it was done she poured the dregs which remained in the bottom of the pitcher into the goblet and considered them a moment before dipping her finger in them and gently touching her finger with her tongue.

She smiled complacently at the company.

'As I have said, the poison is not in the wine,' she reiterated. 'The poison was placed in the goblet itself.'

'Then how was it placed there?' demanded Gérroc in exasperation.

In the silence that followed, Fidelma turned to the attendant. 'I do not think that we need trouble you further, Ciar, but wait outside. We will have need of you later. Do not mention anything of this matter to anyone yet. Is that understood?'

Ciar cleared his throat noisily.

'Yes, Sister.' He hesitated. 'But what of the Brehon Olcán? He has just arrived. Should I not inform him?'

Fidelma frowned.

'Who is this judge?'

Marbán touched her sleeve.

'Olcán is a friend of Nechtan's, a chief judge of the Múscraige. Perhaps we should invite him in? After all, it is his right to judge this matter.'

Fidelma's eyes narrowed.

'Was he invited here this night?' she demanded.

It was Ciar who answered her question.

'Only after the meal began. Nechtan requested me to have a messenger sent to Olcán. The message was to ask the judge to come here.'

Fidelma thought rapidly and then said: 'Have him wait then but he is not to be told what has happened here until I say so.'

After Ciar had left she turned back to the expectant faces of her erstwhile meal guests.

'So we have learnt that the poison was not in the wine but in the goblet. This narrows the field of our suspects.'

Daolgar of Sliabh Luachra frowned slightly.

'What do you mean?'

'Simply that if the poison was placed in the goblet then it had to be placed there after the time that Nechtan drained one goblet of wine and when he called Ciar to refill his goblet. The poison had to be placed there after the goblet was refilled.'

Daolgar of Sliabh Luachra leant back in his chair and suddenly laughed hollowly.

'Then I have the solution. There are only two others in this room who had the opportunity to place the poison in Nechtan's goblet,' he said smugly.

'And those are?' Fidelma prompted.

'Why, either Marbán or Gerróc. They were seated on either side of Nechtan. Easy for them to slip the poison into the goblet which stood before them while we were concentrating on what he had to say.'

Marbán had flushed angrily but it was the elderly physician, Gerróc, who suffered the strongest reaction.

'I can prove that it was not I!' he almost sobbed, his voice breaking almost pathetically in indignation.

Fidelma turned to regard him in curiosity.

'You can?'

'Yes, yes. You have said that we all had a reason to hate Nechtan and that implies that we would all therefore wish him dead. That gives every one of us a motive for his murder.'

'That is so,' agreed Fidelma.

'Well, I alone of all of you knew that it was a waste of time to kill Nechtan.'

There was a pause before Fidelma asked patiently: 'Why would it be a waste of time, Gerróc?'

'Why kill a man who was already dying?'

'*Already* dying?' prompted Fidelma after the exclamations of surprise had died away.

'I was physician to Nechtan. It was true that I hated him. He cheated me of my fees but, nevertheless, as physician here, I lived well. I did not complain. I am advancing in years now. I was not going to imperil my security by accusing my chieftain of wrongdoing. However, a month ago, Nechtan started to have terrible headaches, and once or twice the pain was so unbearable that I had to strap him to his bed. I examined him and found a growth at the back of the skull. It was a malignant tumour for within a week I could chart its expansion. If you do not believe me, you may examine him for yourselves. The tumour is easy to discern behind his left ear.'

Fidelma bent over the chief and examined the swelling behind the ear with repugnance.

'The swelling is there,' she confirmed.

'So, what are you saying, Gerróc?' Marbán demanded, seeking to bring the old physician to a logical conclusion.

'I am saying that a few days ago I had to tell Nechtan that it was unlikely he would see another new moon. He was going to die anyway. The growth of the tumour was continuing and causing him increased agony. I knew he was going to die soon. Why need I kill him? God had already chosen the time and method.'

Daolgar of Sliabh Luachra turned to Marbán with grim satisfaction on his face.

'Then it leaves only you, *tánaiste* of the Múscraige. You clearly did not know that your chieftain was dying and so you had both the motive and the opportunity.'

Marbán had sprung to his feet, his hand at his waist where his sword would have hung had they not been in the feasting hall. It was a law that no weapons were ever carried into a feasting hall.

'You will apologise for that, chieftain of Sliabh Luachra!'

Cuill, however, was nodding rapidly in agreement with Daolgar's logic.

'You were very quick to offer your newfound wealth as chieftain to pay the compensation should anyone else confess. Had they done so, it would have solved a problem, wouldn't it? You would emerge from this without a blemish. You would be confirmed as chieftain of the Múscraige. However, if you were guilty of causing Nechtan's death then you would immediately be deposed from holding any office. That is why you were so eager to put the blame on to me.'

Marbán stood glowering at the assembly. It was clear that he now stood condemned in the eyes of them all. An angry muttering had arisen as they confronted him.

Sister Fidelma raised both her hands to implore silence.

'Let us not quarrel when there is no need. Marbán did not kill Nechtan.'

There was a brief moment of surprised silence.

'Then who did?' demanded Dathó angrily. 'You seem to be playing cat and mouse with us, Sister. If you know so much, tell us who killed Nechtan.'

'Everyone at this table will concede that Nechtan was an evil, self-willed man who was at war with life. As much as we all had reason to hate him, he hated everyone around him with equal vehemence.'

'But who killed him?' repeated Daolgar.

Sister Fidelma grimaced sorrowfully.

'Why, he killed himself.'

The shock and disbelief registered on everyone's faces.

'I had begun to suspect,' went on Fidelma, 'but I could find no logical reason to support my suspicion until Gerróc gave it to me just now.'

'Explain, Sister,' demanded Marbán wearily, 'for I cannot follow the same logic.'

'As I have said, as much as we hated Nechtan, Nechtan hated us. When he learnt that he was to die anyway, he decided that he would have one more great revenge on those people he disliked the most. He preferred to go quickly to the Otherworld than to die the lingering death which Gerróc doubtless had described to him. If it takes a brave man to set the boundaries to his own life, then Nechtan was brave enough. He chose a quick-acting poison, realgar, delighting in the fact that it was a substance that Cuill, the husband of his current mistress, often used.

'He devised a plan to invite us all here for a last meal, playing on our curiosity or our egos by saying that he wanted to make public reparation and apology for those wrongs that he had done to us. He planned the whole thing. He then recited his wrongdoing against us, not to seek forgiveness, but to ensure that we all knew that each had cause to hate him and seek his destruction. He wanted to plant seeds of suspicion in all our minds. He made his recitation of wrongdoing sound more like a boast than an apology. A boast and a warning.'

Ess was in agreement.

'I thought his last words were strange at the time,' she said, 'but now they make sense.'

'They do so now,' Fidelma endorsed.

'What were the words again?' queried Daolgar.

'Nechtan said: "And now I will raise my goblet to each and every one of you, acknowledging what I have done to you all. After that, your law may take its course and I will rest content in that knowledge . . . I drink to you all . . . and then you may have joy of your law.'

It was Fidelma who was able to repeat the exact words.

'It certainly does not sound like an apology,' admitted Marbán. 'What did he mean?'

It was Ess who answered.

'I see it all now. Do you not understand how evil this man was? He wanted one or all of us to be blamed for his death. That was his final act of spite and hatred against us.'

'But how?' asked Gerróc, confused. 'I confess, I am at a loss to understand.'

'Knowing that he was dying, that he had only a few days or weeks at most, he set his own limits to his lifespan,' Fidelma explained patiently. 'He was an evil, spiteful man, as Ess acknowledges. He invited us to this meal, knowing that, at its close, he would take poison. As the meal started, he asked Ciar, the attendant, to send for his own judge, Brehon Olcán, hoping that Olcán would find us in a state of confusion, each suspecting the other, and come to a wrong decision that one or all of us were concerned in his murder. Nechtan killed himself in the hope that we would be found culpable of his death. While he was talking to us he secreted the poison in his own goblet.'

Fidelma looked around the grim faces at the table. Her smile was strained.

'I think we can now speak with the Brehon Olcán and sort this matter out.'

She turned towards the door, paused and looked back at those in the room.

'I have encountered much wrongdoing in this world, some of it born of evil, some born of desperation. But I have to say that I have never truly encountered such malignancy as dwelt in the spirit of Nechtan, sometime chieftain of the Múscraige.'

It was the following morning as Fidelma was riding in the direction of Cashel that she encountered the old physician, Gerróc, at a crossroads below the fortress of Nechtan.

'Whither away, Gerróc?' she greeted with a smile.

'I am going to the monastery of Imleach,' replied the old man gravely. 'I shall make confession and seek sanctuary for the rest of my days.'

Fidelma pursed her lips thoughtfully.

'I would not confess too much,' she said enigmatically.

The old physician gazed at her with a frown.

'You know?' he asked sharply.

'I know a boil which can be lanced from a tumour,' she replied.

The old man sighed softly.

'At first I only meant to put fear into Nechtan. To make him suffer a torment of the mind for a few weeks before I lanced his boil or it burst of its own accord. Boils against the back of the ear can be painful. He believed me when I pretended it was a tumour and he had not long to live. I did not know the extent of his evil mind nor that he would kill himself to spite us all.'

Fidelma nodded slowly.

'His blood is still on his own hands,' she said, seeing the old man's troubled face.

'But the law is the law. I should make confession.'

'Sometimes justice takes precedence over the law,' Fidelma replied cheerfully. 'Nechtan suffered justice. Forget the law, Gerróc, and may God give you peace in your declining years.'

She raised a hand, almost in blessing, turned her horse and continued on her way towards Cashel.

I admire Ellis Peters for breaking new ground with historical mysteries, for showing us the distant past as urgently and compassionately as the present, and for creating characters we can love. I never read one of her books without a sense of having been in company I truly enjoyed.

I wanted to write a story in tribute to her, and create a historical detective no one had yet used, as far as I know. I cast about for someone to catch the imagination, someone Ellis Peters might have liked, perhaps not too far from her period, and yet utterly different from Brother Cadfael.

I also wanted any excuse to set a story here in the north-eastern Highlands of Scotland. Who better than Lady Macbeth, not as Shakespeare would have us see her, but as history records her, a brave and compassionate woman, a fitting wife for the last High King of Scotland, when it stretched as far south as Yorkshire and Lancashire.

And this is Macbeth country. Cawdor is only a few miles away (although the castle where the bloodstains of Duncan's murder are supposed to be was not built until three hundred years afterwards!). Portmahomack, then the Haven of St Colmac, is actually at least four thousand years old, and was thriving in Macbeth's time. It seemed the perfect answer, and I had great fun writing it.

Anne Perry

The Last High Queen

Anne Perry

The score of horsemen reached the top of the hill and at
their head Macbeth drew rein and stared across at the
height of Ben Wyvis shimmering in the midsummer sun. To
the west lay the long valley and the blue-purple mountains
beyond mountains into the high heart of Scotland. Before
them was the cobalt water of Cromartie.

Beside him Gruoch smiled. In spite of all its memories of
bloodshed and loss, this was a land she loved. Gillecomgain,
her first husband, had been murdered near Inverness, only
twenty miles behind them. He and fifty of his men had been
burned to death when old Malcolm II's troops had locked
them in and set fire to the tower. She was used to wars.
In the bitter struggles for the crown between the houses of
Athol and Moray she had lost her father and all four of her
brothers to Malcolm's ambition that of all his grandsons it
should be Duncan who succeeded him.

That was in the past. Duncan had been a weak king, both
tyrannous and incompetent. He had fought against England
to the south, and Orkney to the north. That would not
have mattered had he been a good soldier, but he was not.
One disaster had followed another, until at last the people
themselves had risen and overthrown him, electing Macbeth
in his place.

She glanced at Macbeth beside her, sitting tall in the saddle, the light on his fair hair, his skin burned by wind and sun. He smiled at her, and they moved forward and down the long slope towards the water and the ferry. It would be a slow business crossing but to ride around by Connon would be far slower. The firth cut deep into the land and it would add thirty miles to their journey.

They had set out from Cawdor the previous day, and were riding to Fearn Abbey where Gruoch especially had matters to discuss with the Abbot. The care of widows and orphans was her particular interest. She understood only too well their loneliness and fear, and the need they felt. After Gillecomgain's death she and her son, Lulach, who had escaped the slaughter, had been in just that plight. True, her grandfather had been King, and her father a legitimate contender for the succession, but they were dead, like her brothers, and she and her son were alone.

That was one of the many things she had in common with Macbeth. He too had lost many of his family to Malcolm's ambition. Theirs had been a wise dynastic marriage, uniting the claims of Athol and Moray, but it was also one of love, and Macbeth had been happy to adopt Lulach as his own.

The kingdom stretched from Caithness to Lancashire, and broadly speaking they were at peace. Certainly they were rich. Food was plentiful. The rule of law prevailed. Now and again there were skirmishes, but that was the nature of men. In England Edward the Confessor harboured the son of the deposed Duncan. Across the Channel William of Normandy had eyes on the English crown, and Norman barons sheltered in the court of Macbeth. In the north Harold Hardrada was poised for more raids along the coast, his eyes also on a fat and sunlit land, ripe for looting.

Ahead of her now, Crinan, her kinsman, was moving more swiftly down the slope to call the ferryman's attention and begin the boarding of horses and men. It was wise to travel with those whose loyalties you knew, whose blood was the same as your own. It was the surest trust. She had learned that long ago, and had it reinforced when Macbeth had made his pilgrimage to Rome, and the governance of Scotland had been in her hands for a space. Celtic law was far wiser than Anglo-Saxon, and certainly than Norman. It allowed the best person, the most able, courageous and wise, to be chief of the clan. If it fell that that was a woman, then so be it. Her inheritance was hers, her dowry was hers always.

The horses were splashing in the shallow water now, pulling back, uncertain of the swaying raft of the ferry. Crinan waved the men forward. It would require several crossings to carry them all but was still far quicker than going all the way inland around the head of the firth. She dismounted and stood patiently in the sun, a sense of peace filling her.

Macbeth came over and put his arm around her shoulders. He did not speak; the silence was companionable. They knew each other well enough; she understood his thoughts. This was one of the rare times when he could forget wars and dissensions, judgements, decisions of state. In this wide, shining land, more home to them than the cities of the south, they could be simply a man and a woman, riding with friends. No matters of state need be thought of at all until they reached Fearn, and that was another thirty miles.

There was no sound in the motionless air but the clatter of hooves on wood, and the slurp of water barely turning over on the shingle.

Then someone shouted.

Gruoch swivelled round. Over the hill of the Black Isle behind them a lone horseman was moving swiftly downward. Macbeth slipped his arm from around her and walked up the slope, watching the figure. A man coming at that speed could only mean a message, and no news so swift could be good.

The other score of men now turned also. Even the ferryman stopped working with the horses. No point in struggling to get them settled if they were all going back again anyway.

A red kite circled above them, its forked tail sharp against the blue sky.

The rider increased his pace and reached them in a flurry, leaping to the ground only yards from Macbeth.

'My lord! I bring word from Fergus. There is news from the English court. A messenger awaits you at Cawdor.'

Macbeth was not troubled. There was no fear in his face or the stance of his body.

'Malcolm again?' he asked, referring to Duncan's eldest son.

'And the Norman barons,' the messenger replied. 'De Bohun and Gilbert.'

Macbeth turned to Gruoch. 'If it is de Bohun I must return. You go on to Fearn. Your meeting with the Abbot is important. I'll see you in four days.'

'I'll go with you, my lady.' Crinan stepped forward, closer to Gruoch's side. 'Five men should be enough.' He did not look at the wide, calm sea, almost motionless in the sun, but his gesture was eloquent. 'We'll come to no harm.'

It was true. This was Moray land, Macbeth's own birthright, and hers. She was loved here, as well as honoured.

The messenger was waiting.

Macbeth regarded her steadily for a long moment, saw her smile, then leaned and kissed her, gently, on the mouth. He turned and mounted his horse and spurred it up the incline, ahead of the messenger, and fifteen men mounted and rode behind him.

With only seven horses the crossing could be made in one journey. Gruoch, Crinan and the five men splashed ashore on the far side and continued east and north along the water's edge. Seals were basking on the tidal rocks, and once a sea eagle swooped low, rising out of the water with a fish in its talons. The sun was hot, and Gruoch was glad of the sweet air off the incoming tide.

'That Malcolm's just like his father,' Crinan said after a while. 'Never at rest unless he's making trouble.'

'He's been at the English court so long he's hardly a Scot any more,' she replied. 'He wouldn't recognise these hills if he saw them.'

'Please God he doesn't see them!' Crinan said with feeling. 'And I wish Macbeth would send those Normans home where they belong. As long as they're here, Edward has his eye on us.'

'It's a balance against Thorfinn,' she countered.

'Orkney won't trouble us,' he said confidently. 'Not while Macbeth is King. Anyway, Thorfinn will have enough to do to keep Hardrada off his shores.'

Her horse slithered on the stones at the mouth of the shallow river that opened out into the firth. She held its head high and moved out into the stream, waded across, and clattered out of the far side.

They spoke of other things, laughing a little, recalling people and events in the past, joys and fears shared.

By four o'clock, the sun still high, they crossed another river and entered the forest. The cool depth of green enclosed them.

They reached Fearn Abbey a little after six. The sky was still mid-blue, no gold colouring the northern horizon, no pink blush to the few threads of cloud.

The Abbot welcomed them with enthusiasm. He was a large man, broad-shouldered and barrel-chested, descended from Norse and Saxon blood. He had defended his church with both sword and tongue, and now in his later years he had been rewarded with this far northern abbey rich in land, and seldom troubled by more than the usual domestic squabbles and trials of faith.

'My lady!' He spread his arms expansively, his face lighting with joy. 'Come in! How blessed we are by your presence. Here, Aiden will take your horse. Hop to it, boy! Don't stand there and let the Queen wait for you!'

A red-faced boy scrambled to obey, mumbling apologies, too shy to offer her a hand to dismount.

The Abbot stepped forward hastily and she accepted, more from courtesy than need, and thanked them both.

'My Lord Crinan,' the Abbot went on cheerfully. 'Welcome to Fearn. All we can offer is at your disposal.' He looked at Gruoch. 'Food? A good chair? Inside, or in the garden? Mead, ale or wine? The mead is very good, if I say so myself. Nothing else quite like heather honey. Best in the world.' He led the way in. The old stone building was warm in the sun and the smell of baking drifted from the kitchens. There were plum trees in the walled garden, and the first fruit were already darkening to purple. The stones reflected both the heat and the heavy scent of flowers.

The meal was excellent, even lavish: fish, meat, vegetables and pastries, particularly the mead which the Abbot had praised – as it turned out, with good cause.

'My lady,' he said when the fish was served. 'Can you tell me of the King's pilgrimage to Rome? I would dearly like to hear of it. Myself, I have barely left Scotland. I have been to Northumbria several times, to Holy Island, and to Jarrow, even as far as York. But that is a small thing compared with France, let alone Rome! Did he see the Holy Father? What news is there of the East? Shall we ever recover Jerusalem from the Turks?'

She was startled, but she could not rebuff his eagerness. His great face was alight with interest and his food all but forgotten.

Macbeth had told her much about it. They had sat up long hours while he shared with her his amazement at the terrible and magnificent ruin that was the Eternal City, sacked nearly six centuries before by barbarians, and now a weed-strewn skeleton of its Imperial glory.

She had seen it through his eyes, felt his awe, and his sorrow, his frustration at the waste and the indifference to all that it had meant to mankind. It was the centre of the world, but to ignorant hands it had been no more than another pile of stones to smash, another way to vent their hatred of what they did not understand.

She found herself smiling as she answered, using Macbeth's words, reliving her own vision and the warmth she had felt in listening to him.

Crinan did not interrupt. He had been to England and to Normandy but they did not hold the magic of Rome. Who wanted the provinces compared with the heart?

'Ah, wonderful!' the Abbot sighed at last, folding his hands across his very generous stomach. 'To have seen such things!' He poured more mead for them without bothering to ask. An empty goblet was an affront to his hospitality. 'But a long way to travel, and dangerous. Months on the road.' He looked at her with considerable respect. He knew that while Macbeth had been away she had ruled in his stead. 'A hard time for you,' he added, echoing her thoughts.

'Yes,' she agreed. Had he any idea how hard? It was far worse than loneliness. There had been difficult decisions to make, quarrels to settle, diplomacy to maintain with Edward in England, William in Normandy and Thorfinn in Orkney. Worst of all there had been a rebellion to suppress, minor, certainly, because she had acted quickly. She had seen too much bloodshed to be indecisive. Justice must be swift and complete.

'I suppose you were expecting someone to take advantage of the King's absence,' the Abbot went on thoughtfully. His broad face broke into a smile. 'But if they thought you were softer or weaker, they picked the wrong woman. If the House of Athol had had Scotland's peace at heart instead of their own glory they'd have left well alone. Few will mourn Maldred, or his kin.'

'His daughter, Doada,' Crinan said quietly. 'She was innocent of any wrong.'

'Perhaps,' the Abbot agreed with a sigh. 'But blood tells.

She was loyal to her father, and wilful enough to gather support for vengeance. Fair too, by all accounts.'

'You can't spare a rebel against the Crown because she is a woman,' Gruoch said with real regret. 'I did not do it willingly. But I had to judge her strength of will, as I knew my own. We can't bear arms like a man, but we can think as quickly and hate as deep. If I spared a man because he was handsome, you'd call it weakness, and not thank me when he plunged the country into war again.'

'Oh aye!' the Abbot said fervently. 'God bless your spirit!'

'No one wants war,' Crinan added, his voice tight and hard. 'We've seen too much of it with Duncan. God knows how many were killed in his idiotic battles!'

They sat in silence for several minutes, remembering old times of fear and grief, and thankful for the present.

A little after ten Gruoch walked alone in the abbey garden. The sun was sinking low in a splendour of gold and fire to the north, but the whole sky was still suffused with light and it would be clear enough to read by for another two hours, or close to it.

She woke with a start, her breath catching in her throat, her heart pounding. There was a dull thud outside the door, as of someone falling. A moment's silence, then a groan, loud and sharp. It was as much of warning as of pain.

She slipped out of bed and reached for the dagger she wore at her belt when she rode.

There was a clatter of feet outside and a cry of alarm, swiftly followed by one of horror.

Someone banged loudly on her door, calling her name.

'What is it?' she answered, holding the dagger tightly, ready to fight if she had to.

'Are you all right? Are you hurt?' the voice demanded.

'No! Findlay?' It had not sounded like him. He was the

322

guard left at her door, a kinsman of Macbeth's she trusted as her own.

'No, lady . . . it's Donald. Findlay's dead. God save us.'

She flung open the door. Donald was standing in front of her, sword in hand, his face pale in the light of the rush torch on the wall. At her feet the body of Findlay lay crumpled, blood pouring from a great wound in his side.

Violence was back again. In a flood, memory washed over her of her father, her brothers, all slain by the sword, and of Gillecomgain burned to death. This was meant for Macbeth! The murderer had expected him here, as he would have been, had not the messenger called him back to Cawdor. The old hatred in the House of Athol again, or something new?

She tried to speak, but at first her voice would not come.

The Abbot appeared at the end of the corridor, his hair wild around his head, his robes flung on so hastily they were all in disarray.

'Oh, thank God!' He crossed himself fervently when he saw her. He gulped. 'Thank merciful God you are alive!' He saw Findlay. 'Poor man. God save his soul.'

'Who was it?' Her voice came at last. 'Who did this?'

'I don't know,' Donald answered. 'He fled when Findlay raised the alarm. Crinan went after him with Einar and Angus.'

'One?' she demanded. 'One man did this? How did he get in?'

A monk came along the passage, skirts swirling, his breathing hard. He had a wooden cudgel in his hand.

'There were three of them, lady. Two of our men are badly beaten, but with God's help they'll recover.' He regarded her closely. 'Do you need aught, my lady? Are you ill, faint?'

'No, I'm not.' It was less than the truth. She felt sick with shock, anger and grief, and she had to hold the door lintel to steady herself. In the torchlight maybe they would not see she was shaking. 'Thank you,' she added as an afterthought. 'But it will be the King they were after. I must ride back to Cawdor to warn him.'

'Now?' The Abbot's eyes widened with incredulity.

'Yes, now! There is no time to be lost.' She turned to Crinan. 'Have the horses saddled. We'll leave as soon as I have dressed. It will still take us a day and a half. We can only hope they move no more swiftly.'

'Send the others by land,' Crinan answered her. 'The fastest way from here would be to ride to the Port of St Colmac, nine miles to the east of here, and take a boat around Tarbat Ness, and then across the Moray Firth. We'll get horses from Ardersier and ride to Cawdor from there. We'll make it by noon if we leave now.'

'Excellent!' Relief surged up inside her. They would be in time! She could warn Macbeth. 'We'll do it! Saddle horses for us too.' And without waiting to see him obey she turned back to her room and closed the door. There was no time to be lost in pleasantries. Only afterwards did she think of Findlay, and wish she had spoken to the Abbot about him then, asked him to bury him here in Fearn. Her own business, which had hardly been touched on, would have to wait for another opportunity. She would come again, and perhaps send a purse by messenger for the monks to pray for Findlay's soul and keep his grave.

She was dressed, her gown and robe on, her hair drawn quickly back in a braid. There was no time for more. It was half past midnight.

The Abbot was waiting at the gate, his face pale. Crinan stood with their horses ready.

'God speed to you, my lady,' the Abbot said earnestly. 'We will bury Findlay, never fear.'

'I know you will,' she said gratefully. 'My prayers will be with yours. I shall send my thanks in more solid form later, when I have warned the King. In the meantime I trust in your intercession with God. Peace be with you.' And as he crossed the air in answer, murmuring in Latin a prayer for her safety, she mounted into the saddle and Crinan followed after her.

They rode east, hard, out along the peninsula. They were so close to the sea the light of the sky reflected from the water beyond the curve of the land, and it was not hard to make out the path. St Colmac was an ancient port. The Picts had settled it two thousand years before the birth of Christ. They would easily be able to find a boat and the way was clear enough in this limpid light.

They rode in silence, bent forward over the horses' necks, urging them on, eyes to the ground, watching for ruts and pitfalls in the track. They had gone about six miles when they breasted a rise and the sea lay before them like a silver shield, as still as glass, reflecting back the light of the summer sky. To the north beyond the water the mountains of Sutherland rose purple-black with a rim of fire along the edge from the sun just below. There was hardly a breath of wind in the silence. For a moment the beauty of it was so great Gruoch forgot her urgency and the fear inside her. The vast, shining night covered her in glory, drowning her senses. She loved this land with a fierceness that closed over her heart; it was home as no other could ever be.

But Crinan was moving ahead, already on the way down the long slope towards the curve of the port. She could see the black outline of the harbour wall and the silhouettes of ships. She urged her horse forward again and caught up with him. There was no time to waste.

They rode along the hard beach, the bright water barely rippling in the sand.

'Ask at that house,' Gruoch ordered, pointing to the first low stone building close by the slipway. 'Tell him who we are, and give him gold.' She held out money from the leather purse she carried.

'You pull it down to the water's edge; I'll ask.'

When she had made sufficient noise to wake the fisherman,

he was willing enough. He would lose a day's catch, but the gold was in his hand. Anyway, one did not deny queens their will. She thanked him and running back through the sand dunes and sea grass, she sped down to splash through the shallow water and, with Crinan's help, scrambled into the boat. He was on the centre cross-bench, and in moments he was pulling hard on the oars.

There was barely a sound, just the bow cutting through the shimmering radiance of the night. The sea was satin-smooth, the sky too pale for stars. It must be after two o'clock and already the fire of dawn burned red below the horizon to the north-west.

Crinan turned the bow east, parallel with the land, to come as close as he dared to round Tarbat Ness and go south again across the Moray Firth towards Cawdor and warn Macbeth.

'Who is it?' she said, speaking for the first time since they had left St Colmac. 'Someone of Athol still hungering for power?'

'Perhaps,' he answered with a grunt, pulling even harder as the oars and the boat sped through the bright water. 'Heaven knows, old Malcolm would have paid the devil to keep the Crown in his line.'

'Malcolm's dead,' she pointed out. 'And Duncan too. He died in battle in Pitgaveny before Macbeth's name was even put to the vote. Who alive wants an English prince in his place, except Edward?'

'Isn't Edward enough? And Malcolm may have grown up in Edward's court, but he wouldn't call himself English.' He dug the oars in deep and threw his weight against them.

He was right. If Malcolm came it would be with an army, not with murder in the night. Apart from morality, such a way would never win him the Crown. The Council would not sustain as High King any man who came by stealth. And Macbeth was loved; Scotland stretched its borders wider than at any time in the past. He had laid almost a generation of peace on the land, and the wealth that went with it. After Malcolm and Duncan's wars that was blessed indeed.

This was personal, a hatred rooted in some deep envy or fancied wrong. Her thoughts returned to the House of Athol. It was they who had rebelled when Macbeth had been in Rome. She had had to execute Maldred and Doada and their men. She thought back on that now with pain. She had hated doing it, but she had never doubted its necessity. Let treason prosper even once, and the King could never be easy in his bed again.

They were almost level with the point. The glistening sea lay all around them, tide running sharp where the waters met, stranded like satin in the light from the paling sky.

Doada had been young. She could remember her face, and her long fair hair. She had had courage, no one would deny that . . . and hatred. Many men had loved her, but she had never married. Like Crinan. She had refused them all. There was talk that the only man she wanted was of the House of Moray, and her father forbade it. Probably a flight of some minstrel's fancy.

Perhaps someone wanted to avenge her.

'Do you think it's the rebellion when Macbeth was in Rome?' she asked aloud.

Crinan looked up.

The tide was running fast now. The whole Moray Firth was glistening white and silver in front of them. They were far out of sight of St Colmac.

'For Doada?' he said with a slow smile.

He had his face to the dawn. In that instant she saw it, the vengeance in his eyes, and she understood. She knew why they were out here alone on the shining, racing tide. If anyone wanted to avenge Doada, it would be Gruoch they sought, not Macbeth! He had never been the victim. That was a blind!

She rose and lunged forward. He reacted an instant later to take one oar in both hands. She ducked low as he stood up, and threw her weight to the same side of the boat as he. It rocked wildly, all but capsizing. Crinan swayed, the oar swung high in the air as he lifted it to crash it down on her, to sweep her overboard. She pitched over to his side again, and the boat skewed. Crinan's arms flung high and the side of the boat caught him under the knees. He folded up and crashed into the water, taking the oar with him.

He cried out once as the cold tide engulfed him, closing over his head. He struck out, reaching for the boat. She picked up the other oar and started to paddle into the stream of the tide, away from him as quickly as she could, desperate to outstrip the grasping hands that would choke the life out of her if they could reach her even once.

But the water was cold and swift, sucking under towards the rocks. Crinan had not the strength. No one could swim in that, as he had known she could not. Her skirts would have taken her down.

She leant on the oar and heaved until her shoulders were almost torn with the effort of it. The boat was light with only her in it, and swerved first this way then that. She needed two oars to make way. The current was carrying her, but it was also dragging Crinan down, and she feared him far more than the gleaming sea.

She could never make Ardersier, she knew that, but the tide would carry her ashore somewhere on this side of the headland. She could climb the shallow cliffs and walk back to St Colmac. She would explain to them that Crinan had fallen overboard . . . just as he would have said of her. She would tell Macbeth the truth later, when she got home again. Home: that was wherever he was. But it was also all this land, from Caithness to York, even if this was the brightest and sweetest part of it. Was she not High Queen of Scotland?

She smiled, and let the sea carry her as the arch of heaven paled with the coming sun.

Historical mysteries offer an appealing form of escapism. Readers and writers alike can enjoy the pleasure of losing themselves for a while in a different place and time. A well-researched historical mystery provides an insight into the past which is as authentic as that available from a textbook but far more compelling. When the depiction of a society very different from our own is enlivened by strong characterisation and an intriguing mystery, the result is apt to be memorable. I am sure that countless readers have learned much more about medieval life and mores from the work of Ellis Peters than from any documentary or encyclopaedia. A weighty reference book, *The Cadfael Companion*, even includes a lengthy appendix describing all herbs and plants mentioned in her remarkable series. Importantly, too, the Brother Cadfael stories remind us that, whatever changes may have occurred since the reign of King Stephen, fundamental human values remain much as they always have been.

Although my own novels are firmly rooted in present-day Liverpool, I have been increasingly attracted by the historical sub-genre over the past couple of years. To write one or two short history mysteries in between full-length books affords a welcome change of pace and mood. There is the chance to explore aspects of the past with which one was previously unfamiliar, as well as the scope to try out a wide variety of characters and social settings. So I have ventured stories set in Victorian Oxford and war-time Yorkshire as well as a Sherlockian pastiche, an alternative explanation of the death of Queen Caroline and a sequel to the events described in *King Lear*. These experiments have given me a lot of fun.

The idea for 'To Encourage the Others' came from an account in a true crime book of the murder of a girl whose body was dumped in the Bridgewater Canal and washed up at Lymm, the Cheshire village where I live. At much the same time, I was reading about the extraordinary crowds that used to gather to watch executions at Tyburn. When the idea for the story struck me, therefore, my background research was already half done. But even when one works on a mystery set in days gone by, one need not dwell exclusively in the past. To check out the history of canals in Britain, I surfed the Internet and found out a good deal about the early navigations.

This is the darkest of my historical mysteries to date (is there, I wonder, a sub-genre of historical *noir*?). The behaviour of the spectators at the execution is in keeping with many contemporary descriptions. Today the frenzied baying for blood seems unthinkable. It could never happen today. Or could it?

Martin Edwards

To Encourage the Others

Martin Edwards

I never miss a hanging. It is not callousness that impels me to attend every time there is a collar day at Tyburn. Rather, I am driven by the dispassionate curiosity of the philosophically inclined. Death concentrates the mind. One may learn more about the human condition from watching those who are about to meet their maker than from any learned treatise. The behaviour of the wretches on the scaffold is infinitely varied. Some rant, many scream, others merely sob with anguish. Always the spectacle is fascinating for the disinterested spectator to behold.

It matters to me not a jot whether the man or woman about to die is a celebrated criminal or an unknown horse thief. I was amongst the crowd of thirty thousand that watched the execution of Earl Ferrers, but I am as readily seduced by the prospect of the hangman turning off a servant girl. One thing that I have learned over the years is this: a peasant can experience terror just as much as a lord.

It is difficult to exaggerate the sense of satisfaction that is afforded by the prospect of a culprit finally receiving his just deserts. Moreover, personal contentment is reinforced by awareness of the lesson taught by the proceedings. For the work-shy, the greedy or the vicious, I venture to suggest that there can be no more telling reminder of the need to mend their ways than the sight of one of their peers twisting in the wind at Tyburn.

I take an interest in the whole legal process – not surprising, given that my father made his fortune at the Bar – and often a knowledge of the background to the case lends a particular *frisson* to the final act in the drama. So it was with Abe Lewin. He was a humble boatman, master of *The Two Sisters*, a small barge that plied the cut from the River Wey. I had followed the trial from the news-sheets, as is nowadays my custom, and had been struck by the vehemence with which he maintained his plea of not guilty to the killing of Martha Scholes. But he failed to convince the jury and the judge condemned him to swing.

In my younger days, I often followed the cavalcade all the way from Newgate Prison. How many times I have heard with a shudder of anticipation the urging of the bell-man from the churchyard at St Sepulchre's:

'You that are condemned to die, repent with lamentable tears. Ask mercy of the Lord for the salvation of your soul!'

I would ride a short distance behind the cart that conveyed the miscreant to his destiny. He would sit on his own coffin, accompanied by the ordinary charged with offering spiritual guidance and an escort of mounted peace officers and marching constables. An execution is a notable leveller. Rich and poor alike mingle freely together, celebrating the ultimate act of justice in a manner that one seldom sees elsewhere. We would make regular stops for refreshment at taverns and I must confess that upon occasion I have been as intoxicated by the time I reached Tyburn Tree as both the criminal and the hangman.

After attaining the age of sixty, I renounced all that. I have never had much of a head for liquor and I began to tire of having my pockets picked. In any event, as my deafness has worsened, the ringing in my ears is exacerbated by the din of an unruly mob in the confined space of a back street ale house. As I have indicated, my interest in hangings is primarily intellectual. One day, perhaps, I shall prepare a monograph summarising the conclusions of a lifetime's study of my subject. My maiden sister Alice doubts it: she tells people that I have been threatening to become an author these past forty years and have yet to write a word. Yet it may be that putting pen to paper with this account of Abe Lewin's execution will spur me to greater things – although I fear that I can never repeat for public consumption the words from that remarkable day which still lodge in my memory.

On the morning in question I resolved to make my way directly to Tyburn and walked through the dusty and desolate waste of Hyde Park in good time to take up my usual vantage point in one of Mother Procter's Pews. I was the lady's oldest customer and although the land overlooking the gallows has long since passed to her son, he still allows me a preferential rate for a box with an unrivalled view of the execution ground. He gave me a nod of greeting, which I returned, but we did not speak. Since I became hard of hearing I have had little interest in trying to make conversation.

As the crowd grew in size and fervour, I pictured in my mind the shocking discovery that had set in train the events leading up to the hanging fair. A fustian cutter on his way to work one February morning had seen a black object floating in the canal. At first he thought it was the bloated carcass of a dead dog, but a startled second glance made him think again. He drew the object to the bank and found his suspicion confirmed. He was looking at the body of a young woman which had been crudely trussed up by rope in a coarse sack, with the head and feet protruding from either end. Closing my eyes, I strove to imagine the sick feeling in his stomach as he took in the sight of the corpse. I could almost taste the bile on my tongue.

Soon the body was identified as belonging to Martha Scholes, the nineteen-year-old daughter of the landlord of a canalside hostelry called The Compass. She had gone missing three weeks earlier, having been last seen in conversation with a boatman whom she knew well: Abe Lewin, who often called at the tavern for refreshment and who was known to be sweet on her. One of the drinkers there had seen her sitting on Lewin's knee; some time later, she disappeared.

When questioned, Lewin at first denied all knowledge of the girl's fate. He was a gypsy and a poor liar; eventually he admitted that he had persuaded her to join him on board *The Two Sisters*. He was alone on the boat at the time, since he had asked his mate to resolve a dispute with the canal company about some waybills before they continued to transport a cargo of grain to a nearby warehouse. Abe and Martha were both the worse for drink and he said that although they had lain together in his cabin, he had been incapable of fulfilling his lustful intentions towards her. Finally, he had fallen asleep and when his mate returned and woke him, she was nowhere to be seen. Assuming that she had decided to return home, he continued with the journey. Unfortunately for him, it was soon established that the sacking in which Martha's body had been encased had come from a consignment on his barge.

The mate, another gypsy called Chadburn, also gave conflicting statements. In the initial panic of interrogation, he claimed never to have seen Martha. Later, when he could be confident that he was not a principal suspect, he said that he had seen a couple embracing together on a wooden bench not far from where *The Two Sisters* was moored. The girl had possessed the same blonde curls as Martha. He had not seen her companion's face, but he claimed that the hand of his right arm, which was stretched around her back, lacked its thumb; he said the man could not, therefore, have been Abe Lewin. A minute after he had passed them, he had heard the sound of a slap and guessed that the man had pressed his good fortune too far. He heard the girl cry out: 'Stop it, Jack! Stop it!'

Chadburn said that the girl sounded to be far from sober.

He did not turn round: it was not his business to interfere in a lovers' tiff and he was keen to ease his thirst at The Compass before returning to the barge. It was suggested by Abe Lewin's counsel that the girl, tired of the slumbering and impotent boatman, had jumped off *The Two Sisters* and found herself another beau. She had a reputation for liking the company of men, although her father would not hear a word said against her memory. If she had displeased the unknown admirer, he might have killed her in a rage and then, in a desperate attempt to conceal his crime, stolen sacking from the barge and placed her body in it. But the prosecutors dismissed Chadburn as an incompetent liar, trying to help his murdering friend whilst making sure that he did not incriminate himself. Even if he was telling the truth, no one came forward to identify the man whom Chadburn had seen and there was not even proof that the girl had indeed been Martha.

There was more than enough evidence to convict Lewin. As well as the sacking, the rope with which it had been tied had come from the barge. The girl had died from a broken neck, sustained in the course of a severe beating, and Lewin was known to have a temper. Witnesses came forward to say that, a week before her disappearance, the couple had argued outside The Compass and they had heard him threaten violence if she did not accompany him back to the boat in defiance of her father's wishes.

The defence argued that she might have told Jack, the man seen by Chadburn, that the master of *The Two Sisters* was alone on board, drunk and incapable. Having killed her in a temper, Jack might have sought to conceal his crime by wrapping her body up with goods stolen from the barge and then throwing it into the canal with a stone to weigh it down. He had not realised that his precautions were inadequate to prevent the movement of vessels on the cut together with the effect of abdominal gases from bringing the wretched Martha back to the surface.

It was a thin argument, however, and the jury wasted little time in dismissing it. Had I troubled to attend the trial, I would have been compelled to lip-read, but in my mind, I could hear the judge pronounce sentence in tones that were thrillingly clear:

'The law is, that thou shalt return from hence, to the place whence thou camest, and from thence to the place of execution, where thou shalt hang by the neck till the body be dead! dead! dead! and the Lord have mercy on thy soul!'

As I came out of my reverie, I noticed the hangman surveying the gallows. He was a burly ruffian by the name of Heslop. I had watched him turn off perhaps half a dozen miscreants before. Executioners are seldom popular men and I have often seen crowds turn on them. Ten years ago, the then master of ceremonies at Tyburn was stoned almost to death. But it would take a brave fellow to challenge Heslop, a six-footer with the muscles of a prize-fighter whom I had never seen sober.

A roar of approval marked the arrival of the cart bearing the condemned man. The hubbub was as great as ever and I guessed that there would be a rich haul for the pickpockets. People were quarrelling, jostling or simply coughing as the clouds of dust filled their lungs. A few yards away from my pew, a well-dressed woman whom I often saw at executions screamed abuse at Lewin as he mounted the scaffold, waving her fists in rage as the hapless ordinary began to sing a psalm.

Lewin was not, thankfully, an educated man and thus we were spared a lengthy diatribe of the type in which more articulate murderers indulge. As he stood before us, it was plain that his spirit was broken. He simply shouted:

'As God is my witness, I am innocent!'

With that, he fell silent and the people around me began to guffaw in derision. I felt a pang of dismay that there was to be no final confession of guilt from this particular sinner

336

to make the event complete. The chaplain may have been of a similar mind, for he spared us an extended homily. After a few embarrassed words he climbed down from the platform and became lost in the crowd. The hangman moved forward – I could almost imagine that I smelled the beer on his breath – and tied the cord around Lewin's neck.

I felt myself tensing, as I had so many times before, when John Heslop covered the criminal's face. I could not help being aware that my own pulse had quickened. There is something terrible yet deeply gratifying about the thought which inevitably passes through one's mind at such a moment: *within a few seconds, the trapdoor will open and his neck will snap.*

As I watched, Heslop's face suddenly curved into a cruel smile. He leaned towards the blindfolded man and whispered in his ear. Then he pulled the lever, the body jerked and fell and justice was done.

Or was it? For an instant, I was assailed by doubt. But then I reminded myself that hanging an innocent man has as much beneficial effect upon the populace as hanging a guilty one – as long as no one doubts his guilt. At once I realised I must tell no one what I had seen. That is why this must remain an entirely private memoir. For as I pushed my way past the anatomists who were about to collect their trophy, I reflected that I had never before realised that Heslop lacked his right thumb. I had not had cause on previous occasions to examine the hand that opened the trapdoor. Indeed, I would not have done so this time, had I not read on his lips the words which the hangman whispered to Lewin, the last words the boatman ever heard in his life.

'Why don't you beg me, just as she did? "Stop it, Jack! Stop it!" Not that I'd take any more notice of you than I did of the bitch.'

I first made the acquaintance of Brother Cadfael on Euston Station when a train delay sent me scurrying to the bookstall. *A Morbid Taste for Bones* turned an irritated traveller into a grateful reader. In Brother Cadfael, I discovered a true friend and a sure-footed guide through the twelfth century. Born and brought up in Wales, I was delighted to find a protagonist who was a devious and resourceful Welshman.

Ellis Peters' achievement was immense. Long before Umberto Eco burst on to the scene with *The Name of the Rose*, she explored the dramatic potential of the Middle Ages and fired a mass-market audience with her tales. She helped to rescue medieval England from its more usual position as a backdrop for a romantic saga or a target for hilarious send-up. Whether writing as Edith Pargeter or Ellis Peters, she made her readers enjoy and respect the periods of history with which she dealt so knowledgeably yet entertainingly.

It was her success in getting people to take the medieval world seriously which encouraged me to write my own series of Domesday Books. Set over half a century before Brother Cadfael padded his way around Shrewsbury Abbey, they share with the later series a passionate interest in the work and beliefs of the Benedictine Order. It is difficult to write convincingly about an Age of Faith unless you have experienced the joys and frustrations of Christian belief yourself.

Here, as elsewhere, Ellis Peters was an inspiration. Her work is grounded on a set of Christian values which are practical, persuasive and full of deep compassion.

I had the good fortune to meet Edith Pargeter on a number of occasions. The last time was shortly before her death when I recorded an hour-long radio interview with her for broadcast at the Malice Domestic Mystery Convention in America so that their Guest of Honour could be heard if not seen. She was a marvellous talker, ranging over the whole of medieval England with ease and speaking about people as diverse as Bernard of Clairvaux, Owain Glyn Dwr and King John as if they were personal friends who often dropped in for tea.

As I was leaving, I congratulated her on the description of the siege in *Brother Cadfael's Penance*, sadly Cadfael's last outing. 'Ah, yes,' she said with a smile, 'I had a lot of fun with that!' So did her readers. She gave them endless fun. Historical mysteries do not date. The work of Ellis Peters will remain as fresh as when it was first written.

She was a dear lady, a dedicated student of history and a true professional. She threw light on every period about which she wrote. And anyone fortunate enough to meet her soon saw from whom Cadfael had got that mischievous sparkle in his eye.

Edward Marston

Psalm for a Dead Disciple

Edward Marston

We reached our destination by nightfall on the third day. Amok, my bodyguard, as was his wont slept on straw with the animals in the stable of an inn but I sought more wholesome accommodation. She and I were having breakfast the next morning when I heard my first mention of The Healer.

'It is wonderful to see you once more,' she purred.

'You are the perfect woman,' I said with feeling. 'I would travel ten times the distance to sleep in your enchanting arms.' An involuntary yawn. 'Not that we had much sleep last night.' That bewitching smile of hers. 'You are insatiable.'

'Is that a complaint?'

'It's a cause for celebration, Naomi.'

'How long will you be in Galilee?'

'Long enough to come here again,' I said.

'Is that a promise?'

'To both of us.'

'I will hold you to that.'

Naomi is always my first port of call in Galilee. She is a most delightful harbour. Dedicated to pleasure, she does things for me that most women would not dare to contemplate, still less to execute with such delicate precision.

341

Naomi is a place of refuge from a hostile world. A fount of love in a Jewish town where a Samaritan like me is despised, Naomi's love has to be bought but it is all the more reliable for that reason. A merchant by trade, I know how to get value for money.

Tall, slim and sensuous, Naomi is no mere companion for a weary traveller from Sebaste. She is also my intelligencer. She sees and hears everything that happens in Galilee. That is why I pay her so handsomely. To keep watch. A merchant needs to have a ready supply of news.

'Who have you come to see?' she asked.

'You, my angel.'

A lazy grin. 'Who else?'

'Zebedee the Fisherman.'

'He is not in town today.'

'Is he out on the lake?'

'No,' she explained. 'He is going to see The Healer.'

'The Healer?'

'A man from Nazareth. He cures the sick.'

'Oh?' I said, interest quickening. 'Is that why Zebedee wants to visit this man? Is the testy old fisherman ill?'

'No, Iddo. He wants to see The Healer out of curiosity. James and John, his sons, have abandoned their nets to follow this Nazarene. Andrew and Peter, the brothers of Bethsaida, have also declared themselves to be his disciples.'

'Disciples? Of some roadside conjuror?'

'He is much more than that, Iddo. They say that he performs miracles. No other man alive could have enticed Zebedee's sons away.' Her mouth hardened into a rueful line. 'Or stolen one of my best clients.'

'Who is that?'

'Levi, son of Alphaeus.'

'The tax collector?'

'Yes,' she sighed. 'But he will never collect taxes again.

Levi – or Matthew as we must now call him – has renounced everything to follow this Healer.'

'He preferred this itinerant Nazarene to *you*, Naomi?' I said in utter astonishment. 'Why?'

'That's a long story.'

'I can't wait to hear it.'

But I did just that. At that moment, Naomi's divine left breast (my favourite) slipped artlessly into view from beneath her raiment and deprived me of the wish to listen to a story of any length. The olive-skinned mound of flesh had a silken sheen and its gleaming nipple blossomed under my eager gaze. Breakfast was summarily abandoned and we devoured each other instead. It was an hour or more before I had breath enough to ask her a question.

'What is this Healer like?'

'He is dangerous.'

'I want to see him,' I decided.

It was a disastrous mistake.

The road was busy. Amok and I were part of a sizeable crowd which was moving – largely on foot – in the same direction. Could they all be going in search of The Healer? How could he tempt so many men away from their places of work and so many women from their domestic chores? What was the secret of the Nazarene's appeal?

We were an incongruous sight. Short and squat, I was as usual mounted on Jubal, the huge stallion I won in a wager in Cilicia. Amok, by contrast, my big, shaggy, bear-like scribe and protector, sat astride his flea-bitten donkey and let his heels drag idly through the dust.

We rode in silence. There was no point in attempting meaningful contact with Amok. He is a man of few words. Even his grunts are severely rationed. But then I do not employ him for the joy of his conversation. He is there primarily to safeguard me. In a country where Samaritans are hated I need Amok beside me to discourage my enemies from adding blows to the familiar insults. His stench keeps most people at bay. I was grateful that Naomi's perfume still haunted my nostrils.

As the crowd thickened I recognised a sturdy figure on foot ahead of us and nudged Jubal forward until I drew level with him.

'Good morrow, Levi!' I said.

'Iddo!' he replied with uncharacteristic warmth. 'What on earth are you doing here?'

'Looking for The Healer.'

'You are only looking,' he said proudly. 'I was called. He chose me as one of his disciples. Oh, and by the way, he gave me a new name. I am Levi no longer. I am Matthew.'

'Naomi told me.'

'I have put that harlot aside.'

'Madness!'

'I have resolved to live a cleaner life.'

'Whatever for, Matthew?'

'It is a condition of following him.'

'I prefer to be a disciple of Naomi.'

Levi – or Matthew as I will henceforth call him – is an old acquaintance. We knew each other for years before we realised that we had someone in common. Naomi. That indicated to me that he was a man of taste. And moderate wealth. Naomi sets a high price on her favours and rightly so. She does not consort with paupers.

A stocky man of medium height, Matthew dresses well and has an air of seedy prosperity about him. He was a tax collector at the frontier town of Capernaum, a quick-witted fellow with an unctuous charm. Tax collectors are a loathsome species at the best of times but he was also reviled for cooperating with the Roman administration, taking money from his own people to put into the coffers of their overlords.

Jews look upon tax gatherers with the same contempt they reserve for murderers, robbers, rapists and other undesirables. Like Samaritans. It was another bond between

344

Matthew and me. Both of us were despised and shunned. Since his job entailed the collection of customs dues on all articles going in and out of Capernaum, I made sure that we came to an amicable arrangement early on. A merchant must know who to bribe.

Jubal ambled alongside the unlikely disciple.

'Have you really given up all to follow him?' I asked.

'Yes,' he said with glowing certitude. 'I have seen the error of my former ways and renounced them completely.'

'Naomi is an *error*?' I gasped in disbelief.

'She is a sinful woman.'

'That is her attraction.'

'Not to me. I have turned my back on her.'

'That is a terrible sacrifice to make.'

'I do it willingly, Iddo. I serve a new master now. The light of purity shines out of him. He has the gift of healing. He restores sight to the blind and hearing to the deaf. When he laid hands upon a cripple the poor wretch was made whole again and danced with joy. My master has magic fingers.'

'So does Naomi.'

'You have grown coarse, Iddo.'

'I am the same as you once were, Matthew.'

'Yes,' he admitted freely, 'that is true. When I sat behind my table and collected taxes I enjoyed a crude jest to break the monotony of the work. But that man has died. I have been reborn in a more godly image.'

'I liked the old Levi.'

'Wait until you meet our master.'

We came round a bend in the road and saw them ahead of us. There were hundreds of people, gathered in a rough circle around a rocky outcrop, looking upwards at the small group of men on the rock itself. Matthew was so keen to join them that he broke into a trot. Amok and I dismounted near the fringe of the gathering and tethered our animals to an olive tree.

I checked that my knife was in my belt. You can never be

too careful in a public place. Even with Amok beside me, I like to have a means of defence. The knife has a long, curved blade and a decorated handle of the finest ivory. Its copper scabbard is a work of art. The weapon imparts reassurance.

Anxious to see The Healer I soon found my height a severe disadvantage in such a large throng. Amok noted my distress and pushed a way through the press. One hand on the knife, I followed in his wake. A crowd as large as that is normally loud and boisterous but this one was strangely subdued. It was eerie. Nobody even cursed Amok as he bullocked past them. Attention fixed on the rock, they hardly noticed us.

When a man's voice was raised in the singing of a psalm a hush fell on the whole congregation. The mellifluous words floated on the wind like so many doves of peace. Accompanying himself on the lyre, the musician had a deep, resonant voice which lent beauty and authority to his words. Even to ears as sceptical as mine the sound was persuasive and moving. It also helped us to get our bearings. Follow the psalm and it would lead us to The Healer.

> 'The Lord lifteth up the meek;
> he casteth the wicked down to the ground.'

That has not been my experience but the melodious voice almost had me believing in it. The singer was positively beguiling us with his art, investing every phrase of the psalm with the sheer power and harmony of his conviction.

> 'Sing unto the Lord with thanksgiving;
> sing praise upon the harp to God:
> Who covereth the heaven with clouds,
> who prepareth rain for the earth,
> who maketh the grass to grow upon the mountains.'

When we finally reached the singer we found ourselves gazing at a big barrel-chested man of mature years with a red beard and long red hair which hung in ringlets. His fingers plucked deftly as his voice soared.

> 'He giveth to the beast his food,
> and to the young ravens which cry.
> He delighteth not in the strength of the horse;
> he taketh not pleasure in the legs of a man.'

There were thirteen other men on the rock with him. Matthew was directly behind the singer and I also recognised James and John, the sons of Zebedee, but I could not pick out The Healer. Which of those smiling onlookers had brought us all to that hot and dusty place outside the town? My eye ran slowly over the thirteen men. Before I could even guess which one might be the Nazarene, tragedy struck in mid-psalm.

> 'Praise the Lord, O Jerusalem; praise thy God, O Zion!'

As the words rose up into the air there was a sudden movement behind us and we were pushed towards the singer in a surging wave. Hit by the human deluge he let out a cry of agony, dropped his lyre and fell like a stone to the ground. Having spent its force, the wave ebbed quickly back to reveal the victim. Lying on his back, his mouth frozen in praise of his Lord, he gazed up at heaven with a mixture of yearning and reproach. Only angels would accompany his psalms from now on.

When I studied the corpse more closely my shock was tempered with alarm. Sticking out of his chest was the ivory handle of the weapon which had evidently killed him. I identified it all too readily.

The taut silence was broken, improbably, by Amok.

'Look, master,' he said, pointing. 'Your knife.'

It was all the proof that the crowd needed. They attacked with ferocity and fought each other for the privilege of reaching me. My protests of innocence went unheard in the swirling hysteria. The last thought which went through my mind before I was beaten unconscious was that if I survived the onslaught to hold that knife in my hand once more, I would use it to cut out Amok's tongue.

A man of few words had used them to incriminate me.

Thrown into my face with vicious force, a bucket of black, brackish water finally brought me to my senses again. My face was a mass of aching bruises and a continuous avalanche of sharp stones was taking place inside my skull. My apparel was torn, my body throbbing with pain and my legs made of wax. What disturbed me most of all was that my arms were paralysed.

A second bucket of water concentrated my mind and allowed me to open a first wary eye. It liked nothing of what it saw. Arms pinioned, I was perched on a stool in a featureless room, held upright by two Roman soldiers with drawn swords in their other hands. A third soldier stood before me with two empty wooden pails and a grin as broad as the Tiber. He had enjoyed the task of reviving me for interrogation.

The bucketeer stepped back smartly as an officer came marching into the room. My guards kicked the stool from beneath me and jerked me into an upright position. The newcomer was short and muscular with the strutting arrogance of a man in a position of command. My two supporters were Syrians, pressed into service in the Roman army, but their superior was the genuine article. A Roman soldier from Rome itself. A member of the conquering élite.

It put an imperious note into his clipped Latin.

'What is your name?' he demanded.

'Iddo,' I mumbled.

'Speak up in my presence.'

A thorough shake by the guards loosened my vocal cords.

'Iddo,' I repeated aloud.

'Where do you live?'

'Sebaste.'

'What is your occupation?'

'I am a merchant.'

'Why did you come to Galilee?'

'To do business.'

'With whom?'

'Zebedee the Fisherman.'

'Where did you spend last night?'

'At an inn.'

'Alone?'

'With my travelling companion. Amok.'

Arms folded, legs wide apart, he gave a curt nod.

'You have a good command of Latin,' he said with grudging approval. 'Do not use it to lie to me.'

'I am not lying.'

'Then why tell me you slept at an inn with that smelly servant of yours when you spent the night between the thighs of a harlot?' He gave a cold smile. 'True or false?'

'A bit of both,' I confessed, wondering how he could possibly have come by the information. 'The beating I took left me confused.'

'Perhaps you would like another bucket of water to refresh your memory. This time your head will be held in it for a few minutes until you learn the difference between truth and dishonesty.' He let the threat hang in the air for a moment. 'You were lucky,' he added.

I raised an ironic eyebrow. 'This is *luck*?'

'In the hands of the Jewish authorities you would have been killed an hour ago. A Samaritan stabbing a Jew to death in broad daylight? They would have slaughtered you without even the formality of a trial. You were fortunate to escape. But for the courage of your bodyguard you would have been torn to shreds by that mob. Amok saved your life. My men rescued you both in the nick of time but Amok is your real saviour.'

'Where is he?'

'Helping us with our enquiries.'

'He's *talking* to you?' I said in amazement.

'Constantly. Through an interpreter.'

'What has he told you?'

'That is our business,' he snapped. 'All I am concerned to establish now is whether or not your story agrees with his. We have already stumbled on one discrepancy – where and with whom you spent the night. I hope we do not find any more.' He took a step towards me. 'Now, Iddo. Answer me this and be careful with your reply. Why did you kill that man?'

'I did not kill him!' I denied hotly.

'Your knife was in his chest.'

'I swear that I did not put it there!'

'Then who did?'

'Whoever took it from my belt.'

'Amok, perhaps?'

'Of course not. Amok is my bodyguard.'

'He was the one person in the crowd who knew that you carried a knife and he was close enough to take it.'

'It would have been an act of suicide,' I argued. 'You said it yourself a moment ago. A Samaritan murdering a Jew at an exclusively Jewish gathering. Even Amok's strength would not have kept that mob at bay indefinitely.'

'True. He took a buffeting on your behalf.'

'Because he was more concerned with protecting my life than seeking the death of an anonymous musician.'

'Josephus.'

'Who?'

'That is the name of the murder victim,' he explained. 'Josephus of Cana. A fine singer by all accounts.'

'He had a most beautiful voice.'

'Who decided to silence it?'

'Not me. Nor Amok. We were innocent bystanders.'

'That remains to be seen.'

'I had no *reason* to kill the man.'

'None that has so far emerged.'

'I've never seen him before in my entire life.'

'We will need to verify that fact.'

'Speak to Zebedee. He will vouch for me.'

'Do not try to tell me my job,' he warned, 'or I will have you soundly whipped then thrown into a cell to repent your folly. You are my prisoner. That means you have no rights beyond those I choose to grant you. Frankly, Iddo, I've half a mind to throw you back to the Jews so that they can deal with you. It would save me time and trouble. And you would probably get no more than you deserve.' He wagged an admonitory finger. 'Do as I tell you or I'll make you wish you were never born.'

It was time to fight back and my brain had now cleared sufficiently for it to remember the one fact that might save me. I had no chance of justice at the hands of this self-important brute. My only hope lay in appealing to a higher court. Shrugging off the guards, I drew myself up to my full height and managed a semblance of dignity.

'I wish to speak with Caius Marcius,' I said calmly.

He was visibly shaken. 'Repeat that,' he ordered.

'Caius Marcius. The commander of this fort. Your superior. I want him to witness how shabbily I've been treated by one of his underlings. Send my name to him. He will recognise it.'

'You know Caius Marcius?' A note of caution intruded. 'What exactly is the nature of your relationship with our commander?'

'I have often done business with him.'

'Of what nature?'

'That is highly confidential,' I said. 'I could not possibly divulge any details because Caius Marcius trusts me implicitly. I have earned that trust and turn to him now to speak up on my behalf.'

'He will not defend a murderer.'

'Nor will he send an innocent man to his death.'

I spoke with more conviction than I felt but it seemed to do the trick. My interrogator moved away and ran a pensive hand over his smooth-shaven chin. I had planted a doubt in his mind. It was a relief to see that all those favours I had done for Caius Marcius over the years might now bear fruit. A merchant should always ingratiate himself with his political masters. A friend high up in the Roman administration is a friend indeed.

My captor swung round to face me again.

'Caius Marcius is not at the fortress,' he said.

'Then I will come back when he is.'

'He returns from Caesarea tomorrow.'

'Good,' I said. 'Release me at once from this unwarranted imprisonment and you have my word that I will be back here tomorrow to discuss this whole matter with your commander.'

My suggestion was met with a sneer of contempt.

'Lock him up!' he decreed.

'Alone?' asked one of the guards.

'No. Put him in with the others. A night in a cell with real criminals will tell us if he is one himself.'

Lifting me bodily, the two guards carried me out.

'Caius Marcius will hear about this!' I yelled.

'It will be included in my report.'

'He would expect me to be treated with respect.'

'You have been.'

The prison quarters consisted of a series of low, dark, airless stone cells with sunken floors. Dragged through the dust, I arrived in an even more dishevelled state than before. The one concession to my bodily comfort was the removal of my bonds. My hands and arms belonged to me again. Before I could rub them back into life, however, the door of a cell was unlocked and I was hurled unceremoniously in through it.

Somebody punched me as I landed on top of him and I

rolled into a corner for safety. The door slammed shut with awesome finality. I felt as if I would never again savour the sweet taste of freedom. More immediate problems pressed in on me. The first was the stink. The cell was flavoured with the accumulated excrement of its past and present inhabitants, enriched by the reek of rancid food and the stench of despair. I retched for several minutes which afforded some amusement to my companions. Their sniggers buzzed in my ears like angry bees in search of stolen honey.

My fellow-prisoners were the second problem. It took me some time to work out how many of them there were. One tiny slit in the stone, high in one wall, admitted only a finger of light to penetrate the darkness. When my nostrils finally adjusted to the smell I was able to let my eyes get used to the gloom. Shapes were slowly conjured into view but they had no real definition. I was incarcerated with ghosts.

There were two of them. Huddled against the opposite wall, they sat close enough to each other to exchange nudges and whispers. I caught the odd curse in Hebrew. They were talking about me and keeping me under scrutiny. Who were they? What hideous crimes had they committed to get themselves thrown into such a foul prison? Murder? Kidnap? Robbery? Assault? Rape? I shuddered. They were creatures of the pit, denizens of the darkness who were as much at home in that black mire as the rats I could hear snuffling in the clotted straw.

They belonged. I did not. I was trespassing on their territory and they resented it. How would they express their resentment? That was the question which tormented me.

'Amok!' I cried to myself. 'Where *are* you?'

I sat up with a start when I remembered that it was Amok, my own loyal, reliable, incorruptible Amok, who was directly responsible for my arrest. It was he who told the world that the murder weapon which had interrupted a psalm was mine. It was Amok, my closest associate, ridding himself of a week's verbiage in one calamitous speech, who tossed my Samaritan carcass to the ravening Jewish wolves. Had he maintained his habitual silence I would not now be fearing for my life in a military prison. Amok had rebelled against his master.

Evil has its own distinctive odour. It emanated slowly from my companions until it filled the cell and made my head pound. Menace was tangible. They were biding their time. Having sized me up, the two men would know when to strike with maximum effect. Vigilance was essential. Whatever happened, I told myself, I must not fall asleep.

When your body has been pummelled into fatigue such advice is easier to issue than to accept. Sitting upright against the dank wall was an effort in itself. I could feel my strength being sapped by the minute. There was no hope of my being able to stay awake throughout the night to defend myself against an assault. My whole being seemed to be closing its doors on the world one by one. It was impossible to believe that my numb anatomy had so recently thrilled to Naomi's soft caresses.

I clung on until the finger of light drooped, turned grey and waggled a farewell before vanishing through the slit. A blackness deeper than anything I had ever known before enfolded me in its arms and squeezed all resistance from me. I was asleep in an instant. How long my slumber lasted I have no notion but I was brought out of it in the most inconsiderate manner.

The kick in the stomach awakened me then I was hauled upright by a powerful arm and pinned against the wall. Light was just starting to feel its way in through the slit so it must have been dawn but I was given no chance to make an accurate assessment of the time of day. The villain who had me flattened against the wall was bigger, broader, heavier and stronger than me. He also had a weapon.

Grabbing me by the beard, he put the blade of his knife across my throat. From the smell of his breath I knew that we could never be close friends.

'What's your name?' he growled.

'Iddo.'

His eyes narrowed suspiciously.

'Are you a Samaritan?' he accused.

I gave him my most obliging smile.

'Not necessarily.'

It was not the occasion for complete honesty.

'If you were I'd slit your throat right now. We have our standards. We may be criminals but we do not deserve to be locked up with a rotten, lousy, cheating Samaritan. It'd be an insult to us. Understand?'

'Only too well.'

'So what are you in for, Iddo?'

'Murder.'

It earned a momentary respect from them. They nudged and whispered again then the knife was twisted to draw a warning trickle of blood from my neck.

'With us or against us?' hissed my assailant.

'With you,' I affirmed. 'All the way.'

'We mean to escape.'

'But that's impossible.'

'Not with your assistance,' he said. 'We have a plan.'

'How do I come into it?'

'Call for help.'

'Who from?'

'The guards. There are only two of them. Stupid Syrians who come on duty at first light, still half-asleep. Yell out that we're attacking you and they'll stagger over here. When they open that door we'll be ready for them.'

'You'll kill them?' I gulped.

'We'll kill anyone who stands in our way.'

'What about me?'

'You escape with us, of course.'

I know a grotesque lie when I hear it. Merchants are students of character. We develop intuition. I did not need a long acquaintance with the pair to know that they had no intention of letting me leave the cell alive. When I had served my purpose they would dispose of me as callously as they would of the two Syrians. My brain whirred madly.

'Will you do it?' he demanded.

'What must I say?'

'Just howl for help. Say that we're hitting you.'

'Or we will,' added his friend. 'Hard.'

They held the advantage over me but I did have one secret means of fighting back. A merchant needs to speak in many languages. Unknown to them I was fluent in Aramaic. When I battered on the door of the cell and cried out for help in the Hebrew which they understood I also slipped in a warning in words that the Syrian guards alone would recognise.

'This is a ruse!' I cried. 'I'm pretending to be in danger to lure you to the cell. They are behind the door and one of them has a knife. Beware!'

My voice became one long screech of pain and footsteps were heard thundering down the passageway outside. Crouched behind the door, the two villains waited to pounce on the unsuspecting guards but these were Syrians with the benefit of Roman military training. When the door opened they came through it with their shields held before them, giving them complete protection and allowing them to force the two prisoners back against the wall. Other guards came running to their aid. Instead of escaping the men were overpowered and fettered within minutes.

I was taken out of the cell for my own safety.

'You betrayed us!' shouted my would-be assassin.

'Shameful, isn't it?' I teased. 'Learn your lesson.'

'What lesson?'

'Never trust a Samaritan.'

His howl of rage was heard as far away as Sebaste.

I prefer to think that it was my brave action in foiling a prison escape which earned me my release but two other factors were paramount. Amok, my silent associate, suddenly discovered the power of words and used them to persuade the Romans, if not of my innocence then at least of the unlikelihood of my guilt. But it was the return of Caius Marcius which was decisive. We are old trading partners. Over the years I have provided him with rich foods, heady wines and all the other delicacies a soldier needs when he is isolated from the civilised world of Rome. More to the point, I introduced him to Naomi and he has been unfailingly grateful to me.

'You are free to go, Iddo,' he said magnanimously.

'What about Amok?'

'Take him with you. He is charged with no offence.'

'Thank you, Caius Marcius.'

'Ride hard in the direction of Samaria,' he counselled. 'Leave Galilee while you have the opportunity.'

'But I was falsely accused of a murder.'

'The Jews still believe you stabbed Josephus with your knife. Show yourself in the streets and they will take the law into their own hands. Trade elsewhere until this whole affair has blown over.'

'How can it until the crime has been solved?'

'We will look into the matter.'

'I was there,' I reasoned. 'You were not. The only person likely to get to the truth is me. I owe it to myself to track down the killer. And I owe it to Josephus. I have never heard a psalm sung so well.'

'Stay in Galilee and you court danger.'

'I thrive on it.'

'Go now,' he urged. 'While you still may.'

'Only when I have unmasked the real assassin.'

Caius Marcius turned away to ponder. A noble Roman, he has the kind of handsome profile which would grace the imperial coinage and withstand the wear and tear without losing any definition. When he looked back at me he clicked his tongue and shook his head sadly.

'You are a brave fool, Iddo.'

'I want my name cleared.'

'Let others try to do that for you,' he said. 'How can you possibly solve this crime? You would not even know where to start looking.'

'Yes, I would.'

'Where?'

'In the psalms.'

Torn between anger and gratitude, I was not sure whether to berate Amok for bringing the wrath of the mob down on me or to thank him for saving me from their worst excesses. In the end I settled for a brief reprimand followed by a pat on the back. Amok retreated into a hurt silence.

Remaining in Galilee meant assuming a disguise and he was very unhappy about that. As anyone who has stood next to him will testify, Amok has not changed his garments for at least a decade and I had to force him to put on a clean robe. My own flamboyant apparel – a merchant needs to be visible – was traded for the most sober raiment I could find. Our animals had been brought to the fort by the soldiers who arrested us and it seemed sensible to leave Jubal there for the time being. A white horse is a rare sight among the asses and camels of Galilee. For once in my life I did not want people to look at me and take due note of my status.

Two men and a donkey left the fort to solve a murder.

'Your task is simple, Amok,' I told him. 'Watch my back. That is all you have to do. Guard your master. Is that clear? And the next time my knife ends up in someone's chest you are to hold your tongue. Do you hear? Say nothing!'

Amok said nothing.

He waited outside the house while I made my first call. Amok would never dream of crossing such a sinful threshold. Naomi was puzzled until she realised who was concealed beneath the black burnoose. Relief gave way to sheer delight and she showered me with kisses.

'Thank heaven you are safe!' she said.

358

'You heard what happened?'

'Everyone in Galilee has heard.'

'I did not kill him, Naomi.'

'I never thought for a moment that you did.'

'Somebody used me as his scapegoat,' I said, taking her by the shoulders. 'I need you to help me find him.'

'How?'

'Tell me all you know about Josephus of Cana.'

'It is little enough,' she apologised. 'Report has it that Josephus was a lawyer, a learned man of good reputation. When he heard The Healer preach, however, Josephus lost all interest in his clients and talked only of the law of the Lord. His ambition was to become one of the disciples but twelve had already been chosen. Josephus found it difficult to cope with rejection. Why should an upright man like himself be turned away while a rogue like Levi, son of Alphaeus, was accepted as a fit companion to The Healer?'

'A good question.'

'It preyed on his mind.'

'What action did he take?'

'You witnessed it for yourself, Iddo,' she said. 'He elected himself as one of the chosen. Whenever and wherever The Healer went to preach Josephus of Cana went also and inspired the crowd by singing them a psalm. It was his way of being part of The Healer's ministry.'

'I think I hear what you are telling me, Naomi.'

'Josephus was an interloper.'

'An unlucky thirteenth disciple.'

After a visit to the temple I set off in search of Matthew. It took an age to track him down. In the old days he would have been easy to find, sitting behind his table in the open air, collecting taxes, dispensing ribald jokes and swindling the gullible citizens with a skill born of long practice. Our search began at his home then took us on a circuitous route through the whole of Galilee. We eventually caught him outside a house on the fringe of the town. When I revealed to him who we were Matthew was duly startled.

'I thought you were languishing in prison,' he said.

'Until this morning I was. Quite unjustly.'

'I know, my friend. Whoever killed poor Josephus, it was certainly not you. I tried to say so at the time but the crowd was in no mood to listen.' He embraced me warmly. 'Your travail is over. God has seen fit to deliver you.'

'With a little help from the Roman army,' I corrected. 'As for my travail it continues unabated. Were it not for this disguise I would probably have been stoned to death by now. In the eyes of your people I am still the prime suspect. Murder is bad for a merchant's business. I must exonerate myself.'

'Count on my full support, Iddo.'

'That is why I came to you.' I glanced up at the fine mansion behind him. 'But what are you doing out here at this splendid residence? I thought you had renounced your rich friends and your life of indulgence?'

'I have, I have,' he insisted. 'My master was summoned here because the daughter of the house is grievously sick and likely to die. Only his healing powers can save her.'

'Are the other disciples here?'

'Some of them. I stayed outside to keep watch.'

'For what?'

'Enemies. My master is not popular in some quarters I fear. His preaching unsettles the Pharisees, his miracles arouse much envy and scorn. After what happened yesterday we feel that it is wise to take certain precautions.'

'Who killed Josephus of Cana?'

'I wish I knew.'

'Do you have no idea, Matthew? You were standing as close to Josephus as anyone. Did you not see the knife being thrust into his chest?'

'It happened so quickly and amid such commotion.'

'What of the faces in the front row of the crowd?'

360

'I recognised none apart from your own.'

'Did Josephus have any particular enemies?'

'Several. He was a lawyer.'

'Has anyone sworn to kill him?'

'I do not know, Iddo. He was not one of the chosen. He merely lurked in our master's shadow and tried to befriend him by singing psalms.' He put an anxious face close to mine. 'This is a desperate business, my friend. I tell you this in confidence. We are appalled at the murder of Josephus of Cana and mourn his demise but some of us, privately, have a deeper fear. Was the hapless Josephus, in fact, the killer's intended target? Might not your knife – stolen deliberately from your belt – have been destined for another heart?'

'Your own, perhaps?'

'Or my master's. They wanted to silence him.'

'They?'

'His enemies.'

'Do you have their names?'

'They are legion.'

'Where was your master standing?'

'Just behind Josephus.'

'Then why was he not stabbed?'

'Who knows?' he said with a shrug. 'All I can suggest is that when the crowd surged forward it was difficult to control the thrust of the knife. My guess is that the murderer had a confederate further back in the press and that it was he who caused that sudden lurch forward in order to conceal the stabbing. You unwittingly provided the murder weapon.'

'Come back to Josephus,' I said.

'Why?'

'Is there any significance in the timing of his death?'

'What do you mean?'

'The thirteenth disciple was killed at the very moment he was about to sing the thirteenth verse of his psalm. Do you know what that verse is, Matthew?'

'Not offhand.'

'For he hath strengthened the bars of thy gates;
    he hath blessed they children within thee.'

'Your knowledge of the psalms astounds me, Iddo.'
    'Even a sinner needs something to sing.'
    'But you are a Samaritan. You only accept the Pentateuch.'
    'The Five Books of Moses could do with a psalm or two to
lighten their tone,' I said with an irreverent grin. 'But I will
not deceive you. The psalm sung by Josephus has a special
meaning for me. I called at a temple on my way here to
seek it out in full lest it should contain some vital clue.'
    'And does it?'
    'I am not sure. I need to sing it to myself a few more
times. And in honour of Josephus of Cana.'
    'Josephus?'
    'A psalm for a dead disciple.'
    'We all grieve at his passing.'
    'What does The Healer say?'
    'My master?'
    'He was there at the crucial moment and in a perfect
position to witness the outrage. Does he not have some idea
who delivered the fatal thrust with the knife and which breast
the blade was really destined for?'
    'He spoke only of you, Iddo.'
    'Me?'
    'With great sympathy.'
    'But he does not even know me.'
    'He knows your situation,' said Matthew gently. 'Knows
and understands. You are a Samaritan, a natural outcast in a
Jewish enclave like Galilee, a man so despised for an accident
of birth that he will be suspected of the most heinous crimes.
You are the ritual sacrifice, Iddo. A man is killed. Your knife
is in his chest. Proof positive of Samaritan villainy.'
    'I am beginning to like your master,' I conceded.
    'Then hearken to his advice.'
    'What is it?'

'Two crimes were committed yesterday, Iddo. The second was the murder of Josephus and it was so hideous an act that it obscured the crime which preceded it.'

'The theft of my dagger.'

'Who knew that you carried it?'

'Amok and myself.'

'Are you sure?'

'What do you mean?'

'Only this, my friend,' he said with a consoling hand on my shoulder. 'Someone deliberately put the blame for this killing on you. Someone who hates you enough to want you dead. Someone who trailed you through that crowd. Someone who knew that you had that weapon in your belt.'

'What are you saying, Matthew?'

'Leave us to worry about who the real target was. All that you need to concentrate on is your own predicament.'

'Give it to me in a sentence.'

'Look to your enemies.'

It was sound advice and we acted on it promptly. The problem lay in the sheer numbers. Success breeds envy and I have been highly successful as a merchant. I have created so many enemies in Galilee that it would take a month or more to get around them all. Speaking aloud, I counted the leading suspects on my stubby fingers. All would be happy to see me dead.

It was Amok who provided the breakthrough. He refused to speak but he did rise to an elaborate mime, taking back one hand before bringing it smartly forward and opening his palm. I saw invisible dice rolling in the dust and let out a cry of triumph.

'Amok!' I congratulated. 'You are a genius.'

A faint smile lit his inscrutable features.

'Nathan!' I continued. 'He must be involved here. Why ever didn't I think of Nathan of Galilee?'

The answer was simple. It would be hard to imagine anyone less likely than Nathan to make the effort to see The

Healer. Nathan is one of the most godless and unscrupulous human beings in existence, the sort of grasping merchant who gives the rest of us a bad name. What Amok had reminded me was that Nathan knew that I carried the knife in my belt. It was something he would not forget because I had won it off him in a game of dice and he had cursed me when parting with it.

Could Nathan be involved in the murder of Josephus?

We set off to find out, trailing him through the dingier parts of the town where he preyed upon the poor and ignorant. As expected we found him at an inn, sharing a jug of wine with a thin, angular man. Nathan was sleek, fat, middle-aged and far too cowardly to wield the murder weapon so he would need an accomplice of sorts. The sly smile of his companion alerted me at once. The two of them were celebrating and had already drunk too much wine to be aware of eavesdroppers.

I stationed Amok outside the inn and went in alone. Taking care to keep my face turned away from them I sat at the adjoining table and ordered food and drink. As time passed their celebration became steadily louder and their comments more indiscreet. I leaned in to hear the tell-tale phrases.

'Iddo,' said Nathan with a chuckle. 'Iddo the idiot.'

'A Samaritan dog!' sneered the other.

'I could not believe our luck when I saw him there.'

'His knife went in like a dream.'

'My knife, Phanuel,' insisted Nathan. 'My knife. That wretch won it off me in a game of dice. I still believe that he cheated. But it was my knife that did the deed. And I caused that ripple. I played my part.'

'Almost too well, my friend. When the crowd surged forward, I was almost knocked off my feet.' His lips parted in a grin. 'But my weapon found its mark.'

'We worked well together.'

'Next time it will be *his* turn.'

'You have not paid me for Josephus yet.'

'Here,' said Phanuel, taking a bag of coins from his belt and slipping it to Nathan with faint disgust. 'There is your wage, hireling. What I did was done out of true conviction but you needed to be bought.'

'I am a merchant.'

'You drive a hard bargain.'

'That is what Iddo the Samaritan found out.'

I had heard enough. Finishing my drink, I went back outside and told Amok what I had discovered. He was all for charging into the building and dragging the pair of them out by the scruff of their necks but I warned against intemperate action. We had to choose a less public place for our confrontation.

As it turned out, Nathan chose it for us. When he and Phanuel rolled out of the inn we simply had to follow them from a discreet distance until they came to a grove of olives. Too much wine prompted both men to step among the trunks in order to relieve themselves. They were standing targets.

I sauntered up behind them on my own.

'Hello, Nathan,' I said jocularly. 'Remember me?'

'Iddo!' he exclaimed, drenching his legs in alarm.

'I wondered if you had time for a game of dice.'

'We thought you'd be dead by now.'

'I know. That's what I wanted to discuss with you.'

Phanuel was quick to recover. Swinging around, he slipped a hand into his sleeve and produced a long dagger. There was a glint of madness in his eye.

'I should have killed you when I had the chance!' he said.

'Tell that to the authorities.'

'It was Phanuel who did it,' bleated Nathan, losing his nerve. 'I'm no murderer. He stole your knife, Iddo.'

'Shut your mouth!' snarled his accomplice.

'Yes,' I said. 'I heard all I needed to back at the inn. You are as guilty as this villain. You'll both hang.'

Phanuel brandished his dagger menacingly.

'Who says so?' he challenged.

'Amok does,' I explained.

'Who?'

'Amok. Let me introduce you.'

But my bodyguard was in no mood for the niceties. His mode of introduction was brutally direct. One blow across the back of the neck felled Nathan then a kick in the groin doubled Phanuel up. Before he could regain his breath his dagger had been expertly snatched away by Amok who lifted him high above his head, rotated him several times, then hurled him against the trunk of a tree with great force.

The killer of Josephus of Cana sat on the ground amid an impromptu hailstorm of olives. Amok reached down to pick one up and pop it into his mouth. It was a deserved reward.

The capture of the two conspirators absolved me from the charge of murder and allowed me to resume my career as Iddo the Merchant. Nobody was more overjoyed at the turn of events than my old friend Matthew, the quondam tax collector.

'Well done, Iddo!' he said. 'You and Amok have done us all a great service. I am surprised that Nathan was implicated but not that Phanuel was involved.'

'You know him?' I asked.

'Only by reputation. A religious zealot. Part of a small but dedicated group who have tried to infiltrate the Sanhedrin in recent years. They see our master as a serious threat. He inspires people with his miracles, leading them away from the influence of Phanuel and his sect.'

'The Healer was their next target, Matthew.'

'So we feared.'

'This first murder was simply a test of their cunning.'

'They will pay the full price for their crime.'

'Caius Marcius had a cell waiting especially for them.'

'Thanks to you a horrible crime has been solved.'

'Amok did his share,' I reminded him. 'He was the one who plucked the name of Nathan from the long list of my enemies.'

'You have won many friends, Iddo. But I daresay you will not wish to linger here among them. Galilee treated you very badly. You will wish to get away as soon as possible.'

'I will stay for the funeral, Matthew.'

'Funeral?'

'I must,' I said. 'I want to pay my respects to Josephus of Cana. After all, he and I have an unfortunate bond.'

Matthew heaved a deep sigh of regret.

'You were both in the wrong place at the wrong time.'

I remembered that beautiful voice raised in song.

'Yes,' I said. 'Wrong place, wrong time, wrong psalm.'

Although a pedant might quibble about the inherent tautology of the term 'historical fiction' the devoted reader of the genre knows exactly what is meant by this elastic term. That reader has already discovered that a clothing of fiction applied to the bare bones of history makes that history immensely more readable.

One of the requirements of the form is that its author decides where he or she stands on matters historical. Historians of fact are allowed the academic luxury of unlimited 'ifs' and 'buts' and, even more importantly, 'don't knows' and 'not enough evidence to say', but the writer of historical fiction has to decide not only on the 'goodies' and the 'baddies' but also where love – and murder – come in.

Just as the field of the Battle of Waterloo has been aptly described as a great day for the study of morbid anatomy so it is true to say that the works of Ellis Peters (to say nothing of those of Brother Cadfael) in cloaking hard fact with splendid fiction have increased interest in the early medieval history of England and Wales – and not only in crime and punishment, too, but in monasticism and herbalism as well. On Ellis Peters' part, this came with an immense capacity for engaging sympathy for those little people who remain when 'the Captains and the Kings depart', left behind by the ravages of battle, disease or famine, folk sometimes unconsidered by the detached and dispassionate specialist.

In much the same way as Josephine Tey in her book *The Daughter of Time* reignited the controversy over the nature of the real Richard III, so Ellis Peters has revived interest in the desperate power struggle between the cousins Stephen and Matilda – happily an unfamiliar field since anarchy has seldom been part of the English condition.

To parody the famous humorist E.V. Knox it may be truthfully stated that 'Historical Fiction As She Is Wrote' doesn't come much better than when Ellis Peters set it to paper.

Catherine Aird

Handsel Monday

Catherine Aird

The little girl lay motionless at the foot of the east turnpike stair. She was sprawled, head downwards, just where the bottom step belayed out into the Great Hall of the castle. How long she had been lying there, tumbling athwart the first three steps, the Sheriff of Fearnshire did not yet know. All he knew so far was that the child's cheek felt cold to the touch of his ungloved hand.

Quite cold. She was dead.

The air, too, was cold, bitterly cold, just as cold as it had been the last time that Sheriff Rhuaraidh Macmillan had come to Castle Balgalkin. To make matters worse – if they could be any worse than they already were, that is – it was snowing hard today as well. The cold, though, was the only thing that Sheriff Macmillan had so far found that was the same on this visit as it had been the last time he had been at the castle.

Then – it had only been the Monday of last week although now it seemed much longer – the whole of Fearnshire had been *en fête* for the Feast of Hogmanay. Or should, he mused as he took off his other glove, he start thinking of Hogmanay by its French name of *Hoguinane* now that everything in Scotland was being influenced by a Queen from France?

That day – Hogmanay, he decided obstinately – there had

been, as there was every year at Castle Balgalkin, a great ceilidh – and he wasn't going to change that good old Gaelic word for any French one – to celebrate the ending of the old year and the coming in of the new one. And that night in the best Fearnshire tradition the Laird of Balgalkin himself had answered the door to the first footers.

Rhuaraidh Macmillan moved his hand from a cold cheek to the girl's outflung arms, the better to see her hands.

Today it was all very, very different. For one thing, when the Sheriff had arrived there had been no welcoming Laird at the door of the Castle Balgalkin. 'The ancient place of the stag with the white head' was what the desmesne had been called in olden times – Scottish times, not French ones. He wasn't surprised: this winter alone had been hard enough to bring any number of stags down off the hill in search of forage.

Macmillan lifted a limp little hand and started to examine small fingers with surprising tenderness.

On New Year's Eve, only the week before, Sheriff Macmillan and his lady wife had been acclaimed as they had arrived from Drummondreach by a piper who had taken up his bagpipes as soon as he saw the couple get near to the castle. There had been no piper at Castle Balgalkin today and no pibroch heralding his approach with ancient tune. Instead there had been only a distraught servant waiting at the gate, anxiously watching out for the coming of himself and his little entourage.

The child's fingers didn't seem broken to him. And the fingernails definitely weren't . . .

At the first sight of the Sheriff the retainer had turned and run back inside the fortillage in a great hurry. Macmillan had heard quite clearly his urgent shout apprising his master of the Sheriff's arrival. His voice had echoed round the castle's sandstone walls with a diminishing resonance though any sound made by the Laird as he crossed the Great Hall towards the Sheriff and his clerk had been muffled by the reeds and the rushes that were strewn about the floor.

Those same rushes, deep as they were, noted the Sheriff automatically, had not been deep and soft enough to save the girl as she had fallen. Even though her head was half-covered by them he could see from where he was standing that her face was badly discoloured by both blood and bruises on the left-hand side.

'It's a bad business, Rhuaraidh . . .' The servant's call had produced the man himself – Hector Leanaig, Laird of Balgalkin. He, too, had presented a very different picture from the genial host of the week before. A veritable giant of a man, he was sufficiently black-a-vised to have gone first footing himself on New Year's Eve. He had come forward to meet the Sheriff, shaking his head sadly. 'A bad, bad business . . .'

'Tell me, Hector.' Macmillan had inclined his head attentively towards Hector Leanaig and waited. It would have been quite impossible to discern from the Sheriff's tone whether this was an invitation or a command.

'My Jeannie's dead,' the Laird had blurted out. Big and strong though he was, nevertheless the man looked shaken to his wattles now. There was an unhealthy pallor about him, too, contrasting sharply with his raven-coloured hair. 'My poor wee bairn.'

The Sheriff nodded. This was what he had been told.

'She's just where we found her.' Leanaig had struggled for speech but only achieved a rather tremulous croak. 'This way . . .'

Although at first the Laird had taken the lead through the castle, he fell back as soon as they neared the broken figure spread-eagled across the bottom three steps of the stair. The Sheriff had advanced alone, his clerk and the Laird lagging behind.

And now Rhuaraidh Macmillan was gently turning the girl's hands over and taking a long look at their outer aspects.

There were grazes here and there on both and some dried blood over the back of the knuckles of her left hand.

'Poor wee Jeannie,' repeated the Laird brokenly.

'Aye, Hector,' agreed the Sheriff non-committally. That, at least, was true enough, whatever had happened to her. He straightened up and changed his stance, the better to take a look at her head.

Seemingly Hector Leanaig could not bear to watch him going about his business because he took a step back and averted his gaze from the sad scene.

The child was in her night-clothes, her gown rucked up on one side. A dreadful bruise disfigured the left side of her face and even without stooping the Sheriff could see that her cheek was broken. He dropped on one knee and, with great care, put his hand to her skull. That, too, might be broken. It was certainly cold to the touch and what blood was visible there was brown and dried: the girl, he concluded, must have been dead for several hours.

Hector Leanaig licked dry lips. 'She's just where we found her.'

'We?' queried Rhuaraidh Macmillan sharply. 'Who was it exactly who found her, then?'

'One of the women,' said Leanaig, jerking his head roughly over his shoulder but not turning round.

The Sheriff's gaze followed the direction of his gesture. In the far corner of the hall a buxom young woman was lurking in the shadows. She was weeping, stifling her sobs as best she could. Her face was almost invisible under a woven kirtle but what he could see of her visage was swollen by tears. Here and there strands of blonde hair extruded from under the woollen garment. She would have been comely enough, he thought, had it not been for her obvious distress.

'Morag,' amplified the Laird, still not letting his gaze fall on her. 'Jeannie's nurse.'

Rhuaraidh Macmillan, though, took a good look at the weeping woman. Irony of ironies, she was standing under

374

the traditional Christmas osier and evergreen Kissing Bough – the ivy and the holly there to ensure new growth in the spring to come. This had been suspended from a handy rafter – not too low to kiss under, not too high to be too difficult to secure. The apples and mistletoe in the Kissing Bough would have been an important part of the Hogmanay Festivities until those had come to an end the night before – Handsel Monday, as ever was. The Kissing Bough would have been fixed firmly enough for sure: it was considered to be very bad luck if it were to touch the ground because in nature the parasitic mistletoe plant always hung downwards.

Perhaps, he thought, that was what had happened at Castle Balgalkin because there was 'nae luck aboot this house, nae luck at a'': that was beyond doubt, whatever had befallen the girl.

The young woman under the Kissing Bough let forth a loud sob as she saw the Sheriff's eye rest upon her. Wrapped tightly round her shapely shoulders was a shawl; this she held with its edges closed together as if for greater protection against the outside world. Rhuaraidh Macmillan, no amateur in these matters, was well aware of how frightened she was. And no wonder, if the dead child had been left in her charge.

'Morag Munro,' said Hector Leanaig roughly. 'She'll tell you herself.'

'The bairn wasna' there in her bed when I woke up,' said the young woman between chattering teeth. 'Handsel Monday or no'.' She stared wildly at the Sheriff. 'And I'd warned her . . .'

'What about?' asked Macmillan mildly. No good ever came of frightening witnesses too soon. He'd learned that a long time ago.

'Handsel Monday, of course,' said Morag, visibly surprised. 'Did ye not mind that yestre'en was Handsel Monday?'

'Tell me,' he invited her. Nothing was to be assumed

when Sheriff Macmillan was going about his business of law and justice, nothing taken for granted. Not even the ancient customs attached to Handsel Monday.

'"When all people are to stay in bed until after sunrise",' she quoted, '"so as not to be meeting fairies or witches".'

Hector Leanaig said dully, 'The first Monday in January, that's Handsel Monday. You know that, Rhuaraidh Macmillan, as well as I do.'

'Jeannie knew it,' Morag Munro gulped. 'And I told her she wasna' to leave her bed until I came for her in the morning.' The young woman dissolved into tears again. 'And when I did, her bed was empty.' Her shoulders shook as her sobs rang round the hall. 'She was gone.'

'And Mistress Leanaig?' asked Sheriff Macmillan, suddenly realising what it was that was missing from the *mise-en-scène* and what it was that he had been subconsciously expecting as a backdrop to this tragedy: the unique and quite dreadful wailing of a mother suddenly bereft of one of her children.

'She's away over at Alcaig's,' said Leanaig thickly. He jerked a shoulder northwards in the direction of the firth. 'They say her father's a-dying.'

Macmillan nodded his ready comprehension. Mistress Leanaig, he knew, was the only daughter of the Lord of Alcaig's Isle.

'Her brothers came for her yesterday afternoon,' said Hector. 'She went at once.'

'In her condition?' asked Macmillan. If he remembered rightly, Mistress Leanaig was in the 'interesting condition' that the French called *enceinte*. At least, that was the reason the other guests had been given for Hector Leanaig spending most of New Year's Eve dancing with a high-spirited young woman called Jemima from Balblair. There had been a memorable Orcadian version of 'Strip the Willow' which no pregnant woman could have danced with safety. And which he for one, Rhuaraidh Macmillan, wouldn't forget in a hurry – even though he himself had danced it featly with his own lady-wife. Nor, he thought judiciously, would the fair-haired young woman from Balblair called Jemima with whom Hector Leanaig had danced most of that evening be likely to forget it soon either.

'Old man Alcaig was asking for her.' The Laird pointed up through a gun loop at the leaden sky. 'We could see that there was snow on the way and they were anxious to be well beyond Torgorm in daylight.'

'So . . .' invited the Sheriff, bringing his gaze back to the pathetic little form at his feet. He had no need to ask why the Laird of Balgalkin hadn't gone with his wife to her dying father's the day before. It was no secret in Fearnshire that old Alcaig and his fine sons didn't like his son-in-law. And never had.

'So she went with them,' said Leanaig.

'Leaving the bairn with you.' If the Sheriff had remembered rightly old Alcaig had quibbled for a long time over his daughter's tocher going with her to Leanaig. That it had gone there in the end was a triumph of tradition and usage over personal inclination.

'She said Jeannie was too young to be crossing the water on a night like last night.' Hector Leanaig ran a hand over his eyes. 'God!' he said distractedly. 'She'd have been safer with her mother.'

The Sheriff didn't answer this. Instead he started to examine the child's clothing. Though her nightgown was caught up under one knee, it did not look to him as if it had been really disarranged other than by the tumble down the stairs. Then he started to pull it to one side, lifting it clear of her piteous body.

A hectic choler took over Hector Leanaig's pale visage. 'Rhuaraidh, I swear by all that's holy, that if there's a man in this place who's laid so much as a finger on her, I'll kill him myself with my bare hands, kinsman or not.'

'Whisht, man,' said the Sheriff soothingly. 'There's no call for that. No one's been near her in that way. Her goonie's quite clean and there's no sign of interference.'

A low moan escaped Morag, the nurse. 'The poor mite.'

'And there's no sign of a struggle,' added Rhuaraidh Macmillan, turning his attention to the turnpike stair which curled up clockwise from the hall on their left. He put his foot on the bottom step and peered up. The stone steps curled away upward out of his sight in an endless spiral. Above them the turret tower was capped by a conical wooden roof. The stonework and wood of the turret, he noted, looked in reasonable condition. Some of the dowry which had come with Alcaig's daughter in the end had no doubt been spent on her new home, the castle at Balgalkin.

'Wait you, here,' the Sheriff commanded, motioning to his clerk to keep everyone where they were. 'All of you,' he added firmly as Leanaig started forward to join him.

The Sheriff stepped delicately round the inert figure on the lower steps and started to climb the round stair tower. In the first instance it took him up from the Great Hall to the second floor of the castle but he could see that it went further up and beyond still. As he mounted the stair he ran his left hand over the wall but only a fine red sandstone dust marked his fingers.

He took his bearings afresh when he stepped off the stair at the first landing and reached the rooms above.

He came first to a little room hung about with fine linens and women's things which he took to be Mistress Leanaig's retiring room. The French fashion these days was to call a ladies' place something quite different – by a new French word which he couldn't call to mind just this minute. His wife would know the name of it – and would be wanting one herself at Drummondreach soon, too, he'd be bound.

He came next to the nursery. Here, against the longest wall of the room, was the child's bed and over in the corner a little truckle bed where he supposed the nurse, Morag Munro, slept. Macmillan took a careful look at both.

Neither showed any sign of great disturbance. The bedding on the child's bed had been turned back as by its occupant slipping out of it quite normally.

There was nothing unusual about the other one either. He put a hand in the child's bed and then did the same between the rugs on the servant's one. There was no residual warmth to be felt now in either sleeping place.

Leaving the nursery he went to the master bedroom where the Laird and his lady slept – when she was at Balgalkin, that is. He paused on the threshold, the French name of Mistress Leanaig's own room having suddenly come to him after all. Boudoir – that was it.

The room here was a much grander affair than the others. Not only was there a great bed against the further wall and a garderobe, but there were hangings on all the walls and in the corner a small privy stair which did not climb to the upper floors like the turnpike one. Instead, it descended in a clockwise spiral from the main bedroom to the Great Hall. This west turret, he deduced, was the Laird and his lady's stair and theirs alone.

The Sheriff advanced on the bed and pulled aside the curtains hanging from the tester – and found another bed covered in thick rugs from which all interior heat had gone. This one, though, did show signs of someone in it having had a rude awakening. To him, the bed coverings had all the look of having been thrust aside in great haste by its occupant.

Rhuaraidh Macmillan walked across to the window. To the north under a lowering sky lay a snow-clad Fearnshire and somewhere in that wilderness was a woman whose young daughter was unaccountably dead at the foot of the other stair, her skull broken.

Unaccountably to him, that is.

So far.

Taking his time, Rhuaraidh Macmillan went round the second floor all over again, and then climbed up to the top level by the turnpike stair. Here, without any refinements at all, slept the other retainers of Castle Balgalkin. A persistent curious flapping sound he traced not to pigeons but to an old flagstaff from which was already flying the flag of the Leanaigs at half-mast.

He felt a spasm of pity for Mistress Leanaig who from all accounts would be leaving one deathbed only to find another. And unless Hector had sent a messenger to Alcaig's Isle, she would read the flag's message as she neared Torgorm but not know for whom it was flying so low.

Macmillan came down to the main bedroom again and stood there thoughtfully before making for the privy stair. Again he put his left hand out and ran it over the wall, this time as he went down rather than up the stair. This time, too, a fine red sandstone dust marked his fingers.

But so did something else.

He paused and considered his hand. There was no doubt about it. He was looking at blood. Not a lot, but blood for all that. Macmillan stood for a long quiet minute on a step just above the last turn of the stair but still out of sight of those waiting at the foot of the other stair at the east end of the Great Hall.

Where the body lay.

Then the Sheriff put his hand down again on the wall of the privy stair.

Low down.

The sandstone felt slightly damp to his touch. He would have been the first to admit that the walls of Castle Balgalkin probably always felt slightly damp to the touch in winter – it was no wonder that the Queen from France was finding Scotland not to her liking after warmer climes. But this dampness was different. He crouched down to consider the patch. Unless he was very much mistaken someone had taken a wet cloutie to the stone and rubbed it as clean as they could before he reached the castle.

Rhuaraidh Macmillan straightened up and turned silently

back up the privy stair. He then walked through the master bedroom, and past the nursery and Mistress Leanaig's boudoir to the main east turnpike stair. He descended this and rejoined the dejected group waiting beside the distressful body at the bottom of the stairway.

Hector Leanaig was standing where he had left him although his head was now sunk on his chest as if he was afraid to look up. The child's nurse, Morag Munro, was still standing under the Kissing Bough, well away from the others. As the Sheriff appeared down the turnpike stair her weeping changed to a more primitive keening.

'It wasn't only me,' she said when she managed to speak. 'The Mistress warned her about Handsel Monday, too. She told her that on Handsel Monday night everyone has to keep to their beds until sunrise. Made her promise her mother she would stay there.' She gulped. 'I heard her say that myself.'

'I wonder why the child didn't stay in her own bed then,' mused Sheriff Macmillan aloud, addressing nobody in the Great Hall in particular.

'It's a dangerous night, Handsel Monday,' growled Hector Leanaig.

'I ken that right enough, Hector,' agreed Macmillan. 'But I don't believe in the fairies and witches myself, that's all.'

'Not believe?' echoed the Laird of Balgalkin, astonished.

'No, Hector.' The Sheriff shook his head. 'I'm afraid Handsel Monday is just an ancient way of putting an end to the feasting of Hogmanay, that's all.'

Hector Leanaig said obstinately, 'Jeannie believed in it.'

'The English,' remarked the Sheriff, ignoring this, 'call the time when the kissing has to stop by the name of Twelfth Night.'

'Oh, the English,' said Leanaig dismissively. 'They're not right-minded folk at all.'

'But it's still when the kissing has to stop,' said the Sheriff, adding meaningfully, 'All the kissing, Hector.'

The Laird of Balgalkin stared at him, a flush mounting his cheek.

Rhuaraidh Macmillan stared down at the pitiable figure on the floor. 'What, Hector, do you think it could be that would make a wee girlie like this so disobedient?'

'I canna' think, man, of anything at all.'

'And I can only think of one thing myself,' said the Sheriff.

The Laird jerked his head up, the flush suffusing his whole face now. He searched the Sheriff's face. 'You can?'

'I'm afraid so,' said Macmillan very quietly. 'I think that Jeannie woke up in the night and found her nurse gone from her bed.'

Hector Leanaig said nothing while Morag Munro clutched her kirtle round her head even more tightly.

'And,' said the Sheriff evenly, 'I think when that happened Jeannie was naturally frightened that the fairies or the witches must have spirited away her nurse, Morag.'

The wailing under the Kissing Bough stopped abruptly and a palpable silence fell in the Great Hall of Castle Balgalkin.

'But,' continued Rhuaraidh Macmillan in a steely voice, 'I don't think they had.'

'No?' said the Laird hoarsely.

'No, Hector. I think that something much worse than fairies or witches had taken Jeannie's nurse away from her bed in Jeannie's room.'

The Laird moistened his lips. 'Something much worse?'

'You, Hector,' said the Sheriff.

'Me?' spluttered the Laird of Balgalkin.

'I think,' maintained Macmillan unperturbed, 'that when little Jeannie woke up and saw Morag Munro was not in her bed in the nursery, her next thought – her very natural thought – was to find you, her father.'

'Well, that would be understandable, right enough,' responded Leanaig non-committally. 'If she did,' he added lamely.

'Don't forget,' carried on the Sheriff ineluctably, 'that last night – Handsel Monday – was one your daughter had been told on all sides by people she trusted was one to be very afraid of indeed.'

'Aye,' admitted Leanaig, 'that's true.'

'I think,' resumed Macmillan, 'Jeannie was very frightened and did come looking for you – after all, you were only in your own bed in the next room, weren't you, Hector?'

Hector Leanaig said nothing.

'You either were or you weren't in your own bed, Hector,' said Rhuaraidh Macmillan without impatience. 'Which was it?'

'I was,' said Hector Leanaig gruffly.

'The trouble was,' said the Sheriff almost conversationally, 'that though you were in your own bed, I think you were not alone in it.'

Hector Leanaig's face told its own story. The flush on it slowly drained away before the Sheriff's eyes to be replaced by a marked pallor. The man of law pointed to the pathetic bundle at their feet and said, 'Your Jeannie was young all right but not too young to know what makes the beast with two backs.'

The woman under the Kissing Bough screamed. 'We didna' kill her. I tell you, we didna' kill her. She ran away.'

'And her father ran after her,' said the Sheriff calmly.

'To try to explain,' jerked out Hector. 'I swear that's all I did . . . I swear.'

'I know,' said Rhuaraidh Macmillan imperturbably. 'But Jeannie ran away down the stair before you could catch up with her.'

'She fell . . .' said Hector. 'Before I could catch her and explain.'

Morag Munro ran across the Great Hall and flung herself at the Sheriff's feet. 'Believe us,' she pleaded. 'We didna' touch her. It's true.'

'Partly true,' responded Macmillan. He pointed diagonally across the hall. 'But it was the other stair that she ran down. You didn't want anyone to guess she'd come from your room.'

Leanaig brushed his hair away from his eyes. 'How do you know that?'

'How else do you account for the crack on her head being on the left of her skull? This is a clockwise stair going up and a left-hand one coming down. If she'd tumbled down this turnpike stair here her head would have hit the right-hand side of the stairway.' He looked down at the child and then at the step, tapering to the apex of its triangle as it became the central pillar of the stair. 'There's nothing to catch her head on coming down on the left in this turnpike. She would have fallen to the right . . . and it's the left of her head that's stove in.'

The only sound in the Great Hall now was the heavy breathing of the Laird of Balgalkin as he struggled to control himself.

'And the privy stair,' whispered Hector Leanaig as one making a great discovery, 'comes down the other way.'

'Clockwise from the top,' agreed the Sheriff.

'It's a stair that could be defended by a left-handed swordsman,' said the Laird almost absently.

'Jeannie hit her head on the left-hand side of the privy stair as she ran down it away from you.' The Sheriff looked across at Morag Munro. 'From you both. And the pair of you hoped to get away with blaming Handsel Monday.'

Hector Leanaig sagged like a man stuffed with straw reeling from a punch in the solar plexus. 'I may have killed my daughter, Rhuaraidh, but I didn't murder her.'

'But she's as dead,' said the Sheriff bleakly, 'as if you had.'

The Laird made a visible effort to straighten himself up. 'What are you going to do?'

'Me?' Rhuaraidh Macmillan gave a mirthless laugh. 'I'm

not going to do anything, Hector Leanaig. No, I'm going to leave that to poor wee Jeannie here.'

'Jeannie?'

'Aye, man. She's going to haunt you here for the rest of your life . . .'

In 1988 I attended a writers' conference during which the state of the business was discussed. An author of considerable repute said that the mystery field was taking off, but forget about sending out historical mysteries. His reason: Ellis Peters had that field sewn up and nobody wanted to look at historical mystery by anyone else. I was crestfallen. I had just sent *SPQR* to my agent and now figured I had wasted my time and effort.

As it turned out, *SPQR* found a publisher and bagged me a nomination for the Edgar Award. The *SPQR* series now includes nine novels and a number of short stories, with no end in sight. That author was right about one thing, though: Ellis Peters defined the historical mystery novel for us all. The historical mystery field is thriving as never before, with dozens of authors participating in every historical period.

I think, though, that all of them would agree with me that we are all contending for second place.

John Maddox Roberts

An Academic Question

John Maddox Roberts

One of the best things about Athens is that it isn't Gaul.
That year my family wanted me out of Rome. I, in turn,
did not want to go back to Caesar's army in Gaul. For once
the family concurred, not because Gaul was so dangerous and
unpleasant but because nobody was winning any glory there
except Caesar. If you believed the dispatches he sent back for
publication he was conquering the place all by himself.

But to stand for higher office I needed more military time
on my record. This is not to say that Gaul was the only area
of Roman military operations that year. Cassius Longinus was
fighting the Parthians in Syria, and Appius Claudius was,
technically, still at war in Cilicia. But Syria was an ill-starred
place since the defeat of Crassus at Carrhae and bad blood lay
between my family and the Claudians.

Fortuitously, a minor outbreak of piracy occurred in the
waters around Cyprus and I was offered an equally minor
naval command to deal with it. Like any sensible Roman I
detest sea duty, but, upon consideration of the alternatives,
I took it.

The secret of handling such an assignment in those days
was, simply: don't rush it. I had a whole year ahead of me
to crush these nautical bandits so I determined to take my
time getting to Cyprus, be leisurely in my naval operations,

and get back to Rome just in time to stand for next year's praetorship.

So, when on the way to Cyprus my little flotilla put in at Piraeus, I was quick to take the opportunity to laze about for a few days and see the sights. I admired the fortifications of Piraeus, built more than four centuries before by Themistocles, and walked the impressive length of the Long Walls, which connected the port with Athens by a continuous stretch of fortification.

Accompanied by my slave, Hermes, I walked between the walls all the way to the city. I could have hired a horse or been carried in a litter but I needed to stretch my legs after the voyage and, in any case, such luxuries were still frowned upon by my class in those days. A public man of military age was expected to make a show of simplicity, especially among degenerate foreigners.

I presented myself at the house of the Roman prefect, one Publius Serrius, an agreeable drudge, and let him know that I was on no official business in Athens and would be truly happy not to be involved in any during my stay. Hermes stashed our meagre baggage in the room we were given, and I was off to see the sights.

It pains me to admit it, but Athens proved to be as beautiful as everyone said. It has been devastated and sacked a number of times but I saw no evidence of this. Admirers from the world over vie with one another to adorn Athens, and it is full of beautiful works of art and splendid architecture. The city is much smaller than you would expect so it is easy to see everything in a short time. Within two days I had seen the sights of the Acropolis, the Stoa and the Erechtheum and everything else. I had seen so many statues that my sleep was populated with them.

That evening at dinner I remarked to my host that I had run out of noteworthy things to see and asked if he had any suggestions, since I had to depart soon.

He turned to the man reclining to his left. 'What do you

suggest, Androcles?' This man was a philosopher, one of those tiresome people who spend their lives just thinking about things but never doing anything. He wore the requisite shabby robe and untrimmed beard and had clearly put in long hours practising at looking wise.

'Has the senator visited the Academy? It is just a short walk from the city by way of the Dipylum Gate.'

'The Academy?' I said. 'Isn't that where Socrates taught?'

He looked pained. 'Plato, sir. The Platonic school still meets there, as they have for more than three hundred years.'

Serrius must have caught my expression. 'It is one of the most beautiful groves in the world, Decius Caecilius. Besides exquisite plantings and landscaping it contains some wonderful sculptures.'

That was more like it. The last thing I wanted to do was listen to boring old philosophers jabbering at one another, but a fine garden is always a delight to any Roman's heart.

'I will be most happy to be your guide,' Androcles said. Philosophers always have their hands out for a tip.

'The Academy,' Androcles said, 'takes its name from Academus, a hero of the Trojan War. He first planted this grove, and willed it to his native city, Athens.'

We were strolling along outside the city, alongside the river Cephissus. It was more a creek than a river. Like Rome, Athens has spilled outside its old walls and we were not in open country, but rather in a sort of suburb called the Ceramicus, because many of the city's potters had their homes and workshops there. I had given Hermes the day off.

'That was one influential group of veterans,' I said. 'Every city I've ever visited was founded by a Trojan fleeing the sack of Troy or else by someone who fought there on the Greek side.'

'So it seems. The Trojan prince Aeneas founded Rome, according to legend.'

'That's how the story goes,' I said. 'There is ample room for scepticism, but it may soon be inadvisable to voice doubts.'

'Why should that be?'

'Because Julius Caesar himself claims descent from the goddess Venus by way of Aeneas. Casting doubts upon the ancestry of Caesar is a poor idea these days.'

'I shall keep that in mind. Ah, here we are.' We stood before a life-sized statue whose inscription identified it as Plato. This was not one of the wonderfully polished and refined sculptures of the city but a rather plain chunk of marble with a coarse finish. In keeping with philosophical simplicity, no doubt.

The statue stood by an equally simple gate in a stone wall perhaps eight feet high. We passed within and I gazed with some awe, which I took pains to conceal, on the most perfect outdoor setting of my long and varied experience.

The Academy was not at all what I had expected. In my mind I had pictured a garden about the size of a typical country villa's, with a circle of stone seats in the centre where students could listen to the harangues of a teacher and pretend that they weren't bored to death. Instead I discovered a varied grove as big as a good-sized farm, landscaped in low hills so that you could not see the whole thing, but every turn in the many paths revealed a view that made the breath catch in your throat. Light and shade were perfectly balanced, with trained vines arching upon arbors over many of the paths, trimmed so that you could always see through them and plenty of sunlight was available.

Classes took place mostly in little clearings where the students simply sat on the soft grass, though some energetic teachers walked about as they spoke, their students following. Many of these students gave every evidence of paying attention.

The sculptures were small, exquisite, and widely spaced 'so that they become objects of contemplation, rather than distraction,' Androcles explained.

We rounded a curve and came upon a gymnasium where

fifty or sixty naked young men ran, wrestled, jumped, played ball or swam in a pool that looked like the jewel of a god dropped there and forgotten. I had not imagined that the Academy included physical pursuits but Androcles explained that Plato had insisted that it was useless to cultivate the mind if the body was not given equally rigorous training.

There is this to be said about the noble youth of Athens: they are *beautiful*. I had heard this phenomenon described by Cicero, but had never quite believed it. I looked them all over and could not perceive a flaw anywhere. Compared to them, a similar muster of young Romans of my own class on the Campus Martius was a festival of ugliness. I have never shared the Greek erotic fascination with boys, but in this place I could understand its appeal.

'What do you do in these parts?' I asked my guide. 'Drown the ugly ones at birth?'

'In Athens,' he said, 'we have devoted many centuries to cultivating excellence in all things.'

'Well, you've been successful in most areas,' I admitted. 'Too bad you couldn't add politics and military affairs to the lot.'

'Rome's excellence in these areas,' he said drily, 'makes up for many shortcomings.'

I deserved that. I should not have been so belittling. It just seemed unfair that any people should possess so much beauty in one small place.

My attention was drawn toward a patch of shade in a corner of the exercise yard. In an alcove formed by a half-circle of olive trees a truly spectacular youth sat playing the lyre, surrounded by admirers, most of them older men but a few about his own age.

He was fairer of hair than most Greeks, his features so perfectly cut that he could have made a living posing for sculptors as one of the better-looking gods. His physique was superb, but I could detect no scars, so the wonderfully proportioned muscles were all for show. He had never stood in the battle line and, Greek military activity being what it was by that time, was unlikely to.

Androcles caught the direction of my gaze. 'Ah, the incomparable Isaeus is here. You are lucky, Senator. He does not come here often.'

'Well, I wouldn't have made a special trip just to get a look at him but he is striking. Who are those men admiring him? Other than the usual gaggle of pederasts, I mean?'

'These are connoisseurs of art as well as of beauty. The tall man with the near-white beard is Rhoecus. He is a very rich man who sponsors plays at the great festivals. The burly man with the short brown beard is Agesander the sculptor. Some judge him to be the finest of this generation. His *Diomedes and Odysseus*, dedicated at Delphi by the Thebans, is wonderful to behold. The bald one is Neacles, famed teacher of the lyre. Isaeus is his student.'

'Teaches him for free, I'll bet. Who are the younger ones?' I cannot say why I was so curious, except that this scene, civilised as it was, was so far from anything you could expect to encounter in Rome.

'That superb one, only slightly less beautiful than Isaeus himself, is Melanthus, his rival in almost everything. They are close companions, despite the fact that Melanthus comes in second in everything.' This youth, perhaps a year or two older than Isaeus, had features as fine and a body as perfect, but his hair was dark and his complexion a commonplace olive. In truth he was no less handsome than his friend, just less striking.

'The younger boy is Amyntas, the son of Rhoecus, a very promising athlete who displays poetic talent as well.' This lad had curly brown hair and an agreeable, snub-nosed face. He displayed some dark down on his chin and upper lip, but was a year or so from his first shave.

'The rest, young and old, are simply admirers, people of taste but no reputation.'

And every damned one of them, of whatever age or station,

was mooning over that boy like Paris panting over Helen. Well, they were Greeks.

'Would you like to meet him?' Androcles asked.

'Decidedly,' I said, 'just so I can brag about it when I get back home.'

Isaeus paused in his song at our approach. His eyes widened to take in my plain woollen tunic with its senator's stripe, the military boots and belt that proclaimed my warlike status, and last of all my typically Roman face with its numerous scars and long, Metellan nose. To his credit, he did not recoil in horror.

'Isaeus, gentlemen,' Androcles proclaimed, 'allow me to introduce a distinguished visitor. This is the noble Senator Decius Caecilius Metellus the Younger, lately Urban Aedile of Rome, now on his way to Cyprus to crush the pirates in the eastern sea.' One by one they were introduced, took my hand and murmured polite inanities.

We Romans are quite aware that nobody loves us. Greeks, in particular, have had to swallow a lot of pride in bending their necks to the Roman yoke. But the better educated among them, like those men present upon this occasion, knew perfectly well that they were hopelessly inept at managing their own affairs, and that the Roman hand rested very lightly on Greece. We put down their seditions gently, taxed them lightly, and spent great sums repairing and adorning their cities and shrines after we'd looted them in the first place. Only Corinth suffered greatly. We had to make an example of somebody. Nobody ever did as much damage to the Greeks as their fellow Greeks anyway.

So these men were probably not faking extravagantly in proclaiming their pleasure in meeting me.

'Senator,' Rhoecus said, 'you do us honour. Will you honour me further by taking dinner at my house tonight?'

'The honour will be mine,' I told him, having no graceful way out. I knew all too well the austerity of Greek dining habits. However, I might one day find myself governing

Athens and it is always good to have the rich men on your side. It makes the job so much easier. Rhoecus extended his invitation to all those present and all accepted, although Isaeus seemed as reluctant as I.

I turned to the sculptor. 'Agesander, you are famed everywhere I go. On Rhodes I saw your superb *Aphrodite and Eros*, and in Syracuse I was taken to see your *Dionysus Dancing* before I was allowed to see anything else. It is the pride of the city.'

He inclined his head graciously. 'The Muses have guided my hands. But those were early works. I hope that the group I am now completing will surpass all my earlier efforts.'

'What might this project be?' I asked him.

'He's sculpting *Achilles and Patroclus*!' Amyntas cried. 'With Isaeus and Melanthus as his models!' This earned the boy some stern looks. Well-bred Greek boys are not supposed to intrude upon the conversations of their elders unless invited. Amyntas gazed upon Isaeus with adoration.

'A wonderful subject,' I commended. 'And I cannot imagine two finer models for the roles.' No harm in laying on a little flattery, I thought. 'Will this group be in marble as at Rhodes, or in bronze as at Syracuse?'

'I am portraying the heroes in marble,' he said, 'nude, of course, as is the convention in heroic sculpture, and only lightly tinted. The helmets and shields are being executed in bronze to my design and cast by Melanippus, who performs all my bronze casting. The armour of Achilles, of course, was the work of a god, and I hope I will be forgiven if the quality of my shield falls a trifle short of that divine standard.'

'But,' I said, 'the armour of Achilles was not made by Vulcan – Hephaestus, I should say, until Patroclus was dead.'

'Quite perceptive,' the sculptor said. 'In fact, the title of the group is *Achilles and Patroclus reunited in the Fields of Elysium*. I could not resist having a try at sculpting that shield as it is described in the *Iliad*.' He looked about him. 'I always picture Elysium looking rather like the Academy.'

'It is an incomparable place,' I agreed. 'Agesander, would it be too great an imposition to ask to see this sculpture? I know many artists are touchy and never allow anyone to see a work in progress, but I must return to my ships tomorrow and I may never get to Miletus.'

He smiled amiably. 'By all means. I love nothing more than seeing the stone and metal take shape beneath my hands and I would not deny others this pleasure. As it occurs, all is finished except for some details of the pedestal and the bronze work. It would please me if all of you would come to my studio and tell me what you think.'

I would never pose as a connoisseur, and my grasp of other aspects of Greek culture is dismally low, but I have a lifelong love for fine sculpture and this offer alone made the trip to Athens worthwhile.

The younger men donned their clothes, which didn't amount to much – just brief chitons draped from one shoulder and concealing nothing. It was interesting to see the three of them move. Even in the simple act of rising and dressing, I could see that Isaeus had the perfect poise of a dancer, Melanthus the feral grace of a warrior, and Amyntas the springy co-ordination of an athlete.

The walk to the studio was a short one. It was just a simple shed with two open sides, only enough to keep out rain and let in as much light as possible. In its centre stood a magnificent sculpture and we all admired it for a while. The youths were portrayed in incredibly lifelike fashion, symmetrically but naturally posed, each with an arm around the other's shoulder. Each had a hand extended to one side. Clearly, when it was finished, the extended hands would rest upon the rims of their shields. The tops and backs of their heads were unfinished.

'Isn't it conventional,' I said, 'to portray Achilles as some-what larger than any of the other heroes except for Ajax?'

'I have departed from convention here,' Agesander said. 'My models are utter perfection, and taking liberties with such perfection could anger the Muses. I have depicted them as the same size, exactly as in life.'

'Why are the heads not finished?' asked Rhoecus.

'When complete, they will be wearing helmets. These are of the Corinthian design, pushed up to display their faces – in fact, here come those helmets now.'

A crew of workmen arrived at the studio, carrying wooden stretchers which bore weighty objects covered with protective cloths. Agesander drew back the cloths to inspect the work, revealing a pair of imposing helmets and two broad, circular shields. The shield of Patroclus bore a Gorgon mask on its face. That of Achilles, slightly larger, was covered with the incredible design of concentric circles of cities, battles and so forth as described in the *Iliad*.

'Melanippus has done an excellent job, as usual,' Agesander proclaimed. 'When finished, the details will be highlighted in silver and gold. This group was commissioned by the citizens of Miletus, and they have paid for the very best treatment.'

'Such a sculpture,' said Neacles, the lyre teacher, 'would assure the reputation of any city.'

'The Milesians are singularly fortunate,' Rhoecus agreed.

For once, I had no argument with the fulsomeness of the praise. As far as I was concerned, this work was beyond praise.

The house of Rhoecus was a short walk from the studio. His table was as austere as I had feared but the conversation, which in this company was mostly devoted to art, was agreeable enough. I did not understand Neacles' more technical comments concerning the lyre, especially when he dragged in the theories of Pythagoras, but overall it wasn't nearly as boring as I had expected.

It was interesting to study the interplay among the younger men. They were something new in my experience, whereas I had seen numerous specimens of the other types. Isaeus and Melanthus displayed a clear affection, together with that distance which always characterises rivals. Amyntas, on the other hand, showed an almost embarrassing infatuation with Isaeus, constantly fawning over him, serving his plate like a servant and so forth. Oddly, the others did not seem to regard this as improper behaviour. Greeks, you know.

'And now,' said Rhoecus as the plates were cleared away, the drinking bowl was brought in and the wreaths were passed around, 'we must excuse the young men. All three are in training for the next Isthmian Games and have taken a sacred vow not to touch wine and to be abed within an hour of sunset.'

Isaeus, Melanthus and Amyntas took their leave respectfully. The elder two had spoken scarcely a dozen words between them since being introduced to me. Although grown *epheboi*, they were still of an age to keep silence before their elders.

Rhoecus was elected master of ceremonies. He decreed the wine should be mixed with no more than one-third part water and that each of us should regale the party with a story or song, beginning with me.

So I gave them the rousing story of Mucius Scaevola, who, when captured by Tarquin the Proud, thrust his own hand into the brazier of coals and did not flinch while it burned to a stump, to show the Etruscans how contemptuous the Romans were of death and torture. I received polite applause. It is often better to make a point with foreigners than to please them.

'A very – ah, how shall I say – Roman story,' commended Rhoecus. 'And now, Neacles?'

The old man made a production of tuning his lyre and graced us with a wonderful song in praise of Apollo. This, someone whispered to me, was the song with which Neacles had taken the Olympic prize twenty years before.

The applause was just dying down when a slave rushed in, breathless and bug-eyed.

'Murder!' he cried. 'Murder at the studio of Agesander!'

'Who is this?' I asked.

'Why,' Agesander said, 'this is one of my slaves. What are

you babbling about, you fool? Are you drunk? If so, I'll have the hide off your back!'

'No! It is murder! Come look!' The man appeared to be some sort of Asiatic, and in his agitation he forgot his Greek and lapsed into his native gibberish.

'We had better go look,' Rhoecus said.

Everyone rose, doffing their wreaths and looking about for their sandals. I was last out the door, first dipping another cup of wine and draining it. I winced at the taste of the resin Greeks use so excessively in their wine. It never kept me from drinking it though.

Back at the studio, our torches illuminated a dismal scene. At the base of the wonderful sculpture a corpse lay, face-down, its dark hair bloodied. At the order of Agesander, slaves turned him over, revealing the handsome features of Melanthus. It looked as if the evening would be livelier than I had anticipated.

'My friends,' Rhoecus said sadly, 'I fear that we must summon the city Archon and the leading men. Somebody fetch Isaeus and my son as well.'

'Don't forget the Roman governor,' I said, reminding them of who had the real power here.

While various slaves and flunkies scurried to carry out these orders, I examined the studio. All was much as we had left it, save that the shield of Achilles now lay face-down on the floor and one of the helmets lay near it. I squatted by the helmet and looked it over. The bronze crest was clotted with blood and hair. It had been the murder weapon.

Grasping an edge of the shield, I rocked it. It moved ponderously. It was not a battle shield, made of wood and faced with thin bronze. It was a piece of sculpture, made of solid bronze and as thick as a man's palm. Crossing to the statue, I examined the position of the hands. Below each was a slot cut into the pedestal and artfully disguised by carved grass. The lower rims of the shields would rest in these slots.

By the time I finished my examination quite a throng had

gathered, many of the men still wearing wreaths from inter-rupted drinking bouts. As word of the victim's identity spread their mood turned ugly. One of the city's most promising youths had been murdered.

In short order the city's Archon arrived, along with his board of counsellors, all distinguished men. Serrius arrived, and I was happy to see that he had foresightedly brought a strong guard of auxiliaries from the Greek levies. The Archon called for silence.

'We must have an orderly presentation of the evidence,' said the white-bearded elder. 'I call upon all to remain calm. Who last saw this man alive?'

Rhoecus came forward and gave an account of our dinner party and how the young men had withdrawn before the symposium. He spoke with a philosopher's impassivity but I could see the worry on his face. I didn't blame him.

'Isaeus son of Diocles and Amyntas son of Rhoecus,' the Archon said, 'come forward.' I had to hand it to them, these Athenians knew how to conduct a proper inquest. The two young men came forward. Both produced very convincing cries and tears upon seeing the bloody corpse of their late friend.

'Amyntas,' said the Archon, 'tell us how you last saw Melanthus.'

'It was at my father's house!' the boy said through his tears. 'I bid Isaeus and Melanthus goodnight at the door and went to my room to sleep, I swear it!'

'Isaeus?'

'Why, at the door of Rhoecus' house I left Melanthus in conversation with Amyntas and went to my own home. I do not know why my friend has lied about the matter.' He looked at the boy with hurt surprise, which was reciprocated.

'Clearly,' said the Archon, 'though it grieves me to say it, one of these two noble youths is culpable in this crime. Until we can decide which of them is guilty, both must be placed under arrest.'

'It was Amyntas!' shouted someone in the crowd. 'We all know how jealous he was of godlike Melanthus!' A distressing faction of the crowd agreed, loudly.

'My son is innocent!' Rhoecus cried. 'He was the friend of Melanthus!'

'And Melanthus was my friend!' Isaeus shouted. His cheering section backed him up.

'May I speak?' I said in my best Forum voice.

'Senator?' said the Archon. 'What interest have you in this matter?'

'Noble Athenians,' Serrius said, 'the Senator Decius Caecilius Metellus has a certain reputation in Rome for criminal investigations. He has often acted on behalf of our praetors and brought in many convictions.'

'Then we would like to hear his observations,' said the Archon. Rhoecus said nothing but when he looked at me there was pleading in his eyes.

I stepped into the centre of the studio. 'My Athenian friends, I am going to make some observations and demand some actions. I request that none of you ask questions until I am done. First: Isaeus, pick up that shield.' I pointed to the shield of Achilles.

He shrugged, stooped and grasped the massive thing in both hands. Making a show of it, he raised the bronze disc over his head, his muscles flexing prettily. From the audience came murmurs of admiration, even shouts that this proved his innocence.

There is an old Greek story that the sculptor Praxiteles, accused of impiety for sculpting the goddess Aphrodite nude for the first time in the history of Greek art, summoned in his defence the model for the statue, the famous courtesan Phryne. Whipping off her gown, he displayed her naked to the jury and demanded how anyone could find impiety in such beauty. Dazzled, the jury voted acquittal. This sort of jurisprudence would never sway a Roman jury, but it seemed to have its adherents in Athens.

'Amyntas,' I said, 'pick it up.'

The boy went to the shield, stooped, grasped and struggled to raise it, but could not get it higher than his knees. Defeated, he laid it back on the floor.

'Amyntas is a promising young man,' I said, 'but unlike Isaeus, he has not yet achieved his full strength.'

'Why do you go on about the shield?' Isaeus demanded. 'Anyone can see that Melanthus was killed with the helmet. Amyntas would have no trouble picking that up.'

'Quite true,' I said, picking up the object in question. 'Like the shield it has been cast of thick bronze and designed to last for ages. It probably weighs forty pounds, ten times the weight of a battle helmet. The narrow edge of the arching crest was brought down upon the head of Melanthus from behind. Quite within the physical abilities of this youth.' Isaeus began to smile, but I sobered his face with my next statement: 'The shield, though, provided the motive for this murder.'

'This will require some explanation, Senator,' said the Archon.

'Easily provided. One of you –' I pointed to a counsellor, a man in the prime of life who kept himself in good condition – 'you, sir. If you please, pick up that shield and set it in its place.'

Mystified, the man hoisted the shield without too much effort and carried it to the sculpture. With great care he tried to set it in its slot, but the figure's hand was set too low. Now truly puzzled, he stepped back. 'It doesn't fit!'

'That,' I said, 'is because you, like the rest of Athens, like the models themselves, assumed that Isaeus was to be Achilles.' I turned and pointed theatrically to the beautiful young man. 'You just couldn't wait, could you, Isaeus? You and Melanthus had to come back down here and see how this superb sculpture would look in its full glory, with the shields and helmets in place, with you in the dominant role of Achilles, your superiority immortalised in marble and bronze, surpassing the second-best-looking man in Athens for eternity! I would give much to have seen the look on your face when you discovered that you were to be not Achilles, but Patroclus!'

The godlike face was stricken. 'But I should have been Achilles! I surpassed Melanthus in everything!'

Agesander came forward, scandalised. 'Isaeus, your golden hair and swiftness of foot and your touch upon the lyre raised you above your friend in this generation, but what would that mean sculpted in imperishable marble a hundred Olympiads from now? Anyone could see that Melanthus had the stance and physical address of a perfect warrior! Of course he deserved to be Achilles, and you to be his companion, Patroclus.'

'But you didn't tell your models that, did you?' I said. 'Too bad. Isaeus might have gone off in a huff but Melanthus would be alive and Athens wouldn't be out two contenders for the next Isthmian Games.'

Guards led the shattered Isaeus off to the local lock-up, followed by a troop of loyal mourners who worshipped him still. Poor Amyntas wept with a combination of relief and grief, and Rhoecus came up and took my hand solemnly. As I said before, it is never a bad thing to have the rich ones on your side.

These things happened at Athens in the year 703 of the City of Rome, the consulship of Servius Sulpicius Rufus and Marcus Claudius Marcellus.

I don't normally write short stories; 300,000 words is about the minimum length I need to feel quite comfortable. There's a reason for this, beyond simple inability to shut up – and that's the fact that I write historical fiction.

When you write contemporary fiction, you can say, 'He put on a blue suit, got into his car and drove to his office,' without the need to define 'suit', 'car', or 'office'. Everyone who might read the book has experienced all three things, and will easily supply the necessary details themselves. 'Suit' in the thirteenth, eighteenth, or nineteenth centuries, though, would have meant very different things – and an author needs to describe just what is meant, in order to give a reader a clear picture.

Historicity goes well beyond the details of physical life, though – and this is what makes historical fiction so interesting; the chance to experience a mental make-up and social norms that may have been quite different than our own – or perhaps not so different.

In eighteenth-century London, homosexuality was a matter of moral outrage, of gossip and public scandal – and yet little or nothing was done in terms of official prosecution, and everyone knew what went on in the back rooms of mollyhouses and the shadows of the Royal Arcade. Don't ask, don't tell?

Why historical crime fiction, though? Well, this is the combination of two loves of mine – historical fiction and crime fiction. My husband once asked me why I read murder mysteries all the time – some sort of vicarious urge to walk on the dark side? I suppose all the books about poisons, magic, and hideous methods of archaic torture (don't let anyone tell you historical people didn't have lots of imagination!) make him slightly nervous. After all, he reads books about building engines because he actually intends to build engines.

I suppose, in a way, he's right; there's some component of morbid curiosity involved. And being able to run someone through with cold steel on the page certainly relieves any small feelings of domestic stress, to be sure.

Still, the appeal of historical crime fiction is a matter of perspective and definition, I think. Looking backward to see where we have come from gives us a better idea of how we got to be who, what, and where we are. Likewise, it's both instructive and reassuring to realise that many of our present values and concerns are the same as they have been in previous times and distant places: murder is the most grievous of wrongs, and justice is a social necessity. These things have always been true, and – by implication – always will be.

To work out the details of crime and punishment in the context of times past gives us a frame of reference in which to evaluate our own notions of social justice and individual responsibility, both in terms of violation and resolution. It's no coincidence that most murder mysteries, at their most basic level, come down to a confrontation (whether explicit or indirect) between murderer and detective; between Good and Evil. The resolution may fall in one direction or the other for any one story – but the conflict is eternal.

Diana Gabaldon

Hellfire

Diana Gabaldon

Part I

London, 1756
The Society for Appreciation of the English Beefsteak, a
gentlemen's club

Lord John Grey jerked his eyes away from the door. No. No, he mustn't turn and stare. Needing some other focus for his gaze he fixed his eyes instead on Quarry's scar.

'A glass with you, sir?' Scarcely waiting for the club's steward to provide for his companion, Harry Quarry drained his cup of claret then held it out for more. 'And another, perhaps, in honour of your return from frozen exile?' Quarry grinned broadly, the scar pulling down the corner of his eye in a lewd wink as he did so, and lifted up his glass again.

Lord John tilted his own cup in acceptance of the salute, but barely tasted the contents. With an effort, he kept his eyes on Quarry's face, willing himself not to turn and stare, not to gawk after the flash of fire that had caught his eye in the corridor.

Quarry's scar had faded; tightened and shrunk to a thin

white slash; its nature was made plain only by its position, angled hard across the ruddy cheek. It might otherwise have lost itself among the lines of hard living, but instead remained visible, the badge of honour that its owner so plainly considered it.

'You are exceeding kind to note my return, sir,' Grey said. His heart hammered in his ears, muffling Quarry's words – no great loss to conversation.

It is not, his sensible mind pointed out, *it cannot be*. Yet sense had nothing to do with the riot of his sensibilities, that surge of feeling that seized him by nape and buttocks, as though it would pluck him up and turn him forcibly to go in pursuit of the red-haired man he had so briefly glimpsed.

Quarry's elbow nudged him rudely, a not unwelcome recall to present circumstances.

'. . . among the ladies, eh?'

'Eh?'

'I say your return has been noted elsewhere, too. My sister-in-law bid me send her regard, and discover your present lodgings. Do you stay with the regiment?'

'No, I am at present at my mother's house, in Jermyn Street.' Finding his cup still full, Grey raised it and drank deep. The Beefsteak's claret was of excellent vintage but he scarcely noticed its bouquet. There were voices in the hall outside, raised in altercation.

'Ah. I'll inform her, then; expect an invitation by the morning post. Lucinda has her eye upon you for a cousin of hers, I daresay – she has a flock of poor but well-favoured female relations, whom she means to shepherd to good marriages.' Quarry's teeth showed briefly. 'Be warned.'

Grey nodded politely. He was accustomed to such overtures. The youngest of four brothers, he had no hopes of a title, but the family name was ancient and honourable, his person and countenance not without appeal – and he had no need of an heiress, his own means being ample.

The door flung open, sending such a draught across the

room as made the fire in the hearth roar up like the flames of
Hades, scattering sparks across the Turkey carpet. Grey gave
thanks for the burst of heat; it gave excuse for the colour that
he felt suffuse his cheeks.

Nothing like. Of course he is nothing like. Who could be?
And yet the emotion that filled his breast was as much
disappointment as relief.

The man was tall, yes, but not strikingly so. Slight of build,
almost delicate. And young, younger than Grey's thirty-odd
by nearly ten, he judged. But the hair – yes, the hair was
very like.

'Lord John Grey.' Quarry had intercepted the young man,
a hand on his sleeve, turning him for introduction. 'Allow
me to acquaint you with my cousin by marriage, Mr Robert
Gerald.'

Mr Gerald nodded shortly, then seemed to take hold of
himself. Suppressing whatever it was that had caused the
blood to rise under his fair skin, he bowed, then fixed his
gaze on Grey in cordial acknowledgement.

'Your servant, sir.'

'And yours.' Not copper, not carrot; a deep red, almost
rufous, with glints and streaks of cinnabar and gold. The
eyes were not blue – thank God! – but rather of a soft and
luminous brown.

Grey's mouth had gone dry. To his relief, Quarry offered
refreshment, and upon Gerald's agreement, snapped his fingers for the steward and steered the three of them to an
armchaired corner where the haze of tobacco smoke hung
like a sheltering curtain over the less convivial members of
the Beefsteak.

'Who was that I heard in the corridor?' Quarry demanded,
as soon as they were settled. 'Bubb-Dodington, surely? The
man's a voice like a coster-monger.'

'I – he – yes, it was.' Mr Gerald's pale skin, not quite
recovered from its earlier excitement, bloomed afresh, to
Quarry's evident amusement.

'Oho! And what perfidious proposal has he made you, young Bob?'

'Nothing. He – an invitation I did not wish to accept, that is all. Must you shout so loudly, Harry?' It was chilly at this end of the room, but Grey thought he could warm his hands at the fire of Gerald's smooth cheeks.

Quarry snorted with amusement, looking around at the nearby chairs.

'Who's to hear? Old Cotterill's deaf as a post, and the General's half-dead. And why do you care in any case, if the matter's so innocent as you suggest?' Quarry's eyes swivelled to bear on his cousin by marriage, suddenly intelligent and penetrating.

'I did not say it was innocent,' Gerald replied drily, regaining his composure. 'I said I declined to accept it. And that, Harry, is all you will hear of it, so desist this piercing glare you turn upon me. It may work on your subalterns, but not on me.'

Grey laughed, and after a moment, Quarry joined in. He clapped Gerald on the shoulder, eyes twinkling.

'My cousin is the soul of discretion, Lord John. But that's as it should be, eh?'

'I have the honour to serve as junior secretary to the Prime Minister,' Gerald explained, seeing incomprehension on Grey's features. 'While the secrets of government are dull indeed – at least by Harry's standards –' he shot his cousin a malicious grin – 'they are not mine to share.'

'Oh, well, of no interest to Lord John in any case,' Quarry said philosophically, tossing back his third glass of aged claret with a disrespectful haste more suited to porter. Grey saw the senior steward close his eyes in quiet horror at the act of desecration, and smiled to himself – or so he thought, until he caught Mr Gerald's soft brown eyes upon him, a matching smile of complicity upon his lips.

'Such things are of little interest to anyone save those most intimately concerned,' Gerald said, still smiling at Grey. 'The fiercest battles fought are those where very little lies at stake, you know. But what interests you, Lord John, if politics does not?'

'Not lack of interest,' Grey responded, holding Robert Gerald's eyes boldly with his. *No, not lack of interest at all.* 'Ignorance, rather. I have been absent from London for some time; in fact, I have quite lost . . . touch.'

Without intent, one hand closed upon his glass, the thumb drawing slowly upward, stroking the smooth, cool surface as though it were another's flesh. Hastily, he set the glass down, seeing as he did so the flash of blue from the sapphire ring he wore. It might have been a lighthouse beacon, he reflected wryly, warning of rough seas ahead.

And yet the conversation sailed smoothly on, despite Quarry's jocular inquisitions regarding Grey's most recent posting in the wilds of Scotland, and his speculations as to his brother officer's future prospects. As the former was *terra prohibita* and the latter *terra incognita*, Grey had little to say in response, and the talk moved on to other things; horses, dogs, regimental gossip and other such comfortable masculine fare.

Yet now and again Grey felt the brown eyes rest on him, with an expression of speculation that both modesty and caution forbade him to interpret. It was with no sense of surprise, though, that upon departure from the club, he found himself alone in the vestibule with Gerald, Quarry having been detained by an acquaintance met in passing.

'I impose intolerably, sir,' Gerald said, moving close enough to keep his low-voiced words from the ears of the servant who kept the door. 'I would ask your favour, though, if it be not entirely unwelcome?'

'I am completely at your command, I do assure you,' Grey said, feeling the warmth of claret in his blood succeeded by a rush of deeper heat.

'I wish – that is, I am in some doubt regarding a circumstance of which I have become aware. Since you are so

411

recently come to London – that is, you have the advantage of perspective, which I must necessarily lack by reason of familiarity. There is no one . . .' He fumbled for words, then turned eyes grown suddenly and deeply unhappy on Lord John. 'I can confide in no one!' he said, in a sudden passionate whisper. He gripped Lord John's arm with surprising strength. 'It may be nothing, nothing at all. But I must have help.'

'You shall have it, if it be in my power to give.' Grey's fingers touched the hand that grasped his arm; Gerald's fingers were cold. Quarry's voice echoed down the corridor behind them, loud with joviality.

'The 'Change, near the Arcade,' Gerald said rapidly. 'Tonight, just after full dark.' The grip on Grey's arm was gone, and Gerald vanished, the soft fall of his hair vivid against his blue cloak.

Grey's afternoon was spent in necessary errands to tailors and solicitors, then in making courtesy calls upon long-neglected acquaintance, in an effort to fill the empty hours that loomed before dark. Quarry, at loose ends, had volunteered to accompany him, and Lord John had made no demur. Bluff and jovial by temper, Quarry's conversation was limited to cards, drink, and whores. He and Grey had little in common, save the regiment. And Ardsmuir.

When he had first seen Quarry again at the club he had thought to avoid the man, feeling that memory was best buried. And yet . . . could memory be truly buried, when its embodiment still lived? He might forget a dead man, but not one merely absent. And the flames of Robert Gerald's hair had kindled embers he had thought safely smothered.

It might be unwise to feed that spark, he thought, freeing his soldier's cloak from the grasp of an importunate beggar. Open flames were dangerous and he knew that as well as any man. And yet . . . hours of buffeting through London's crowds and hours more of enforced sociality had filled him

412

with such unexpected longing for the quiet of the North that he found himself seized suddenly with the desire to speak of Scotland, if nothing more.

They had passed the Royal Exchange in the course of their errands; he had glanced covertly toward the Arcade, with its gaudy paint and tattered posters, its tawdry crowds of hawkers and strollers, and felt a soft spasm of anticipation. It was autumn; the dark came early.

They were near the river now; the noise of clamouring cockle-sellers and fishmongers rang in the winding alleys, and a cold wind filled with the invigorating stench of tar and wood-shavings bellied out their cloaks like sails. Quarry turned and waved above the heads of the intervening throng, gesturing toward a coffee house; Grey nodded in reply, lowered his head and elbowed his way toward the door.

'Such a press,' Lord John said, pushing his way after Quarry into the relative peace of the small, spice-scented room. He took off his tricorne and sat down, tenderly adjusting the red cockade, knocked askew by contact with the populace. Two inches shorter than the common height, Grey found himself at a disadvantage in crowds.

'I had forgot what a seething anthill London is.' He took a deep breath; grasp the nettle, then, and get it over. 'A contrast with Ardsmuir, to be sure.'

'I'd forgot what a misbegotten lonely hellhole Scotland is,' Quarry replied, 'until you turned up at the Beefsteak this morning to remind me of my blessings. Here's to anthills!' He lifted the steaming glass which had appeared as by magic at his elbow, and bowed ceremoniously to Grey. He drank, and shuddered, either in memory of Scotland, or in answer to the quality of the coffee. He frowned, and reached for the sugar bowl.

'Thank God we're both well out of it. Freezing your arse off indoors or out, and the blasted rain coming in at every crack.' Quarry took off his wig and scratched his balding pate, quite without self-consciousness, then clapped it on again.

'No society but the damned dour-faced Scots, either; never had a whore there who didn't give me the feeling she'd as soon cut it off as serve it. I swear I'd have put a pistol to my head in another month, had you not come to relieve me, Grey. What poor bugger took over from you?'

'No one.' Grey scratched at his own fair hair abstract-edly, infected by Quarry's itch. He glanced outside; the street was still jammed, but the crowd's noise was mer-cifully muffled by the leaded glass. One sedan chair had run into another, its bearers knocked off-balance by the crowd. 'Ardsmuir is no longer a prison; the prisoners were transported.'

'Transported?' Quarry pursed his lips in surprise, then sipped, more cautiously. 'Well, and serve them right, the miserable whoresons. Hm!' He grunted, and shook his head over the coffee. 'No more than most deserve. A shame for Fraser, though – you recall a man named Fraser, big red-haired fellow? One of the Jacobite officers – a gentleman. Quite liked him,' Quarry said, his roughly cheerful countenance sobering slightly. 'Too bad. Did you find occasion to speak with him?'

'Now and then.' Grey felt a familiar clench of his innards, and turned away, lest anything show on his face. Both sedan chairs were down now, the bearers shouting and shoving. The street was narrow to begin with, clogged with the normal traffic of tradesmen and 'prentices; customers stopping to watch the altercation added to the impassibility.

'You knew him well?' He could not help himself; whether it brought him comfort or misery, he felt he had no choice now but to speak of Fraser – and Quarry was the only man in London to whom he could so speak.

'Oh, yes – or as well as one might know a man in that situation,' Quarry replied offhandedly. 'Had him to dine in my quarters every week; very civil in his speech, good hand at cards.' He lifted a fleshy nose from his glass, cheeks flushed ruddier than usual with the steam. 'He wasn't one to invite pity, of course, but one could scarce help but feel some sympathy for his circumstances.'

'Sympathy? And yet you left him in chains.'

Quarry looked up sharply, catching the edge in Grey's words.

'I may have liked the man; I didn't trust him. Not after what happened to one of my sergeants.'

'And what was that?' Lord John managed to infuse the question with no more than light interest.

'Misadventure. Drowned by accident in the stone-quarry pool,' Quarry said, dumping several teaspoons of rock sugar into a fresh glass and stirring vigorously. 'Or so I wrote in the report.' He looked up from his coffee, and gave Grey his lewd, lopsided wink. 'I liked Fraser. Didn't care for the sergeant. But never think a man is helpless, Grey, only because he's fettered.'

Grey sought urgently for a way to enquire further without letting his passionate interest be seen.

'So you believe—' he began.

'Look,' said Quarry, rising suddenly from his seat. 'Look! Damned if it's not Bob Gerald!'

Lord John whipped round in his chair. Sure enough, the late afternoon sun struck sparks from a fiery head, bent as its owner emerged from one of the stalled sedan chairs. Gerald straightened, face set in a puzzled frown, and began to push his way into the knot of embattled bearers.

'Whatever is he about, I wonder? Surely – Hi! Hold! Hold, you blackguard!' Dropping his glass unregarded, Quarry rushed toward the door, bellowing.

Grey, a step or two behind, saw no more than the flash of metal in the sun, and the brief look of startlement on Gerald's face. Then the crowd fell back, with a massed cry of horror, and his view was obscured by a throng of heaving backs.

He fought his way through the screaming mob without compunction, striking ruthlessly with his sword hilt to clear the way.

Gerald was lying in the arms of one of his bearers, hair fallen forward, hiding his face. The young man's knees were drawn up in agony, balled fists pressed hard against the growing stain on his waistcoat.

Quarry was there; he brandished his sword at the crowd, bellowing threats to keep them back, then glared wildly round for a foe to skewer.

'Who?' he shouted at the bearers, face congested with fury. 'Who's done this?'

The circle of white faces turned in helpless question, one to another, but found no focus; the foe had fled, and his bearers with him.

Grey knelt in the gutter, careless of filth, and smoothed back the ruddy hair with hands gone stiff and cold. The hot stink of blood was thick in the air, and the faecal smell of pierced intestine. Grey had seen battlefields enough to know the truth even before he saw the glazing eyes, the pallid face. He felt a deep, sharp stab at the sight, as though his own guts were pierced as well.

Brown eyes fixed wide on his, a spark of recognition deep behind the shock and pain. He seized the dying man's hand in his, and chafed it, knowing the futility of the gesture. Gerald's mouth worked, soundless. A bubble of red spittle swelled at the corner of his lips.

'Tell me.' Grey bent urgently to the man's ear, and felt the soft brush of hair against his mouth. 'Tell me who has done it – I will avenge you. I swear it.'

He felt a slight spasm of the fingers in his, and squeezed back, hard, as though he might force some of his own strength into Gerald; enough for a word, a name.

The soft lips were blanched, the blood-bubble growing. Gerald drew back the corners of his mouth, a fierce, tooth-baring rictus that burst the bubble and sent a spray of blood across Grey's cheek. Then the lips drew in, pursing in what might have been the invitation to a kiss. Then he died, and the wide brown eyes went blank.

416

Quarry was shouting at the bearers, demanding information. More shouts echoed down the walls of the streets, the nearby alleys, news flying from the scene of murder like bats out of hell. Grey knelt alone in the silence near the dead man, in the stench of blood and voided bowels. Gently, he laid Gerald's hand limp across his wounded breast, and wiped the blood from his own hand, unthinking, on his cloak.

A motion drew his eye. Harry Quarry knelt on the other side of the body, his face gone white as the scar on his cheek, prying open a large clasp-knife. He searched gently through Gerald's loosened, blood-matted hair, and drew out a clean lock, which he cut off. The sun was setting; light caught the hair as it fell, a curl of vivid flame.

'For his mother,' Quarry explained. Lips tightly pressed together, he coiled the gleaming strand and put it carefully away.

Part II

The invitation came two days later, and with it, a note from Harry Quarry. Lord John Grey was bidden to an evening's entertainment at Joffrey House, by desire of the Lady Lucinda Joffrey. Quarry's note said simply, 'Come. I have news.'

And not beforetimes, Grey thought, tossing the note aside. The two days since Gerald's death had been filled with frantic activity, with enquiry and speculation – to no avail. Every shop and barrow in Forby Street had been turned over thoroughly, but no trace found of the assailant or his minions; they had faded into the crowd, anonymous as ants.

That proved one thing, at least, Grey thought. It was a planned attack, not a random piece of street violence. For the assailant to vanish so quickly, he must have looked like any member of the *hoi-polloi*; a prosperous merchant or a noble would have stood out by his bearing and the manner of his dress. The sedan-chair had been hired; no one recalled the appearance of the hirer, and the name given was – not surprisingly – false.

He shuffled restlessly through the rest of the mail. All other avenues of enquiry had proven fruitless so far. No weapon had been found. He and Quarry had sought the hall porter at the Beefsteak, in hopes that the man had heard somewhat of the conversation between Gerald and Bubb-Dodington, but the man was a temporary servant, hired for the day, and had since taken his wages and vanished, no doubt to drink them.

Grey had canvassed his acquaintance for any rumour of enemies, or failing that, for any history of the late Robert Gerald that might bear a hint of motive for the crime. Gerald was evidently known, in a modest way, in government circles and the venues of respectable society – but he had no great money to leave, no heirs save his mother, no hint of any romantic entanglement – in short, there was no intimation whatever of an association that might have led to that bloody death in Forby Street.

He paused, eye caught by an unfamiliar seal. A note, signed by one G. Bubb-Dodington, requesting a few moments of his time, in a convenient season – and noting *en passant* that B-D would himself be present at Joffrey House that evening, should Lord John find himself likewise engaged.

He picked up the invitation again, and found another sheet of paper folded up behind it. Unfolded, this proved to be a broadsheet, printed with a poem – or at the least, words arranged in the form of verse. 'A Blot Removed', it was titled. Lacking in metre, but not in crude wit, the doggerel gave the story of a 'he-whore' whose lewdities outraged the public, until 'scandal flamed up, blood-red as the abominable colour of his hair,' and an unknown saviour rose up to destroy the perverse, thus wiping clean the pristine parchment of society.

Lord John had eaten no breakfast and sight of this extinguished what vestiges he had of appetite. He carried the document into the morning room and fed it carefully to the fire.

*   *   *

Joffrey House was a small but elegant white stone mansion just off Eaton Square. Grey had never come there before but the house was well known for brilliant parties, much frequented by those with a taste for politics; Sir Richard Joffrey, Quarry's elder brother, was influential.

As Grey came up the marble steps, he saw a Member of Parliament and the First Sea Lord, close in converse ahead of him, and perceived a considerable array of discreetly elegant carriages standing at a distance in the street. Something of an occasion, then; he was a trifle surprised that Lady Lucinda should be entertaining on such a scale, on the heels of her cousin's assassination – Quarry had said she was close to Gerald.

Quarry was on the *qui vive*; Grey had no sooner been announced than he found himself seized by the arm and drawn out of the slowly moving reception line into the shelter of a monstrous plant that had been stood in the corner of the ballroom, where it consorted with several of its fellows in the manner of a small jungle.

'You came, then,' Quarry said, unnecessarily.

Seeing the haggard aspect of the man, Grey said merely, 'Yes. What news?'

Fatigue and distress tended merely to sharpen Grey's fine-cut features, but gave Quarry an air of snappish ferocity, making him look like a large, ill-tempered dog.

'You saw that – that – unspeakable piece of excrement?'

'The broadsheet? Yes; where did you get it?'

'They are all over London; not only that particular excrescence – many others, as vile or worse.'

Grey felt a prick of deep unease.

'With similar accusations?'

'That Robert Gerald was a pederast? Yes, and worse; that he was a member of a notorious sodomitical society, a gathering for the purpose of . . . well, you'll know the sort of thing? Disgusting!'

Grey could not tell whether this last epithet was applied to the existence of such societies, or to the association of Gerald's name with one. In consequence, he chose his words with care.

'Yes, I have heard of such associations.'

Grey did know, though the knowledge was not personal; such societies were said to be common – he knew of taverns and back rooms aplenty, to say nothing of the more notorious mollyhouses, where . . . still, fastidiousness and caution had prevented any close enquiry into these assemblies.

'Need I say that – that such accusations have no truth – not the slightest pretension to truth?' Quarry spoke with some difficulty, avoiding Grey's eye. Grey laid a hand on Quarry's sleeve.

'No, you need not say so. I am certain of it,' he said quietly. Quarry glanced up, giving him a half-embarrassed smile, and clasped his hand briefly.

'Thank you,' he said, voice rasping.

'But if it be not so,' Grey observed, giving Quarry time to recover himself, 'then such rapid profusion of rumour has the taste about it of an organised calumny. And that in itself is very strange, do you not think?'

Evidently not; Quarry looked blankly at him.

'Someone wished not only to destroy Robert Gerald,' Grey explained, 'but thought it necessary also to blacken his name. Why? The man is dead; who would think it needful to murder his reputation, as well?'

Quarry looked startled, then frowned, brows drawing close together in the effort of thought.

'Strewth,' he said slowly. 'Damn, you're right. But who . . . ?' He stopped, looking thoughtfully out over the assemblage of guests.

'Is the Prime Minister here?' Grey peered through the drooping foliage. It was a small but brilliant party, and one of a particular kind; no more than forty guests, and these all drawn from the echelons of power. No mincing fops or gadding henwits; ladies there were, to be sure, providing grace and beauty – but it was the men who were of consequence. Several ministers were in attendance, the Sea Lord, an assistant Minister of Finance. He stopped, feeling as though someone had just punched him hard in the belly.

Quarry was muttering in his ear, explaining something about the Prime Minister's absence, but Grey was no longer attending. He fought the urge to step back farther into the shadows.

George Everett was looking well – very well indeed. Wig and powder set off the blackness of his brows, and the fine dark eyes below them. A firm chin and a long, mobile mouth – Grey's index finger twitched involuntarily, tracing the line of it in memory.

'Are you well, Grey?' Quarry's gruff voice recalled him to himself.

'Yes. A trifling indisposition, that is all.' Grey pulled his eyes away from Everett's slim figure, striking in black and primrose. It was only a matter of time, after all; he had known they would meet again – and at least he had not been taken unawares. With an effort, he turned his attention back to Quarry.

'The news you mentioned. Is it—'

Quarry interrupted, gripping his arm and pulling him out from the shelter of the trees, into the babble of the party.

'Hark, here is Lucinda. Come, she wishes to meet you.'

Lady Lucinda Joffrey was small and round, her dark hair worn unpowdered, sleek to the skull, and her ringlets fastened with an ornament of pheasant's feathers that went well with her russet gown. Her face was plump and rather plain, though it might have some claim to character, had there been much life to it. Instead, swollen lids drooped over eyes smudged with shadows she had not bothered to disguise.

Lord John bowed over her hand, wondering again as he did so what had caused her to open her house this evening; plainly she was in great distress.

'My lord,' she murmured, in response to his courtesies. Then she lifted her eyes and he found himself startled. Her eyes were beautiful, almond-shaped and deep amber in colour – and despite their reddened lids, clear and piercing with intelligence.

'Harry tells me that you were with Robert when he died,' she said, softly but clearly, holding him with those eyes. 'And that you have offered your help in finding the dastard who has done this thing.'

'Indeed. I offer you my most sincere condolences, my lady.'

'I thank you, sir.' She nodded toward the room, bright with guests and blazing candles. 'You will find it strange, no doubt, that we should revel in such fashion, and my cousin so recently and despicably slain?' Grey began to make the expected demur but she would not allow it, going on before he could speak.

'It was my husband's wish. He said we must – that to shrink and cower before such slander would be to grant it credence. He insisted that we must meet it boldly, or suffer ourselves from the stain of scandal.' Her lips pressed tight, a handkerchief crumpled in her hand, but no tears welled in the amber eyes.

'Your husband is wise.' That was a thought; Sir Richard Joffrey was an influential Member of Parliament, with a shrewd appreciation of politics, a great acquaintance with those in power – and the money to influence them. Could the killing of Gerald and this posthumous effort to discredit him be in some way a blow at Sir Richard?

Grey hesitated; he had not yet told Quarry of Gerald's request at the club. 'There is no one I can confide in,' Gerald had said – and presumably included his cousin by marriage therein. But Gerald was dead, and Grey's obligation was now vengeance, rather than confidence. The musicians had paused; with a tilt of the head, Grey drew his companions back into the privacy of the jungle.

'Madam, I had the honour of a very brief acquaintance with your cousin. Still, when I met him . . .' In a few words, he acquainted his hearers with Robert Gerald's last request.

'Do either of you know what his concern might have been?' Grey asked, looking from one to the other. The musicians were starting up again, the strains of fiddle and flute rising above the rumble of conversation.

'He asked you to meet him on the 'Change?' A shadow passed over Quarry's face. If Gropecunt Street was the main thoroughfare for female prostitution, the Royal Exchange was its male counterpart – after dark, at least.

'That means nothing, Harry,' Lucinda said. Her grief had been subsumed by interest, plump figure drawn erect. 'The 'Change is a meeting place for every kind of intrigue. I am sure Robert's choice of meeting place had nothing to do with – with these scurrilous accusations.' Lady Lucinda frowned. 'But I know of nothing that would have caused my cousin such concern. Do you, Harry?'

'If I did, I would have said so,' Quarry said irritably. 'Since he did not think me fit to confide in, though—'

'You mentioned some news,' Grey interrupted, seeking to avert acrimony. 'What was that?'

'Oh.' Quarry stopped, irritation fading. 'I've gleaned a notion of what Bubb-Dodington's invitation consisted.' Quarry cast a glance of unconcealed dislike toward a knot of men gathered talking at the opposite side of the room. 'And if my informant be correct, 'twas far from innocent.'

'Which is Bubb-Dodington? Is he here?'

'Indeed.' Lucinda pointed with her fan. 'Standing by the hearth – in the reddish suit.'

Grey squinted through the haze of hearth smoke and candleglow, picking out a slender figure in bag-wig and rose velvet – fashionable, to be sure, but seeming somehow slightly fawning in attitude as he leaned toward another of the group.

'I have enquired regarding him,' Grey said. 'I hear he

is a political, but one of no great consequence; a mere time-server.'

'True, he is nothing in himself. His associations, though, are more substantial. Those with whom he allies himself are scarcely without power, though not – not yet! – in control.'

'And who are those? I am quite ignorant of politics these days.'

'Sir Francis Dashwood, John Wilkes, Mr Churchill . . . Paul Whitehead, too. Oh, and Everett. You know George Everett?'

'We are acquainted,' Grey said equably. 'The invitation you mentioned . . . ?'

'Oh, yes.' Quarry shook his head, recalled to himself. 'I finally discovered the whereabouts of the hall porter. He had overheard enough of Bubb-Dodington's conversation to say that the man was urging Gerald to accept an invitation to stay at West Wycombe.'

Quarry raised his brows high in implication, but Grey remained ignorant, and said so.

'West Wycombe is the home of Sir Francis Dashwood,' Lady Lucinda put in. 'And the centre of his influence. He entertains there lavishly – even as we do –' her plump mouth made a small moue of deprecation – 'and to the same purposes.'

'The seduction of the powerful?' Grey smiled. 'So Bubb-Dodington – or his masters – sought to entice Gerald? To what end, I wonder?'

'Richard calls the West Wycombe assemblage a nest of vipers,' Lucinda said. 'Bent upon achieving their ends by any means, even dishonourable ones. Perhaps they sought to lure Robert into their camp for the sake of his own virtues or –' she paused, hesitant – 'for the sake of what he might know, regarding the Prime Minister's affairs?'

The music was starting afresh at the far end of the room, and they were interrupted at this delicate moment by a lady, who, spotting them in their leafy refuge, came bustling in to claim Harry Quarry for a dance, waving aside all possibility of refusal with an airy fan.

'Is that not Lady Fitzwalter?' Buxom and high-coloured, the lady now pressing Quarry's hand provocatively to her breast was the wife of Sir Hugh, an elderly baronet from Sussex. Quarry appeared to have no objections, following up Lady F's flirtations with a jocular pinch.

'Oh, Harry fancies himself a great rake,' Lady Lucinda said tolerantly, 'though anyone can see it comes to nothing more than a hand of cards in the gentlemen's clubs and an eye for shapely flesh. Is any officer in London greatly different?' A shrewd amber eye passed over Lord John, enquiring as to what his own differences might be.

'Indeed,' he said, amused. 'And yet he was sent to Scotland for some indiscretion, I collect. Was it not the incident that left him with that slash across the face?'

'Oh, la,' the lady said, pursing up her mouth in scorn. 'The famous scar! One would think it the Order of the Garter, he does flaunt it so. No, no, 'twas the cards that were the cause of his exile – he caught a Colonel of the regiment a-cheating at loo, and was too much gone in wine to keep a decent silence on the point.'

Grey opened his mouth to enquire about the scar, but was silenced himself by her grip upon his sleeve.

'Now, there's a rake, if you want one,' she said, low-voiced. Her eyes marked out a man across the room, near the hearth. 'Dashwood; him Harry spoke of. Know of him, do you?'

Grey squinted against the haze of smoke in the room.

The man was heavy-bodied but betrayed no softness of flesh; the sloping shoulders were thick with muscle, and if waist and calves were thick as well, it was by a natural inclination of form, rather than the result of indulgence.

'I have heard the name,' Grey said. 'A political of some minor repute?'

'In the arena of politics, yes,' Lady Lucinda agreed, not taking her eyes from the man. 'In others . . . less minor. In fact, his repute in some circles is nothing short of outright notoriety.'

A reach for a glass stretched the cloth of Dashwood's broidered plum-silk waistcoat tight across a broad chest, and brought into view a face, likewise broad, ruddy in the candleglow and animated with a cynic laughter. He wore no wig, but had a quantity of dark hair, curling low across the brow. Grey furrowed his own brow in the effort of recall; someone had said something to him, yes – but the occasion escaped him, as did its content.

'He seems a man of substance,' he hazarded. Certainly Dashwood was the cynosure of his end of the room, all eyes upon him as he spoke.

Lady Lucinda uttered a short laugh.

'Do you think so, sir? He and his friends flaunt their practice of licentiousness and blasphemy as Harry flaunts his scar – and from the same cause.'

It was the word 'blasphemy' that brought back recollection.

'Ha. I have heard mention . . . Medmenham Abbey?'

Lucinda's lips pursed tight, and she nodded.

'The Hell Fire Club, they call it.'

'Indeed. There have been Hell Fire clubs before – many of them. Is this one more than the usual excuse for public riot and drunken licence?'

She looked at the men before the fire, her countenance troubled. With the light of the blaze behind them, all individuality of lineament was lost; they appeared no more than an assemblage of dark figures; faceless devils, outlined by the firelight.

'I think not,' she said, very low-voiced, glancing to and fro to assure they were unheard. 'Or so I *did* think – until I heard of the invitation to Robert. Now . . .'

The advent near the jungle of a tall, good-looking man whose resemblance to Quarry made his identity clear put an end to the clandestine conference.

'There is Richard; he is looking for me.' Poised to take

flight, Lady Lucinda stopped and looked back at Grey. 'I cannot say, sir, what reason you may have for your interest – but I do thank you for it.' A flicker of wryness lit the amber eyes. 'Godspeed you, sir, though for myself, I should not much respect a God so petty as to be concerned with such as Francis Dashwood.'

Grey passed into the general crowd, bowing and smiling, allowing himself to be drawn into a dance here, a conversation there, keeping all the time one eye upon the group near the hearth. Men joined it for a short time, fell away, and were replaced by others, yet the central group remained unchanged.

Bubb-Dodington and Dashwood were the centre of it; Churchill, the poet, John Wilkes and the Earl of Sandwich surrounded them. Seeing at one point during a break in the music that a good many had gathered by the hearth, men and women alike, Grey thought the moment ripe to make his own presence known, and unobtrusively joined the crowd, manoeuvring to a spot near Bubb-Dodington.

Mr Justice Margrave was holding the floor, speaking of the subject which had formed the meat of most conversations Grey had heard so far – the death of Robert Gerald, or more particularly, the rash of rumour and scandal that followed it. The judge caught Grey's eye and nodded – his worship was well acquainted with Grey's family – but continued his denunciation unimpeded.

'I should wish that, rather than the Pillory, the stake be the punishment for such abominable vice.' Margrave swung a heavy head in Grey's direction, eyelids dropping half-closed. 'Have you read Holloway's notion, sir? He suggests that this disgusting practice of sodomy be restrained by castration or some other cogent preventative.'

Grey restrained the urge to clasp himself protectively.

'Cogent, indeed,' he said. 'You suppose the man who cut down Robert Gerald to be impelled by moralistic motives, then?'

'Whether he were or no, I should say he has rendered signal service to society, ridding us of an exponent of this moral blight.'

Grey observed Harry Quarry standing a yard away, gleaming eyes fixed on the elderly justice in a manner calculated to cause the utmost concern for that worthy's future prospects. Turning away, lest his acknowledgement embolden Quarry to open violence, he found himself instead face to face with George Everett.

'John,' Everett said softly, smiling.

'Mr Everett.' Grey inclined his head politely. Nothing squelched, Everett continued to smile. He was a handsome devil, and he knew it.

'You are in good looks, John. Exile agrees with you, it seems.' The long mouth widened, curling at the corner.

'Indeed. I must take pains to go away more often, then.' His heart was beating faster. Everett's perfume was his accustomed musk and myrrh; the scent of it conjured tumbled linens and the touch of hard and knowing hands.

A hoarse voice near his shoulder provided welcome distraction.

'Lord John? Your servant, sir.'

Grey turned to find the gentleman in rose velvet bowing to him, a look of spurious cordiality fixed upon saturnine features.

'Mr Bubb-Dodington, I collect. I am obliged, sir.' He bowed in turn, and allowed himself to be separated from Everett, who stood looking after them, a faint smile upon his lips.

So conscious was he of Everett's eyes burning holes in his back that he scarcely attended to Bubb-Dodington's overtures, replying automatically to the man's courtesies and enquiries. It was not until the rasping voice mentioned the word 'Medmenham' that he was jerked into attention, to realise that he had just received a most interesting invitation.

'. . . would find us a most congenial assembly, I am sure,'

Bubb-Dodington was saying, leaning toward Grey with that same attitude of fawning attention he had noted earlier.

'You feel I would be in sympathy with the interests of your society?' Grey contrived to infuse a faint tone of boredom, looking away from the man. Just over Bubb-Dodington's shoulder, he was conscious of the figure of Sir Francis Dashwood, dark and bulky. Dashwood's deepset eyes rested upon them, even as he carried on a conversation, and a ripple of apprehension raised the hairs on the back of Grey's neck.

'I am flattered, but I scarcely think . . .' he began, turning away.

'Oh, do not think you would be quite strange!' Bubb-Dodington interrupted, beaming with oily deprecation. 'You are acquainted with Mr Everett, I think? He will be one of our number.'

'Indeed.' Grey's mouth had gone dry. 'I see. Well, you must allow me to consult . . .' Muttering excuses, he escaped, finding refuge a moment later in the company of Harry Quarry and his sister-in-law, sharing cups of brandy punch at the nearby buffet.

'It galls me,' Harry was saying, 'that such petty time-servers and flaunting jackanapes make my kin to be the equal of the he-strumpets and buggerantoes that infest the Arcade. I've known Bob Gerald from a lad, and I will swear my life upon his honour!' Quarry's large hand clenched upon his glass as he glowered at Mr Justice Margrave's back.

'Have a care, Harry, my dear.' Lucinda placed a hand on his sleeve. 'Those are my good crystal glasses. If you must crush something, let it be the hazelnuts.'

'I shall let it be that fellow's windpipe if he does not cease to air his idiocy,' said Quarry. He scowled horridly, but suffered himself to be turned away, still talking. 'What can Richard be thinking of, to entertain such vile scum? Dashwood, I mean, and now this . . .'

Grey started, and felt a chill down his spine. Quarry's blunt features bore no trace of resemblance to his dead cousin by marriage; and yet – his face contorted with fury, eyes bulging slightly as he spoke . . . Grey closed his eyes tightly, summoning the vision.

He left Quarry and Lady Lucinda abruptly, without excuse, and made his way hastily to the large gilded mirror that hung above a sideboard in the dining room.

Leaning over the skeletal remains of a roasted pheasant, he stared at his mouth – painstakingly forming the shapes he had seen on Robert Gerald's mouth – and now again on Harry Quarry's; hearing in his mind as he made them the sound of Robert Gerald's effortful – but unvoiced – last word.

'Dashwood.'

Quarry had followed him, brows drawn down in puzzlement.

'What the devil, Grey? Why are you making faces in the mirror? Are you ill?'

'No,' said Grey, though in fact he felt very ill. He stared at his own image in the mirror, as though it were some ghastly spectre.

Another face appeared, and dark eyes met his own in the mirror. The two reflections were close in size and form, both possessed of a tidy muscularity and a fineness of feature that had led more than one observer to remark in company that they could be twins – one light, one dark.

'You will come to Medmenham, won't you?' The murmured words were warm in his ear, George's body so close that he could feel the pressure of hip and thigh. Everett's hand touched his, lightly.

'I should . . . particularly desire it.'

Part III

Medmenham Abbey, West Wycombe

430

It was not until the third night at Medmenham that anything untoward occurred. To that point – despite Quarry's loudly expressed doubts beforehand – it had been a house party much like any other in Lord John's experience, though with more talk of politics and less of hunting than was customary.

In spite of the talk and entertainment, though, there was an odd air of secrecy about the house. Whether it was some attitude on the part of the servants, or something unseen but sensed among the guests, Grey could not tell, but it was real; it floated on the air of the abbey like smoke on water.

The only other oddity was the lack of women. While females of good family from the countryside near West Wycombe were invited to dine, all of the house guests were male. The thought occurred to Grey that from outward appearance, it might almost be one of those sodomitical societies so decried in the London broadsheets. In appearance only, though; there was no hint of such behaviour. Even George Everett gave no hint of any sentiment save the amiability of renewed friendship.

No, it was not that kind of behaviour that had given Sir Francis and his restored abbey the name of scandal. Exactly what *did* lie behind the whispers of notoriety was yet a mystery.

Grey knew one thing; Dashwood was not Gerald's murderer, at least not directly. Discreet enquiry had established Sir Francis' whereabouts, and shown him far from Forby Street at the time of the outrage. There was the possibility of hired assassination, though, and Robert Gerald had seen *something* in the moment of his death that caused him to utter that last silent accusation.

There was nothing so far to which Grey could point as evidence, either of guilt or depravity. Still, if evidence was to be found anywhere, it must be at Medmenham – the deconsecrated abbey which Sir Francis had restored from ruins and made a showplace for his political ambitions.

Among the talk and entertainments, though, Grey was conscious of a silent process of evaluation, plain in the eyes and manner of his companions. He was being watched, his fitness gauged – but for what?

'What is it that Sir Francis wants with me?' he had asked bluntly, walking in the gardens with Everett on the second afternoon. 'I have nothing to appeal to such a man.'

George smiled. He wore his own hair, dark and shining, and the chilly breeze stroked strands of it across his cheeks.

'You understimate your own merits, John – as always. Of course, nothing becomes manly virtue more than simple modesty.' He glanced sidelong, mouth quirking with appreciation.

'I scarce think my personal attributes are sufficient to intrigue a man of Dashwood's character,' Grey answered drily.

'More to the point,' Everett said, arching one brow, 'what is it in Sir Francis that so intrigues *you*? You have not spoke of anything, save to question me about him.'

'You would be better suited to answer that than I,' Grey answered boldly. 'I hear you are an intimate – the valet tells me you have been a guest at Medmenham many times this year past. What is it draws *you* to seek his company?'

George grunted in amusement, then flung back his head, breathing in the damp air with enjoyment. Lord John did likewise; autumn smells of leaf mould and chimney smoke, spiced with the tang of ripe muscats from the arbour nearby. Scents to stir the blood, cold air to sting cheeks and hands, exercise to stimulate and weary the limbs, making the glowing leisure of the fireside and the comforts of a dark, warm bed so appealing by contrast.

'Power,' George said at last. He lifted a hand toward the abbey – an impressive pile of grey stone, at once stalwart in shape and delicate in design. 'Dashwood aspires to great things; I would join him on that upward reach.' He cast a glance at Grey. 'And you, John? It has been some time since

432

I presumed to know you, and yet I should not have said that a thirst for social influence formed much part of your own desires.'

Grey wished no discussion of his desires; not at the moment.

'"*The desire of power in excess caused the angels to fall*",' he quoted.

'"*The desire of knowledge in excess caused man to fall.*"' George completed the quote, and uttered a short laugh. 'What is it that you seek to know then, John?' He turned his head toward Grey, dark eyes creased against the wind, and smiled as though he knew the answer.

'The truth of the death of Robert Gerald.'

He had mentioned Gerald to each of the house party in turn, choosing his moment, probing delicately. No delicacy here; he wished to shock, and did so. George's face went comically blank, then hardened into disapproval.

'Why do you seek to entangle yourself in that sordid affair?' he demanded. 'Such association cannot but harm your own reputation – such as it is.'

That stung, as it was meant to.

'My reputation is my own affair,' Grey said, 'as are my reasons. Did you know Gerald?'

'No,' Everett answered shortly. By unspoken consent, they turned toward the abbey, and walked back in silence.

On the third day something changed. A sense of nervous anticipation seemed to pervade the air, and the air of secrecy grew heavier. Grey felt as though some stifling lid pressed down upon the abbey, and spent as much time as possible out of doors.

Still, nothing untoward occurred during the day or evening, and he retired as usual, soon after ten o'clock. Dismissing the valet, he undressed alone. He was tired from his long rambles over the countryside but it was early yet. He picked up a book, attempted to read, but the words seemed to slide

433

away from his eyes. His head nodded, and he slept, sitting up in the chair.

The sound of the clock striking below in the hall woke him from uneasy dreams of dark pools and drowning. He sat up, a metal taste like blood in his mouth, and rubbed away the sleep from his eyes. Time for his nightly signal to Quarry.

Unwilling to allow Grey to risk such company alone, Quarry had followed Lord John to West Wycombe. He would, he insisted, there take up station in the meadow facing the guest wing each night, between the hours of eleven and one o'clock. Lord John was to pass a candle flame three times across the glass each night, as a sign that all was so far well.

Feeling ridiculous, Grey had done so on each of the first two nights. Tonight he felt some small sense of reassurance as he bent to light his taper from the hearth. The house was silent but not asleep. Something stirred, somewhere in the abbey; he could feel it. Perhaps the ghosts of the ancient monks – perhaps something else.

The candle flame showed the reflection of his own face, a wan oval in the glass, his light blue eyes gone to dark holes. He stood a moment, holding the flame, then blew it out and went to bed, obscurely more comforted by the thought of Harry outside than by the knowledge of George Everett in the next room.

He woke in darkness to find his bed surrounded by monks. Or men dressed as monks; each wore a rope-belted robe and a deep-cowled hood, pulled far forward to hide the face. Beyond the first startled exclamation, he lay quiet. He might have thought them the ghosts of the abbey, save that the reassuring scents of sweat and alcohol, of powder and pomade, told him otherwise.

None spoke, but hands pulled him from his bed and set him on his feet, stripped the nightshirt from his body and helped him into a robe of his own. A hand cupped him intimately, a caress given under cover of darkness, and he breathed musk and myrrh.

No menaces were offered, and he knew his companions to be those men with whom he had broken bread at dinner. Still, his heart beat in his ears as he was conducted by darkened hallways into the garden, and then by lanternlight through a maze of clipped yew. Beyond this a path led down the side of a stony hill, curving into the darkness and finally turning back into the hillside itself.

Here they passed through a curious portal, this being an archway of wood and marble, carved into what he took to be the semblance of a woman's privates, opened wide. He examined this with curiosity; early experience with whores had made him vaguely familiar but had afforded no opportunity for close inspection.

Once within this portal, a bell began to chime somewhere ahead. The 'monks' formed themselves into a line, two by two, and shuffled slowly forward, beginning to chant.

'Hocus-pocus,

Hoc est corpus . . .'

The chant continued in the same vein – a perversion of various well-known prayers, some merely foolish nonsense, some clever or openly bawdy. Grey restrained a sudden urge to laugh, and bit his lip to stop it.

The solemn procession wound its way deeper and he smelt damp rock; were they in a cave? Evidently; as the passage widened, he saw light ahead, and they entered eventually into a large chamber, set with candles, whose rough-hewn walls indicated that they were indeed in a catacomb of sorts. The impression was heightened by the presence of a number of human skulls, set grinning atop their crossed thigh bones, like so many Jolly Rogers.

Grey found himself pressed into a place near the wall. One figure, robed in cardinal's red, came forward, and Sir Francis Dashwood's voice intoned the beginning of the rite. The rite itself was a parody of the Mass, enacted with great solemnity, invocations made to the Master of Darkness, the chalice formed of an upturned skull.

In all truth, Grey found the proceedings tedious in the extreme, enlivened only by the appearance of a large Barbary ape, attired in bishop's cope and mitre, who appeared at the Consecration. The animal sprang upon the altar, where it gobbled and slobbered over the bread provided, and spilt wine upon the floor. It would have been less entertaining, Grey thought, had the beast's ginger whiskers and seamed countenance not reminded him so strongly of the Bishop of Ely, an old friend of his mother's.

At the conclusion of this rite, the men went out, with considerably less solemnity than when they had come in. A good deal had been drunk in the course of the rite, and their behaviour was less restrained than that of the ape.

Two men near the end of the line seized Grey by the arms, and compelled him into a small alcove, around which the others had gathered. He found himself bent backward over a marble basin, the robe pushed down from his shoulders. Dashwood intoned a prayer in reverse Latin, and something warm and sticky cascaded over Grey's head, blinding him and causing him to struggle and curse in the grip of his captors.

'I baptise thee, child of Asmodeus, son of blood . . .' A kick caught Dashwood under the chin and sent him reeling backward. A hard punch in the pit of the stomach knocked the breath from Grey and quieted him for the remainder of the brief ceremony.

Then they set him on his feet, bloodstained, and gave him drink from a jewelled cup. He tasted opium in the wine, and let as much as he dared dribble down his chin as he drank. Even so, he felt the dreamy tendrils of the drug steal through his mind, and his balance grew precarious, sending him lurching through the crowd, to the great hilarity of the robed onlookers.

Hands took him by the elbows and propelled him down a corridor, and another, and another. A draught of warm air, and he found himself thrust through a door, which closed behind him.

The chamber was small, furnished with nothing save a narrow couch against the far wall, and a table upon which stood a flagon, several glasses . . . and a knife. Grey staggered to it, and braced himself with both hands to keep from falling.

There was a strange smell in the room. At first he thought he had vomited, sickened by blood and wine, but then he saw the pool of it, across the room by the bed. It was only then that he saw the girl.

She was young and naked and dead. Her body lay limp, sprawled white in the light, but her eyes were dull and her lips blue, the traces of sickness trailing down her face and across the bedclothes. Grey backed slowly away, shock washing the last remnants of the drug from his blood.

He rubbed both hands hard across his face, striving to think. What was this, why was he here, with the body of this young woman? He brought himself to come closer, to look. She was no one he had seen before; the calluses upon her hands and the state of her feet marked her as a servant or a peasant.

He turned sharply, went to the door. Locked, of course. But what was the point? He shook his head, his brain slowly clearing. Once clear, though, no answers came to mind. Blackmail, perhaps? It was true that Grey's family had influence though he himself possessed none. But how could his presence here be put to such use?

It seemed he had spent forever in that buried room, pacing to and fro across the stone floor, until at last the door opened and a robed figure slipped through.

'George!'

'Bloody hell!' Ignoring Grey's turn toward him, Everett crossed the room and stood staring down at the girl, brows knit in consternation. 'What's happened?' he demanded, swinging toward Grey.

'You tell me. Or rather, let us leave this place, and then you tell me.'

Everett put out a quelling hand, urging silence. He thought

437

for a moment and then seemed to reach some conclusion. A slow smile grew across his face.

'Well enough,' he said softly. He turned and reached toward Grey's waist, pulling loose the cord that bound it closed. Grey made no move to cover himself, though was filled with astonishment at the gesture, given the circumstances.

This astonishment was intensified in the next instant as Everett bent over the bed and wrapped the cord round the neck of the dead woman, tugging hard to draw it tight, so the rope bit deep into flesh. He stood, smiled at Grey, then crossed to the table, where he poured two glasses of wine from the flagon.

'Here.' He handed one to Grey. 'Don't worry, it's not drugged. You aren't drugged now, are you? No, I see not; I thought you hadn't had enough.'

'Tell me what is happening.' Grey took the glass, but made no move to drink. 'Tell me, for God's sake!'

George smiled again, a queer look in his eyes, and picked up the knife. It was exotic in appearance; something Oriental, at least a foot long and wickedly sharp.

'It is the common initiation of the Brotherhood,' he said. 'The new candidate, once approved, is baptised – it was pig's blood, by the way – and then brought to this room, where a woman is provided for his pleasure. Once his lust is slaked, an older Brother comes to instruct him in the final rite of his acceptance – and to witness it.'

Grey raised a sleeve and wiped cold sweat and pig's blood from his forehead.

'And the nature of this final rite is—'

'Sacrificial.' George nodded acknowledgement toward the blade. 'The act not only completes the initiation, but also ensures the initiate's silence and his loyalty to the Brotherhood.'

A great coldness was creeping through Grey's limbs, making them stiff and heavy.

'And you have . . .'

'Yes.' Everett contemplated the form on the bed for a moment, one finger gently stroking the blade. At last he shook his head and sighed.

'No, I think not.' He raised his eyes to Grey's, clear and shining in the lamplight. 'I would have spared you, I think, were it not for Bob Gerald.'

The glass felt slick in Grey's hand, but he forced himself to speak calmly.

'So you did know him. Was it you who killed him?'

Everett nodded slowly, not taking his gaze from Grey's.

'It is ironic, is it not?' he said softly. 'I desired membership in this Brotherhood, whose watchword is vice, whose credo is wickedness – and yet had Bob Gerald told them what I am, they would have turned upon me like wolves. They hold all abomination dear – save one.'

'And Robert Gerald knew what you were? Yet he did not speak your name as he died.'

George shrugged, but his mouth twitched uneasily.

'He was a pretty lad. I thought – but I was wrong. No, he didn't know my name, but we met here – at Medmenham. It would have made no difference had they not chosen him to join us. Were he to come again, though, and see me here . . .'

'He would not come again. He refused the invitation.'

George's eyes narrowed, gauging his truth; then he shrugged.

'Perhaps if I had known that, he need not have died. And if he had not died, you would not have been chosen yourself – would not have come? No. Well, there's irony again for you, I suppose. And still, I think I would have killed him under any circumstance; it was too dangerous.'

Grey had been keeping a watchful eye on the knife. He moved, unobtrusively, seeking to get the corner of the table betwixt himself and Everett.

'And the broadsheets? That was your doing?' He could, he

439

thought, seize the table and throw it into Everett's legs, then try to overpower him. Disarmed, they were well-matched in strength.

'No, Churchill's. He's the poet, after all.' George smiled and stepped back, out of range. 'They thought perhaps to take advantage of Gerald's death to discomfit Sir Richard – and chose that method, knowing nothing of his killer or the motive for his death. The greatest irony of all, is it not?'

George had moved the flagon out of reach. Grey stood half-naked, with no weapon to hand save a glass of wine.

'So you intend now to procure my silence, by claiming I am the murderer of this poor young woman?' Grey demanded, jerking his head toward the still figure on the bed. 'What happened to her?'

'Accident,' Everett said. 'The women are drugged; she must have vomited in her sleep and choked to death. But blackmail? No.'

Everett squinted at the bed, then at Grey, measuring distance. 'You sought to use a noose for your sacrificial duty – some dislike blood – and though you succeeded, the girl managed to seize the knife and wound you, severely enough that you bled to death before I could return to aid you. Move a little closer to the bed, John.'

A man is not helpless, only because he is fettered. Grey flung his wine into Everett's face, then smashed his glass against the stones of the wall and lunged upward, jabbing with all his might.

Everett grunted, one side of his face laid open, spraying blood. He growled deep in his throat and ripped the blade across the air where Lord John had stood a moment before. Half-blinded by blood and snarling like a beast, he lunged and swung again. Grey ducked, was hit by a flying wrist and fell across the woman's body. He rolled sideways, but was trapped by the folds of his robe.

The knife gleamed overhead. In desperation, he threw up

his legs and thrust both feet into Everett's chest, flinging him backward.

Everett staggered back, then froze abruptly. The expression on his face showed vast surprise. His hand loosened, dropping the knife, and then drew slowly through the air, graceful in gesture as the dancer that he was. His fingers touched the reddened steel protruding from his chest, acknowledging defeat. He slumped slowly to the floor.

Harry Quarry put a foot on Everett's back and freed his sword with a vicious yank.

'Good job I waited, wasn't it? Saw those buggers with their lanterns and all, and thought best I see what mischief was afoot.'

'Mischief,' Grey echoed. He stood up, or tried to. His knees had gone to water. 'You . . . did you hear?' His heart was beating very slowly; he wondered in a dreamy way whether it might stop any minute.

Quarry glanced at him, expression unreadable.

'I heard.' He sheathed his sword, and came to the bed, bending down to peer at Grey. How much had he heard, Grey wondered – and what had he made of it?

A rough hand brushed back his hair. He felt the stiffness matting it, and thought of Robert Gerald's mother.

'It's not my blood,' he said.

'Some of it is,' said Quarry, and traced a line down the side of his neck. In the wake of the touch, he felt the sting of the cut, unnoticed in the moment of infliction.

'Never fear,' said Quarry, and gave him a hand to get up. 'It will make a pretty scar.'

I have known this story since I was a child.

Aston Hall is a superb Jacobean-style mansion, which now lies in the heart of Birmingham, nose to nose with Spaghetti Junction and the Villa Football Ground. The story of Sir Thomas Holte, the Hall's builder, and his cook is often dismissed as a myth. However, when I went to university I heard friends who read law discussing a famous precedent with a rather startling judgement: William Ascrick's trial for slander and subsequent appeal certainly took place. Did a murder occur, or am I perpetuating an injustice? The details in the court case are extremely specific. The final verdict strongly indicates that the judges thought Ascrick had a point . . .

In retelling the story I don't imply that the Parliamentarians' siege in 1643 was a direct consequence of what had – or had not – happened in a kitchen in 1606; that would be simplistic and inaccurate. But the social confrontations do seem to be connected. Whatever the truth, researching all these events was great fun, taking me back to the local history section of Birmingham Reference Library where I first dreamed of becoming a writer, and then to the Hall itself. The curators went to endless trouble to help supply background information and most kindly allowed me to visit when the Hall was officially closed in winter – a very special experience.

I gained my interest in the Civil War when I was a passionate reader of historical novels, among them those of Edith Pargeter, little thinking that one day as Ellis Peters she would give my own first novel a generous accolade. She was one of the authors who fixed my standards for popular fiction, high standards which are all too often ignored by authors and publishers alike but which readers do value and to which in the long run they are loyal. I mean excellence in writing, an authentic historical flavour, and above all a sound ethical base.

The story I have written in Edith's memory is not a pure mystery, though the murder is crucial to what I have to say. For me Edith/Ellis was far more than the author of Brother Cadfael. This story seems appropriate because it has a local flavour – something I can write about with particular joy and I hope a decent insight. She was constantly fascinated by the interplay of national politics and more private domestic events. So many of her books involve this, where individuals who are trying to lead lives of their own are affected – and perhaps have their quandries resolved – whilst they are caught up in some great historical struggle. She would, I feel, also approve of not allowing the rich and powerful to hide their crimes, simply on account of their position; the idea of an indignant local man challenging Sir Thomas and forcing the cook's fate to be examined publicly would certainly appeal to her sense of justice.

Lindsey Davis

The Party May Yet Be Living . . .

Lindsey Davis

There might have been better things to do on Christmas Day. However, those who believed they were about the Lord's work were glad enough to respond to orders from the County Committee in Warwick to relieve the new threat to Bromidgeham. So they spent Christmas Day 1643 on the march in a column from Coventry, knowing that they would almost certainly pass that night and perhaps several others out in the open in the great park of Aston Hall.

At least they were favoured by the weather. The years of the Civil War were to become notorious for the foulest conditions, adding greatly to the miseries endured by the troops on both sides, and sometimes affecting the outcome of assaults. November that year had produced serious snow and rainstorms, with fogs that hampered manoeuvres even more filthily than the sulphurous gusts of gunsmoke. But in December the skies cleared. This had allowed the royalist Sir Thomas Holte to ask for and receive a detachment of forty musketeers from Dudley Castle to help him fortify his house against the perceived hostility of his neighbours. The Parliamentary town of Bromidgeham was producing in its numerous forges the swords that armed his enemies, and went further than that; it had earned itself a lively reputation as 'a town so generally wicked that it had risen upon small parties of the King's and killed or taken them prisoners, and sent them to Coventry, declaring a more peremptory malice to His Majesty than any other place'. Indeed the numbers of prisoners that Bromidgeham managed to capture in this way and dispatch to secure cells were enough to make 'sending to Coventry' a lasting proverb.

There had already been a stiff punishment administered by the King's nephew, Prince Rupert of the Rhine. In April that year he had passed through Bromidgeham on his way to relieve the siege of Lichfield. Undaunted by the Prince's dashing reputation, the townsfolk dug a trench across the road, set up their colours and, with only a handful of troops, prepared to defy him. The Royalists unsportingly rode around the end of the trench, entering the town through a back route. After a wild night which left dead on both sides and many local people affronted, the cavaliers had left, first lighting fires which destroyed a large number of houses around Digbeth and Deritend. This only hardened the attitude of those who supported Parliament so that by the end of the year life had become uncomfortable for Sir Thomas Holte, living but two miles away at Aston. In response he sought to protect the Hall, which he had built, and at huge expense.

Garrisoning the Hall was a typical gesture. He must have known that when he obtained his forty musketeers he had issued a challenge. With their weapons, which were nearly as long as a man was tall, their coils of match and the prepared gunpowder charges slung around them on bandoleers, their swagger and – as it turned out – their foreign bluster, the troops from Dudley hardly went unnoticed. Holte immediately stood at risk of attracting the firepower of his enemies. And so the troops from Coventry arrived on Christmas Day.

Colonel Godfrey Bosville was charged with capturing the house. When he rode up with his twelve hundred men he found Aston Hall as handsome as a great house should be. It stood on an elevation, a site perfectly chosen so that the complicated roofline would be outlined against the Warwickshire sky. Seventeen years in construction and completed a bare decade before, the fine symmetrical building comprised a central block flanked by equal wings, each provided with Dutch gables, balustrades, groups of tall chimneys, and square towers topped with graceful pinnacles. Its diapered red brick was picked out with sharp quoinstones; its windows were all well-proportioned. Behind one, caught by the low winter sunlight, a glint of metal flashed, almost certainly from a musket.

The defenders' preparations had been made at a scramble. Sir Thomas proved difficult, refusing at first the officers' requests to fell trees in the park to provide a clear field of fire and their proposal to dig earthworks. His scruples had been overcome and hasty trenches had been thrown up. The church was occupied by Royalist troops too, so approaching the redoubt would be very dangerous for the attackers. They had no choice but to start a siege.

It was the defenders who sounded a challenge. Bosville at once responded, demanding use of the Hall for Parliament. The defenders roared back the customary brave answer that they would not yield while they had a man alive. Bosville shrugged and turned away.

This ended the first exchange. The light was fading and Bosville's ordnance had yet to arrive. Everyone stood down. The soldiers of the attacking force prepared to endure their first night on the bare ground, sustained by meagre marching provisions from their knapsacks and any tobacco they had brought privately, with only the faint hope that women from the town might bring them some bellarmine jugs of wine. Their officers accorded themselves their traditional privilege of retiring for the night; they rode off into Bromidgeham, where they billeted themselves on houses that might possess featherbeds and roast beef.

While the Colonel and his chiefs of staff found themselves soft lodgings with the Porters, Jennens and other wealthy families, their most junior companion, one Captain Hopewell, was dispatched alone to take refuge with a forge owner named Ascrick, reported to be sympathetic to their cause. Only when the Captain found the address he had been given by the troop's quartermaster did he learn that William Ascrick's house at his forge in Deritend had been one of those fired to a cinder in what the locals jovially called Prince Rupert's Burning Love to England; as a result Mr Ascrick, who must be a man of substance, currently resided elsewhere, amongst large quantities of salvaged chattels and iron-working equipment, with rebuilding work to excuse any amount of poor hospitality. The Captain had, by force of arms, the right to billet himself on any luckless householder he chose – though it was wise to exercise discretion in a friendly town. Unfortunately for him, he found himself detained with great determination by his host, who evidently entertained a vivid desire to hear how the Coventry men were breaking heads at Aston Hall.

Having to confess they had only exchanged challenges placed Hopewell at a disadvantage that he could see he would regret.

Reluctantly he accepted that he stood no chance of slipping away to the warm welcome of the Old Crown in Digbeth – a hostelry that had been good enough for Prince Rupert. Instead he let himself be drawn into a kitchen where he was squeezed on to an old low nursing stool between stacks of fire-damaged chairs and boxes of rescued tureens. His hopes of a hot dinner dwindled as he came under the caustic eye of Ascrick's elderly female servant Temperance. And his heart sank still further as he recognised that he had placed himself with a man who was gripped by an obsession that went back across two generations and for nearly forty years.

'Are ye interested in legal debates?'

Captain Hopewell, a quiet, modest young man, realised these were fatal words. He was trapped alone in a strange town, with a long night to endure before a cold morrow when he would stand in danger of a bullet through the breast. He should have denied any such interest – which would have been the truth. Natural courtesy forced him to nod and to smile.

'You've done it now!' scoffed Temperance, a forceful woman, which was to be expected since she came from Bromidgeham. Although Hopewell was risking his life for righteousness, he was a soldier and in obtaining his billet he might have hoped for something comely in the domestic environment. Any winsome maids had been whisked out of sight. Temperance was a tart old terror. She wore a dark mulberry gown with a plain collar coming well down over her breast and an equally severe apron. At first he had wondered if she were Ascrick's wife, but Temperance lacked the docility of a wife; she led her own life. Her thin-lipped scowl proclaimed it.

Her employer, William Ascrick, was of medium build, balding, with a bright eye and a maverick demeanour. Though his scrawny body and the haggard neck inside his crumpled falling band implied poor scratchings at his table, he was gulping down a posset thickened with Naples biscuit and scented with a good strewing of cinnamon; he devoured this strengthening brew with gusto and did not cease from it even when confronted with a guest.

'We have nothing to feed you on,' Temperance declared to Hopewell, cutting across her master's legal story with the same casual brutality she was using to slice onions. 'You must make shift with a hard egg on some sippets of bread. I have indoors barely one collop for Master Ascrick—'

'The collop must go to the Captain, to sustain him for the good work he will be about,' Ascrick himself interrupted. 'Done up prettily in onion gravy?' he offered, so the Captain's heart dared to rise. He let himself wonder if the veal fillet might be accompanied by a bottle of sack, though his wits told him not to hope for it.

'And what am I to find for you then?' Temperance chivvied her master, undaunted. Captain Hopewell heard himself therefore politely decline the collop, at which Ascrick announced he could not sit and eat it alone in front of so good-mannered a guest, and at once Temperance put away the meat uncooked – almost certainly, thought Hopewell, intending to devour it later secretly herself. In the meantime it was eggs on toasts all round.

Captain Hopewell cleared his throat. Ascrick was surveying him with beady intent while Temperance glared at them both. Enough had been said on his arrival for the Captain to have gleaned that whatever issue his host was burning to discuss was connected with Aston Hall. He heard himself venture to ask what connection or interest the forge master had with Sir Thomas Holte.

'Aye, aye, don't be impatient; there is plenty of time for that!'

Hopewell kept his face neutral. He was yearning for bed but feared he would be required to sleep curled up in great discomfort on the very settle that was currently occupied by his leisurely host. That Ascrick himself had a soft mattress and warm coverlets waiting was in no doubt; Temperance had taken away a cinder-filled copper bedpan earlier, while her master sighed and muttered an insincere apology that they were living in such hurly-burly conditions after the Royalist fire. Uncertainty about his night's rest preyed on the Captain, making him tense when he should be conserving his strength and energy for the fighting tomorrow.

The meagre supper had barely dented his appetite, and to add to his discomfort he was now forced to watch Temperance preparing a cauldron for her master's luncheon the next day: a net of neatly trimmed vegetables, a fowl swimming in a pottery vessel with butter and broth, and a round fat pudding tied in a cloth. All these were placed together in the cauldron where they would be boiled to sweet tenderness throughout the next morning, then consumed by Ascrick while Hopewell would be braving noise, shot, smoke and Royalist insults at the Hall.

'So you want to hear of my father's rare adventure?' demanded William Ascrick just as the Captain began to nod off in the warmth from the hearth.

Hopewell roused himself a little, though after that day's journey from Coventry and the tension of arriving at the site of the coming siege, he was as drowsy as ever in his life. 'Was this to do with Sir Thomas Holte?'

'A violent and vindictive man!' nodded Ascrick, reflecting both qualities in his own tone.

'He is of some consequence in this locality?' enquired the Captain cautiously. Sir Thomas Holte had been, he knew, Sheriff of the County in his younger days. Holte was extremely wealthy and evidently regarded the possession of extensive lands as a signal of his importance.

'That's his opinion! My family was never afraid of him.'

'Is he a man who inspires fear?'

'In the kitchen, maybe,' replied Ascrick obscurely, relishing some private jest. Captain Hopewell raised an eyebrow, trying hard to feign curiosity though he was wishing he could ease off his great leather thigh boots and relieve his aching toes, perhaps resting them on the brass fender among the trivets and jacks.

'Kitchens are dangerous places,' remarked Temperance darkly, letting her great bone-handled knife crunch savagely through a turnip like an executioner at work.

'So what happened in the kitchen at Aston?' queried Captain Hopewell, anxious to move the story on.

'It was at Duddeston,' Temperance corrected him.

'If it happened!' added Ascrick, with a peculiar grin.

'Which we are not allowed to say,' returned Temperance equally knowingly.

'Then how am I to hear this tale?' inserted Hopewell,

hiding his exasperation and pretending to laugh at the riddle. 'And what sort of tale is it?'

'The most terrible kind. One of dark deeds and their concealment,' answered Ascrick in a sombre tone.

'Yet you may not say so?'

'*The court was of the opinion –*'

' *– Slander ought to be direct!* Aye,' rebuked Temperance, butting in once again. 'We can all sing the roundel.'

As if taking up what she said, Ascrick then quoted what seemed to be a court verdict: '*In a declaration that A cleaved B's head so that the one part lay upon one shoulder and the other part—*'

'God's Blood!' exclaimed Hopewell. They now had his full interest. A year of war had given him full knowledge of the hard strength required for a blow that could wreak such damage on a human skull. He could envisage the resultant mess of brains, bone shards, and blood. Split heads were terrible enough amidst the carnage of a battlefield, but it was clear the event under discussion was far more domestic in character.

Both Temperance and Ascrick stared at him. After living with the tale for nigh on forty years, its gruesome aspects no longer shocked them. The soldier's honest squeamish reaction made them reassess the violence that had happened – that was *supposed* to have happened – all that time ago.

'So who was killed in this gruesome manner?'

'Perhaps nobody,' crowed Ascrick triumphantly. It was a Bromidgeham habit to enjoy being perverse. 'We have that on the authority of the Chief Justice, sitting on the King's Bench!'

Hopewell resented being teased, and chose to play no part in his own gulling. He remained stubbornly silent.

'Nay then.' Ascrick smiled gently. 'It was said to be just a story.'

His hearer could bear no more. This time Hopewell actually rose and yawned openly, pulling straight his buff jerkin with the brusque air of a soldier who was minded to leave the company for his bed. Ascrick took the hint, also clambering to his feet. The Captain was relieved to see him signal that Temperance should bring a light, which she did, though it was not even a stump of a candle but a thin rush balanced in a greasy holder. Without a word more Hopewell was led to a small, barely furnished chamber which contained a joint stool, an empty wash jug on a dusty windowsill, and a narrow, uncurtained bed which appeared to have been left unmade since the time of Queen Elizabeth. Grateful to have reached any haven of sleep, he smiled his thanks.

He waited until Ascrick and his servant were both tiptoeing out of the door. 'I shall rest the more sweetly if ye will spare me from puzzling over what it is that never must be said.'

William Ascrick turned back, relishing the moment. 'My father said it. That he never denied: "*Sir Thomas Holte took a cleaver and smote his cook with the same cleaver upon the head, and clave his head, that one side of his head fell upon one shoulder, and the other side on the other shoulder.*"'

'He killed his cook?'

William Ascrick merely smiled, then closed the door behind him quietly as he left.

A musket shot cracked. While Temperance and William were still blinking at the flash from a third-floor window in the Hall, the soldiery ducked. There was laughter as the shot lost itself harmlessly among the leaves of a stately oak tree but then an infantry man ran up, red-faced with alarm. Colonel Bosville himself rode at a brisk trot to the scene. He ordered the men to move back members of the public who had walked out from the town to watch the attack. Doing his best not to bluster, the infantry man rounded on Ascrick; then, sensing where the power lay, it was Temperance he addressed: 'Madam, in the name of God, stand further off – for your own safety!' To nobody in particular he added irritably, 'This is not some entertainment at a fair—'

'That's your opinion,' chortled William. 'I like it well enough! How long do you suppose you brave fellows will be at it here?' he demanded of the Colonel.

Bosville, dismounting, gave him a look that said, *first* he had no idea, *second* it was nobody's business but that of the brave fellows (who were beginning to look less brave as shot smacked into the turf around them), and *third* the occasion was acquiring the smell of one that was running out of hand. Like most commanders, he had service abroad behind him and he had been assigned plenty of men for this duty, but the Parliamentary force would be derided by its enemies as a troop of undisciplined irregulars. Reality was that most Civil War troops were irregulars for England had no standing army. All anyone could muster for this kind of local engagement were the old weekend trained bands, the hopeless home-guard, beefed up by whatever could be raised by local subscription and recruitment; ploughmen, tapsters and released prisoners were favourite offerings. Butchers, who would be used to blood, were what commanders preferred.

Intelligence had gleaned that the Royalist soldiers in the Hall were French and Irish: seasoned mercenaries. They would be veterans, survivors of damnable miseries in the Thirty Years War in Europe. Colonel Bosville displayed the blank-faced aspect of a man who knew he might be immured in fiasco.

William gave him an indulgent smile just as a flurry of new shot burst from the house. This time a cry rose from a close knot of troopers. Several were on the ground. Colleagues pressed around them. When they remained in a huddle, obviously engaged in urgent attentions to the wounded, others began to shout more sternly for the townspeople to withdraw. Bromidgeham people preferred not to stand where they might be killed. Those who were not part of the attacking force were already deciding to go home.

Ascrick lingered, though he allowed Bosville to urge

him back further from the house. Muskets fired bullets of fearsome weight, an ounce and a quarter if they were made at full size; they could kill at four hundred yards, though their effective range was less. Against the snipers from the Hall the Parliamentarians could make no advance at present, though they were doing good work, nonetheless. Their ordnance had arrived: light three-pounders, and a great brass demi-culverin, pulled by eight horses, and capable of firing balls of up to twenty pounds, at ten or twelve an hour. With these, well-sited on the south-west side of the Hall, they had begun a fierce bombardment. They would pound the building to submission eventually, though while it was happening most of the soldiers stood in ranks simply waiting for action that could be hours or even days away. Ascrick and Temperance found the tedium too much; they departed, leaving with the Colonel a small parcel of fresh-made Shropshire cakes, which they had brought for their lodger, the Captain. Since Hopewell had devoted himself to supervising the cannon (in order to avoid conversation), Colonel Bosville was well into the large biscuit-like confections before his officer came to take charge of them. It was all the more galling since Captain Hopewell had already been forced to hear more than he wanted of the rare Dutch pudding (stewed beef, served most daintily with saucers of mustard) which had been lavished on his Colonel the previous night.

A lull allowed Hopewell to stand by the Colonel, patiently hoping to be offered a share in his own gift. Watching Bosville eat three cakes for every one that came his way, he mentioned what he had heard of the quarrel between Ascrick's father and Sir Thomas Holte. 'Old scores are rankling. There was a trial, apparently, though I gathered it was Ascrick who was sued, and by the baronet.'

'Aye. It was a famous case in Warwickshire.' Bosville was in a philosophical mood. 'Look around you, Captain. The seeds of animosity are all here; we have, in little, the whole matter of the conflict that brings our armies to war.'

Obediently Hopewell let his eyes roam across the great park which Sir Thomas had enclosed, with little local complaint, and beyond it to what had once been open countryside, now completely given over to a conglomeration of smallholdings, again all fenced in by Holte, then leased out to artisans for his own profit. Having land beside both the Rivers Bourne and Rea, he owned more than a few watermills and furnaces, which were leased to the iron masters of Bromidgeham who were now so opposed to him politically. The house he had built on his profits, a grandiose architectural novelty, declared to the world in general and the nearby town in particular that its owner deemed himself a great man.

'The Holtes have been a well-connected and well-endowed family for many generations,' said Colonel Bosville, who either knew, or had chosen to discover, the sensibilities of the county in which he was serving, and especially of the particular members of the squirearchy at whom he was aiming his ordance. 'But our challenger here believed himself to occupy an exceptional position. His father died and he inherited before he was twenty-one, then when King James first came south he was one of the welcoming party for the new King and was knighted on that occasion. He married well – which meant wealthily.'

'And managed his estates well too,' Hopewell suggested. 'His reputation is that of an energetic and astute man of business.'

'A fortune builder as well as a house builder. Though not popular?'

'He is thought proud.'

'And acquisitive?'

'And he bears grudges. He was at odds with his own son and heir for twenty years. It is said even the King attempted to intervene and reconcile them, to no avail. The son was wounded at Edgehill and though he recovered he died a few months ago at Oxford, even then a stranger to his father.'

'What was the quarrel?'

'That the son had married in defiance of his father's wishes, though the wife he took was the daughter of the Bishop of London – perfectly respectable, yet she had little dowry.'

A soldier nearby who had been listening in shamelessly spoke up: 'It is said that Sir Thomas hath also locked up one of his daughters for refusing to marry as he wished. People believe she is kept in a small attic here, and has been for fifteen years. Or else that she has become deranged,' he added, somewhat taking away force from his tale.

'If she is there,' said Colonel Bosville rather crisply, implying he disbelieved it, 'her time of deliverance is nigh. We shall discover the poor maid and release her from her trouble.'

He finished the last Shropshire cake then walked off to another spot in the park, in a huff at being interrupted.

'What you say is well known,' the soldier continued to Hopewell, unabashed by the Colonel's discomfiture. The Parliamentary forces were much given to outspokenness. Like most rude and difficult people they were mightily proud of their honesty of heart. It could be tricky when political negotiations were delicate. The man leaned on his pike, a frightful sixteen feet of iron-spiked pole with which a well-drilled soldier could disembowel an enemy. 'He killed his cook. He concealed it and was never brought to account for the black deed – except that William Ascrick accused him and was himself tried for saying so.'

'And what did Sir Thomas say?' asked Captain Hopewell mildly.

'He said he was innocent! Well, he would,' commented the soldier, with the logic that would ring down the centuries and be famously used by another person from Bromidgeham commenting sourly upon the judiciary. 'He said Ascrick was seduced and provoked by the instigation of the devil. But

Holte was charged to wear a badge of his guilt forever, in the bloody red hand.'

'I believe,' Hopewell intervened cautiously, 'there may be another explanation for that badge on his coat of arms.' He knew this to be the emblem of Ulster, which was awarded to those who had purchased the new rank of baronet from King James. The title was sold for the price of one thousand and ninety-five pounds, which would maintain thirty foot soldiers in the army in the north of Ireland; the red hand signified the bearer's loyal support for Ulster.

The soldier was having no truck with explanations. 'It means he has bought himself precedence above all others except the peerage – and that he is an overbearing tyrannical upstart.'

'Well, that sounds a reason for us to knock in his windows!'

Captain Hopewell took himself off to bombard a few more of them. The new expensive panes burst into most satisfying cascades of broken glass.

Cannonballs were crashing through gaping holes and well into the body of the Hall, though it was thought the defenders had protected themselves from harm by keeping to the upper rooms. Musket fire from above prevented any attempt at an advance. And whatever Sir Thomas Holte might have done to a cook in his younger days, now he was in his seventies he seemed able to inspire loyalty from his domestic servants; pot shots from members of his household using antique ship's guns also helped keep the attackers back. Keeping up the pressure and hoping the defenders would run out of ammunition, Colonel Bosville passed the opinion that there would be a change of strategy the next day.

Poaching was forbidden in the Orders of War. When some soldiers were found to have acquired dogs and to have caught one of Sir Thomas Holte's deer, which they were roasting, it fell to Hopewell to remonstrate.

*　　*　　*

On his return to his billet, fired up by a day's action and by joy at his surviving it, Captain Hopewell took a firmer attitude with his hosts. He brushed aside curious questions by suggesting that tactics at the Hall were a military secret which he could not betray on pain of a court martial. Then he broached the issue of supper with a briskness that would have caught offguard a feebler servant – though Temperance proved a match for him.

'Master Ascrick has enjoyed so fine a pipkin of fowl at his mid-day table, we are settled on a light cheesecake for supper.'

Captain Hopewell was about to demand whether anything remained of the jointed chicken he had seen being prepared in its pipkin yesterday evening when his eye lighted on the brown glazed vessel, obviously empty, washed and upended to dry at the edge of the hearth. Taking himself an apple from a heaped charger, he crunched the fruit and plunged into bitter thoughts. Colonel Bosville, he knew, had been promised beef carbonado and an almond tart tonight, while the men left in the park at Aston Hall would undoubtedly be dining on a sovereign meal of venison despite the reproofs their young officer had showered on them.

All he was offered for consolation was a spread of large documents, with which Ascrick covered the kitchen table while Temperance at the other end poked at some limp leaves for a winter salad.

'I have looked these out for you, Captain, that you may learn the true matter of my father's controversy.'

'The dead cook,' commented Hopewell, glaring at Temperance as if he were wishing her a similar fate. She ignored him.

Hopewell took one look at the scrawled pages in faded ink, thick with legal technicalities and Latin terms, then he had the sense to wave an arm, signalling that his weariness as a soldier unluckily prevented him giving close attention to such a complex text. Ascrick looked briefly disappointed, but rallied, since this left him the floor. Lighting a pipe of tobacco, he leaned back in his chair and explained: 'By these, which are copies of the Pleas, which my father had made for him, you may see that the case was heard at Warwick, in the fifth year of King James. Here it tells that Sir Thomas Holte, by Richard Jackson –'

'His attorney?'

' – Avers that he, Sir Thomas, has been a good, true, and faithful liegeman of the King from his birth, and on account of his good name, fame, credence, estimation, and conversation, and the favour of the King, he has been appointed one of the Justices of the Peace for Warwick.'

'The same county,' commented Hopewell, drawn in despite his initial reluctance, 'where his plea is being heard? Was he his own judge?'

'Nay,' said the younger Ascrick in an equally dry tone. 'But you may be assured his friends judged him!'

Hopewell had leaned forward over the papers. 'Discharging their office,' he pronounced, 'with the same lack of fear, malice, or favour which it is claimed Sir Thomas customarily used?'

'I doubt it not,' smiled Ascrick.

'So it is said here that your father, also called William Ascrick, on the twentieth of December – a nice anniversary of our own visit to these parts – did at Birmingham, openly, publicly, maliciously, and in the hearing of diverse persons, utter with a loud voice the false, seditious, scandalous, and opprobrious words—'

'That Sir Thomas clave his cook's head.'

'And was your father, as he is accused, provoked by the devil?'

'Certainly not. My father could agitate without suggestion from others!' cried Ascrick. Bromidgeham folk were proud of their forthright expression of opinions and grimly pleased when it offended other people.

'Then we may wonder if the extremity of the language

used against him may show some unusually hot aggravation on the part of Holte?'

'Guilt?' suggested Temperance.

'And the Plea says,' commented Hopewell, feigning deafness in a stout masculine manner, 'that your father was also moved to make his claim by envying the happy and prosperous state of the said Sir Thomas.'

'My father's family was long established in these parts, people of renown and standing, makers of good marriages and holders of local office.'

And owners of money, thought Hopewell. He had himself been kept to the kitchen, the customary fate of billeted soldiers, who were seen as loiterers and lewd-livers. Nonetheless his sharp eyes had noticed that there was a parlour containing a fine set of chairs with turkeywork cushions, and a carved buffet that bore silver salts and shakers, a great gilded fruit dish, and a row of delicate engraved wine glasses. This kitchen was groaning with shelves of copper and pewter. The staircase by which he ascended to his small chamber was hung with crude medieval and Elizabethan portraits of family members, both men and women looking self-satisfied and in their best ruffs.

Even so, this did not match the brazen opulence of the Great Hall at Aston, or the flamboyance of the man who had built it. Hopewell remembered Colonel Bosville's belief that in such a disparity lay the seeds of the war – not simply meaning that the fullness of a man's coffers caused offence to the industrious, but that arrogance and display were out of tune with the new mood of the times.

So too was any feudal notion that a man who had committed a murder should escape justice because he was rich and powerful, and because the deceased was in his employ.

'The story ran thus,' Ascrick at last explained: 'Sir Thomas Holte was ever a quarrelsome, violent man. He was a young man, still living then at Duddeston Hall, the old family seat, which was itself a magnificent manor house in extensive and beautiful grounds. One day when out hunting, he made a proud boast to his companions. He claimed his cook was so diligent that whatever time they returned, the man would have dinner ready and on the table. A large wager was struck.'

'I can guess the remnant of the tale—'

'This was the one occasion when the cook failed his master. The dinner was *not* ready.'

I know how the baronet felt, thought Captain Hopewell.

'Then, Captain, occurred that melancholy event at which my father became so indignant. While his companions jeered, Sir Thomas, incensed, ran to the kitchen, seized the cleaver and dispatched the cook.'

'Though nobody must say so!' smiled the Captain. *Recipe for a Rare Scandal: Take one cook, and chop him through the bone . . .* 'Was your father present?'

'No, but the truth was well known in Bromidgeham – though Sir Thomas tried to conceal his crime.'

Hopewell was silent, imagining the scene in that kitchen: the panic, the unplanned nature of the occasion, the physical problems of concealing a dead body, the ghastly mess of blood to be washed clean. He wondered what the hunting friends had done. Did they hear the commotion? Were they given wine and amusements to keep them from the scene – or were they drawn in as co-conspirators? And did they then claim their wager money, or was the matter allowed to drift? What, he allowed himself to speculate facetiously, had become of the uncooked dinner? 'Were there witnesses?'

'None who would own to it.'

'Did the cook have family?'

'If so they were suborned and made no protest.'

'Did a body exist to be examined, according to the rule of *habeas corpus*?'

'None that was publicly produced.'

'Afterwards Sir Thomas was able to continue his life, pretending nothing had happened?'

'He never expected to be challenged.'

'Yet he was. And when he became incensed a second time, at your father speaking out, he did not produce the cook alive. That would have been the best way to prove his innocence.'

'If the cook was dead, he could not. It's certain the cook was never seen again.'

'Even so,' argued the Captain slowly, 'there could be a valid reason for the servant disappearing. Had the wager gone awry as the tale has it and Sir Thomas burst into the kitchen in a towering rage, the cook may have taken to his heels and escaped. If his fear of his employer's displeasure was so great he fled the district, that would indeed prevent Sir Thomas showing that his cook lived on unharmed.'

'You are a fair man,' agreed Ascrick, though they both knew what they thought.

'Were the other servants questioned?'

'Who could pursue the issue? Holte was the County Sheriff, the rector of Aston parish, and a Justice of the Peace. Enquiries were made informally by people who thought the business shameful, but the servants refused to co-operate.'

'Paid off?' queried Hopewell.

'To say so might lead to another slander suit.'

'Let us at all costs avoid uttering opprobrium! What then was the legal outcome, Master Ascrick? Holte entirely escaped justice, yet your father, being innocent of the deed, was summoned to court?'

'Holte claimed damages of a thousand pounds.'

'*Whew!*' It occurred to the Captain that this was the strongest proof that the Ascricks were themselves substantially set up. Sir Thomas, the wily businessman, must have believed he stood a chance of them paying such large compensation. In fact a thousand pounds would have nearly paid for his subsequent purchase of the rank of baronet. While the sum was perhaps fair compensation for a man of standing who had been wrongly accused of a heinous crime, it was flagrant opportunism of an astonishing kind had he actually murdered the cook.

'My father responded that he was not guilty and put himself on his country. The case was heard at Warwick. The jury returned a verdict of Guilty against my father, but reduced damages to thirty pounds, with one shilling costs.'

'Did he think himself lucky to escape the full damages?'

'He thought himself wronged and he appealed.'

'That would move the case away from Warwick?'

'Indeed it did, to the King's Bench in London. Fleming, who was the Chief Justice, and Williams heard it.' The younger Ascrick sat up straighter as he reached the climax of the story. 'And here it was proved that by persistence justice may yet be obtained, for they judged for the defendant and quashed the damages. But it was a strange quirk by which they acquitted him.'

'Which was?'

'That the declaration "*A cleaved B's head and one part lay upon one shoulder and another part upon the other shoulder*" must positively aver that B was killed.'

'It must follow that he would be!' Captain Hopewell exclaimed.

'But slander, they adjudged, must be direct. It was their conclusion – for which my father was enduringly grateful – that notwithstanding the logical outcome, it was but a trespass; yea, "*notwithstanding such wounding, the party may yet be living*".'

Captain Hopewell laughed out loud.

'I would call that not a trespass but a technicality!'

'It was the opinion in my family,' said Ascrick demurely, 'that the Chief Justice and the other judge believed Sir Thomas had undoubtedly killed his cook in the manner described.'

'Then he was an errant knave to have pursued the slander case.'

'He had no choice,' said Ascrick. 'Silence would have condemned him.'

'True. So what happened then?'

'Everyone carried on their lives. A few years later Sir Thomas was able to acquire the rank of baronet. A decade after the court case my father died, and straight after that Sir Thomas began to build Aston Hall.'

'Perhaps he could not abide living at Duddeston where he faced the memory of his crime?'

'Perhaps!' smirked Ascrick. 'Though I doubt that. He wished to build a great house to demonstrate his status – and he wished to build it close to Bromidgeham to affirm his ascendancy over the town. He spent much on Aston Hall, though he remains wealthy. Though he is supposed to be well regarded, he has quarrelled bitterly with his children. His first wife bore him fifteen of them.'

'So he has other occupations than hunting?'

'Captain Hopewell!' Temperance rebuked him.

Ascrick tried to distract her by introducing a new topic: 'There was one curious event which may be pertinent. In the first year of the reign of King Charles, Sir Thomas sought and obtained a royal pardon which would absolve him of any crime which had occurred prior to the death of old King James.'

'Aha!'

'I believe it is not specific to the cook,' said Ascrick, 'but my attorney, John Harborne, the same as acted for my father, has made diligent enquiries concerning the document.' He rummaged amongst the papers on the table and produced a letter from which he read out in a sombre voice: '"The pardon, which may be pleaded in any court as a complete answer to any charge, remitting almost every kind of crime – including *all kinds of homicides, felonies, robberies, and accessories of the same. And also all kinds of escapes and*

465

evasions, as well as voluntarily as involuntarily and negligently, and each of the aforesaid murders, homicides, and felonies, or accessories, or suspicions of the same."'

'Well, that covers everything!' quipped Temperance, dragging a boning knife through meat. 'It only fails to mention a guilty conscience – but we may read that in.'

Captain Hopewell laced his hands together and pursed his lips thoughtfully. 'Not many of us would feel the necessity of obtaining such a document.'

'Perhaps Sir Thomas feels he may be vindictively pursued,' suggested Ascrick, as if he would like to do it.

'Or needs an indemnity from just prosecution?'

The two men laughed, quietly and without malevolence. Holte was an old man now. The scandal had never died, perhaps never would. Besides, twelve hundred Parliamentary troopers were about to take away from him the house which symbolised his position and a great part of his fortune.

'Justice has come knocking in the form of a bright demiculverin,' said Hopewell. 'Tomorrow he will be forced to surrender or we'll batter the Hall around his ears. If he survives he will be fined into oblivion.'

'Not him,' scoffed Ascrick. 'Half the sequestration committee is in his pocket. Those who are not his cousins are his godsons. Mark my words, he will delay and protest his enfeebled and elderly condition, until little by little the case loses impetus.'

'His house will still be in ruins,' replied the Captain matter-of-factly.

'Make sure you spare the cook,' said Temperance.

The next day came the final assault upon the Hall.

Colonel Bosville drew up his forces, and although he was not a man who rode before them with a Bible in one hand and his sword in the other, being of a quieter disposition than some of the godly psalm singers, he primed them for action bravely. Horse and foot marched up with great valiance,

466

with their first objective to storm the church. This they did, carrying it by assault and taking prisoner forty French and Irish soldiers, among them one woman. Despite the reputation of the rebel forces for destroying church property, no damage was done to the fabric or contents.

Taking the church ended the crossfire which had previously raked the park. That allowed the Parliamentarians to seize the earthworks and approach the house. Then they burst in through the windows, at which the defenders indoors finally called out for quarter. It was granted, yet two Parliamentarians were then shot in the mouth as they entered. This barbarous breach of the rules of war so enraged their colleagues that they determined to put all the enemy to the sword, and had killed or seriously wounded twenty of them before remonstrations from their officers could halt the slaughter.

Eighty prisoners were rounded up, stripped, and made secure. The dead were collected for burial, the wounded were attended to. Through the gunsmoke, troops invaded the Hall, seeking money, other plunder, plate, and incriminating papers. Their boots thundered up the Great Stairs where one baluster post lay shattered by a cannonball ricochet. Shouts rang out as the soldiers ransacked the house, still keyed up in case of unexpected surprise as they moved from room to room. Already from the park came the rumbling of cartwheels as transport arrived to carry off the prisoners and plunder.

Hopewell found himself running through the building with a pounding heart, hardly aware of what he sought. He had acquired a cut eye and was filthy from the smoke and rubble dust. It was his first serious engagement. This was also the largest mansion he had ever explored. He passed through an astonishing array of rooms, parlours and withdrawing rooms, bed chambers grand and informal, dressing rooms and lobbies. There were three main levels to the Hall, but winding stairs came to various confusing mezzanines and turn-offs. He skidded around corners, pausing only to gape at the Nine Worthies looking down at him from niches in the frieze of the Great Dining Room, curious and unusual figures in high relief plasterwork of striking quality. On he went like a soul with a mission. Eventually he stumbled through a doorway into the Long Gallery; he had heard it discussed but was quite unprepared for such a wonder, though at that moment it was completely empty. Floored and panelled in oak like most of the house, with a spectacularly fine plaster ceiling in contemporary strapwork and a rather less glorious fireplace in soft local sandstone, the broad apartment ran the whole length of the west side, just then lit through its nearly full height windows by the low winter sun.

Hopewell stood alone, struck by a mood of unexpected melancholy. He felt bemused and lost. Then, leaving the deserted gallery, he made his way slowly back down to ground level. Soldiers passed him, bearing armfuls of curtains and pictures. Avoiding their triumphal bustle, he found his way to the domestic quarters. It was there in the kitchen that hunger overcame him and he allowed himself some plunder of his own, falling upon a stale loaf that he discovered in a bread crock.

And as he stood, rather guiltily searching for an implement to carve the loaf, two soldiers came in escorting a prisoner. They found Captain Hopewell looking wry as he realised the knife box must already have been carted off when the kitchen was searched.

The prisoner was stripped even of his shirt, and barefoot; soldiers always stole the clothing and footwear of those they captured because they were often ill supplied themselves. He was not protesting, so they were not manhandling him cruelly. Even so he was furious and looked ready to struggle violently. Why they had brought him this way through the house Hopewell could only conjecture; perhaps some delicacy made them spare such an old man the sight of their comrades carrying away so much Royalist pictures, plate, and furniture.

He had a Jacobean beard, full lips, a long nose, and haughty dark eyes. Even naked and defeated, he thought himself far superior to the begrimed young captain who stood at the table in his sixteen-shilling army suit. Before the soldiers told him, Hopewell knew the prisoner must be Sir Thomas Holte.

Their eyes met. Hopewell still had the loaf in his hand, subtly destroying his authority. He did wonder whether, if he asked the question, Sir Thomas would tell him if he had really killed the cook. He did not ask, because he knew the answer. Never. The man was arrogant and obdurate. He would deny it to the end. He had been right to challenge the slander, however; his reputation had been permanently scarred by Ascrick's forthrightness. The death of his cook would be remembered at least as a legal curiosity. He could probably see that the Captain was thinking of it now.

Hopewell slowly drew his sword. It was a good, serviceable blade, made in Bromidgeham. Whatever the baronet expected, he merely ordered the soldiers, 'The transport is waiting. Take him away.' He glanced down at the weapon, and back to Sir Thomas Holte. He moved the loaf slightly upon the table, deliberately measuring it with his eye. 'Times change, Sir Thomas.'

Then he swung the sword and smote the loaf, neatly slicing it in two.